The Lost Angel

OTHER BOOKS BY JAVIER SIERRA

The Secret Supper
The Lady in Blue

The Lost Angel

A NOVEL

Javier Sierra

Translated by Carlos Frías

ATRIA BOOKS

NEW YORK   LONDON   TORONTO   SYDNEY   NEW DELHI

ATRIA BOOKS

A Division of Simon & Schuster, Inc.
1230 Avenue of the Americas
New York, NY 10020

First Atria Books hardcover edition October 2011

ATRIA B O O K S and colophon are trademarks of Simon & Schuster, Inc.

Illustrations by ED.

Document image on page 175: *Monas hieroglyphica*, John Dee, Amberes, 1564.

For information about special discounts for bulk purchases, please contact Simon & Schuster Special Sales at 1-866-506-1949 or business@simonandschuster.com.

The Simon & Schuster Speakers Bureau can bring authors to your live event. For more information or to book an event, contact the Simon & Schuster Speakers Bureau at 1-866-248-3049 or visit our website at www.simonspeakers.com.

Designed by Paul Dippolito

Manufactured in the United States of America

10   9   8   7   6   5   4   3   2   1

Library of Congress Cataloging-in-Publication Data
Sierra, Javier, date.
    [ángel perdido. English]
    The lost angel : a novel / Javier Sierra.
        p.   cm.
    Summary: "Bestseller Javier Sierra presents a new historical enigma: a mysterious pair of 16th-century stones used for communicating with God"—Provided by publisher.
    Includes glossary.
    I. Title.
    PQ6719.I54A4213 2011
    863'.7—dc22   2011019248

ISBN 978-1-4516-3279-8
ISBN 978-1-4516-3281-1 (ebook)

To Eva, Martín and Sofía,
my own guardian angels

... the sons of God saw that the daughters of man were beautiful; and they took wives for themselves of all whom they chose. And the Lord said, "My Spirit shall not strive with man forever, for he is indeed flesh; yet his days shall be one hundred and twenty years."

—GENESIS 6:2–3

Qui non intelligit, aut taceat, aut discat. (He who does not understand, let him either remain silent or learn.)

—JOHN DEE (1527–1608)

The Lost Angel

Twelve hours earlier

An enormous flat-screen monitor lit up in the National Security Agency director's office as the electric blinds darkened the room with a whispered hum. A man in a tailored suit sat across a rich mahogany desk from the all-powerful Michael Owen, waiting to be told why he had been summoned so hastily all the way from New York.

"Colonel Allen." The towering man with obsidian skin cleared his throat. "Thank you for coming so quickly."

"I don't think I had much of a choice, sir," he answered.

Nicholas Allen was battle tested in these circles. He had spent two decades navigating the bureaucratic maze that is Washington, DC, and yet, he could count on one hand the number of times he had been in this room. If Owen, the agency's director, had called him to his office in Fort Meade, Maryland, it was because he was in a bind. A big one. Rushing here was the least he could do.

"You'll understand in a minute why I needed you here so quickly, Colonel Allen," Owen said, his eyes fixed squarely. "Six hours ago, our embassy in Ankara sent me a copy of a videotape I need you to see. I want you to pay close attention to every detail and give me your thoughts when it's over. Can you do that?"

"Of course, sir."

Nick Allen had been trained to do just that. To follow orders without question. From every angle, he was the perfect soldier: a powerful physique, six feet tall, a square jaw and angular face bearing the scars of combat, and a piercing blue-eyed stare that could in a flash dart from kindness to merciless fury. He focused that gaze and leaned his tall frame back in the chair, waiting for the monitor with multicolored test bars to reveal its first image.

What he saw made him start.

A man in a room with cracked and stained walls sat with his hands tied in front of him and a black hood draped over his head. Someone had dressed him in an orange prison jumpsuit, of the kind worn by US federal inmates. But those hovering around him weren't "friendlies." Between the shadows, Allen could make out two, maybe three men dressed in Middle Eastern–style tunics, head scarves covering all but their eyes. *From the border between Turkey and Iran,* Allen thought. *Maybe Iraq.* As the jittery camera moved about, Allen finally saw graffiti written in Kurdish. The video had obviously been shot with a handheld camera. Maybe a camera phone. Once he heard the men speak again, he was certain where they were from. "Near the Armenian border," he said. Plus, two of the men were carrying AK-47s, and, on their waistbands, each wore a curved scimitar, typical of that region. He wasn't surprised to hear the cameraman also directing the scene. Nor that he spoke to the hostage in English with a heavy northeast-Turkish accent.

"All right. Now, say what you're supposed to," the voice ordered.

The prisoner struggled as menacing hands grabbed him by the back of the neck and roughly angled his face toward the camera, whipping off the black hood.

"Say it!"

The hostage looked shaken, unsteady. His whole demeanor told of abuse. Unkempt beard. Mussed hair and a gaunt, dirty, sun-scorched face. Nick Allen thought it odd that the lighting was so poor he couldn't get a good look at the man's face. The room looked lit by a single bulb. And yet, something about this man seemed strikingly familiar.

"In the name of the Forces of Popular Defense . . . I urge the government of the United States to cease supporting the invading Turks," the hostage said in perfect English. Somewhere behind him, a swell of disgruntled yells called out, "Keep going, you filthy dog!" The poor man, whom Allen couldn't identify no matter how hard he tried, began to tremble. He leaned forward and held up his bound wrists for the camera to see. Several of his fingers were black, perhaps frostbitten, but they appeared to be grasping a small stone pendant. The irregularly-shaped opaque stone dangling between the man's tortured fingers caught Nick

Allen's eye. "If you ever want to see me alive again, please do what these men ask," the hostage said, his voice choking back a deep sadness. "The price . . . the price for my life is the immediate withdrawal of all NATO troops within 150 miles of Mount Ararat."

"Mount Ararat? Is that all? They're not asking for a ransom?" Allen said.

The two men in the background began chanting in Kurdish and moving aggressively toward the hostage. One of them pulled a dagger and held it against the hostage's throat, looking as if he were ready to plunge it into the man at any second.

"Now, watch closely," Owen whispered.

Colonel Allen rubbed his nose and waited for the video to continue.

"Say your name!"

Allen had seen many similar videos in the past. They would force the hostage to give his name and rank and possibly the name of the town he was from, then they would press his face close to the camera so there would be no doubt about his identity. If at that moment the hostage was not important to the terrorist group, they would wait for him to cry and plead for his life and, finally, to say good-bye to his family before they bowed his head and slit his throat. The lucky ones would get a gunshot to the head to end the agony. Others would simply bleed to death on camera.

But this hostage must have been of considerable importance. Otherwise, Michael Owen wouldn't have called Allen here. Nick Allen was, after all, an expert in special operations. His résumé included rescue missions in Libya, Uzbekistan and Armenia, and his unit was the agency's most secretive. Is this what the director wanted him to do? To rescue this man?

The voices on the video surged up again:

"Didn't you hear me?" the cameraman yelled. "Say your name!"

The prisoner raised his gaze to reveal dark circles under his eyes.

"My name is Martin Faber. I'm a scientist—"

Michael Owen froze the tape. Just as he had expected, Nick Allen was dumbstruck.

"Now do you understand, Colonel?"

"Martin Faber . . ." Allen muttered the name, still not believing it. "Of course . . ."

"And that's not all, Colonel." Still holding the remote, Owen pointed at the frozen figure on the screen and motioned a circle around the man's hands.

"Did you notice what he's holding?"

"Is that . . . ?" Nick Allen said, squinting in disbelief. "Is that what I think it is, sir?"

"Yes."

Nick Allen pursed his lips as if he couldn't believe what he was seeing. He stood within an inch of the screen to get a closer look.

"If I'm not mistaken, sir, that's just one of the stones we need."

A malevolent gleam flashed in the eyes of the man who commanded the most powerful intelligence agency on earth.

"You're right, Colonel," Owen said with a smile. "The good news is this last will and testament gives us the location of the missing stone. Pay close attention."

Michael Owen aimed the remote at the screen and pressed play. The frozen image of Martin Faber returned to life. His icy blue eyes watered on the verge of tears.

"Julia," he whispered, and then said in Spanish, "We may never see each other again . . ."

"Julia?" Allen said to himself.

Seeing his most trusted soldier's face light up made the director of the National Security Agency smile. Even before the video had ended, the bureau's finest agent knew his orders.

"Julia Álvarez—find her, Colonel Allen. Immediately."

1

For some strange reason, I had my mind made up the day I died, my soul would leave my body and float weightlessly to heaven. I was convinced that once there, guided by an irresistible force, I would come face-to-face with God and I would look into his eyes. And in that moment, I would understand it all. My place in the universe. My origins. My destiny. And even why he gave me a gift for perception that was so . . . unique. This is how my mother had explained it to me when I asked her about death. So did the priest of my church. They both knew how to quiet my restless Catholic soul. I envied their determination in defending all that had to do with what was on "the other side," life after death, and the nature of our existence. And now I was starting to understand why.

On the evening of that first day in November, I was, of course, not dead. But nevertheless, I found myself face-to-face with the Creator. His giant face stared back at me serenely, his body more than fifteen feet tall, his arms spread wide, inviting, as I hovered inches from his nose.

"Don't stay here too late, young lady."

Manuel Mira, the head of security for the Cathedral of Santiago de Compostela, shook me out of my trance with a yell from below. He had spent the afternoon watching me set up my scaffolding and rigging around the statue of Christ in the Pórtico de la Gloria, the Portico of Glory, atop the archway just inside the church's westernmost façade. And now that his shift had ended, I think he worried about leaving me there alone, dangling and at the mercy of ropes and pulleys he didn't understand.

In truth, he had nothing to worry about. I was in excellent shape, an expert with these harnesses, and the alarm in this wing of the cathedral alerted security every time I climbed down from my scaffolding, usually before midnight.

"It's not safe to work in a place so secluded," he said to himself, but loud enough so that I could hear him.

"Don't worry about me, Manuel. I don't plan to have my last rites said for me here," I said with a smile, without turning from my work.

"Be careful, Julia. If your harness gives way and you come crashing down, no one will know about it until seven in the morning. Think about that."

"I'll risk it. This is not Mount Everest or anything. Besides, I've always got my cell phone with me."

"I know, I know...," he grumbled. "Still, be careful. Have a good night."

Manuel, who was at least twenty years older than me and had a daughter my age, tipped his cap and gave up his warnings as a lost cause. Besides, he knew that given my present situation—dangling from a second-story height, enraptured with my work, wearing safety goggles and a hard hat crowned with LEDs and emblazoned with the logo of the Barrié de la Maza Foundation, tethered to a PDA and to the wall just below the statue of Christ—it was better to just let me be. My work required surgical precision, nerves of steel and total concentration.

"Good night," I said, appreciating his concern.

"Oh, and, uh, beware of the ghosts, will you?" he said flatly, just as he was turning to leave. "Remember, it's All Souls' Day, and they love to haunt this place. They seem to like this spot, in particular."

I couldn't even bother to smile. I was holding a $60,000 endoscope designed in Switzerland specifically for this work. Death, despite my earlier daydreams, was still a long way off.

Or maybe not.

After months of writing articles about how to preserve masterworks of the Romanesque period, I knew I was on the verge of being able to explain the deterioration of one of it's most important sculptures. What did I care that it was All Souls' Day—the Day of the Dead? Deep down, I saw it as a fortunate coincidence. For centuries, pilgrims had traveled the Way of St. James, the oldest and most journeyed spiritual pilgrimage in Europe, to visit the very sculptures I was analyzing in the shrine to St. James at the Cathedral of Santiago de Compostela. They made this trek to revive their faith, reminding themselves that to cross under this archway meant ending their sinful life and beginning another one that was more sublime. And that's how it received its name, the Pórtico de la Gloria, the pathway to heaven.

The more than two hundred sculptures here truly were a collection of immortals, an army impervious to man and time. And yet, since the year 2000, some inexplicable disease was causing these statues to crumble. Isaiah and Daniel, for example, seemed to be peeling in layers, while the musicians strumming their instruments above them threatened to come crashing down in chunks, had we not reinforced them. Heralding angels, characters from the book of Genesis, sinners and the convicted—all of the sculptures showed worrisome signs, a darkening, an aging that seemed to be sapping the life from them.

Not since the time of the Crusades had anyone examined these sculptures as closely as I had. The Barrié Foundation thought they had been damaged by humidity, mold or bacteria. But I wasn't so sure. That's why I came back here after hours when there were no tourists to wonder why I was obscuring the masterworks with my maze of scaffolding. And, of course, when there were no other experts to challenge my ideas.

Because I had another explanation.

One so controversial it had brought me nothing but trouble.

I was the only one of our crew who had grown up nearby, in a town along the Costa da Morte. And I knew—or rather, I felt in my bones—that there was more to the rapid crumbling of these ancient works than merely some strange lichen or acid. Unlike my colleagues, I didn't let my scientific background blind me to other explanations that were more . . . let's say *unconventional*. Any time I mentioned concepts like tellurism, the power of Earth's magnetism, or magnetic fields or earthly radiation, they rolled with laughter. "There isn't any credible research on that," they'd scoff. Luckily, I wasn't alone in my supposedly wild ideas. The dean of the cathedral agreed with me. He was a crotchety old clergyman whom I'd grown to love. They all called him Father Fornés. But I called him by his first name, Benigno—Spanish for "benign." I guess I just loved how it contrasted with his personality. He was the one who always stood up to the Foundation for me and encouraged me to follow my instincts.

"Sooner or later," he'd say, "you'll prove them wrong."

Someday, I thought.

At about one forty in the morning, after I'd spent who-knows-how-long using the endoscope to probe each of the nine cracks our team had mapped, my PDA chirped three times, signaling it was finally transmitting data to the computer we had set up opposite the Pórtico. I breathed a deep sigh of relief. If everything went as planned, tomorrow the University of Santiago de Compostela would process the data from the stone in the department of mineralogy at its School of Geological Sciences. Then, thirty-six hours later, we could discuss the results.

Tired but hopeful, I lowered myself and untied my harness to make sure the information was transmitting. We couldn't afford any mistakes. I was relieved to hear the five-terabyte hard drive purring like a satisfied kitten, filling the cavernous room with a rewarding hum that put me in a good mood as it finished registering all the information—the topography of each crevice, the spectrographic analysis and the video files recorded by the endoscope. Everything seemed to be going according to plan. So with satisfaction at a job well done, I finally relaxed after untangling myself from my ropes, and started picking up my equipment. I fantasized about taking a hot shower, eating a hot meal and massaging lotion onto my tired muscles before curling up with a book to distract me.

I deserved it.

But destiny has a way of toying with our best-laid plans, and that night, it had something unexpected in store for me.

Just as I disconnected the powerful headlamp and removed my helmet, a darting movement at the back of the church made me start. The hairs on the back of my neck stood on end as if the cavern had been charged with static electricity. The entire room—all of its ninety-six meters in length and its one hundred eighteen towering mullioned balconies—seemed to come alive with a "presence." My mind tried to make sense of what I was seeing. In the depths of the cathedral, I imagined I saw a flash. A fleeting spark. Soundless. A glow that emerged from the ground and traveled a lighted path toward the center of the intersecting aisles about a hundred feet away.

I'm not alone. My pulse quickened.

"Hello? Is someone there?"

A vast echo swallowed my words.

"Can anyone hear me? Is someone there? Hello . . . Hello . . . !"

Silence.

I tried to stay calm. I knew this place like the back of my hand. And I knew where to go in case I had to make a run for it. Besides, I had a cell phone and a key to the gate that led outside to the Plaza del Obradoiro. I had nothing to fear . . . I tried to convince myself that maybe I'd seen a flicker of light reflected from my metal lab tables into the moonlit cathedral. Sometimes, lights can play tricks on you. But I couldn't convince myself. And I couldn't manage to shake this feeling. That had not been a reflection in the strict sense of the word. Nor a lightning bug. Nor a falling ember from a church candle.

"Hello . . . ? Hello . . . !"

More silence answered.

As I peered into the cathedral's shadowy darkness, it felt as if I were staring deep into the jaws of some massive whale. The emergency lights at the exits were scarcely enough to give shape to the leviathan. Without proper lighting, it was hard to even imagine where the altar was. Or, for that matter, the crypt. The gilded altar and the ornate wooden bust of St. James remained veiled in darkness.

Should I dial the emergency number? I wondered as I rifled inside my pocket for my cell phone. *What if this is all in my head?*

What if it's some tortured, wandering soul . . .

I shook that idea out of my head. I tried to keep the window of fear in my mind from opening even a sliver. Still, I couldn't control the runaway pounding in my chest.

There was only one way to face down the shaking inside me. I grabbed my coat and backpack, flipped on the LED headlamp and headed for the darkened area where I thought I'd seen the light. *We only exorcise our demons when we face them head-on,* I told myself. Still shaking, I headed up the aisle toward the transept of the cross-shaped church, praying all the way I'd find no one there. Saying my Hail Marys, I finally reached the door to the Plaza de Platerías, one of the cathedral's main entrances, which, of course, was locked at this time of night.

That's when I saw it.

Rather, I almost *ran into* it.

And yet, even seeing it up close, I couldn't believe my eyes.

"Oh, God!"

The shadowy figure's face was obscured by a black hood, like a monk's. He looked to be rooting around for something he had just deposited at the base of the only modern statue in the entire cathedral, a sculpture by Jesús León Vazquez that marked the Campus Stellae. Thank God, he was skittish, not aggressive, as if he had just snuck into the church and was still trying to get his bearings.

I should have turned and run and called the cops. Instead, maybe on instinct, or maybe because we locked eyes for a second, I built up the courage to open my mouth.

"Hey! What are you doing?" I heard myself say before I knew it. "Didn't you hear me? Do you have permission to be in here?"

The thief—at least, that's what he looked like to me—casually stopped whatever he was doing, but not because I had scolded him. I saw him zip closed a black nylon bag as he turned toward me, as if he couldn't care less who was watching him. Actually, it felt like he had been crouching there . . . waiting for me to find him. Unfortunately, it was too dark to make out his face. That's when he mumbled something—something that shook my insides—in a language I didn't recognize as he slowly walked toward me.

"*Ul-a Librez?*"

"Wha . . . What did you say?"

"*Ul-ia Alibrez?*"

Seeing my confusion, he formed the words once more, finally making them understandable—and equally disturbing.

"Are you . . . Ju-lia Álvarez?"

2

Outside the cathedral, rain was falling. The *orballo* is the characteristic precipitation of northern Spain, inconspicuous until it had soaked through everything it touched. The cobblestones in the Plaza del Obradoiro were this rain's favorite victims, and at the moment, the streets couldn't absorb another drop. So when the elegant, burgundy sedan crossed the most celebrated esplanade in Galicia, it sent a wave crashing against the side of the Hostal de los Reyes Católicos before stopping at its front door.

Inside, the hotel concierge peeked out the closest window and shut off the television. His last guests for the night had arrived. He stepped outside, toward the car, just as the cathedral's bells tolled two in the morning. Just then, the driver shut off the engine to the Mercedes, turned off the lights and set the time on his watch to exactly two, as if it were a daily ritual.

"We've arrived in Santiago, my love."

The woman in the passenger seat unbuckled her seat belt and stepped out into the damp evening. She breathed a sigh of relief at seeing the concierge rushing toward her with a wide black umbrella.

"Good evening, sir . . . madam," he said in perfect English. The scent of freshly soaked earth filled the rental car's interior. "They told us you would be arriving late."

"Excellent, thank you."

"Let me escort you to your suite. We'll take care of parking the car and making sure your luggage is delivered to your room as soon as possible," he said, smiling. "We've also delivered a basket of fresh fruit to your room since the kitchen is closed at this hour."

The driver looked out across the plaza noting the harmonious atmosphere conferred on it by the stones. It was amazing how the space seemed to flawlessly bridge the divide between the fifteenth-century cathedral with its Baroque facade and the neoclassical palace in front of him.

"Tell me," he whispered as he handed the keys and ten euros to the valet, "have they finished restoring the Pórtico de la Gloria yet?"

The concierge glanced over at the cathedral. He hated that all the scaffolding disfigured the grand old church and scared away tourists.

"No, it's a shame, sir." He sighed. "The newspapers say that even the experts can't agree on how long it'll take. But it's sure to be a long time."

"You think so?" the man said, shaking his head. "Even with people working around the clock?"

He motioned toward the two enormous windows over the entrance to the cathedral, beneath the colossal statue of the apostle St. James, where a powerful orange light flickered menacingly inside.

The concierge's face paled.

Those didn't look like any work lights he had ever seen. They flashed and flickered with an ominous orange glow. He needed to call the police. And fast.

3

"Julia Ál-varez?"

It took me a moment to realize that the "monk" was pronouncing my name. It was clear he didn't speak Spanish. And his accent didn't sound French or English, either. To make matters worse, my first efforts to communicate with him through gestures didn't seem to be working. Still, call it a gut feeling, but I could tell from his calm, almost timid behavior that this apparently lost stranger meant me no harm. It wouldn't have been the first time a person on a pilgrimage here had gotten locked inside the cathedral walls. Some of the ones who came from faraway countries couldn't understand the signs written in Spanish. Every now and then, someone would stay behind lost in prayer in one of the twenty-five smaller chapels, emerging from their meditation to find themselves trapped with no one around . . . until they eventually set off a motion detector.

Still, there was something about this man that just didn't fit. Being so close to him made me feel odd, dizzy. And it bothered me—not just a little—that he knew my name and repeated it every time I tried to ask him a question.

When I finally dared to shine my light on him, it revealed a lithe young man of a dark complexion with slightly Asian features and a small tattoo of a snake below his right eye. His demeanor had an infinite gravity. He was roughly my height, muscular like a soldier. Even attractive.

"I'm sorry," I said, a little embarrassed as I studied him. "You . . . can't stay here. You should go."

But he didn't budge.

"Ju-lia Ál-varez?" he repeated.

I attempted to stay calm and motioned toward my work space, trying to show him the way out. I gestured for him to pick up his belongings and follow me, but only managed to make him more nervous.

"Come on. Follow me," I said, taking his arm.

Big mistake.

The young man shook his arm free as if I'd attacked him, held his black bag tight and yelled a bloodcurdling scream, something like *"Amrak!"* that put me on edge.

Just then, I had a terrible thought: *Is he carrying some stolen artifact in that bag? Something valuable? One of the cathedral's treasures? And if so, how unpredictable might he be?* The idea terrified me.

"Listen, calm down," I said, pulling my cell phone out of my pocket and showing it to him. "I'm going to call for help. They'll get us out of here, okay?"

The young man held his breath. He looked like a cornered animal.

"Juli-a Álva-rez?" he repeated.

"Nothing's going to happen to you, okay?" I said, ignoring him. "I'm just going to dial the emergency number. See? You'll be out of here in no time."

But seconds passed and still the phone wouldn't connect.

I tried a second time. Then a third. Without success. All the while, my new scary friend stared at me with a vacant expression, clutching his bag. Finally, on the fourth try, just as the call went through, the stranger bent over and placed his bag on the ground, motioning for me to look at it.

"What is it?" I asked.

He smiled. And for the second time that night, this man managed to confound me with his answer. Another name. A name I knew very well.

"Mar-tin Faber."

4

Just a few yards away, two police cars, a private security van and a fire truck raced across the Plaza de la Quintana. They had come up Calle Fonseca, following another squad car of officers who were already there monitoring the flickering lights inside the cathedral after receiving a call from the Hostal de los Reyes Católicos about a fire.

"Doesn't look like a fire to me, Inspector Figueiras," one officer muttered, standing outside the Puerta de Platerías, the Goldsmith's Door, getting soaked in the rain, but never for a moment taking his eyes off the cathedral.

The inspector, a rough-hewn type, hardened by the war against drug trafficking in Galicia, looked skeptically at him. There was nothing he hated more than being caught in the rain and having his glasses fog up. Needless to say, he wasn't in a good mood.

"And how did you come up with that brilliant assessment?"

"Well, I've been standing here for a while, sir, and I still haven't seen any smoke. Plus," he added, "doesn't smell like anything's burning. And you know the church is filled with all kinds of flammable stuff."

"Has anyone called the diocese?" Antonio Figueiras asked, annoyed. He hated dealing with church officials.

"Yes, sir. They're on their way. But they've told us the conservation crews often work late into the night and the lights might be theirs. Do you want us to go inside?"

Figueiras hesitated. If his men were right and there was no sign of fire other than some light flickering in the windows from time to time, then breaking the door in would only mean problems. He could already read the headlines the next morning in La Voz de Galicia: COMMUNIST COMMISSIONER DEFILES SANTIAGO CATHEDRAL. Fortunately, before he could answer, he was approached by an official in a navy blue fireman's uniform.

"Okay, so what does the fire department have to say?" Figueiras asked him.

"Your man's got a point, Inspector. Doesn't look like a fire," the assistant fire chief, a man with thick eyebrows and a catlike appearance, said confidently. "The fire alarms haven't gone off and we checked them less than a month ago."

"So what do we think it is?"

"Probably an electrical surge. The network in this area has been overloaded for the past half hour."

That only managed to pique the inspector's interest.

"Why didn't anyone tell me about this?"

"I thought you would've figured that out on your own," the firefighter said flatly, gesturing around him. "The streetlights have been out for a while now, Inspector. Only the buildings with emergency generators have any power, and the cathedral's not one of them."

Antonio Figueiras took off his glasses to wipe them with a handkerchief, cursing under his breath. So much for his keen sense of observation. He looked up and saw that the plaza was, in fact, barely lit by the headlights of his patrol cars. Not a single neighboring house had a light on. Only the flickering lights inside the cathedral could be seen. They seemed random, like flashes in a lightning storm.

"An area-wide power outage?" he said.

"More than likely."

Out of the corner of his eye, despite the driving rain and the low light, Figueiras noticed the outline of a large, towering figure rushing toward the Platerías door, as though he was about to force open the lock.

"Who's that?" he shouted.

His deputy inspector, Jiménez, just smiled.

"Oh, that guy . . . Yeah, I forgot to mention him to you. He showed up late this afternoon from some United States law enforcement agency. With an official letter. Said he's working on a case and has to find some woman who lives in Santiago."

"Well, what's he doing here now?"

"Well . . . ," Jiménez replied, "turns out the woman he's looking for works for the Barrié Foundation, and tonight's her shift at the cathedral. When he heard there was a fire he followed us here."

"So what's he doing?"

Jiménez looked over and shrugged his shoulders.

"Well, Inspector . . . It looks like he's going inside."

5

"Stop right where you are, and put your hands up!"

The words thundered throughout the cathedral, making me lose my balance for a moment. I fell to my knees on the hard marble floor as a cold rush of wind blew in.

"Don't move! I'm armed!"

The new voice erupted from somewhere behind the intruder in black. I'm not sure what rattled me more, hearing that outburst in perfect English or hearing the young man with the tattoo whisper the name of my husband Martin Faber. But I had no time to think. Purely on instinct, I dropped my helmet and put my hands on my head. But the young man didn't follow my lead.

It all happened so fast . . .

The young "monk" turned on his heel, whipped off the black habit and dove behind a row of benches to his right. He wore a running suit under his garment and brandished an object that I didn't immediately recognize.

But if his reaction startled me, it was nothing compared to the series of silent explosions along the wooden bench that sent clouds of splinters into the air.

"Julia Álvarez?"

The same voice that had ordered us to put our hands up was now pronouncing my name. His pronunciation was better than the young monk's. I heard the voice coming from behind me, but I was so shocked by what I assumed was gunfire that I failed to be surprised that, on that night, everyone seemed to know my name.

"Get down!"

Oh, God . . .

I hit the ground hard again and managed to crawl into a confessional against a wall. What sounded like three or four thunderclaps resounded through the cathedral, followed by flashes of light. But this time, the shots were coming from the young, tattooed monk. He was armed, too!

And then, for several seconds frozen in time, everything stood still.

A deathly silence fell over the cathedral. I curled up in the fetal position with my heart threatening to pound out of my chest, not daring to breathe. I wanted to cry, but fear—a visceral, gripping terror like I had never felt—had wrapped itself around my throat. *What is going on? What are they doing firing at each other in a church filled with . . . Jesus Christ! . . . filled with priceless artifacts?*

It was when I looked up at the roof to find a reference point, something that could help point me toward an exit, that I saw it. It's still hard to describe . . . In the center of the cathedral, flowing the length of the aisle from the keystone of a crypt decorated with the Eye of God, was an ethereal substance, as a translucent veil some sixty feet in the air, flashing with bolts of orange light. I'd never seen anything like it. It was like a tiny storm cloud had slipped into the cathedral and came to float exactly over the tomb of the apostle St. James.

God, would Martin love to see this, I thought.

But then my survival instincts kicked in. I had to find a way out of there.

I was about to leave my hiding place to crawl toward one of the stone columns for better cover when an enormous hand pressed down on my back, keeping my nose to the floor.

"Ms. Álvarez, don't even think about moving," the voice said, as his hand pressed against my ribs.

I was frozen with fear.

"My name is Nicholas Allen, ma'am. I'm a colonel with the United States military and I've come to rescue you."

"To rescue me?"

Had I heard him right?

That's when I realized that this Colonel Allen had been calling out all of his orders in an English flecked with a mild southern accent. Like Martin's.

"Martin . . . !"

But before I could ask another question, a fresh volley of what I assumed was gunfire exploded above us, splintering the wooden confessional and ricocheting off the stone wall.

"We better get out of here, fast," the colonel said. "He's got a gun!"

"Nicholas Allen, Inspector. He flew in from Washington on a chartered flight to the Santiago airport."

"And they let him through customs with a weapon?"

"Looks like it, sir. He must have had high-level clearance."

"Well, I don't give a shit who the hell he is, you hear me? Go back to the car and call for backup. Tell them to send an ambulance . . . and a helicopter! Have them land it in the Plaza del Obradoiro and send another unit to cover the northern exit. Go!"

Jiménez withdrew to carry out his orders. Figueiras's plan—unless things went awry—was just to hang tight, cover the exits and wait for the American to show his face so they could arrest him. Better that no one should have to fire another shot.

So much for the best-laid plans . . .

Three powerful, hollow thuds caught everyone by surprise. Then just overhead, along the so-called Treasury façade, which runs from the Platerías door all the way to the Caballos fountain, a window shattered into a thousand pieces.

"What the hell . . . !"

Figueiras barely had time to look up. Above them, past falling shards of glass, he saw a scene that left him dumbstruck: the wiry silhouette of a man with an athletic build, his hair tied into a long ponytail and clutching something under his arm, leaped along the five-hundred-year-old rooftop, trailed by a cloud of strange, luminous dust.

The inspector, an atheist raised by leftist Spanish communists, felt the blood drain from his face, and shouted only a single phrase from his mother's native language.

"*O demo!*"

The devil.

Antonio Figueiras's face grew pale.

"Were those gunshots?" Everyone froze. "Holy shit, those are gunshots!"

The six police officers and two security guards next to him looked at each other, confused, as if they doubted that the hollow volley of explosions could have come from a gun's barrel.

"That son of a bitch got himself into a gunfight inside the cathedral!" Figueiras shouted, shooting a look at Jiménez, as if he were, to blame. He whipped out his sidearm, a nine-millimeter Heckler & Koch Compact he kept under his trench coat. "We have to arrest him . . ."

Jiménez just shrugged.

"Then you'll explain to me exactly who this character is," Figueiras spat. "Now, cover me. I'm going in!"

Four officers followed his lead, cautiously approaching the Platerías entrance, careful to stand on either side in case someone opened fire. Three others stood guard, covering the other exits, including the nearby Puerta Santa, the Holy Door, located behind the main altar. The driving rain was blinding and made it almost impossible to see the cream-colored awnings of the nearby Otero jewelry store. Moreover, the darkness caused by the blackout gave the oldest entrance to the cathedral a haunting feel. Almost sinister. The Old Testament scenes depicted above it didn't help: the statue of an adulterous woman holding her lover's severed head, famous among those who make the pilgrimage as a warning of divine justice. The scene of Adam and Eve being cast out of the Garden of Eden. And on the spandrels of the main archway, glistening in the rain, the angels of the apocalypse sounding their trumpets.

"What did you say this character's name was?" Figueiras whispered as he leaned against one of the archway's fluted columns.

When I finally left the cathedral, I was doused by a curtain of rain. The storm had plunged the street into total darkness and only lightning flashes lit the doorways of nearby homes. I felt stunned, like I'd lost the hearing in my left ear, and I couldn't keep my arms and legs from shaking. It felt good to be soaked through by the rain. It reminded me that I was alive . . . and that anything could still happen. I clung to the sea of smells that washed over me—the smell of moss, of soaked earth, of wood burning in nearby chimneys. That and the rhythmic pounding of the rain helped calm my heart.

Not everyone was as lucky.

The man who led me out of the cathedral was raging. I could hear him arguing with someone who was waiting for him just outside the door. Luckily, someone quickly got me away from him. Two firefighters whisked me to an arcade to shelter me from the incessant rain, and then covered me with a blanket.

"Look!" one of them said as a nearby streetlamp flickered. "The power's back."

The firefighters thoughtfully brought me a plastic chair and a bottle of water that I downed in seconds.

"Don't worry, miss. You'll be all right."

"Will I?"

The stress of this recent commotion, combined with nine uninterrupted hours of tedious work, should have shown on my face. Maybe it sounds superficial, but I instinctively looked for a place to check my reflection. I guess I was trying to busy my mind with something, anything, other than monks, gunshots and mysteriously glowing thunderclouds. And for at least a little while, it worked. The glass door of the only café still open at this time of night was all I needed to see the sorry shape I was in. There, in the reflection, was a girl with wild, tangled hair who seemed totally out of place. Her flame of red hair barely showed its usual fire in this dim, fading light, and her piercing green eyes faded into dark circles that made me shudder.

What have you gotten yourself into, Julia?

What worried me most about my reflection was what I didn't see: suddenly I'd lost all my muscle tone. And I must have slammed hard into something during the commotion, because my upper back ached as if I'd fallen off my scaffolding . . .

The scaffolding!

I prayed that the gunshots hadn't knocked anything loose. My work space was set up just below it, all the data from my experiments co-cooned in that hard drive.

"The police will want to talk with you," the nearest of the firefighters said. "Wait right here, okay?"

A cop wrapped in a beige trench coat, dripping wet and desperately trying to wipe the moisture off his white thick-framed glasses, trudged over, grumbling under his breath as he greeted me halfheartedly. He dried his hands on the back of his coat and reached out to shake my hand with a rather stiff formality.

"Good evening, miss," he said. "My name is Antonio Figueiras of the Santiago police department. Are you okay?"

I nodded.

"This whole situation is a little . . ." He hesitated. "A little embarrassing for us. The man who rushed you out of the cathedral said you were ambushed. He told us in his broken Spanish that you're Julia Álvarez—is that right?" I nodded and the annoyed inspector continued. "Look, it's my job to question you immediately about all this, but this character—he works for the U.S. government—says he has something important he needs to discuss with you."

"The colonel?"

The inspector looked surprised to hear Nicholas Allen's rank. He seemed to process the information before nodding his head. "That's right. Do you mind speaking with him first? If you do, I could always—"

"No, no, not at all. As a matter of fact, I have a few questions for him, too."

The inspector called him over.

I saw Nicholas Allen emerge from a car parked at the far end of the plaza and make his way toward me. When I saw him in the light for the first time, I was a little surprised. He was about six feet tall, about fifty years old, and had the demeanor of a perfect gentleman. His suit had been crumpled in the fracas, but his designer tie and crisply starched shirt still gave him an air of distinction. He carried a leather briefcase and pulled up a chair next to me before greeting me again.

"You can't imagine how glad I am that I got to you when I did, Ms. Álvarez," he said with a sigh of relief, reaching out to hold my hands.

"Do we . . . know each other?"

The colonel turned his face toward the light, as if pretending to model his face for me. But up close, I could see an alarming scar running the length of his brow and disappearing beneath his slicked-back salt-and-pepper hair.

"Well, I know you," he said. "I was a friend of your husband's. He and I worked together on several government projects, long before the two of you met. And since . . . well, let's say I've followed your careers."

Something about the colonel's admission caught me off guard. I'd never heard Martin mention this man. For a moment, I wondered whether I should bring up the monk—or whatever he was—who had mentioned Martin to me. But I decided to hear the colonel out first.

"I need to ask you some important questions. But I think you and I should have this conversation in private," Allen said, shooting a sideways look at Inspector Figueiras, who was lurking a couple of feet away.

"Whatever you think is best," I said, shrugging my shoulders.

"Great, just let the inspector know and we'll get to it," he said, smiling.

I hesitated for a second, but my curiosity had gotten the better of me. I walked over to the disheveled-looking inspector and asked him for a few minutes alone with Allen. He agreed, even though he looked uneasy about it.

"Thank you," the colonel whispered.

We ducked inside the nearby La Quintana café, where the staff was buzzing about, recovering from the recent blackout and hoping to close soon. The espresso machine whirred in the background while the remaining waiter sat us near the back.

"Julia . . ." He sounded hesitant. "I know you and Martin met in 2000, when he made the Way of St. James pilgrimage. That he left everything for you. His work. His parents. That you were married near London and—"

"Wait a minute," I said. "You want to ask me about Martin after everything else we've just been through?"

"That's right. He's the reason I'm here. Well, he and that man I saved you from tonight."

The waiter brought us cups of coffee.

He continued. "Tell me, when was the last time you spoke to your husband?"

"A month ago. He was in a mountainous region in Turkey, gathering data for a study on climate change."

"Near Mt. Ararat?"

"How did you know?"

"I know a lot more than that, ma'am," he said, pulling an iPad out of his briefcase and setting it in front of me as the screen came to life. "Your husband is in serious danger. He's been kidnapped."

8

"What are you waiting for? Send me that information immediately!"

Despite his sloppy appearance and lack of social graces, the inspector wasn't the type of man to sit around waiting for things to happen. He hung up the phone hastily even before the person on the other end could even answer. It was bad enough that some foreign cop was interviewing his only witness to the shooting in the cathedral and had a better idea of what was going on than he did. But after an enlightening conversation with the dean of the cathedral while his men picked up shell casings and noted the damage to the sacred building, Inspector Figueiras had a much better idea about who Julia Álvarez was.

Father Fornés described her as strong-willed—perhaps even too much so. She wasn't much for church dogma and, in Fornés's opinion, might have let herself stray into pagan ideas. "'Spiritual,' New Age–y, that kind of thing," the priest said, unsolicited. "But I will tell you, she's the best there is at her job. I know that girl is going to make a huge discovery one day."

What surprised Figueiras most about the conversation was the revelation that Julia Álvarez was married to an American.

That's why he had called the police station and asked them to send him everything they could find out about the couple. Figueiras was focused on the portable computer in his patrol car when he felt the beating of helicopter blades pulsing through the air and rattling the windows of every building in the plaza. He'd almost forgotten his impulsive order to call for his only helicopter in the driving rain. He barely had time to regret it when the chief of police called.

"We have that information you asked for," he said. "First off, we don't have anything on Julia Álvarez. She's got no prior arrests. Not even a parking ticket. But we do know she has a doctorate in art history and wrote a book on the Way of St. James pilgrimage. But that's about all we found."

"Her husband, however, is a lot more interesting. Martin Faber is a climatologist. One of the best, Figueiras. Actually, no one really understands why he lives here. In 2006, the United Nations awarded him a prize after he published a study on the melting permafrost in the European and Asian mountain ranges. And all of his predictions seem to be coming true. This guy's well respected, Inspector. The interesting thing, though, is that he studied at Harvard and was recruited by the National Security Agency, where he worked until he married Julia Álvarez and retired here with her."

"Her husband is a spy?"

"Technically? Yes," the chief said, lowering his voice, "but the bad part is the rest of his file is labeled 'classified.'"

"How convenient . . ."

The inspector's eyes came alive behind his white-rimmed glasses. How convenient, indeed, that the man interrogating his witness and her husband both worked for the same intelligence agency, the NSA. *There's something big going on here,* he decided.

"Do we know when they got married, Chief?"

"I haven't been able to find it yet. But when I looked in the register of US citizens living in Spain, I noticed they were married in Great Britain. And there's a pretty interesting little fact in their customs file . . ."

"On with it, Chief!"

"Well, it seems they lived in London for a year, working on something that was a complete departure for the both of them. They were antique dealers. But after moving here, they sold everything. Except for two Elizabethan-era stones, which they declared when they moved into the country."

"Two stones?"

"Two ancient relics. Strange, right?"

9

The images flashing before my eyes seemed unreal. It was like something out of a brutal Gulf War movie. It was almost too hard to watch, yet I couldn't look away—because I instantly recognized the film's main character, dressed in an orange prison jumpsuit, whose face filled the entire screen. *Oh, God* . . . I recognized his sharp features; the profile of his face; the big, strong hands that were now bound; and that look he got on his face when something had gone terribly wrong. And I knew immediately I couldn't watch any more.

"What . . . is this?" I pleaded.

The colonel froze the video.

"It's a 'proof of life,' Ms. Álvarez. It was found last week in the northeastern part of the Anatolia region of Turkey. As you can see, it shows—"

"My husband, I know," I said, stopping him from saying anything I could not bear to hear, as my throat tightened. I wordlessly fingered the gold wedding band on my ring finger, fighting back tears. "Who's done this? Why . . . ? What do they want from him?"

"Please, try to stay calm."

"Calm? How can you expect me to stay calm?"

The waiter glanced our way as I shouted at the colonel, my eyes swimming with tears and an invisible hand squeezing the breath out of my chest. He gently took my hands as the waiter disappeared into the next room.

"I'll answer all of your questions, Ms. Álvarez, as much as the US government knows. But I need you to try to stay calm and answer my questions too, okay?"

I couldn't make a sound. My eyes just kept going back to Martin's frozen image on the screen. He was almost unrecognizable. Days' worth of stubble on his face, his hair matted, his skin covered in sun blisters. An ocean of remorse washed over me, threatening to drown me. *How could I have been so stupid? Why did I let him make that trip alone?* The memory of our last conversation flashed in my mind. It was just before he left for Kars, near Ararat. For five years, he'd used me to help him with his experiments. Finally, I told him I wouldn't do it anymore.

"Not even for love?" he said, surprised at my anger.

"No . . . not even for love!"

Now I was regretting my decision. Was I the one who got him into such danger?

"First thing you should know is that a terrorist group has claimed responsibility for his kidnapping," Allen said, oblivious to my thoughts. "The Kurdistan Workers' Party, an illegal Marxist faction that's been at war with the Turkish government for decades. The good news"—and he grinned as he said it—"is that they have a long history of kidnapping hikers and returning them safely. The not-so-good news is that in this case, they've been very careful and left no traces of their whereabouts. Not even our satellites have been able to find them."

"Sat . . . ellites?" I said, chocking back my sobs.

"Our government has come to you as a last resort, Ms. Álvarez," he said. "Before Martin met you, he worked on some very important projects for our country. He knows sensitive information that cannot fall into the wrong hands. That's why I'm here. To help you find him, but also so you can help us. Do you understand?"

"I'm not sure."

A wave of realization engulfed me. Martin had never said much to me about his time in Washington. He barely mentioned that part of his life. It's like there was something about it he just wanted to forget, like an old girlfriend you just don't mention to your new wife. Then Nicholas Allen brought me back to the present by turning the conversation toward something I couldn't have imagined.

"Now, I need you to watch the rest of the tape," he said.

"What?"

"I'm not showing this to you to torture you, believe me. I need you to help us decipher a message your husband sent you."

"To me? In the video?"

A slight tremor shot through my tired hands.

"Yes, a message to you."

The device came back to life, bathing the back corner of the café in a bluish glow. Colonel Allen slid his finger across the touch screen and the video jumped to minute seven. I clasped both hands to my stomach, as if that would help me control my emotions. When the screen showed my husband's emaciated face, frozen in time, I prepared myself for the worst.

The first sounds were from a man's voice with a broken English accent.

"I said, say your name!"

The voice was hostile, impatient, and came from somewhere off-screen.

"Didn't you hear me? Your name!"

Martin raised his tired face, as if he'd finally heard the order.

"My name is Martin Faber. I'm a scientist—"

"Do you have a message for your loved ones?"

My poor husband nodded. His inquisitor hissed his orders, venom dripping with every syllable accentuated in Russian, as if he'd just walked off the set of *The Hunt for Red October*. Martin fixed his gaze straight ahead, as if he were talking directly to me and we were the only ones in the room.

"Julia," he said, speaking to me in Spanish, my native language. "We may never see each other again . . . And if I don't get out of this alive, I want you to remember me as a happy man, a man who found his other half at your side . . ."

A single restless tear rolled down my cheek. And I saw his hands tightly grasp the symbol of our love. The object that had given our lives—or mine, at least—an unexpected purpose. With his voice trembling and the sound cutting in and out, he continued.

"If you squander your remaining time, all will be lost. The discoveries we made together. The world that opened up to us. All of it. Fight for me. Use your gift. And though others may strive to steal what was ours, keep envisioning a way for these two halves to be made whole again—"

The video ended abruptly.

"There's nothing else?" I said, feeling as if the wind had been knocked out of me.

"No."

I was confused, my mind spinning. And Colonel Allen, who hadn't stopped holding my hands, gripped them tighter.

"I'm sorry," he said, whispering still lower, "I'm truly sorry."

As Martin's words were still ordering themselves in my mind, the colonel, whose intentions I wasn't completely clear on, asked me a question so unexpected that it only managed to confuse me further.

"Ms. Álvarez," he asked, "what gift was your husband referring to?"

10

Miguel Pazos and Jaime Mirás had only been working at the Santiago de Compostela police department for a year after whisking through the police academy with stellar grades. They loved their job, in the county seat, with the largest tourist population in northern Spain, even though almost nothing worth mentioning ever happened there.

Inspector Figueiras had posted them at the stairway leading to the entrance to the cathedral and the Pórtico de la Gloria, and they couldn't help gossiping excitedly about the commotion. But there was no reason to worry, not really, they figured. After all, the gunshots that sent everyone scrambling had passed. Thank goodness the cathedral wasn't on fire and no one had been hurt in the gunfight. Still, Figueiras wanted them on high alert for anything suspicious. An armed suspect was still at large, maybe hiding somewhere down one of the alleys leading to the wide open Plaza del Obradoiro, and he needed to be found.

At the door to the Hostal de los Reyes Católicos, everything seemed quiet. The state-run hotel was shut tight, as it always was at this hour of the night. Power had been restored, bathing the cathedral and the façade of the Palacio de Rajoy in a pale light. The constant rain played in the young officers' favor. They could sit inside the dry patrol car, parked along the Calle San Francisco, where they had a perfect view of anyone who looked suspicious.

Neither of them expected that, exactly at two forty in the morning, the ground would begin to tremble.

It was just a soft tremor at first, as if the rain simply had started pounding harder against the roof of their Nissan X Trail. The young cops looked at each other wordlessly. But when a deafening rumble thundered all around them, they started shaking in their seats.

"What the hell is that?" Pazos said.

His partner tried to calm him down. "It's probably just the helicopter," he said.

"You're probably right."

"Man, you have to have some balls to fly that thing in this kind of weather."

"Big ones . . ."

The rumbling grew louder. Nearby puddles rippled in rhythm and blew apart as a downward windstorm beat the air around the officers.

"Jaime . . . ," Pazos said, pressing his face against the windshield to watch. "Is that *our* chopper?"

A huge black aircraft, fifty feet long with two sets of spinning rotors and a third on its rudder, descended in front of them, its power levitating their two-ton all-terrain truck a hair's breadth off the ground.

The helicopter's powerful engines came to a halt, producing a deafening, high-pitched whistle that forced them to cover their ears.

"Who called in the army?" Pazos yelled over the noise.

But his partner wasn't listening.

He was too distracted by the sight in his passenger window. A man with olive skin, his hair pulled back into a braid and a scar just below his right eye, gave a few quick taps against the patrol car's window. Mouth still hanging half-open, lowered the glass.

"Hey! What's going—"

He didn't have time to finish his sentence.

Two silent blasts, lost in the fading whistle of the helicopter's engines, flung the officers' skulls against their headrests. The shots from the stranger's Sig Sauer pistol were so quick, so precise, that the two young men never saw it coming. And they never heard their executioner mumble something in a strange, unintelligible language—"*Nerir nrants, Ter, yev qo girkn endhuni!*"—before he crossed himself and left their motionless bodies in his wake.

11

"It's a long story, Colonel. And I'm not even sure it's appropriate for me to be telling you," I said, swallowing hard.

Nicholas Allen took a long, slow drink of coffee and leaned back in his chair before putting his massive hands on the table.

"All right," he said, his voice shifting into a serious tone. "I want you to think hard about this. Your husband used a kidnapper's proof of life to send you a message. And also a warning. You're aware of that, aren't you?"

I nodded without being completely sure.

"When I first saw this video in Washington," he said, tapping the iPad, "I understood that the allusion to someone stealing what was yours was a message. Do you have something valuable that you need to protect?"

Allen asked in such a way that he seemed to know the answer to the question. In fact, he didn't even wait for me to respond.

"One thing's clear," he said. "Your husband's right about you being in danger."

My pulse quickened. "Do you think that 'monk' from the cathedral was going to . . . ?"

"Don't you? He was after you, I'm sure of it. Did he speak to you? Did he say anything at all?"

"Well, he mentioned Martin . . ."

"In what regard?"

"I don't know," I said, frustrated. "I couldn't understand him!"

"It's okay. Don't worry. We'll go step-by-step. I'd like you to go back and answer my first question."

So we started again.

"Fine . . ." I sighed.

"What 'gift' was your husband referring to in the video, Ms. Álvarez?"

"I have visions, Colonel."

I said it without thinking, without caveats or provisos, and I felt as if a great weight had been lifted off my shoulders. And just as I'd expected, Nicholas Allen looked perplexed. Just like everyone else.

"I guess it is going to be a long story . . . ," he said, shaking his head.

"It runs in my family. Like something innate, you know? My mother had it. My grandmother, too. In fact, every woman on my mother's side of the family has had it, as far as I can tell. Sometimes I've wondered whether it's some kind of genetic mutation. I've tried to repress the visions with medication, but it's no use. I don't know how, but Martin knew that I had this gift. It's a lot like what people call clairvoyance, but it's not that, exactly. You can imagine, I kept it secret. When I was in college, it was a struggle to keep it from my professors and classmates. We'd walk into a museum or some historical site and my visions would come flooding over me. At first, it was something I could feel. I could presage that something was going to happen."

"What kind of visions do you see?"

"It's hard to put into words," I said, twisting a napkin into knots. "I never talk about it, and I've never done it in public. I could pick up an object and 'see' its history. I could see where it had been and who it had belonged to. Martin told me it's called 'psychometrics.' But I could do more than that. Sometimes, I would forget my own language and slip into other languages, some of them unrecognizable. One time, my grandmother relaxed me into a deep trance and I started speaking in perfect Latin. This gift of speaking in tongues is called 'xenoglossy.' It was Martin who helped me develop my gift, to not be afraid of it."

If the colonel doubted my story, he didn't let on. "How did you and your husband meet?"

"Is that important?" I asked.

"It might be."

"Fine." I sighed. "It was several years ago. Martin came to my town as just another pilgrim making his journey along the Way of St. James.

I was a tour guide then at a church in Noia, along the Costa da Morte. He visited the church and we got to talking. We hit it off right away, and he started telling me about things in *my* life. Personal things, about my work, my friends . . . I thought it was some kind of magic trick he used to pick up women. But it was more than that. He told me I could do that kind of thing, too. That I had a natural ability for it. He told me he could teach me to develop my gift to its full potential. He stayed in my town, and as time went on, little by little, we fell in love. Simple as that."

I glanced up and noticed "the look" on the colonel's face, the look everyone got whenever I told this story. But I decided to press on.

"I need you to find Martin, Colonel. If you promise me you'll find him, I'll tell you anything you want to know about my gift. But help me."

Allen's gaze turned from worried to compassionate. Even sweet. His silvery eyebrows arched sympathetically.

"I promise," he said finally. "That's why I'm here."

And with an innocence he hadn't shown until that moment, he added, "I imagine that 'teaching you to reach your full potential' has something to do with that stone he showed in the video, right?"

"Right. When I finish my story, I think you'll understand."

"Where were we?"

"The gift of visions. Can you imagine what that kind of gift means in a world like ours, a world of facts and reason? I always felt out of place because of my gift. I was convinced that if I didn't find a way to muffle it, it would drive me insane."

"And Martin Faber was interested in this gift of yours?"

"Mesmerized."

"Do you know why?"

"Y-yes," I stuttered.

"Please." He smiled, noticing my hesitation. "Go on. Don't hold anything back. I've given you my word that I'm going to help you find Martin. But I need your collaboration."

"Well, it has to do with a family secret."

"Another family secret?"

"Yes. From the Fabers . . . That stone Martin is holding in the video? It's actually a talisman, a stone with immeasurable power."

Allen's face took on its most serious gaze yet.

"I learned about it for the first time the day before Martin and I were to be married. It's an incredible story. Though it'll probably take all night to tell it."

"Go ahead, Ms. Álvarez. I want to hear all about it . . ."

12

It was late and it had been a long night already, but Inspector Figueiras needed to get some work done. He headed for the police station to start filling out the mountain of paperwork from the night's incident and to put out an APB on the monk from the cathedral.

The old city was deserted. He turned the wrong way down Calle Fonseca with his police lights flashing and left a standing order for his men to keep an eye on whatever might be happening at La Quintana. They were to bring the witness to him as soon as the American was through with his interrogation. *She can sleep in the holding cell, for all I care,* he thought. *But I need her in custody until I have answers about what the hell's going on here.*

As the cathedral's spires disappeared in his rearview mirror, he looked out on the plaza and could see the profile of an enormous airship in the center of the courtyard. Between the swipes of his wiper blades, he guessed it was the helicopter he had called in. He figured it must be waiting out the storm before returning to base.

"Hmm. Better that way," he said.

As he cruised down Avenida de Rodrigo de Padrón, out of the historical district and came to rest at the police station's underground parking lot, his only thoughts were on what role the Fabers' precious talismans played in this whole mess. Because they *must* play some role, he figured. *Something worth that much,* he said to himself, *two million pounds, to be exact, according to the customs documents . . .*

"A couple of stones from the sixteenth century?" The voice on the other end of the line couldn't believe he had been awakened at this time of night for a professional opinion.

"That's right, Marcelo. Elizabethan. English, at least."

Marcelo Muñiz was Figueiras's friend and Santiago's best-known jeweler. Any precious gem bought or sold anywhere in Galicia first passed across his desk.

"I don't remember seeing anything like that," Muñiz said firmly. "Who were the owners?"

Figueiras gave him the information on Martin Faber and Julia Álvarez, and Muñiz went to work. He put down the phone, flipped open his laptop and sifted through his professional database. After a few minutes, Muñiz came back on the line with bad news.

"Sorry, Figueiras. Nothing. But I can assure you of this: Those stones didn't pass this way. Any chance they didn't sell them?"

"Maybe," Figueiras said. "But let me ask you something. If you were moving from England to Spain and you had something like that in your possession, why would you even declare it at customs?"

"For the insurance, of course," Muñiz said. "If they're incredibly valuable and you want your insurance company to cover them when you leave the country, you have to have a paper trail."

"And if you had something that valuable, would you keep working? Would you keep up a crazy schedule that had you toiling away inside an old church in the middle of the night?"

"Well, maybe its owners didn't want to call too much attention to themselves," Muñiz said. "Maybe their interest in the stones isn't purely monetary. You'd be surprised how much some people value objects beyond what they're worth."

"Maybe . . . ," Figueiras said, exhaustion finally setting in. "I guess I'll figure that out tomorrow."

13

It *was* a long story. I'd warned him. But Nicholas Allen was determined to hear it. He asked for a double espresso and whatever pastry the café had left at this hour. The waiter, resigned at seeing local and federal police cars parked out front, had no choice but to wait these two customers out—no matter how long it took.

"Start wherever you like," Allen said.

"Okay. How about I start with the day I saw these stones for the first time? It was the eve of our wedding . . ."

I'd never seen my fiancé as excited as he was on that early summer morning. It was toward the end of June 2005, and we'd arrived at our hotel in the West End with a little time to rest before the ceremony. We were going to get married in a small Norman church in Wiltshire, a beautiful place. It was to be a simple service, just a handful of guests. We called a priest who was a friend of Martin's family, quickly filled him in and asked him to preside over our ceremony.

I was madly in love with this man. In all other areas of my life, I was tough, determined. But not when it came to Martin. He was like a sculptor who could chisel and mold the world around us, bringing beauty to all aspects of my life.

Everything happened so quickly between us. Within ten months we were hurrying down the aisle. Martin left his job in the United States and frankly, I didn't even think twice about leaving mine.

You're going to think this is ridiculous, Colonel. But shortly before I met Martin, I'd read somewhere that if you asked the universe for guidance and wrote down the things that you wanted in life, you could achieve them. Just writing things down helps order them in your mind and makes the goals seem attainable. So I wrote a three-page letter the day I turned twenty-nine, summarizing everything I wanted in a man. I asked for my soul mate. A good man. Someone to share adventures with. He had to be someone who was pure of heart and capable of making my heart soar with his words.

I tucked the message inside a sandalwood box that I stashed in the back of my closet. And just when I'd forgotten about it, Martin came to Noia. You should have seen him. Behind the ragged clothes he wore for his pilgrimage, he glowed with the most radiant smile in the world. He was so magnetic, so perfect. Down to the letter, he was the man I'd described in my letter to the cosmos.

The day before our wedding, on the flight from Santiago to London's Heathrow, Martin showed me a couple of pictures of the church he'd chosen for the ceremony. He'd kept it all a secret. And just as you'd expect, I thought it was perfect.

That afternoon, in London, we took a cab south because there was something important he wanted to show me. As we left behind the busy city, he asked the driver to take us to an address on Mortlake Road in Richmond upon Thames. When we finally reached our destination—a modern brick four-story apartment building in a quiet residential neighborhood—I felt a little disappointed. I'd imagined he was taking me to some exotic restaurant where we'd make all sorts of exciting plans for our future. But Martin had something else in mind that afternoon.

"Have you ever heard of John Dee?" he asked me flatly as the cab left us in front of the building.

"Is he a family member of yours?"

"No, no," he laughed. "Dee was a magician and the personal astrologer to England's Queen Elizabeth the First. He was considered a master of the occult and his fame was rivaled only by his contemporary Nostradamus."

"Martin, are you going to talk to me about wizards again?" I said in protest. "I thought all that stuff—"

"I need to tell you about this. It's time," Martin said, aiming a serious gaze at me.

"Oh, enough . . ." I sighed.

The only times Martin and I had ever fought was when he brought up his obsession with the science of the occult. He was fascinated with it in a way I never was. At that point, I hadn't yet written my book about the hidden symbols on the Way of St. James. Anything that remotely approached the supernatural, I just ignored. I'd lived through some . . . *strange* things in my youth, and I didn't want to admit there were some phenomena that science couldn't explain. It was easier to believe those topics were for the superstitious and the ignorant. I guess it just went against everything I grew up hearing at home. Yet here was a man steeped in science—he had a doctorate in physics from Harvard University—and he believed blindly in things like clairvoyance and mediums. He said they were the world's science before actual science. But I just couldn't follow Martin down that path of reasoning.

"I'm begging you to listen to me, Julia," he said, holding me by the shoulders. "Just this once."

"Okay."

"Before we go inside, there's something else you should know about John Dee. He was one of the world's most important mathematicians, cartographers and philosophers during the sixteenth century. And, like any good Catholic—like you—he was skeptical about anything supernatural. He translated Euclid, Greece's foremost scholar in geometry, into English for the first time. He was the first man to apply geometry to navigation. His discoveries helped make the tiny island of England into one of the world's greatest empires."

"But I don't get it. Why do you care so much about some old, dead warlock, Martin?"

"There's a part of John Dee's work that's always fascinated me," he said, skirting my question and taking a deep breath. "He devised a way to speak to angels. His method is still a mystery."

What was this man, this man who was going to be my husband in a few hours, trying to tell me?

"You have to believe in this, Julia. At least, you have to open yourself to the possibility," he pleaded. "In 1581, a solar storm occurred and a real angel of flesh and blood, a being who blended in so seamlessly with humans that he might cross this street without you giving him a second look, came to see John Dee—and taught him how to speak to angels. And from that day, Dee became an ambassador to the angels, learning incredible, marvelous things that would inspire a golden age of technology for centuries to come."

Martin's eyes were on fire. I couldn't have stopped him if I'd wanted to.

"What you don't know about me is a family secret that we only speak of when we welcome a new member, someone like you. After Dee's death, our family inherited all of his research, all of his books and all of his spells. Although, through the centuries, we've lost most of his ability to communicate with the divine."

"Wait. Are you telling me that your family speaks to angels?" I asked, frightened.

"Tonight, you're going to meet a group of people who have seen more and done more than anyone else in that realm, Julia. And then you're going to understand why I brought you here to meet them. All I'm asking for is a little patience . . . and faith."

14

The massive airship that had landed in the center of Plaza del Obradoiro was not your run-of-the-mill helicopter. An experimental prototype, it was one of only three in the world, and could fly smoothly in this kind of hammering weather. It was clad in bulletproof armor and loaded with heavy artillery. It could fly at an altitude of more than sixteen thousand feet—unheard-of for a warship of this kind—and slice through the skies at more than three hundred miles an hour, remaining airborne for twelve hours straight without refueling. Its alloy coating made it impervious to extreme temperatures and it was equipped with one of the world's most advanced navigation systems.

That flying beast had no flight plan and no ID. Officially, it didn't even exist. So naturally, no one expected it to turn up in Galicia. It had come out of nowhere, bisecting Europe and holing up in a little-known hangar near the Fervenza reservoir, awaiting this very moment.

When its side door whooshed open, the man who'd ended the lives of the two young officers jumped inside, still dripping with rain as the door zipped closed behind him.

"What happened out there?"

Waiting inside was a man in his midforties, his eyes dark and piercing, and the parts of his face not covered in a long, neat beard were toughened from the sun. And he wanted answers. The soldier lowered his weapon, bowed at his feet and spoke in his native Armenian, barely raising his voice.

"*Tsavum e.* I had to do it, Sheikh."

The bearded man remained silent.

"If I hadn't neutralized them, they would have detained me and it would have cost us the entire mission. I'm sorry, master."

"It's all right . . . ," his superior said, placing his hand gently on the kneeling man's head as if bestowing a blessing. "And how did it go in the church? Did you see her?"

The young man's eyes filled with tears.

"You were right, Sheikh," he said, now breathing heavily, his eyes fixed on the ground in front of him. "It's her. That woman can activate the *Amrak*. In the cathedral, she did it without even noticing."

"She wasn't aware of it?"

"That's how great her power is, master."

The sheikh simply stared down at his kneeling disciple for a moment, shaken by this information. What would his ancestors have said about this? How would they have explained a foreigner having such power over one of their most sacred heirlooms? Fortunately, he no longer resembled his predecessors. If anything, he was more like a doctor impatiently awaiting the results of a critical lab test. Not what you might expect from the supreme leader of one of the world's oldest and most secret societies.

"What else did you learn?" he asked, holding his voice steady.

"*Votsh*. Nothing. I didn't have a chance, Sheikh. They arrived before I could—"

"They? Do you mean . . . ?"

The young man nodded.

"The Americans . . ."

The master lifted his hand from his disciple's head and the young man's gaze rose to meet his.

"Then we have no other choice, my son," he said intently. "We must intervene before evil has its way."

15

"Is that when you saw the stones, Julia? Didn't you say that was the first day you ever saw them?"

Nicholas Allen was getting anxious. He made it seem vital that he understand my connection to the stones.

"I'm getting there," I said, unwittingly feeding his suspense. "If you want to understand, you have to let me tell the story step-by-step."

"Right. Of course," he said. "Go on . . ."

After his careful speech, Martin brought me toward a white aluminum door that led to the building's apartments nine through sixteen on the Mortlake side of the road. Above the door frame was a metal plaque with white letters against a blue background that read JOHN DEE HOUSE.

"This is it," he said.

"John Dee's house?"

A sly grin ran across his cherubic face and chased away my anxiety. I could see his excitement in his sweet dimples and in the way he looked at me.

"What are you waiting for? C'mon!" he said.

We ran up the first flight of stairs two at a time and came to a wide, airy hallway bathed in warm light. If a necromancer's house once stood here, none of that darkness remained. I was just about to say that to Martin when the apartment door right in front of us swung open.

"Martin, my boy!"

An older woman stepped out of the door and flung herself into Martin's arms. She was about sixty, elegant, her brown hair cut into a neat bob that framed her smooth, made-up skin, and she wore a conservative blue dress.

"We've been expecting you!"

"God, Sheila, how many years has it been? You look incredible!"

They hugged each other for a long time, long enough for me to notice her name, Sheila Graham, engraved on a small golden plaque flanked by a pair of angels hanging on her door.

"So this must be . . ."

"Julia," Martin said, finishing her sentence. "And as of tomorrow, my dear aunt, she'll be the newest member of the family."

"Such beautiful red hair," she said, whistling and running her eyes over my print dress. "You have chosen wisely . . ."

She flashed me a knowing grin and led us inside. We followed her down a long, dimly lit hallway into her lavish home. We passed bookcases whose shelves seemed ready to burst under the weight of their countless tomes and went into a quiet living room whose large bright windows opened up to the street below. Waiting for us there was a young man reclining on a wingback sofa, his attention focused on a heavy book in his lap. He was tall but muscular with a curly beard and curly hair framing his ruddy face. When he saw us come in, he nodded in our direction.

"Hello," he said simply. "Sit wherever you like, love."

Love?

That young lion perched on his rock was named Daniel. "Like the prophet," Sheila said. "Daniel Knight. And if you think I'm some old cougar who's gotten herself a boy toy twenty years her junior, think again, my dear," she said, and I blushed because it was exactly what I'd thought.

Martin and Sheila went down the hall to bring back drinks and I was left with Daniel, who was again engrossed in his reading. At least it gave me time to get a good look at my surroundings. The room was large, about two hundred square feet, divided between this sitting area and the adjacent dining room. The long table at its center, with its high-backed chairs, must have hosted some interesting dinner parties. Against the window was an antique curio cabinet whose glass doors enclosed a motley collection of trinkets: a pan flute; a crystal sphere; a strange, long pipe carved with the image of a Bedouin nomad; several lithographs organized neatly in a row, and four plaster figurines covered in black lacquer . . .

But what really caught my attention was the opposite wall, which was covered in old photographs. Sheila was a young woman in several of them, and she clearly had been attractive. There were pictures of her posing at historical sites all over Great Britain. The Glastonbury Tower, which shows up on the cover of all the King Arthur books. The British Museum. The monoliths at Stonehenge. Riding on a white horse over the rolling Wiltshire hills. And in another picture, she was posing next to a group of smiling hippies in white tunics holding large, extravagant walking sticks.

"Those are Druids, love," Daniel murmured as I leaned in for a closer look. "One of them is John Michell."

"Druids. Right. Of course," I said, not knowing what a Druid was. "Can I ask you what Sheila does for a living?"

Daniel looked up from his book.

"Your fiancé hasn't told you?"

I shook my head.

"We study the occult," he said flatly. "And, I must say, we're quite good at it."

Daniel was looking for a reaction. And although he clearly got it from the dumbstruck look on my face, he left me swinging in the wind. He let Martin, who came into the room balancing a tray of petit fours, tell me exactly who our hosts were.

"Julia, Daniel Knight works for the Royal Observatory in Greenwich. He's an astronomer. But he's also the world's foremost expert on John Dee. He's just published a book in which he breaks down how Dee communicated with angels. Right now, he's studying the language they spoke. Care for a wedge of baklava?"

"Wait, didn't we just agree that Dee was a scientist?" I asked ironically as I chose one of the delicious pastries.

"He was. And one of the great ones! But you have to understand, during the Renaissance, they had a very different definition of what

constituted a 'scientist.' We owe a tremendous amount of our fundamental understanding of science to the early alchemists. Paracelsus,
for example, was the first to apply the scientific method to medicine.
Robert Fludd, a famous Rosicrucian mason, invented the barometer.
And another alchemist, Jan Baptiste van Helmont, coined the term
'electricity' while he was studying magnets . . ."

"Well done, Martin," Daniel said proudly.

"Daniel, maybe you can convince her. Julia refuses to believe me
when I tell her the world has a rich history of occultism as important
as anything we learn in school."

Finally, something seemed to light a fire in the aloof astronomer.

"Very well. I'll try," Daniel said, eager to take up the challenge. "You
should know that until the Industrial Revolution, this country's bur-
geoning scientists were more concerned with questions of spirituality
than of the physical world. Just look at Sir Isaac Newton. He put all of
his time and energy into trying to reconstruct the Temple of King Solomon. His writings show he was obsessed with trying to re-create the
only place in the Old World where man could speak 'face-to-face' with
God. *The Principia Mathematica,* which asured him a place in the history
of science, was to him only a rudimentary accomplishment. To Newton, mathematical principles were just a tool, the means to a greater
end. He believed numbers were the basis of God's language and that
we had to learn mathematics if we ever hoped to speak to Him."

"He really wanted to reconstruct King Solomon's Temple?" I said,
munching on a pastry.

"He wrote all about it," Daniel said. "We have his notes and they
prove he was trying to find a way to communicate with the universe's
architect. Newton imagined the Temple to be a kind of telephone
switchboard we could use to talk to God."

"Well, according to Martin, Dee got closer than even Newton to
speaking to God. Well, to angels, anyway," I said with a wry smile.

"Make no mistake, Julia: Sir Isaac Newton believed in angels."

I blushed. "I'm sorry. I didn't mean to offend you . . ."

"It's not me you're offending," he grumbled. "Many men

throughout history have died searching for this secret. All of humanity's greatest mysteries are tied to the search for direct communication with God. What were the Ark of the Covenant, the Holy Grail, and the Kaaba, if not tools to get closer to Him? Dee was the last man in history to accomplish it. He achieved unrivaled fame in England for being able to communicate with heavenly beings. And it all happened on this patch of land where we're standing. That's why Sheila moved here."

"You think the actual ground is important?"

"It very well could be. We've never fully understood how Dee opened this pathway to the world of angels. That's why we have to respect even the ground he stood on when he established contact."

"So you truly believe John Dee spoke with the angels?"

Daniel twisted in his chair while Martin watched in amusement.

"To me, he has provided us proof beyond a shadow of a doubt," Daniel said, as if his ego had been wounded. "These celestial beings told him about hundreds of events that were yet to take place. They were able to move through time to see them happen—it's one of the reasons Queen Elizabeth the First was in this very house, to seek his guidance."

"So . . . did he guess right?"

"I'm not sure 'guess' is the word you're looking for."

"Okay." I humored him. "Did he predict correctly?"

"Judge for yourself, love," Martin interjected. "Dee predicted the decapitation of Mary Queen of Scots and the deaths of Spain's King Philip II, the Holy Roman Emperor Rudolf II, and even Queen Elizabeth herself. So, yes. I'd say he was extraordinarily successful."

Martin sat down beside me, trying to provide some cover from Daniel. "Twenty years ago, when my parents moved to the United States, they charged Daniel and my aunt Sheila with looking into every aspect of John Dee's life and history. Particularly the tools he used to communicate with the angels. We know Dee employed at least two 'seers' who were able to use the tools the angels gave him. At first we had no idea what those clairvoyants might have seen when they used the instruments. But apparently, it was something extraordinary."

Martin paused to gather his thoughts.

"Those tools were simple but powerful. On the outside, they were plain-looking stones, but they contained unimaginable power. Dee was able to learn the secret to fine optics, geometry, medicine . . . He was so convinced of the stones' power that he spent his fortune to build a sort of altar, an 'invocation tablet,' in which he embedded the stones. He adorned it with an obsidian mirror that the Spaniards brought back from the New World and encrusted it with a treasure trove of jewels from around the world, so that his mediums could receive the clearest messages from the angels. He followed every instruction he received from the other side, particularly from a spirit named Uriel, to open a free-flowing line of communication that hadn't existed since ancient times."

Sheila then came into the room with a steaming teapot that smelled of spearmint and set it down on the table before us.

"My girl," she said, "what's important is that we have the two stones, the very ones that Dr. Dee used in his experiments. Oh, there are others, including the ones on display in the Department of Medieval Antiquities at the British Museum. But none are as powerful as ours. We are the keepers of the true adamants of John Dee."

"Ada . . . what?" I said.

"Oh, really, Martin!" Sheila said, slapping the back of my fiancé's head with a smile. "You mean to tell me you haven't told her anything? Really?"

"I told you I wouldn't! Not a single word."

"Good boy," she said, smiling.

As I poured the mint tea into a set of small cups, Daniel took up the conversation.

"Okay, then I'll tell her," he said, first biting into his wedge of baklava and sipping some tea. "Julia, Dr. Dee's writings say these stones, or adamants, were the most important gift the angels gave him. They were forged in heaven. They're more special and rare than any moon rock NASA ever brought back to Earth. In fact, before the angels entrusted the adamants to him, they told him explicitly that they were taken from paradise. From the Garden of Eden itself."

16

Colonel Allen broke in, no longer able to contain himself. "So you're telling me that you fell in love with a man who came to your town on the Way of St. James and instantly discovered your most closely guarded secret, your gift of 'sight.' And you agreed to marry him and didn't find out until the day before your wedding that he also had a secret?"

"That's right. John Dee's seer stones."

"So if you have this gift, why didn't you see any of this coming?"

"I already told you! I didn't acknowledge my gift, much less use it. I tried to hide it. God, I prayed. I prayed so hard that one day I would wake up and this curse would be gone. If I had any kind of premonition, I ignored it. I just wanted to be normal, like any other person. Until Martin came along."

"I have to tell you I find that hard to believe, miss."

"This whole damn story is hard to believe!" I said, pounding the table. "Up to and including the point where you show up and get into a gunfight inside a church with some monk, or whatever the hell he was, who hadn't even tried to hurt me."

"He was about to. I can promise you that."

The colonel remained calm and that allowed me to get ahold of myself.

"So you think any of this will help you find Martin?" I asked.

"Without a doubt."

"Okay. Then I'll go on . . . What happened that day with the adamants was just the beginning. That was the day I finally accepted my gift. Although I probably never should have . . ."

I stared at him openmouthed.

"Of course, you don't have to believe anything we tell you. But ever since Martin's father gave them to us, they haven't ceased to amaze us."

"What do you mean?"

"Well, although we've never gotten them to do what Dr. Dee's private papers tell us they did, they do some . . . unusual things. Sometimes, they become heavier. Sometimes they're lighter. Sometimes they change color. At times, we can see symbols in the adamants that disappear just as mysteriously as they appeared. And they're so hard not even diamonds can cut into them."

"But what does any of that have to do with communicating with angels?"

"Well, we put them in the hands of psychics, seers with a real reputation—the way Dee did in the sixteenth century—and they managed to get them to emit bursts of sound and light. But nothing more."

"What about a gemologist? Have you taken them to an expert?"

"That's another curious little fact," Daniel said with a quizzical smile as he stroked his beard. "Let's just say that all efforts to learn their secrets have failed. Only certain people with special psychic gifts have taught us anything about them. And that's what we're hoping you can do, Julia. Isn't that right, Martin?"

I watched Daniel's eyes widen, his pupils dilate as he said those words.

"Martin believes," he added, "that you are one of those gifted seers."

"Me?"

I felt my heart instantly begin to race. *What is this? Some kind of a setup?* I looked for answers on Martin's face. He knew I'd spent my life running away from this kind of thing, the "gift" he always believed I had. How could he do this to me, especially on the eve of our wedding?

"Julia," Martin said finally, "I think it's time you see these stones for yourself . . . and show us all what you're capable of."

17

Sheila walked over to the curio cabinet that had caught my attention, carefully opened its doors and took out a small wooden box decorated with silver. When she opened the box and placed it gently next to the teapot, I thought she'd made a mistake. I was expecting a pair of shimmering emeralds or rubies. I was surprised to see displayed on the red felt inside the box a pair of innocuous black stones that looked like they'd been recently removed from the bottom of a riverbed. They seemed to be the most ordinary rocks you've ever seen.

Plus, they weren't faceted the way you'd expect from a jewel. They were kidney shaped, smooth and slender, unpolished and opaque, and about the size of a coin.

"Choose one and take it over to the window, dear," Sheila said.

I chose the larger one and walked over to stand in the sunlight.

"Now, hold it up and look through it."

I did as she said, and she continued to speak.

"Some mediums say they come alive in the sunlight as you turn them clockwise. The sun's rays change their molecular structure and spark a reaction inside them."

I turned the stone between my fingers but saw nothing. The one I'd chosen was opaque. Heavy. And just as lifeless as any other stone.

"Look closer," Sheila said insistently in a calming, measured tone. "Try to steady your breathing and keep turning it."

The more I studied it, the more I was convinced it was just another rock—and that Martin's friends were either charlatans or nuts.

"One of three things can happen," Sheila said, "as you gaze at the stone: You might not feel anything, because your mind is not ready to accept this talisman. Or, on activating, its power will cloud your thinking temporarily . . . or it might kill you."

"It can . . . kill me?" I asked with a sarcastic smile on my face.

"I'm sure you know the story of Uzza," she said.

"Uzza . . . ?"

"According to the Old Testament, Uzza was one of the men who carried the Ark of the Covenant. He was a slave and didn't know the history of the ark the way the Levites did. They warned him time and again never to touch the ark directly. But one day, as was recorded in several ancient texts, he couldnt avoid doing so. As they rolled the ark in a cart, it bounced against a stone and began to fall. Instinctively, Uzza rushed to grab it to keep it from crashing into the ground."

"I remember," I said without taking my eyes off the stone. "He was struck down by lightning, right?"

"Yes. But not by the ark."

"Oh, no?"

"The ark contained the Ten Commandments, the very laws God himself had etched in stone. Those tablets were made of the very stone you are holding in your hands at this moment. And that's why I say they could kill you."

I feigned a shiver. And just as I was about to return the adamant to its wooden box, I noticed something in it. I'm not sure how to describe it. It was like a brief spark, the way a prism catches the light. But it seemed impossible from this flat, unfaceted stone. I brought it back up to my eyes to take another look and noticed something I hadn't before. As I turned it, I saw a spot on the black adamant where it seemed to become translucent, looking grayish-green. And I know this is going to sound crazy, but at one point it felt as if Dee's adamant was coated in some kind of leathery flesh. A thin membrane that, as I held it up to the light, allowed me to see something inside it, like the pit of a date.

"Did you see something, dear?"

I nodded vaguely, astonished. "Why? Didn't you?" I said.

Hypnotized by what had happened, I looked closer at the stone. I turned it again, at different angles, so it was bathed in sunlight, trying to convince myself there was no way that pitch-black stone was actually becoming transparent before my very eyes. And I realized it was no longer just a lifeless rock. I admired it as if it were a diamond.

Daniel, Martin and Sheila were watching me, looking satisfied.

"You saw it, didn't you?" Sheila asked.

I nodded again.

Martin couldn't contain his excitement. He'd stopped drinking his tea and was cracking his knuckles the way he always did when he was nervous. "See, I told you," he said. "Julia has the gift."

"It certainly seems that way," Sheila said, still watching me.

But before I could say anything, something else happened. Something brief, and stranger still—if that's even possible. Something I didn't understand then but that came to change the course of my life forever: That once-lifeless stone began to tremble in my hands. It was clear and unmistakable, like a cell phone that's set on vibrate. I looked up and saw the stunned look on Daniel's and Martin's faces. But that was just the beginning. The adamant began to feel lighter in my fingers. Lighter, and lighter still, until it had left my hand altogether, floating. It began to glow and flash with tiny bolts of lightning that illuminated the entire room, casting our shadows against the wall.

"It . . . it flies?" I stammered.

"Dear God!" Daniel roared. "What are you doing?"

And just as he said it, the stone came to rest gently in my hands again. It was warm. Silent. And lifeless again.

"I . . . I don't know!" I said.

Sheila stared at me with a piercing gaze but wore a wide, satisfied smile.

"It has antigravitational properties," Daniel mumbled to himself.

"I have to congratulate you, Martin," Sheila said, positively glowing. "She's exactly the woman we'd expected. There's no doubt." She turned to me and added, "The adamant is now yours to keep, my dear. It's clear that it obeys you. From now on, it will be your talisman. The other will belong to Martin. This will be your wedding gift."

18

Pazos and Mirás had been dead for half an hour before their CB radio squawked for them to check in. But it only managed to chirp before it fell silent. The officer making the rounds had reached the front door of La Quintana café when the power grid went down for the second time that night.

"Son of a . . ."

And now, for some reason, his walkie-talkie wasn't working, either. He smacked the radio a couple of times but it remained silent. Even the "low battery" signal was out. And then he remembered it was still the Day of the Dead.

"Ghosts," he mumbled, and tried to contain a shiver as he crossed himself.

Nearby, at the end of the block, next to the Benedictine monastery Antealtares and across from the old restaurant O Galo d'Ouro on Rúa de la Conga, three shadowy figures plotted their next move. They kept a constant watch on the two patrol cars with armed police officers stationed precisely in front of their target.

"We will not fail this time," said the leader. "We need the woman."

"And if she doesn't have the adamant?"

"It doesn't matter. We'll still take her," he said, unflinching. "Remember that just an hour ago in the cathedral, our brother needed only to bring the *Amrak* close to her for it to activate. And that only happens in the presence of a human catalyst, an adamant, or when both of them together come close to the *Amrak*. So there's a fifty-fifty chance that everything we need is in there," he said, pointing at the café. "And that's more than we have right now."

"And what if she left the adamant in the cathedral?"

For a moment, no one spoke.

"No," one of them said finally. "If she has it, she'll be carrying it."

"I'm surprised you're so sure—"

"Just look at what's happened," he said, interrupting. "We haven't done anything but come close to her and already the power's gone out again. Any time the *Amrak* senses a medium, it drains all the nearby energy to function."

"Look! Over there. Another sign the sheikh is right," the third shadow said.

He pointed into the sky and they all looked up, shielding their eyes from a million freezing raindrops that were like icy daggers against their skin. There, about fifteen feet above them, grazing the tops of the buildings, a shapeless fog had blocked out the storm clouds. It gathered with an iridescent orange glow, wispy fingers stretching in all directions.

"Should we activate the *Amrak*?"

The sheikh nodded.

"It is the only way to be sure. And this time, brothers, let us pray that no one else need be killed."

19

This latest blackout caught us off guard. Nicholas Allen swiped his iPad's screen to give us some kind of light, but it only flickered for a moment before going black. The waiter found a candle and matches under the bar.

"Do you have the adamant with you?"

"What if I do?"

"Well . . . ," he said, smiling ironically. "You could use it to give us a little more light, no?"

"Are you making fun of me?"

"I'm sorry, I didn't mean to," he said. "Look, I've come a long way to find you. My government knows this. But before I make another move, I need to know you have one of the seer stones. In your husband's video, he spoke of your reunion, and it seemed to me he wasn't just talking about the two of you. Did he tell you whether he had hidden the adamants someplace?"

Things were taking an uncomfortable turn. The colonel was drawing his own conclusions now, and that was my fault. Before he assumed I knew more than I did, I needed to tell him something important. Something I never thought I would ever tell anyone. Something about which Martin swore me to secrecy before he left.

"I'm sorry to tell you this, Colonel Allen, but I don't have the adamant you're looking for."

His expression was so disbelieving, I felt I had to tell him more.

I continued. "A lot of things happened after Sheila Graham entrusted me with her adamant. Too many to explain in one sitting. But suffice it to say that during the training Martin and his family subjected me to, I discovered that the adamants were a powerful source of energy."

"I'm listening . . ."

"I don't know quite how to describe it. The adamants are a force all their own—a spring of powerful but unpredictable energy. Even my husband was scared of their potential."

"But were you able to use them? Were you able to communicate with angels?"

"We tried, of course. Many times. Too many. Until I just got tired of the whole game."

"You got tired?"

I quickly sipped the last of my cold coffee before going on. I still wasn't sure how far I should trust this man.

"Yes, Colonel. Tired. Exhausted. I spent months staring into the adamants, trying to visualize a location where the connection to the world of angels was strongest. I tried to find what they called 'portals.' Niches on Earth where a divine connection is strongest. Can you imagine what my life was like? I felt like a guinea pig, a prisoner to my own husband! The second I gave him some new coordinates, we were off again to some distant country. We traipsed all across Europe before finally returning to Santiago."

"So, you were tired and gave up."

"Well . . ." I hesitated. "There was one other minor detail."

"And that is . . . ?"

"Martin was raised in a Protestant home, and not a very religious one at that. And I was raised in a deeply Catholic family. All the times he tried to get me to make the adamants move or give us signs, he insisted on having me gaze upon them endlessly . . . and, well, it scared me. It started to feel like something . . . demonic. We were toying with strange and powerful forces that I didn't understand. S-so . . . ," I stammered, "just before he left for Turkey, after five disjointed years of wrestling with the adamants, we had a huge fight."

"Because of the adamants?"

"I told him I was tired of his witchcraft and that I was through helping him. That his days of experimenting were over, at least for me."

"I bet that really rattled him."

"More than you can imagine," I admitted. "When he realized my decision was final, he decided to separate me from my adamant and hide it someplace secret. And he took his with him to Turkey to find one of the locations that had come to me in a vision. He wanted to hide that one, too. He promised me he was through with the adamants and that he would make sure no one would ever touch them or use them again. But he said we had to be careful. He was obsessed with them not falling into the wrong hands. He wanted to make sure no one except his family could find the adamants. That's why he decided to split them up."

"But now we need your adamant to find Martin."

"Why?" I shot back. "Why would you think we'd ever need it to find Martin? Those stones can burn in hell, for all I care!"

"That's where you're wrong, Ms. Álvarez," he said. "I think your talismans are actually remnants of a mineral from outer space, one that crashed to Earth as a meteor and is emitting high-frequency electromagnetic radiation. And I think Martin knew it. If we could find yours, the one your husband hid before he left, we could take it back to the lab, identify the exact frequency of the radiation, and use that information to search the Ararat region, where your husband was taken captive, for a similar signature frequency. We can triangulate that position from one of our satellites and send in a special ops team to rescue him."

"This sounds like science fiction, Colonel."

"Ms. Álvarez, your husband is familiar with these techniques, and he knows very well what the US government is capable of. He knows that adamant is the only way we have of finding him. And that's why he sent you that cryptic message."

"Are you sure?"

"It can't hurt to try, can it?"

I stayed quiet for a moment, thinking.

"All right, Colonel," I said finally. "But the problem is, even if your theory's right, I have no idea where he hid my adamant."

Allen patted his trusty iPad with a sideways grin. The device had sprung back to life.

"Are you sure?" he said. "Don't you think Martin might have hidden the location in his message?"

20

Inspector Figueiras's heart leaped out of his chest when one of his men burst into his office and shook him repeatedly.

"Inspector, Inspector, wake up!"

Antonio Figueiras had stretched out in his office chair and nodded off, hoping to rest for the five or six hours until morning when he could begin making his calls. But he wasn't so lucky.

"Wha . . . what's going on?"

"The chief has been trying to call you on your cell phone for hours," the nervous officer said. "He said it's urgent."

"Son of a . . . What time is it?"

"Three thirty, sir."

"In the morning?"

Figueiras looked incredulously out his window. It was still pitch-black outside, the rain pounding the glass mercilessly. He rushed over to his trench coat and dug around for his cell phone, which he remembered he had turned off. He cursed under his breath and chased the man out of the room before he dialed the chief, only to find his boss much more alert than he was.

"Where the devil have you been, Figueiras?"

"Sorry, sir. My cell phone battery died," he lied.

"Okay, enough with the flimsy excuses. I've got some information on your case."

"About the cathedral?"

"What else? I got a call from our embassy in Washington a half hour ago. I'd asked them to poke around quietly about this spy married to our countrywoman."

"And . . . ?"

"You're not going to believe this. Martin Faber's been kidnapped by a group of Turkish terrorists from the PKK in the northeastern part of the country. The United States' NSA has launched an international search-and-rescue operation."

"Kidnapped? Are you sure?"

"That's the word. The PKK is a sect of radical, leftist terrorists who've been destabilizing Turkey's Kurdish territories for years."

Figueiras twisted in his chair as his boss went on.

"The shooting in the church wasn't some random act of violence. Don't you see? Someone's trying to get to your witness. Protect Julia Álvarez at all costs. Understand me?"

"Yes, Chief."

21

"There are a couple things you should know about your husband . . . ,"
Nick Allen said.

"What kinds of things, Colonel?"

"Martin worked for the National Security Agency. The branch of
our government that monitors communications all over the world and
reports to our country's Department of Defense."

Allen must have seen my eyes widen in surprise. This total stranger
knew things about my husband that I never would have imagined.

"Don't worry, Ms. Álvarez. Martin wasn't someone like me, involved in tactical operations. He was only a scientist."

"He never mentioned any of that . . . ," I mumbled.

"There's a good reason for that: your own safety, ma'am. Even if
you're a janitor at the NSA, when you join the agency there are two
major rules. The first: absolute discretion. Anything you see, do or
learn while part of the agency stays inside the agency. And you, Ms.
Álvarez, are outside the agency. We're taught that any slipup, no matter how small, can endanger covert operations and risk innocent lives."

"And the second rule?"

"Working for the NSA means accepting certain risks. If you're captured by the enemy, they will try to wheedle every last bit of information from you. Even divulging the location of some menial field office
can give them insight into how we move and operate. Since we're always targets, we're taught to do things like bury cryptic messages inside
innocent-sounding phrases. Slipping a code into an innocent telephone
call could be enough to save your life."

"Martin knows to do that?" I asked, shocked.

Allen nodded. "Didn't you notice anything strange in the video?
Something about the way he delivered the last line?"

Allen clicked the button of his video player, and Martin's emaciated face returned to the screen to deliver the last line.

". . . and though others may strive to steal what was ours, keep envisioning a way for these two halves to be made whole again," he said in Spanish.

Hearing the words again, this time they seemed redolent of dark omens.

"Here's what I think, Julia. I think the code is in the words 'envisioning a way for these two halves to be made whole again.' Does that trigger anything in your mind? Do you remember your husband ever saying those words to you before? Maybe during some important moment or in some place that might give us a clue to where he might have hidden your adamant? The structure of the phrase highlights the instructions to you. It sounds like he's saying that if you want to be reunited with him, there is a particular method or path you can envision."

"Maybe he's referring to my gift?"

"Hmm. Too simple."

"Well, what if it's a play on words? Martin loves word games."

"Could be. Do you want to experiment with mixing up the letters?" he said, reaching into his pocket for a scrap of paper and a pen.

Just then, the lights flicked back on, and the café's appliances came to life. The cigarette dispenser by the window flashed on. The coffee grinder began whirring. Even the coolers clanked back on. But it was a fleeting burst. A second later, they were off again, plunging us back into darkness.

22

Something was happening to the phosphorescent cloud floating above the three strangers.

The youngest of them was enthralled by it, amazed that it started to morph at the very moment the sheikh ordered him to open the black nylon bag he was carrying, allowing the rain to penetrate its contents. All he had said was simply, "It's time to activate the *Amrak*."

Instantly, the shapeless cloud floating over the ancient city of Santiago grew into a dense fog, expanding and pulsating with a sporadic rhythm, as if some creature were alive at its center, struggling to break free. A creature that reacted to the contents of that black bag. And when the young man saw the plaza's lights flicker yet again, he knew it had something to do with this ethereal beast. To thrive, it would suck every last ounce of the surrounding energy. Maybe even his own.

"Are you ready?" the sheikh asked, oblivious to his apprentice's worries.

The young man, who was named Waasfi and was descended from one of Armenia's most influential families, nodded. So did the other man, a soldier who'd been in countless battles since his country slipped from the yoke of the Soviet Union.

And then the sheikh did some something strange. Without moving the black bag, he held his hands over it, as if preparing to cast a spell, and brought his face within an inch of it.

He could immediately sense the subtle aroma and the surprising breeze that always seemed to appear when he was about to tap the power of the object he handled so carefully. Bringing the object so close to Julia Álvarez, he felt, was like completing an ancient circle. His *Amrak*—the name he gave to his ancient charm—would finally show all the power it was capable of.

The other two men stood an equal distance from the bag and began to hum with a constant monotone voice, like a mantra. *Mmmmmm-mmm*. The sheikh had taught them to use the resonance in their chest to awaken the *Amrak*. As strange as it might seem, the idea was based wholly in science. The *Amrak* was a squarish tablet made of a mineral whose atoms were arranged in hexagonal molecules. At the right frequency, the stone would resonate, altering its atomic structure—the way a soprano's particular pitch can shatter a crystal champagne flute, or a focused ultrasonic blast can pulverize a kidney stone.

And in just the same way, the mysterious relic inside the bag soon began to hum, as if in sync with the serenade. At first, it was barely audible. But the humming grew, filling them with all the determination they needed.

Their leader trained his eyes on the bag until he deemed the moment just right to begin an incantation of unintelligible phrases. He could see wisps of smoke begin to form. And he knew he would soon feel its enrapturing power, an invisible but brutal force that would knock out anyone who hadn't insulated themselves in garments lined with lead—as their clothes were.

Neither of the sheikh's young soldiers knew exactly what was happening. But a tingling was starting to wash over them from head to toe. It wasn't painful or even entirely unpleasant. It was like a mild static electricity that filled the air.

"*Zacar od zamran; odo cicle qaa . . .*"

They followed their orders and repeated the sheikh's strange words, whatever they meant. It wasn't Armenian, but some other arcane and mysterious tongue.

"*Zorge lap sirdo noco Mad . . .*"

A fresh wave of goose bumps ran across their flesh as they repeated those alien words.

"*. . . Zorge nap sidun . . .*"

No one who might have happened upon that bizarre scene—three strangers dressed in black, praying around a black bag on the street in the driving rain—could ever have imagined what was happening. Nor would they have believed that this ritual was, in fact, a way to conjure a connection to the Supreme Being, to the very center of the universe—and that they were on the verge of crossing over beyond the realms of faith and theory. They repeated this ancient incantation, born of a forgotten and inscrutable language, hoping to draw the protection of the *Amrak*.

. . . *Hoath Iada.*

It was three thirty-five in the morning when the old city of Santiago fell into darkness for the third time that night. The cloud above had started just above the roofline but was now spreading out into the sprawling plaza toward the cathedral.

The sheikh was stunned as he watched it grow. "The power of God." "His all-consuming fire." "The glory of Yahweh." It was known by many names. Yet few in the history of man had managed to extract such a force from that relic, which was now a weapon at their service. In fact, the sheikh had known only one person, one man, who could tap into its power. A brilliant scientific mind who had talked about using a combination of naturally occurring electromagnetic energies—the friction from tectonic forces, underground currents, atmospheric disturbances and even solar flares—to tap into the *Amrak's* almost supernatural force and turn it into a fountain of inexhaustible power. Or into a powerful beacon of light. He had called it geoplasmic energy.

And now, the sheikh would use this knowledge ostensibly to rescue that very scientist—one Martin Faber.

The moment the lights went out again, I started to feel sick.

A nausea rose from the pit of my stomach until my mouth was swimming with saliva. I could hardly focus on Colonel Allen's claim that the answer to Martin's disappearance was encoded in his kidnapping video. I held on to the edge of the table in the café to keep steady. But when I looked across to Nicholas Allen by the last flash of the iPad's screen, I could tell he, too, was about to faint. He scrunched his face in a way that made his scar seem gruesome, and he swayed from side to side in his chair. I only managed to notice a fleeting look in his blue eyes, a subtle look of panic. I could tell right away from the terrified look on his face that the soldier who had come to rescue me from God-knows-what had realized what was causing these symptoms.

But I didn't have a chance to ask him about it.

I felt my last bit of strength leave me. My lungs had forgotten how to take in a breath. My muscles relaxed, and I suddenly stopped caring about the world around me. *God, what's happening to me?*

I felt a last stab of pain and noticed that the hot coffee had spilled onto my lap. But my body couldn't even respond involuntarily. Not even to react to the scalding coffee. Not to put my hands out before I crashed to the oak parquet floor.

A millisecond before everything went black, I had one final moment of lucidity. A terrifying last thought that felt all at once like a condemnation and a sweet release:

I am dead.

Father Benigno Fornés's room overlooked the northern entrance to the cathedral. From his balcony in the San Martín Pinario seminary, he could see down to the gardens surrounding Bishop Gelmirez's palace and into the Plaza de la Inmaculada. He always had a clear view of the cathedral and could see right away whether anything was amiss. Maybe it was his unobstructed view that kept the priest from being able to get to sleep that night. He was more worried than usual after the first ruckus at the cathedral. Despite the biting cold, he kept the window open and his cell phone turned on. If anything else happened in his cathedral that night, he wanted to be the first to know.

The old man had a bad feeling about all of it. He had grown up just steps from those walls and he knew how quickly things could go from bad to worse. It wasn't something he could put his finger on. He could just feel it in his bones. So he wasn't too surprised when a series of events that night robbed him of his sleep.

First, it was the power failures that got him out of bed, the lights outside flickering before plunging the street into darkness. His mind was still spinning from the false threat of fire earlier in the night. Smart and discerning, and already unable to sleep, the seventy-one-year-old decided to take action.

He dressed quickly and quietly, grabbed his coat and flashlight and tiptoed past the other dormitories as he stepped out into the night. He hurried across the passageway along the Calle de la Azabachería to the cathedral, stopping just outside the abbey's doors, hoping the crotchety old wiring inside him was wrong for once.

"I hope I'm wrong, Lord," he muttered. "I hope I'm wrong . . ."

Father Fornés punched a six-digit code into the keypad by the door and turned off the alarm. Inside, he moistened his fingers in the holy water by the door and crossed himself before feeling his way down one of the cathedral's aisles, looking for anything out of the ordinary.

At first glance, everything looked fine.

There was no trace of the haunting orange glow that had caused such a fuss. Even in the overwhelming darkness there was an imposing solemnity about the place. Only the flicker of a few fading candles highlighted niches around the old church: the baptismal font and the chapel to Santa María de Corticela. The old dean could still let himself be overwhelmed at the memory of a time when the eighty-six-thousand-square-foot cathedral kept its doors open around the clock for every man, woman and child who believed. But that was another time. A time when Christian pilgrims kept sacred the heirlooms of St. James, the "Son of Thunder," who took the reins of the early church after St. Peter's death. Modern times had moved beyond the old ways, unfortunately. And gunshots in the ancient church certainly didn't help matters.

Father Fornés silently walked the length of the church, shining his flashlight toward the Platerías door and back toward the altar. The fiery-looking cloud had left no traces of smoke or ash on the walls.

"What if it was a sign from God?"

The old priest had meant it as more than a mere question when he spoke to the archbishop. It was a warning. But the young theologian who had been made head of the Catholic Church in Santiago just a year ago had disappointed him again. The old ways were foreign to him, too. He was more concerned about the apparent gunfight than about the mystical storm that had gathered in the sacred old church. But that was to be expected from Archbishop Juan Martos. Take away the robes and the ring, and he could pass for any cold and calculating corporate CEO. He was—unfortunately, as Father Fornés saw it—more concerned with managing the mundane than with caring for the eternal souls of their flock.

"A sign from God?" the archbishop had asked. "How do you mean, Father Benigno?"

"Your Grace, remember that this cathedral was founded in the ninth century when mystical lights signaled the presence of a sacred object to

Pelagio, the old hermit. He told your ancient predecessor, Bishop Teo-domiro, about the sacred object. And the bishop came here to find one of the greatest treasures of the Christian faith."

"The ark containing the bones of the apostle St. James," Archbishop Martos said flatly, as if reciting the words to a fairy tale.

"Precisely, Your Grace. We mustn't forget that our Lord has used these mystical lights as signs to His people. To open our eyes."

Archbishop Martos didn't seem to pay much attention. He was, after all, too young, too much of an outsider to Santiago and its rich history to understand the old dean's concerns. That's when Fornés realized his archbishop wasn't aware of the cathedral of Santiago's hidden function. He wasn't "a man of the tradition." Otherwise, he would never have ordered the church closed until the police finished their investigation.

No, he wouldn't expect Martos to understand Father Fornés's role as the keeper of the cathedral's secrets. And maybe that's why he went against his superior's orders and entered the cathedral to examine it with his own eyes that night. He was the one whom Divine Providence had chosen to keep watch over this house. And nothing was going to keep him from fulfilling his duty. Not even the archbishop.

The church was still that night.

Its darkest corner was the main entrance, which housed the Pórtico de la Gloria, so Father Fornés decided to start vigil there. Scaffolding, makeshift tables covered in notes and computers and chemicals were positioned all about. But that sacrosanct place seemed just as Julia Álvarez—the prodigy—had left it.

Julia was special. Fornés had noticed it the first time he met her. And it wasn't just her intellect; it was her fire, her will and her open mind in the face of the others working on the restoration. Without knowing it, when she suggested that what was affecting the stone was some other force—some kind of underground, seismic invisible energy—she was never closer to the secret of Compostela that he so closely guarded.

A stray beam from his flashlight lit the whiteness of the intricately carved stone column at the center of the doorway, bringing the priest's mind back to the task at hand—he needed to finish his rounds. If only people knew that the very reason for Compostela's existence was hidden in that historic column: Images of different people seemed to climb a representation of Jesus's family tree, beginning with the figure closest to the ground, a bearded man grabbing two lions around the neck. The carvings stretched upward like a climbing vine, like an ancient DNA double helix tracing a path through the ages, through St. James and, above him, to Jesus Christ himself.

The priest looked around. Everything seemed to be in its place. The gunshots had not damaged any of those splendid sculptures, thank God.

Feeling more at ease, he made his way to the center of the church, where the gunfight had taken place. The police had cordoned off the area with yellow crime tape, but the priest slipped beneath it for a better look. Even with the thin beam of his flashlight he could begin to see the damage. The projectiles had chipped several handrails, littering the floor with centuries-old splinters. Several of the holes were numbered by police, shell casings still lay where they came to rest and fingerprinting equipment sat where police would return to it in the morning. Fornés dodged the evidence as best he could and headed for the area that interested him the most.

And that's when he saw it.

A smaller perimeter had been taped off near the Platerías doorway, just below the monument to the *Campus Stellae*. He knew better than anyone else that that was the oldest section of the cathedral. Only a handful of scholars were aware that the spot marked the birthplace of the world's oldest and most important Christian temple after St. Peter's Basilica in the Vatican. And even fewer would recall it as the site of any number of miracles. Most important, it was the very spot where Bernardo the Elder, *magister admirabilis,* placed the cathedral's foundation stone in the year 1075, guided—according to tradition—by a chorus of God's angels.

So when Father Fornés saw police tape cordoning off that sacred area, his pulse immediately quickened.

"My Lord . . . !"

Embedded in that ancient wall was one of the bullets.

The impact had split the stone block, pulverizing part of its surface. Fornés crossed himself at the sight. That, he knew, would definitely call for the restorers' attention. But that wasn't all. The impact had also chipped several of the surrounding blocks, revealing a strange shadow beneath the stone. To the priest, it looked like some kind of inscription. The remnants of old paint. Maybe a quarry mark. Whatever it was, it only made the old priest's heart pound harder.

It looked like this: 𝖳

Father Fornés inched closer for a better look. He shone his light on it and traced the mark with his fingertips. It looked to have been freshly made and seemed to have been scored into the wall. It was recessed a bit and stood out from the surrounding Compostela granite because it shimmered with iridescent gold flecks. And if he wasn't mistaken, it was still warm.

Good God! he thought. *I have to get the monsignor right away!*

25

It's said that when someone dies, the soul begins its most difficult journey. Just before crossing over, it comes face-to-face with a sort of ethereal "black box," a flight data recorder for every experience the soul has had while living in that body, from the very moment the umbilical cord is cut and the lungs take in their first breath. What the soul experiences at that moment exceeds anything it has known in the physical world. For the first time, it is able to see the entire life it has lived from the outside, from the viewpoint of others. Despite what the major world religions might say, at that moment, there are no judges. No trials. No outside voices to validate or reject what it is experiencing. The soul becomes pure energy and is able to judge for itself all the good and the bad it has lived through in that earthly body. Only then will it be able to follow its path to the afterlife.

The only positive of this whole process is learning that there is, in fact, an afterlife. But whether the soul ascends to heaven or descends into hell is nothing more than a state of being, how the soul feels attuned after experiencing the summary of its life inside that earthly form: Is the soul buoyed by its successes on earth, its virtues, its spirit? Or is it anchored by the weight of its failures, its errors, its darkness?

No matter what religion we grew up in, we've all been told about that moment. The moment of final judgment. And although the world's religious leaders have confused the issue, predicting an actual celestial trial or great absolution or even a resurrection of the dead, all I know is that this final review of our lives is real.

I learned it that night at La Quintana café when I found myself lying facedown just inches from a motionless Colonel Allen.

I was surprised at how easy it was for me to die. What I first thought was a painless fainting spell soon became a torrent of memories flashing before my eyes. And I'm not sure why, but I was convinced that I had died the way Uzza from the Bible had after placing his hand on the Ark of the Covenant, as if ten thousand volts had rushed through my body. And now that jolt had launched me into a sea of images and thoughts.

I tried to make sense of everything around me: Why hadn't I felt any pain when I hit the ground? What had become of the café? And Nick Allen? And the waiter?

There was just nothingness.

It was as if I was slowly dissolving into a soothing calm. I wasn't cold anymore, and little by little, I could feel the life force peacefully draining out of me. It made it easy to watch the memories of my lifetime play effortlessly, randomly, beneath my closed eyelids.

My first memory sprang to the surface in a powerful burst.

It was my wedding day. I figured that came to mind first because the colonel had me rooting through those old emotions just before my death.

I could see Martin and me arriving in Wiltshire. It was Sunday morning, the day after I'd had my first encounter with John Dee's adamants, and we'd spent the rest of the evening rushing to get the details of the wedding in place. Our emotions were on edge. We hadn't managed to sleep all night. As a matter of fact, we argued.

I'd almost forgotten about that . . .

Our quarrel started the day before, after I met Sheila and Daniel. And it was all because of those damn *adamantas*.

The first sparks came when we got to our hotel room.

"Hasn't this been the most eye-opening day of your life?" He sighed as he fell back on the bed.

"Oh, I'll say," I said, stewing in a slow simmer. "I realize you know more about me than I ever imagined."

"You mean because of your—"

"Yes, because of *that!*" I said, cutting him off. "You fell in love with me because you thought I was a psychic. Isn't that right? Why didn't you tell me that before?"

Martin cocked his head. "Aren't you, though?"

"No! I certainly am not!"

"Are you sure?" he said, biting back. "You were the one who told me you used to speak with your dead great-grandmother when you were a little girl. And didn't you tell me your mother saw that ghostly procession of the dead, the one people claim to see around your home . . . what did you call it?"

"The Holy Company," I muttered.

"Right. That's it. And weren't you the one who offered up that you were descended from a long line of Galician witches who know all about medicinal herbs? You even told me you brew a rum that's supposed to cure arthritis!"

Martin tried to confuse the issue, but I wouldn't let him.

"So why didn't *you* tell me about the seer stones?" I said, now in a full rage.

"W-well," he stammered, "until now, the stones have been a family secret. And since from tomorrow on you'll be part of the family, I thought you should know. Didn't you like the surprise?"

"Surprise? I felt like your goddamn guinea pig! A circus freak! And what about those . . . those *friends* of yours?"

"Daniel is an expert. And Sheila . . . well, she's someone like you—"

"What do you mean, *someone like me?*"

"Well, until today, she was one of the few who could get the *adamantas* to react. But not like you did. Right away, I knew I was right about you. You can make them speak! You have the gift!"

"Make them speak? Martin, do you really think a pair of rocks can talk?"

He leaped off the bed to stand next to me. "These can. Look, Julia, in twenty years, no one has seen the adamants react the way they did with you today. It's like they were alive! You should have seen Sheila's face. You have the gift," he said again. "The same gift as Edward Kelly,

John Dee's favorite seer. You could look through them and make them vibrate, at your will. You *are* their medium!"

At that moment, it was as if I didn't know Martin at all. "You're scaring me, Martin, you know that?" I said, my eyes filling with tears. "I thought you were a scientist, rational. I've put my whole life in your hands and I don't even know who you are!"

"Julia, please . . . You're scared," he whispered. "But you have nothing to be scared of."

"I'm not so sure, Martin . . ."

"After our wedding, you'll have time to learn how to use the adamants. And you'll see that I'm still the scientist—the man—you've always known. We'll study them together. I promise. You'll breathe life into them. And then I'll interpret them."

I stayed quiet.

"You'll understand everything. Even though this may look like witchcraft now, you'll see there's a very scientific explanation to all of this. Sheila and Daniel just want to help you understand."

"And what if I can't trust you anymore?" I said, looking at him as sternly as I dared. "I feel lied to, used . . ."

"Please, Julia. You're not serious."

I looked down at my hands. His big, strong hands were now holding mine, squeezing them, as if trying to reassure me. But I was unsure about everything now.

"No. No, I guess I'm not."

26

Something strange was going on.

How was Antonio Figueiras supposed to protect the witness when everything seemed to be conspiring against him? The power was out. So was the radio. Even the damn cell phone network was down. There was no way to get a team in place. So Figueiras didn't waste any more time. He jumped into his own car and plotted the quickest route to the Plaza de la Quintana. Julia Álvarez would probably still be talking with the American. Thankfully, he'd left some of his best men in charge, and a helicopter at the ready, to make sure no one got anywhere near her. No Kurdish terrorist, no matter how resourceful he was, would dare try to kidnap Julia with that kind of protection around her.

Thank goodness, he thought as the rain finally started letting up. It had eased just enough so that the first rays of morning sunlight reflected off the cathedral's baroque spires in the distance.

But if Figueiras had bothered to look at the clock on the dashboard as he sped through town, he would have seen it was far too early for daybreak.

27

My second postmortem memory came without warning.

A man dressed in gray, his face weathered by time and the elements, stared at us unflinchingly. Martin and I had just arrived in Biddlestone, the town where we were to be married, and Father James Graham, his family's longtime friend, couldn't believe his ears.

"This is an important decision," he murmured. "Are you sure this is what you want?"

We both nodded. We had arrived early in the morning, having left the hotel while it was still dark because neither of us could sleep.

"And when did you decide this?"

"She agreed the day before yesterday," Martin answered with a half smile.

"I'm not surprised . . ."

Although the priest sounded disapproving, he said nothing else. He sat next to us and invited us to breakfast. Somehow, his mere presence was comforting. And I soon understood why.

"How long has it been since we've seen each other, my son?" he asked Martin.

"Not since my first communion. Thirty years!"

"As long as it's been since I've seen your parents."

"I know. I'm sorry it's been so long since they've visited."

"You know, deep down, I'm actually flattered that you chose me. Because I know you still trust me. Because I know they still trust me," he said, brushing aside any hurt. Martin didn't flinch either. "So tell me, son, do you still want that reading included in the ceremony? Your phone call the other day worried me, frankly. These kinds of requests are rare. Especially in a Christian church."

"I understand, Father," Martin said, taking the old man's hand. "But there shouldn't be a problem, right?"

"No. Not as long as she doesn't object."

"And why should I?" I smiled. "It's *our* wedding."

"My child . . . Your fiancé has asked me to include a particular reading in your wedding ceremony that does not come from the Bible. Did he tell you that?"

"Uh . . . actually, no."

Martin shrugged his shoulders as if this were another one of his surprises.

"He's as stubborn as a mule," the priest said. "He wants an ancient parable read during the ceremony, but the story doesn't exactly paint women in the best light. That's why I was wondering whether you, as a Spanish woman who I assume is a little hot tempered—"

"Is that right? Temperamental, are we?"

I looked over at Martin, amused.

"You have to agree, Martin, it's not your average text," the priest said. "Maybe even inappropriate for a wedding."

"Inappropriate?" I asked, soaked in curiosity. "And how is it inappropriate, Father Graham?"

"Oh, don't listen to him, Julia," Martin said, trying to make light of the priest's comment. "This man has married the people in my family for generations and he always grumbles about the same thing. I think he's just trying to sabotage our tradition," he added with a wink.

"But what kind of reading is this?"

"It's a very ancient text—and very important, mind you—but it's definitely not part of church canon. It's just my obligation to let you know that. Martin told me you're a historian and an art expert. Let me show it to you, so you can judge for yourself."

The old man got up and walked over to a bookcase in the kitchen filled with precious leather-bound books and pulled out a large, thin book.

"The Book of Genesis mentions in passing the very deeds in this tome's sixth chapter," he explained, holding a book that was wrapped in vellum and appeared very old. "Unfortunately, the Bible only briefly discusses the topic that this book expounds on, as if our sacred text wanted to avoid going into the lurid details."

"What book is this?"

"The Book of Enoch. And your husband wants chapters six and seven read at the ceremony."

"Book of Enoch? I don't think I've ever heard of it."

Martin stirred in his chair. At first, I thought he was excited. But as Father Graham started to explain, he wriggled in his seat, as if wondering whether to interrupt.

"The Book of Enoch," the priest said, placing the plain-covered book in front of me, "is a prophetic work that foretells the future of mankind, from the moment man first came into being. The oldest copies came from Abyssinia, modern-day Ethiopia."

"How interesting," I said, drawing out the word, infinitely curious, which made Martin squirm even more. "And what is it about this story that paints women in a bad light, Father?"

"I'm getting to that," the old priest mumbled. "It tells what happened to man after we were cast out of Eden. And what led to the Second Fall from Grace."

"The Second Fall?"

"Well, according to the Scriptures, we tested God's patience twice. The first time was when Adam and Eve were kicked out of paradise and into the mortal world. The Lord could have stricken down our forefathers at that very moment but instead forgave them. They adapted to their new reality and went forth and multiplied."

"So the Second Fall came when . . . ?"

"When those descendants perished in the Great Flood," he said.

Father Graham recounted the story of creation like an anchor reading the evening news. And I wanted to know more.

"Let me see if I understand what you're saying, Father. You're trying to tell me this Book of Enoch is antediluvian, written before Noah and the ark?"

"Not exactly. The author writes about antediluvian occurrences between the time of the First and Second Falls from Grace. But when the text was actually written is a mystery. The text doesn't mention Adam and Eve, which is surprising, but it does go into great detail about why God sent the Great Flood. And the text indicates the information came from none other than the prophet Enoch.

I pressed on, giving my fiancé a sideways glance. "So tell me, Father, why do you think Martin wants this read at our wedding? Does it speak of love?"

James Graham stared at me gravely with his steely blue eyes, as if readying to warn me about some great danger ahead.

"What your soon-to-be husband wants read during the ceremony is at the beginning of the book, my child . . . Actually, why don't you read it for yourself? I'm not sure I can say whether it speaks of love or not."

The priest handed me the open book. A silken blue bookmark marked the page.

Beautiful calligraphy set off the first letter of the text, which was divided into concise paragraphs. It had been printed in an ornate, Gothic script, mixing red and black letters against rich, resplendent paper. I read the title of that section out loud:

> The fall of the angels; the demoralization of mankind; the intercession of angels on behalf of man. God's judgment against the angels. The Messianic Kingdom.

Just reading that made me uneasy. At first, I couldn't see how this had anything to do with my wedding. And as Father Graham and Martin both fell silent to listen to me read, I pressed on:

> And it came to pass, when the children of men had multiplied, and unto them were born the most beautiful of daughters; the angels, the sons of God, saw them and lusted after them, and said to each other, "Let us choose from the daughters of man so that we may have children of our own."

Ah, so this is the part about love, I thought.

So I continued to read:

And the leader among them said to them, "I fear you will not carry out your plan, and thus I, and I alone, will bear the burden of this great sin."

They all responded: "Let us all swear an oath to each other, that we be cursed lest we carry out our deed."

And together, they swore under penalty of anathema to execute their plan. They were two hundred in their number, and they descended to Ardis, the peak of Mount Hermon. And they would recall this as the place where they had made an oath to one another.

"Now, flip to the next bookmark. The green one," Father Graham said. "Read the entire page, please."

Martin interrupted. "We're not using that next part in the reading . . ."

"No. But your fiancée should at least know this part. Julia"—he touched my hand gently—"please read it."

I obeyed and continued.

He and the others each took women. Each chose one and would go to her. And in time, they would teach the women many things, spells and incantations, the cutting of roots and the science of plants and herbs.

And together, their unions brought forth onto the world giants, Titans three thousand ells tall. They devoured all of the fruits of man's labor until there was nothing left to consume.

And then, the giants turned against man and devoured them, as well. And they sinned against the birds and the beasts, the reptiles and the fish, until they eventually ate each other's flesh and blood.

And the earth condemned the violence.

For a long time, the three of us remained silent.

Father Graham seemed to respect that silence. But it scared me. The story seemed to be about a sinful union, one that brought forth an abominable new species that needed to be extinguished.

"Well, Julia, there you have it," Martin said brightly, trying to ease the tension. "See? It's just an old story of love. In fact, the oldest love story, after Adam and Eve's."

Father Graham had a different opinion. "It's a story of a forbidden love, Martin. It never should have been."

"Oh, Father," Martin griped. "Thanks to that love, the sons of God, a species of angels superior to the human race, were able to share their knowledge of science with Adam and Eve's descendants. And if the book is right, they married women on earth, bettering our species. What's wrong with that? Their bloodlines benefited all of humanity. Those were the first instances of marriage in human history. Sacred marriages—hierogamy. Unions between God and man."

"*Impure* unions, Martin!" the priest shouted, before quieting again. "They brought us only misfortune, and that's why God decided to wipe them from the earth with the Great Flood. Hardly an appropriate story to tell on a wedding day."

"But, Father," I said softly, trying to ease the tone the conversation had taken, "this is all just a myth . . ."

I regretted saying those words as soon as they left my mouth.

Father Graham shot up from the kitchen stool and snatched the Book of Enoch from my hands. If he was holding back before, he certainly wasn't anymore.

"A myth?" he scoffed. "I only wish it were all a myth! This book is the only thing we have that truly tells us what happened before the Flood. There's no other text to tell us our true origins."

"But even the Flood is a myth, Father," I said insistently.

"Now, wait just a minute," Martin cut in. "Remember what I told you about our family's interest in John Dee?"

I nodded. It was still burning in my mind.

Martin sighed. "Well, let me let you in on something else. They study him because he was the first person from the Western world to use the Book of Enoch to look scientifically at the Great Flood. That episode, whether it was confined to the Mesopotamian area or whether it was as widespread as climate change, was real. And it happened not once but twice. The last time was some eight or nine thousand years ago. Dee was the first to deduce that from the book that was just in your hands."

"You *really* believe the Great Flood happened?" I asked, stunned.

"Of course."

"Still, why do you want this read at our wedding?"

"My family's spent generations studying Dee, Enoch and the origins of mankind. My mother learned extinct languages just so she could read the Book of Enoch in its original form. Dad studied physics just so he could apply technical, scientific terms to the metaphors for heaven and how Enoch might have traveled there. And I studied biology and climatology so I could confirm that what the prophet writes about in the book actually happened sometime between the first and second floods, between 12000 and 9000 B.C., more or less. This is my way of . . . paying homage to my roots. My parents and I are last in a long line of caretakers of this legacy."

"Is that right?" I said, not believing a word of it.

"He's telling the truth, Julia," Father Graham said. "John Dee was just a link in the chain. So was Roger Bacon, a brilliant Franciscan monk from the thirteenth century. And Paracelsus, the doctor. Emanuel Swedenborg, the mystic. Sir Isaac Newton. And lot of others who remain anonymous in history."

"Julia, two hundred years before a Scottish explorer named James Bruce found the first known copy of the Book of Enoch, John Dee had already learned all its secrets."

"With the adamants," I said.

"Exactly!" Martin said, a smile making his face glow. "Dee discovered that because the holy angels ignored God's will and bred with our ancestors, divine blood courses through our veins . . . And he learned something else: that God's ire did not end with Adam and Eve's expulsion from Eden or with the Great Flood."

"What do you mean?"

"The adamants told of a third Fall from Grace, one that the Book of Enoch also foretells. One that, sooner or later, will be fulfilled in a trial of fire . . . Our species is in danger again, Julia. And that's why I wanted to mark our wedding day with this story. Because one day, you and I may have to save our world together . . ."

28

The iridescent cloud that had been wafting over the Cathedral of Santiago de Compostela descended to ground level like a dense fog that filled every corner and recess. It spread in all directions until it seemed everything was thick with its energy.

And once it spread over man and machine, its effects were immediate. That radiant plasma could sap the energy from any electrical device and the strength from man or beast. Only special clothing, like that worn by the men from the helicopter in the plaza, could withstand its supernatural force, to a degree. The material was designed to redirect electrical charges into the earth beneath them.

"Okay. Let's move!"

The sheikh knew what had to be done as soon as the *Amrak* was activated. He had ordered his men to snap special lights covered in lead-lined fabric onto their submachine guns and double-time it toward the only building the police had been guarding. It was clear that was where Julia Álvarez was being kept.

The three of them darted between the fallen bodies of police officers. Some of them had collapsed against the door to the café, staring vacantly and glassy eyed into nothingness. Inside, they found the waiter slumped on the floor, his face twisted in a grotesque expression, broken dishes all around him.

"How long will the *Amrak*'s effect last, master?"

The question from Waasfi, the young man with the ponytail and the snake tattoo on his cheek, made the sheikh stop in his tracks. "It's not a matter of how long it lasts, but rather how long a person can withstand its effect. Some of them may never wake from this, brother. That's how powerful it is."

Their lights swept back and forth across the foggy café.

"Find the woman you saw in the cathedral," the sheikh said to the young man.

They walked silently toward the back of the café. All of the tables were empty, except one. A tall man, thick and brawny, lay facedown on the ground. Next to him, there was the body of a woman. She had collapsed into a kneeling position. Her head was pinned into her chest, like a broken doll's.

Waasfi lifted her chin.

It was her. Julia. She stared blankly into the void, as if death—or whatever it was the *Amrak* caused—had caught her in midconversation. *She has the most beautiful eyes,* he thought.

When the beam of his light flashed across her face, her pupils shrank.

The Armenian smiled.

"She's over here," he called out.

The sheikh barely noticed. He was squatting over the large American in the black suit and was trying to roll him over to get a better look.

When he finally did, a shadow passed over the sheikh's face.

"Is something wrong?"

Their leader shook his head, worried. "You were right, Waasfi. They're on Martin's trail. I know this man . . ."

29

Images came rushing back, flowing over my eyes and flooding my mind.

I've died, I said to myself, over and over. *All that remains is the darkness.*

But I was wrong.

Another memory flashed across my eyes, one so strong my head spun. I'd always imagined that when your life flashed before your eyes, it played from the beginning, like a movie. But I guess I was wrong about that, too. Because now I was seeing Martin pulling one of his damn seer stones out of my purse and slapping it onto Father Graham's kitchen table.

"Here it is!" he said.

Instinctively, I pulled my own out and placed it next to his.

"Is that what I think it is, Martin?"

"John Dee's. Both of them."

"The adamants?"

Martin nodded.

"I'd heard your mother talk so much about them. But I never imagined they'd look like this."

"Everyone always expects a polished gemstone. Ostentatious. Regal. Something like Dee's smoking mirror."

"What the hell is a smoking mirror?"

The two of them just smiled at me.

"When John Dee died, most of his library and his collection of artifacts ended up in the hands of a British antiques dealer named Elias Ashmole," Martin said. "He was one of the founders of the Royal Society of London and a champion of modern science. But he had a secret: He also believed it was not only possible but necessary to communicate with angels. And then he stumbled onto the 'smoking mirror' among

Dee's knickknacks and tried to use it for that very purpose. It actually wasn't a mirror as we know it today, but a highly polished obsidian slate, probably made by the Aztecs. It's housed in the British Museum today."

"But at least the mirror looks somewhat exotic," the priest scoffed. "These stones look just . . . ordinary."

"You're absolutely right, Father. If someone didn't know about their origin, they might look right past them—until someone taps their power. That's why every time we move, we declare them at customs, leaving a trail in case we ever lose them."

"Do you plan to take them out of England?"

"Maybe . . ."

"Have you been able to determine if the adamants are earthly?"

The priest's question surprised me, but no more than Martin's answer.

"They only look that way, Father," he said. "My mother might say she hasn't been able to find anything like them anywhere else on Earth."

The old priest rubbed one of the adamants again eagerly.

"And where did she find them?" I asked.

"They came with an old copy of the Book of Enoch, which had been handed down in our family. They had been embedded in the leather binding. In the old days, it was customary to decorate the cover of a book with precious stones."

"Do you know if other copies of the book had similar stones embedded in the same way?"

"I don't. If there are any, they've never been found. My parents spent years looking for other adamants, and all they could find were historical references to similar stones. Mostly as part of legends or in journals of the conquistadors, that kind of thing. Actually, they're pretty popular in American folklore."

"In America?" I asked.

Father Graham, who had been fiddling with the adamants, handed them to Martin before responding. "References to the adamants are as ubiquitous as the Great Flood, my child," he said. "Have you ever heard the story of Naymlap? It's famous in Peru."

The priest seemed pleased to tell the story.

"Naymlap was a mysterious sailor—before the time of Columbus— who landed on the coast of Peru after he was guided by a stone similar to these. He told the natives he could hear his gods through it and never lost his way."

"Interesting . . . Father, do you know what the earliest mention of the stones is?"

"That's easy," he said, smiling. "The Sumerians were the first to use them. The best-known of them was a so-called Adapa—Sumer's version of Adam—who ascended into the land of the gods. The parallels between him and Enoch are so great that many scholars think they were one and the same."

Then Father Graham fell silent for a moment, as if trying to order his thoughts before continuing.

"Ancient books are filled with those kinds of unexplainable parallels. Regardless of their culture or country of origin."

"What exactly did you study, Father?" I asked.

"Comparative mythology. Stories about the Great Flood, to be exact." He continued.

"The Flood is the most widespread ancient story of humankind, my child. And the details are similar the world over. Every version, be it Babylonian or Central American, tells the same story and speaks to a similar primal fear. Sumer's Utnapishtim, for example, could be Noah's identical twin. So was Greece's Deucalion, the son of Prometheus. Or Manu, the protagonist in Hindu's Rig Veda, whose ark ran aground on a mountaintop during the flood. According to the stories, all of them survived the Great Flood because God warned them ahead of time and told each of them to build an ark of very precise measurements."

"Not *an* ark. *The* ark," Martin said. "The Sumerian clay tablets that tell the epic of Gilgamesh also refer to the building of a boat with the same dimensions as the one in the Bible. The only difference is that the Sumerian epic tells the story of King Gilgamesh's effort to meet the only survivor of the Great Flood: Utnapishtim."

Although I'd heard about the story of Gilgamesh, it was from a different time period—about four thousand years earlier—than the one I'd focused on in my work as a historian.

"Please, go on," I said.

"It's really a fascinating story. Gilgamesh learns from Utnapishtim about the Great Flood, how it was supposed to cleanse humanity after our species was contaminated. As far as I've been able to determine, our genetic split began some eleven or twelve thousand years ago, when our species mixed with divine blood."

"The 'sons of God' that Enoch wrote about," I said.

"Precisely," Martin added. "And, from a paleoclimatological stand-point, that's about the time in history when a worldwide catastrophe like the Great Flood would fit in the fossil record."

"But why are you so interested in this? You're not a historian or a geneticist . . ."

He smiled. "Julia, hidden in all these different myths are the keys to the first time in human history that people had to adapt to a global climate shift."

"And that's the only reason?"

"Here, let me continue, and you'll see what I mean. In that meeting, Utnapishtim tells Gilgamesh that the god Enki was the one who kept our species from dying a watery death. Enki told Utnapishtim to build an ark so he could save himself and humanity. And he bestowed upon Utnapishtim two stones that he could use to communicate with him."

"Two stones . . . ," I muttered.

"The stones were made by the hands of gods. Living proof of the existence of divine beings," Martin said with a faraway look in his eyes. "Gilgamesh would go on to say that the stones were only used during very special ceremonies, when their energy would be strong enough to let them communicate with heaven."

"And that's why you intend to use them today. As part of our wedding," I said, finally seeing the point of his story.

Martin nodded. "Exactly, my love."

30

Benigno Fornés was breathless by the time he had rushed down the hallway toward the archbishop's palace. He banged on the archbishop assistant's door until the man answered. The cathedral's dean must have looked a mess: He was sweating as he carried his flashlight and his eyes were frantic. He must have seemed a little out of his mind, too. Fornés hurried the assistant to wake the archbishop. And fast.

"At this time of night?" the assistant whispered.

"I'm sorry. But it's a dire matter between the archbishop and me."

"Dire? To whom, Father?"

"To the Church."

The man was struck wordless and nodded. "Well, it better be, Father Benigno. I'll call him, but I'll warn you that I'm not accepting any of the consequences."

"Please, hurry."

It was just before four in the morning when a pale, stumbling archbishop arrived at his assistant's quarters. He'd clearly rushed to dress in his black robes and was still buttoning his priest's collar when he greeted Fornés. He found the old dean a bundle of nerves, pacing in circles, his hands clenched together, as if in urgent prayer.

"All right, Father, what's so important?"

"I'm sorry, Your Grace. But this is something I have to show you. Something you have to see to believe."

"To show me? Where?"

"In the cathedral."

"I thought I was clear that it should remain closed until the police complete their investigation."

Fornés ignored him. "Remember the 'sign' we were talking about?"

Archbishop Martos was caught off guard. He had figured Father

Benigno, the cathedral's keeper, had a more earthly concern. Maybe regarding the shooting this afternoon.

"Uh, yes, of course," he said. "But, Father, couldn't we wait to have a discussion about legends over breakfast?"

"Legends?" Fornés grimaced. "No. No, it can't wait. Your Grace has spent three years here. I've been here forty. This is something you need to see right away, before I try to explain what's going on. What's happened in our church is no coincidence. Now I'm sure of it . . ."

Intrigued, the archbishop followed the wild-eyed priest out the door and into the night. They hurried down the darkened path to the church and headed toward the Platerías door, until Fornés stopped exactly in front of the spot he wanted to show the archbishop.

"Four decades ago, one of my predecessors in charge of the cathedral told me an interesting story, Your Grace," he said. "He explained to me that for more than five hundred years, this sanctuary was considered Christianity's westernmost place of worship, and, as such, it was seen as the church at the end of the world."

The archbishop quietly listened to the priest.

"In the twelfth century, the keepers of the cathedral were so convinced that Compostela would be the first place from which you could see the kingdom of heaven returning to Earth that they decided to secretly decorate it as such. They started replacing the Roman ornamentation with apocalyptic symbols. And that, Monsignor, is how our Pórtico de la Gloria became the quintessential piece in that project. As you know, the images carved in it foretell the coming of the New Jerusalem, the city that will establish a new order on earth."

"Okay, Father, where are you going with this?"

"Your Grace, they believed the day would come when the seven seals that John mentions in the Book of Revelation would open. The book gives us instructions for how to reach the kingdom of heaven when we arrive at the End of Days. But to follow those instructions, Your Grace, first we would have to find the seven seals."

The archbishop started in disbelief. "And you believe this is one of those seals, Father?"

"It's not a matter of believing. It's a fact that one of the seals has just appeared in your cathedral, Your Grace. That's what I want you to see."

"Father Fornés, I don't—"

"Please, Your Grace. Don't say anything else. Just look."

Juan Martos leaned in to look at the spot on the stone wall, disbelieving. There, he found a marking, perfectly carved—or scorched, he couldn't tell—with a skill level that no medieval stonecutter could have ever hoped to achieve. It was shaped like an upside-down "L," about a foot tall. He traced the outline with his fingers. He wasn't ready to validate the old priest's claims. Still he couldn't figure out what language this letter might be in.

"Is it Celtic?"

"No, Your Grace. Not Hebrew, either. And not any other language of this world."

"Do *you* know what this is, Father?"

Fornés hesitated.

"I'm betting the man who was in here earlier tonight could tell you. The police said one of the restorers caught him kneeling over here, as if praying or looking for something."

The priest paused, his face grave.

"Do you know what I think, Your Grace? Someone has set out to open the seven seals. And he's found one of them in our church. I think the police need to find him and bring him back here. We have to talk to him, immediately."

Martos gazed at the dean sadly. The poor old man had lost his mind.

31

"My children, I feel we should open this ceremony with a story."

It was noon on a brilliant June morning when Father Graham presided over our wedding. He seemed to have moved on from the heated discussion he and Martin had had and was ready to make our day memorable. He looked over the handful of guests with that hawkish gaze. The entire congregation fit inside the first three rows of the small chapel, huddled cozily around the bride and groom. All those memories, the sights, the sounds, are forever etched in my mind.

Father Graham looked over the top of his glasses toward Sheila and Daniel, who were seated to my left.

"They would like to share something on behalf of the groom's family. Please," he said, motioning to them, "come up to the altar."

Sheila straightened the brilliant corsage of yellow flowers she wore and headed for the altar. She looked splendid in a black sequined gown, her creamy, white skin seeming to radiate light. A cloud of soft, intoxicating perfume floated around her as she moved, followed by Daniel, his hair as wild as ever, but looking slightly more professorial in a tweed jacket. It was he who addressed us first.

"Father Graham, invited guests . . . ," he said, clearing his throat as he looked around the room.

"One of the Faber family's longest traditions is reading from the Book of Enoch, which tells just how difficult it was in the olden days to distinguish the angels among us."

"What is this, some kind of lecture?" I whispered to Martin.

"Hmm, I thought you liked myths," he said with an ironic grin, never taking his eyes off the altar. "So I thought I'd ask Daniel to give us a little background on angelology."

"Martin!" I hissed under my breath.

"Shh, shh, my love."

Daniel eyed us without interrupting his speech.

"Let me tell you what those angels actually looked like," he said, raising his voice to the crowd. "In the final few chapters of the Book of Enoch, we hear the story of Lamec, Noah's father, who was gravely concerned about these lovely blond creatures who walked among us, unnoticed. He called them 'the Watchers,' because he believed God had sent them to earth to look after us after Adam and Eve were cast out of paradise. Those divine protectors ensured man would never again fall into God's disfavor. They admonished those who broke God's laws and all mankind respected them, heeded their warnings . . . until one day, when a terrible rumor about them spread among the masses," Daniel said, arching his bushy eyebrows and creating a palpable tension with every word. "It seemed that several of the Watchers had taken human brides, mixing their divine flesh with ours. And that's why Lamec grew suspicious when his own wife gave birth to a dazzling young child with crystal-blue eyes and fair skin. He called that child Noah, which means 'comfort.' Lamec died without knowing that God had chosen his hybrid son and family to save man from the Great Flood. And that he had chosen Noah specifically because the child would be able to do something others could not: He could hear the voice of God. And communicate with Him. Like a medium to mankind . . ."

"All right, all right . . . ," Father Graham grumbled, making the audience laugh and lightening the mood. "That's all fine and dandy, but it's time to get on with the ceremony and you still haven't gotten to Enoch and his book."

"Sorry, Father."

Daniel Knight glanced at Martin, as if looking for permission to continue, and moved on.

"Noah had quite a predecessor in Enoch. He was one of the few humans before the Great Flood who had direct contact with the Watchers and he learned from them, even though he was a simple shepherd. Enoch learned their strange language, became their trusted confidant and was rewarded by being allowed to ascend into the heavens without dying or even aging. He returned from paradise not only with endless knowledge, but with a rare wisdom. He insisted a terrible catastrophe awaited man and that we must be prepared. But his contemporaries ignored him. In fact, his warnings were forgotten until his great-grandson Noah broached the topic generations later and he, too, was ignored."

"I'm sorry, Mr. Knight," Father Graham said, "but can you explain to us exactly who Enoch was? Whether he actually existed?"

"Certainly he did, Father," Daniel Knight said, using a handkerchief to wipe beads of sweat that had started to form on his brow. "My partner Sheila and I have spent years studying him and certain stones he is said to have brought back with him from the heavens. And we've come to learn that his journey is nearly identical to that of another hero, one born in the first great civilization after the Great Flood—in Sumer. That's where man invented the wheel, writing, laws, astronomy and mathematics. It's where they first spoke of angels, which they drew with wings, as a symbol of their celestial connection. And it's also the place where man was robbed of his greatest gift: immortality. That hero, who has a longer track record than our Enoch, was a king called Gilgamesh. He also managed to communicate face-to-face with the gods and set foot in the kingdom of heaven—without having to face the unfortunate reality of death. I'd like to give you a brief summary of his odyssey, as it was recorded in those ancient cuneiform tablets.

"It all began more than five thousand years ago, in the times after the Great Flood.

"Gilgamesh, whose name means 'he who has seen the profound,' had just been crowned king of Uruk. His kingdom was extensive, stretching from the eastern shores of the Euphrates. But Gilgamesh was more than just a great warrior. He was also a great thinker. He had watched his parents and close friends die and realized the ravages of time were even more destructive than war. All of us, rich or poor, soldier or farmer, would end up merely bones in a coffin. As would he. And that certainty terrified him.

"Tortured by these thoughts, Gilgamesh decided to journey to the kingdom of Anu, the fatherland of his creators, to demand that the gods make him immortal, the way humanity had been before the Great Flood. He came across the name of the only human ever to have achieved that goal, a foreign king named Utnapishtim, who he believed could teach him the secret to eternal life.

"He journeyed through lands prohibited to humans, defeated terrible monsters and resisted a thousand and one temptations and tricks that the gods hurled into his path.

"Gilgamesh overcame the most difficult challenges, including strangling two colossal lions, one in each arm, a symbol that would come to define him: man dominating beasts with brute force. When Gilgamesh finally reached Utnapishtim in a garden on the far left side of Lifes, the five-thousand-year-old man agreed to hear his pleas.

"Breathless and completely exhausted, Gilgamesh managed to ask just one question. A question that the eleventh clay tablet of the epic takes up with great care. A question that Utnapishtim agrees to answer despite his many doubts: How did you achieve eternal life?"

Daniel paused.

"Would you like to know his answer?"

32

The young man with the tattoo on his cheek looked worried.

"Sheikh, do you know this man?"

His leader, the one with the thick mustache, nodded absentmind-edly. He felt like the walls of the narrow café were closing in on him. It was clear he was trying to hold back a torrent of emotions and memories that came rushing to the surface as he stood next to the enormous man collapsed on the floor in front of him. Waasfi was right when he said that "they"—their ancient enemies—were in the city.

"His name is Nicholas Allen, brother," he whispered. "For years, each of us has been chasing the adamants."

Waasfi looked down again at the fallen soldier. The *Amrak*'s electro-magnetic pulse had left him in a catatonic state that could very well be irreversible. He tried to imagine what kind of challenge he might have posed if Waasfi hadn't managed to give him the slip inside the cathedral. He looked at his battle-tested visage: his sheer size, the imposing scar on his forehead and now a new bruise just below his nose. He must have struck something as he fell and was now bleeding onto the floor. Even still, he was an intimidating sight.

"Is she the one?" the sheikh asked, rousing Waasfi from his trance. He looked down at the woman with fiery red hair covering her face. In the darkness, it was hard to fully make out her features. "Is she the woman you saw in the cathedral?"

The young man nodded.

"Yes, master. But I can't understand how he managed to find her before we did."

"He must have followed the same trail," the sheikh admitted. "Martin Faber's video led him right to her."

"Should I kill him?"

Waasfi tightened his jaw. To him, Allen was a dangerous enemy. His teachers in the mountains of Hrazdan had taught him that a man like this was more than just an enemy from the United States of America: He was evil incarnate. It would give him so much pleasure to squeeze the trigger and ensure there was one less on Earth.

But the sheikh resisted.

"No. Let the *Amrak* decide his fate. A worthy adversary deserves an honorable death."

Waasfi swallowed his bile and picked up the woman. "What should we do with her, master?"

"Frisk her. I don't want any surprises."

Waasfi laid the woman on the ground and patted her down, looking for a weapon, while the sheikh tried to switch on Colonel Allen's device. But it was no use. The cloud's electromagnetic pulse had sapped the power.

Waasfi finished his search by the light of his shielded flashlight and found the woman clean. Doctor Julia Álvarez was harmless. The only metal on her body was a simple necklace with a dangling crucifix and a small, dull medallion. He emptied her purse and laid out its contents but didn't find anything that looked dangerous.

"She's clean."

"Are you sure?"

"Yes, sir."

The sheikh looked over at Julia's lifeless body and the contents on the ground.

"What about that medallion?"

"It's nothing, sir."

"Show it to me."

Waasfi handed it to him. It was a thin silver disk engraved with a picture of a boat and birds flying overhead. Around it were etched the words "Beginning and end."

He couldn't understand why his leader's face suddenly brightened when he saw it.

"You still have much to learn, my son," he whispered with a smile. Waasfi dropped his head in humiliation. "You don't know what this is, do you?"

The young man took a closer look at the little medallion and shook his head.

"This is our clue for where the stone is hidden," he said, putting the medallion back around Julia's neck. "It's too bad the infidels don't know how to read the signs."

33

Something else surprised me in my voyage through the valley of death. Unlike the memories of the living, the memories of the dead are not vague, shapeless far-off mirages. No. They are like life itself, vibrant and immediate and real, but with one main difference: the perspective. It was as if I were seeing my life again through the eyes of God.

Maybe that's why my soul was so intent on reviewing every moment of my wedding. Because I was now able to draw so much meaning from each moment. And now I was focused on what happened as Daniel gave his dark lecture on the meeting between Gilgamesh and Utnapishtim, when one of the guests rose and hurried out of the Biddlestone chapel.

I let the images wash over me again.

The man who rushed out of the church was Artemi Dujok. He was an old Armenian friend of Martin's who, I'd learned that day, was the majority stockholder in a technology company. I hadn't paid much attention at the time when his picture ran in the paper a few days before my wedding under the headline THE DOOMSDAY MAN. It seemed Dujok was behind a project called the Global Seed Vault to build an underground catastrophe-proof bunker to protect a vast variety of the world's plant seeds. Forget Noah's Ark. Martin said Dujok hoped to build Noah's Greenhouse thousands of feet below the Svalbard permafrost, where they could warehouse more than two and a half billion seeds from every continent at below-zero temperatures in case of a worldwide calamity. Dujok's company was in charge of handling the seed bank's security. But the newspaper articles also examined his company's links to military projects and advanced weaponry, bringing into question the benevolent image Dujok tried to project.

Yet the first thing I thought when I met him was that for a brilliant multimillionaire, his clothes didn't match his bank account. He was introverted, hanging in the background, and I don't remember him having a single conversation with another guest. Maybe he felt like he didn't fit in with the others. He'd come alone, without a driver or bodyguards. And maybe he buried his nose in his electronic organizer to avoid calling more attention than his tanned skin and thick, memorable mustache did.

That's probably why no one noticed when he got up after Daniel's speech and hurried to the back of the church, pretending to take a call. He turned his back to us and, when he felt no one was looking, slipped the phone into his coat pocket and headed for the parking lot.

I was surprised to find that in my postmortem state I could follow his every move.

He pressed a key fob and the lights on his BMW flashed in the distance. When the trunk popped open, there was a sight you didn't expect to find in a $70,000 car: a used shovel and pick, covered in mud, and a beige duffel bag that he threw over his shoulder.

He quickly tossed aside his coat and tie and was only in his shirtsleeves, looking around to make sure no one was watching him. The windows of the seven adjacent houses behind the church remained closed and dark. Dujok was alone.

What's he going to do now? I wondered.

Dujok hurried to the church's apse, the curved wall behind the altar, and dropped his bag on the ground. He opened the bag and started taking out all manner of tools. First, he put on a mask and a pair of mud-spattered coveralls. He made sure his pants were tucked into his waterproof boots, then he pulled out a small extendable spade, like the ones mountain climbers use, and he glanced at his watch. I could tell he wanted to work quickly. He stood over a hole in the rocky and muddy ground, about a yard and a half wide and deep, that I somehow knew he had dug the night before. He went to work, continuing to dig as my wedding was going on, behind the back of even his close friend Martin, as if he were looking for something he needed at that very moment.

It didn't take long to find what he was looking for. And he didn't seem too surprised at how quickly he'd heard the sound of metal against metal. As if he knew it was waiting for him.

Artemi Dujok tossed aside the shovel and continued to dig with his hands, revealing the outline of a small lead chest. The metal was aged and rusted, definitely ancient. It didn't seem to have any hinges or locks or identifying marks. Instead, it looked like it had been welded shut, hermetically sealed.

Only before grabbing the metal box did Dujok hesitate. He took off his work gloves and slipped on a thicker, metallic pair. He carefully secured a rope around the box and pulled it out of the hole, until it came to rest at his feet.

I was starting to wonder why I was having this particular vision at the moment of my death when I saw Artemi Dujok start to chisel open the box's top. The smell of ammonia puffed out as the lid popped off, and Dujok covered his face with his arm as a small trail of smoke rose into the air. The Armenian grumbled something under his breath. But when he looked inside the box, I could see his twisted mustache curl up with a smile.

I wasn't close enough to see what was inside, but I did make out the contours of something rough, dark and odd shaped. It was some kind of tablet, engraved with a series of notches and lines. But I didn't have time to see anything else. He quickly picked up the box and placed it under the window of the church's apse. He clearly knew what he was doing.

"*Sobra zol ror i ta nazpsad!*" he whispered in a language I didn't recognize. "*Graa ta malprag!*" he added, raising his voice.

Dujok was no longer that anonymous figure lost in the background. His face glowed with a superhuman intensity.

"*Sobra zol ror i ta nazpsad!*"

His voice now resonated throughout the courtyard. And when he said that phrase a second time, I saw the inside of the box begin to glow and shoot a bolt of light into the sky. It was quick and intense, leaping from inside the lead box toward the window that separated the garden from the altar where Martin and I were being married.

I swallowed hard. He had awoken something inside that box and had done it with an ancient spell, unleashing something I never imagined existed. Never, aside from the night before with Sheila Graham, had I witnessed anything like it.

Who the hell was this Artemi Dujok?

34

Just as Inspector Figueiras floored the accelerator of his Peugeot 307 to take the last hill standing between him and the Plaza de la Quintana, he felt the ninety horses under the hood wheeze and his speed drop.

"Damn it, now what?" he said, pounding the steering wheel.

The engine tried to obey but eventually coughed, shook and came to a silent rest.

Well, at least it had stopped raining.

He coasted the car to the side of the road and set off on foot. There was enough on his mind to quicken his pace. An American spy. Maybe two. A pair of valuable stones. A shooting inside of a church and a woman in danger. If the police commissioner was right, the woman needed to be under police protection, at least until this mess was cleared up. And if that wasn't bad enough, there was that damn rainstorm and a power outage that cut off radio communications between him and his men.

Figueiras adjusted his showy white glasses as he rushed down the block. He cut down a side street, leaving behind the picturesque Pazo archway and the rows of closed souvenir shops. He was so wrapped up in his world that he didn't even notice the helicopter, which was still resting across from the cathedral.

But he snapped back to reality when he turned a corner and saw two men dressed in black rushing down a walkway. Despite the darkness, he immediately recognized them.

"Father Fornés! Archbishop Martos!" he called to them. "Is something the matter? What are you doing out at this time of night?"

Archbishop Martos brightened immediately. "Ah, Inspector." He smiled. "Am I glad to see you."

"Really?"

"A godsend. The dean here just pulled me out of bed to show me something your men found during the shooting at the church, something we hadn't noticed. Isn't that right, Father?"

The old priest's gaunt face tightened, as if he were wishing the earth would swallow him up. He'd never liked Figueiras.

"What is it, Father?"

"W-well . . . ," Fornés stammered. "Remember where the shooting started?"

"Near the *Campus Stellae* monument. I remember. What about it?"

"Well, one of the stone blocks seems to have been damaged . . ."

"Wait, did you breach the secured perimeter?"

Fornés's face reddened.

"What Father Fornés is trying to say is that something has . . . appeared on that wall," the archbishop said. "A sign. The good father saw it while looking over the cathedral a couple of hours ago, and he thinks this might have something to do with the incident."

"A sign?" Figueiras scrunched up his face. "You think that bastard left some kind of signature behind?"

"No, no, Inspector," the priest said, clearly annoyed. "I think the man was looking for that symbol. That symbol wasn't something done on the fly. I think after he discovered it, he didn't have time to cover it back up."

"That's some handy police work, Father. Tell you what: Why don't I give you my detective's shield and you can just go ahead and do my job for me?"

The priest bit his tongue.

"Don't you think he could have gone looking for that symbol while the cathedral was open to visitors, without causing such a fuss?"

"You never were a man of faith, Figueiras," Fornés grumbled. "You'd never understand."

"Understand what?"

Figueiras glared at the priest. In a city dominated by religion, Figueiras derived a strange pleasure from arguing with the clergy.

"That symbol was not made by man, Inspector."

"Of course not. How could it be?" Figueiras said, mocking him.

"It's the mark of the angels—the angels of the apocalypse. And the man who desecrated our temple was trying to invoke them."

"Father, please . . ." the archbishop said, interrupting.

"Angels of the apocalypse, huh?" Figueiras's face lit up.

But the old priest clenched his fist.

"Think whatever you want," the priest spat out, his voice rising. "But don't start praying when the ground begins to shake and the Antichrist himself emerges, and the dragon's tail whips the stars from the sky and brings them crashing to Earth. By then, Inspector . . . you'll already be dead."

"Father!" the archbishop said finally. "Enough!"

The inspector took a step back. The smile had been wiped from his face. Because just then, he noticed the earth had started to shake beneath his feet. And it wasn't his imagination. A hum—first soft, then growing stronger and violent—reverberated throughout the streets, unnerving the three men.

Figueiras looked up. It wasn't the apocalypse, after all.

The helicopter, he thought, looking for the bird's outline in the night sky.

35

By the time Artemi Dujok had returned to the church, Daniel had just finished his speech about the polemical Book of Enoch, and it was Sheila's turn to speak. She looked eager to begin.

"Well, then," she said, looking out at the congregation and letting her eyes fall on the man slinking back into the church. "I'm sure you all want to know how Utnapishtim answered Gilgamesh's question. Am I right?"

The congregation nodded collectively.

Martin was glowing. He seemed proud to have turned our wedding into some kind of lecture on ancient mythology—the mythos of angels.

Utnapishtim did not simply answer his question, Sheila told us. Instead of giving Gilgamesh a straightforward reply about how to reach immortality, he told him a story about himself.

"And I'd like to tell that story now," she said.

"This comes from the Sumerian version of the myth," she began. "Centuries before Gilgamesh was born, Utnapishtim was the ruler of another great city, Shuruppak, whose ruins archaeologists have found. At the height of the city's splendor, civilization had begun to spread throughout Asia and Africa in those antediluvian times. That was about the period when the god Enlil decided it was time to end the spread of the human race. He had been so disappointed with the human species, much like the Bible's Yahweh. And he had reason to be: We were unruly.

"And the manner in which he intended to exterminate us was so cruel that he made the other gods swear not to tell a single mortal soul. Enlil believed the root of our problem was the marriage between divine beings and the 'daughters of man.' Those unions, he said, had corrupted our species. It had made us ambitious, disobedient and, what's worse, stronger and smarter. We were a challenge to the gods themselves. So the god of gods—ruler of skies, winds and storms—decided to snuff out a dangerous genetic deviant. And he had a radical plan: to unleash a worldwide flood that would wipe us from the face of the earth.

"Only one of the gods denounced it: his brother Enki. He believed in the human race. He was the one who helped us spread throughout the earth. He was the one who sent the Watchers to guard over us and allowed them to marry human women. He wanted to improve our species and educate us.

"But Enki was conflicted: How could he save our species without directly betraying his brother?

"Not long before D-day, as seas and skies were changing in anticipation of the cataclysmic event, Enki came up with an answer. He knew he couldn't speak directly to Utnapishtim without breaking his oath to his brother. But what if Utnapishtim overheard the plan? Enki hid behind a wall, waited for Utnapishtim to happen by and began lamenting out loud about his brother's fiendish plan.

"'Tear down your home and use it to build an ark. Leave behind your riches and instead focus on survival. Cast aside prosperity, and seek to save humanity. Take with you seeds from every living thing,' Enki said out loud.

"Utnapishtim immediately recognized his god's voice. He went home that night convinced he had stumbled upon an important conversation, a warning he must heed. He built an enormous armor-plated vessel without a bow or stern or masts, something that would float no matter what the conditions at sea. The twelfth clay tablet of the epic of Gilgamesh goes on to tell the story of the endless days and nights of rain that flooded the city of Shuruppak and terrified the king's crew aboard his ship.

"When the worst had passed, the ship ran aground on a mountaintop. King Utnapishtim led the survivors out and sent them forward to repopulate the earth. And that is how our species was reborn."

Sheila looked over at Martin and me.

"This story is a gift to you," she said. "The couple we honor today in holy matrimony is descended from that ancient sailor and his bloodline. They are the heirs of that sacred union between men and gods. And today, we continue to honor the commandment of the god Enki, to go forward across the land and multiply, ensuring that the genetic code of the Watchers will live on."

"And finally," Daniel said, "it's time to bless this union. May I have the adamants?"

We handed our adamants to Daniel, and Martin and I held hands.

"The 'sons of God' gave stones just such as these to their human wives," he said, raising the stones for the congregation to see. "It was a symbol of the world they came from—paradise—and the world where they so wanted to live."

"These stones," Father Graham added, "are often mentioned in the Bible. The Ten Commandments were carved by the finger of God into two large slabs. Jacob, the patriarch, fell asleep atop one and in his dreams he could see the angels climbing the ladder between Earth and heaven. The ones in your hands proceed from those ancient stones and they remain the symbol of the connection between our two worlds."

"Do you remember, Father, what Jacob said at discovering the ladder?" Daniel asked, cutting back in. "'This is the door to the house of God.' He was telling us the stones unlocked a doorway to this invisible world and opened a line of communication between man and our Father in heaven."

To which Sheila added solemnly, "And your stones are the keys to His door. Keep them close to you. And guard them with your lives."

Father Graham stepped forward and raised his arms to bring the congregation to its feet. He had heard enough.

"It is time," he said, again leading the ceremony. "Martin Faber, by the Stone of Commitment, do you solemnly swear to take Julia Álvarez, daughter of man, as your wife? Do you promise to protect her against all adversity and dishonor for all of your remaining days?"

Martin's eyes flashed with life at Father Graham's choice of words, and he said, "I do."

"And you, Julia. By the sacred Stone of Alliance, do you take Martin Faber, son of the Eternal Father, as your husband? Do you promise to remain at his side in the face of the enemies of light, to support him and comfort him even in the dark days ahead?"

I felt a shiver run down my spine. I felt the intensity of the priest's gaze.

"Do you swear it?" he asked.

"I do."

"In that case," he said, taking the adamants from Daniel's hands and holding them over ours, "these age-old relics will be the witnesses to this union. *Lap zirdo noco Mad, hoath Iaida.* And they will always lead you down the path of righteousness and justice."

He placed the adamants in our hands. And I immediately felt my heart quicken. Mine felt warm, and it jostled like a bird desperate to take flight.

As soon as I closed my hand around my adamant, it stopped humming. But very subtly, it began to glow, pulsing with a soft and calming light in the palm of my hand. And then, it did something unlike anything it had done at Sheila's house and, judging from Martin's face, something he had never seen it do before. Every time it pulsed with light, I could make out the outline of a figure inside, what looked like some kind of letter.

Something like this: 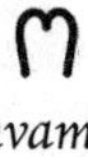

"*Zacar, uniglag od imvamat pugo plapli ananael qaan.* From this day forward, you are husband and wife," Father Graham said, unshaken by what he was seeing.

After that day, I never again saw a symbol appear inside the adamant.

36

Nicholas Allen suddenly opened his eyes.

"Air!" he gasped. "I need air!"

The colonel instinctively grabbed his chest, begging for oxygen. Every cell in his lungs seemed to be screaming for breath. And then, a pain where his heart should have been, an uncontrollable spasm. It felt like he'd been shot in the chest and he actually felt around for a phantom bullet. He coughed, hard, and sat up despite a sickness in his stomach, until he was resting against a brick wall. He tried to gather himself but was disoriented.

"Oh, God . . ."

Someone had dragged him across the floor and left him slumped over like a rag doll. He looked around in the fading light, trying to figure out where he was. And then he saw the lifeless, frozen expression on the waiter's face.

"What . . . what the hell happened here?"

The small café was still. The dim beams from emergency lights bounced off the surrounding furniture. And even though his instincts told him he was alone, he instantly tensed up, every muscle in his gigantic arms and face tightening at the thought of whatever knocked him out still being in the room. Then, he again felt the buzzing of his cell phone in his pocket, which had awakened him in the first place.

"How could I have been so stupid?" he said, rubbing his aching temples as he brought the phone to his ear.

"Allen? Can you hear me?"

The colonel straightened up, still dizzy. He felt cold, frozen to his core. Even his phone felt like a block of ice.

How long had he been out?

"Colonel Allen! Please respond!"

At hearing his name a second time, Allen cleared his throat and answered.

"N-Nick Allen here . . . ," he stammered.

"Colonel? Is that you?"

"Affirmative," he said, wincing.

He noticed a bruise on his forearm. Then his phone beeped, signaling it was running out of power.

"Finally! This is Owen. Where the hell have you been? What's going on? I've been trying to reach you for over an hour. An hour, Allen! Your goddamn phone was off. You know the satellites can't track you if your phone's off. Are you all right?"

"Yes, sir, I . . . I think so."

He could almost feel the NSA director's hot breath through the phone and imagined him stewing behind his desk, almost crushing the phone in his hand. "You *think* so? Where the hell are you?"

Allen looked around, trying to remember what had happened. He was sitting on the floor at La Quintana café, pain shooting throughout his body and a migraine drilling into his temples. When he reached for his service weapon, he realized someone had been there while he was passed out. Someone had emptied the clip of the pistol and had rifled through his wallet. His iPad was gone and the contents of his leather briefcase were spread all over the floor.

What's worse, Julia Álvarez was gone.

"Wha . . . what time is it?" he groaned.

"Time? Jesus, Colonel. It's almost five thirty in the morning in Spain. Do you know what time it is here in Washington?"

Allen's stomach lurched.

"Eleven thirty at night! Where the hell have you been all night, Colonel?"

Allen remained silent. He was numb. Dirty. And his mouth was dry.

"Give me your coordinates, Colonel. I need to get to a meeting but first I need to know exactly where you are."

"Fuck . . . ," Allen grumbled as he tried to lift himself but came crashing back to the ground. "Someone got the jump on me, sir."

"What . . . ?" Owen's voice was muffled on the other end of the line. "What do you mean, Colonel?"

Allen finally picked himself off the ground, despite the dizzying nausea. His old scar was hurting again, and even this dizziness, he thought, seemed familiar. "Your friends, Mr. Director," he said. "Your old friends were here. And they've got Faber's wife."

"How the hell—"

Allen didn't get to hear the rest of Owen's indignation. His phone's lithium battery finally ran out. But the NSA's director already knew what he had to do. His agents at the US embassy in Spain had to find Allen right away.

37

I never figured out how long I spent on the "other side." Or why I had stepped back through the light. I only know that when I finally returned to my body, I felt sick. Really sick. The soothing peace I'd experienced was now shattered, and I seemed to have lost all track of time. When I returned to my earthly body, my brain suddenly switched on every last pain receptor.

The first few seconds of this new life were sheer torture. Indescribable pain.

I felt an explosion in my head, and the jolt traveled to the ends of my toes, cramping every muscle in between. A million pins and needles stabbed me in spasmodic waves. *Oh, God . . . !* And then, it was my lungs' turn to suffer. They filled with oxygen for the first time in God-knows-how-long, and each time I inhaled, it felt like I was breathing fire.

I prayed to God that I could just die again, so I wouldn't have to feel any more. But no one heard my pleas.

I don't know how long I begged for death. But it was long enough for me to understand that I was, in fact, alive again. *Alive.* And I realized it was time to fight to stay that way.

A thousand disjointed thoughts flashed through my mind, but one stood out above all others: the last image I saw before I crossed into the world of the dead. It was the profile of a man, the man who had come to Santiago solely to tell me Martin had been kidnapped in Turkey and that his captors were now coming after me. More specifically, they wanted the one thing that I had no idea where to find.

Dee's adamants.

One of those goddamn stones.

The conduit for speaking to angels.

Still dizzy and unable to open my eyes, I reached up and tousled my hair, a habit I'd picked up from my grandmother. Rotating my head back and forth and massaging my skull was a way of regaining my composure. But that wasn't going to cut it on a day like today. I needed food and a hot shower. And I needed them bad.

But I finally willed my eyes open.

Good God . . .

I'm not sure what scared me more: discovering I was no longer in La Quintana café or finding that someone had taken me from the café and strapped me to a seat. Where, I knew not.

A hand waved in front of my eyes.

"Are you all right, miss? Are you dizzy?" said a shapeless form. Still, I thought I could make out that it was holding a syringe.

His voice sounded muffled, almost synthesized.

I tried to focus my eyes and could see he was wearing a white helmet. He was sitting, facing me, and making a ridiculous gesture toward his ears. *Does he want me to touch my ears?* I couldn't think straight and when I reached up toward them, I felt myself wearing some kind of headphones. I pulled them off, trying to figure out what the hell was going on, but was nearly deafened by a thundering noise.

"Can you hear me?" he yelled above the din. But he didn't even wait for my answer.

"You're okay, miss. You're aboard a helicopter," he yelled. "Don't be alarmed, you have nothing to worry about. We've given you a shot of lidocaine to resuscitate you. The dizziness will pass. Now put your headphones back on so I can talk to you better."

"A helicopter? Lidocaine . . . ? Resuscitate me?"

He nodded while my head spun.

My head pounded with pain. Why was I on a helicopter? And who was this guy?

My headphones crackled to life. This man's voice was now clear in my ears.

"Welcome aboard, Ms. Álvarez," he said in accented English.

"Where . . . where am I?"

I tried to get up, forgetting the seatbelts holding me in my seat.

"Don't overexert yourself, miss. You need to rest," he said. "We're friends of yours. Actually, we just saved your life."

I may not have recognized him, but he seemed to know me. Back in the cathedral, Colonel Allen had spoken to me the same way, but this wasn't him. I looked around to see if he was on the helicopter, too. But I could only see this man in front of me, the one smiling through a thick, bushy mustache, who seemed happy to see me. But for the life of me, I couldn't remember where I'd seen him before, him or the two young men who were at his side. They studied me like I was some kind of oddity. Each was carrying a machine gun with a scope. And when I looked at them more closely, I made a startling discovery: One of them, the one closest to the cabin . . . was the young man with the tattoo on his cheek!

When he realized that I had recognized him, he just stared at me without saying a word.

"Hey . . . you . . ." I struggled against my seatbelt. "Who are—"

"Please, Ms. Álvarez, settle down."

"I know . . . I know that kid."

The man with the mustache looked amused.

"Who *are* you?" I shouted. "What do you want from me?"

"Ohhh," he said, feigning injury. "Don't tell me you don't remember me."

"Do I . . . Do I know you?"

If he was hoping to confuse me further, he succeeded.

"You're breaking my heart, Ms. Álvarez," he said, smiling. "My name is Artemi Dujok. And I can't tell you how glad I am we found you when we did."

"Artemi Dujok?"

It had been five years since I saw him for the first and last time, but my still-numb brain put it all together: I'd just seen him in a deathly dream.

Surprised and curious, I looked at him suspiciously. Yes. It was him, after all.

"Artemi Dujok," I said. "I *do* remember you. Yes. But—"

"I'm glad. I was at your wedding in Wiltshire. I'm a good friend of Martin's."

"Martin! Oh, my God!" My eyes shot open. "Do you know he's been—"

"I know everything, ma'am." Dujok handed me a tissue. "Just try to stay calm. I know what you've just been through. You've been in a coma for more than twenty minutes. Someone who's been blasted with delta brain waves shouldn't be overexerting herself."

"What . . . what do you want from me?" I asked. I had no idea what he was talking about. "What are we doing in a helicopter? The police said Martin's been kidnapped!"

"And that's exactly what I need to talk to you about. Have you seen the proof of life video that his captors made?"

"The video?"

Dujok nodded. "I've figured out what Martin was trying to tell you, Ms. Álvarez."

I was frozen.

"Your husband cleverly got a message to you. A message that only his wife could decipher—"

"Or someone like you?" I said, sarcastically. "What about the colonel? Colonel Allen said he knew Martin too, that they had worked together years ago. Where is he, anyway?"

Dujok ignored my question. "Yes, miss. Someone like me. A friend. A good friend. Someone who knows Martin holds a very coveted stone. And together we'll recover that stone and save your husband."

"You know where he is?"

The helicopter jostled in turbulence as it entered a cloud.

"We'll be on the ground in a few minutes," he said. "Just try to relax."

38

He hadn't given that order! He was sure of it.

That's why, when Antonio Figueiras saw the darkened silhouette of his helicopter rising above the rooftops, he realized there was something else going on that was out of his control.

"You'll have to excuse me," he said, quickly shaking the archbishop's hand before turning to dash off. "You, too, Father. I'll call you later to get your statement . . ."

Figueiras took off in a sprint. God, he hated to do that—not curtly cutting off someone midconversation, mind you, but having to do any kind of physical activity. He was getting too old for this. He didn't have the lungs for it, either. But he had to do it if he was going to catch the helicopter before it took off. *Heads are going to roll today,* he thought. *I swear to God . . .*

The path to the front of the cathedral dropped steeply. Figueiras arrived at La Plaza del Obradoiro—panting, his shirt soaked through with sweat—only to discover that the helicopter wasn't one of his. How had he not realized that before? The chopper now gaining altitude was many times larger than the police station's tiny bird. The blades alone—three of them—were longer than any he'd ever seen. It seemed to have no registration number or markings of any kind and was painted black.

He ducked his head to cut through the downward hurricane the helicopter was causing to get to the patrol car he'd left to guard the square. But when he peeked inside, he couldn't believe his eyes.

"Oh, fuck!" he yelled, instinctively reaching for his gun.

His two young officers sat motionless, a single gunshot wound to each of their foreheads, bleeding against the headrests. Clearly, they'd never seen it coming. Figueiras whipped out his pistol and turned toward the helicopter, but it was already out of range. He'd bet a year's salary that the suspect who slipped right past them was the murderer . . . and that he was aboard that helicopter.

His adrenaline pumping and lungs still burning from a flat-out run, Figueiras was just about to call for backup when his cell phone screen came to life: "Incoming Call."

"Figueiras here."

"Antonio, it's Marcelo Muñiz. I hope I'm not catching you at a bad time."

"I can't talk now!" he yelled to his jeweler friend as he looked over the patrol car. "I'll call you later."

"Whatever you say."

"Wait, why the hell are you calling me at five in the morning?"

"I've been up all night trying to find out something about those stones."

Figueiras didn't want to waste any more time. But he couldn't bring himself to hang up. If Muñiz was calling him at this time, it must be important. "Okay, fine. So what did you find out?"

"I've figured out what kind of stones they are. And you're not going to believe it."

39

It was hard to get used to the helicopter's soft shifting. Fortunately, when it finally leveled out and my stomach was no longer jostling around, I started to feel like my old self again. I had to relax; there was no other choice. Fear and confusion weren't going to help. So I swallowed them down and let my arms and legs hang loose as if I were in my yoga class. It seemed to work a little. But I still felt the blood pounding in my temples and my eyes were still tearing from the pain it took to return to the world of the living.

I tried to distract my mind from the pain that death would have spared me. *What did Dujok say about my body being bombarded with . . . what kind of waves? And why did he take on the task of rescuing Martin when Nick Allen and the embassy are already involved?*

Sitting across from me in a leather seat, Artemi Dujok watched me with an unblinking stare. He offered me something to drink as the rest of us just tried to keep from losing our lunch every time the chopper hopped over a cloud.

"Tell me something, Ms. Álvarez. Did your husband tell you why he was going to Turkey?" he asked.

"More or less," I said, trying not to give too much away. "He said he wanted to study the world's melting permafrost mountain peaks. And since I was going to be busy with the cathedral restoration, we figured it was a good time."

"Then he didn't tell you . . ."

"What do you mean?"

"Martin went to Mount Ararat to return his adamant. The stone originally came from there. Did you know that?"

"Sure," I lied.

"Ms. Alvarez, this is important. Your husband and I have been working together for years. We've been trying to find and bring together the few adamants throughout the world. We both know how extraordinary they are, but you can't imagine how powerful they can be when they are all brought together. In fact, we've been seeing signs that very soon we might need their power to protect us from another global catastrophe. A blow against the biosphere that your husband is well aware of. That's why it's so important that we work together and are honest with each other. Do you understand what I mean?"

"Are you trying to scare me?"

"Actually, yes. Martin is working on a high-level operation, and if he didn't give you all the details, it was only to protect you. Now he's in danger. Circumstances have changed and together, we're going to save him. But I need you to trust me, Julia. I know you barely know me, but I promise, you won't regret it."

"You're going to help me rescue my husband?"

He nodded. "Of course. But to do that, we need your adamant. Do you remember when he asked you for it?"

"It's been a month, give or take." I sighed. "It was just before he left. Actually, we had an argument about it and I told him to take it back."

Dujok nodded as if he already knew that part of the story.

"Then he must have hidden it somewhere safe," Dujok said, thinking out loud. "A special hiding place, where the earth's energy is strong. Somewhere it would be not just safe but charged with power."

"You think so?" I asked, unsure.

"Most important, he would've hidden it someplace where someone like the man you were with earlier could never steal it."

"You think he wanted to steal my adamant? Colonel Allen?" I asked.

"I know it. It was the only reason he was interested in finding you. If he had managed to find the adamant, you probably wouldn't be alive, sitting in that seat."

I felt the helicopter lean to one side, and the blood rushed to my head. Outside the window, I could see the skies lightening, hinting at daybreak. Dujok still had not told me where we were headed.

"And how do I know I can trust *you*, Mr. Dujok?"

"You will," he said, smiling. "It's only a matter of time. Martin told me all about your relationship and all of your . . . let's say *adventures* with the adamants. And he made me promise that if anything happened to him, I would make sure you were safe. I was worried about you. Because I know things about your marriage that maybe even you weren't aware of . . ."

"What . . . kind of things?"

There was a sharpness to his smile now. "Do you know, for example, why Martin wanted to be married at Biddlestone? And why he wanted me at your ceremony?"

I looked Artemi Dujok in the eye. I knew this man with his bushy mustache and courtly manners was trying to gain my trust. And I could see in his warm brown eyes the same man I'd met just a while ago in my preternatural vision.

"Actually, I think I do know why, Mr. Dujok . . . You went to Biddlestone to find something," I said, remembering the last image before I found myself on the helicopter. "Something you dug outside the church, secretly, while we were being married. Isn't that right?"

His eyes flashed. "W-well, I, uh . . . ," he stammered. "You . . . you're absolutely right. Can I ask you who told you about this?"

"I've seen it. Just before you woke me up."

"That's incredible!" he whispered, drawing out the words. "I can't tell you how great it is to know you still have your gift. Have you started using it again?"

God, what else does this man know about me? "I guess so . . . ," I said, looking down.

"All right. I understand that you're suspicious," he said. "But maybe I can help you understand what happened the day of your wedding. You chose to marry in Biddlestone according to a secular angelic ritual; the Book of Enoch was used in addition to the Bible for part of the ceremony, and the adamants used in the wedding were last used by John Dee to communicate with angels during the sixteenth century."

"Are you going to talk to me about angels now?" I said, but Dujok barely skipped a beat.

"John Dee, as your husband I'm sure told you, was one of the last Westerners to successfully communicate with them. And like you, he wasn't exactly a mystic. He didn't float off into trances or anything like that. He was more a man of science than anything else, and that's the approach he took. He used three elements in his experiment: powerful stones, a medium named Edward Kelly who knew how to 'read' the stones and a kind of tablet covered in symbols to help open the channel to the other side. Then, all of those items would have to be brought together at a specific place and time for them to work, and Dee determined when that was."

"I still don't understand what any of this has to do with what you were doing at my wedding."

"It's actually very easy to understand."

"Well . . . go on."

"Toward the end of their lives, John Dee and Edward Kelly were discredited and persecuted by their contemporaries. And it's all because of how they misused their instruments. Kelly became arrogant. He thought himself the heir to the prophets Enoch and even St. John, but with a twist. He sought to make himself rich using the angels' prophecies. It was only a matter of time before fate turned on him. That's why, when they split, Dee set out to make sure his two tools for summoning the angels would never fall into the wrong hands. He concealed the adamants by setting them into the cover of a copy of the Book of Enoch, the one the Faber family has safeguarded for generations. And he buried the tablet at Biddlestone, just outside of the church where you were married. Now do you understand? Dee chose that location for mystical reasons, yes, but also because in an ancient dialect in Wiltshire, Biddlestone means "Bible Stone." And that's how Dee saw his ancient instrument—as an actual Bible, a testament to God's word."

"But how did you know the tablet was buried there?"

"Martin discovered it while studying Dee's last notes at the Ashmolean Museum of Art and Archaeology in Oxford. And shortly thereafter, he met you. When he did, he thought it was a sign that he should rebuild Dee's instrument for communicating with the angels: He had the stones; he knew where the tablet was buried; and then, on a pilgrimage to Spain to travel the Way of St. James, he met you. And he knew right away you had the natural talent to be a medium, that you had the 'second sight' that the English spiritualists talked about."

Dujok paused and took a deep breath.

"It wasn't too much of a stretch for him to want to unearth the tablet when all three of the elements were so close at hand. And with all three together again, after four centuries, he felt it would bring a great blessing on your marriage—a direct line to the heavens."

"But I still don't understand why he called on you."

"I met Martin in Armenia when he still worked for the US government—"

"Which I just learned of today," I said.

"That was about the time I convinced him to stop trying to find other stones for the US government. They certainly weren't going to use the stones for any noble purpose and wouldn't know how to handle them correctly, even if they were. But leaving the NSA only brought him trouble. That's why he decided to separate his adamants and left me in charge of the tablet. He'd hoped to keep them apart—until just recently. Ms. Álvarez, your husband discovered there is a very important reason why the adamants and the tablet should be reunited now to try to communicate with Dee's angels."

"What reason? Why now?"

"The stones respond to vibration. They react to resonance, ultrasound and certain electromagnetic frequencies. And right now, the sun is reacting like never before. Solar storms on its surface are roiling, and the solar flares that have come off the star are the most intense in the last century. All that's missing is for a solar wind to blow those trillions of electrons toward Earth, so that the adamants, the tablet—and you—can use that shower of energy to reopen a gateway to heaven.

"But unfortunately, others have made the same discovery," he said. "And I'm afraid that's why they've kidnapped Martin—to control that conversation with the divine."

The helicopter bounced over another patch of turbulence.

"So . . . you don't think he's been kidnapped by a group of Kurdish terrorists at all."

"Hardly," he scoffed. "That's what Martin's old bosses want you to believe, so you won't ask too many questions."

"But in the video he says they're terrorists."

"That's a ruse. The people orchestrating this are much more power-ful than the Kurdistan Workers' Party. The PKK is a gnat compared to these guys."

"So who are they?"

"I can't talk about that . . . not right now."

"Well, can you at least tell me where we're going?"

"That I *can* tell you," he said, smiling and reaching out to hold the medallion hanging around my neck. "To the place where it all began for you."

He let the words hang in the air, as if waiting for me to finish his thought. But I didn't understand what he meant.

"The last line of Martin's video . . . do you remember it? 'Keep en-visioning a way for these two halves to be made whole again,'" he said, smiling. " 'A way.' Now do you understand?"

"No . . ."

"Where did the two of you meet?"

"In Noia, in Spain. I used to live there. It's exactly at the end of the Way of St. James."

"And this is the coat of arms for your town, isn't it?" he said, caress-ing the medallion around my neck, the one with the boat and the birds flying overhead. "Well, that's exactly where we're headed, Ms. Álvarez."

40

At a quarter to six in the morning, the only light in conference room 603B on the sixth floor of the US embassy in Madrid came from the overhead projector casting an image on one wall. A cloud of cigarette smoke wafted over the picture. This was the only nook in the whole building where you could still smoke indoors without getting reprimanded, but Rick Hale had bigger things on his mind at the moment. The embassy's intelligence attaché had just gotten off the phone with one of his field agents, and clearly, things had not gone smoothly.

Hale had had to slap together this briefing as best he could—and fast.

"This is Julia Álvarez. Spaniard. Thirty-five years old. Separated for the last five months from her husband, Martin Faber, the man the PKK kidnapped several days ago near the Turkish-Armenian border," he said, standing in front of a picture of an attractive redhead taken with a telephoto lens. "These pictures were taken yesterday afternoon in Santiago de Compostela, a city in the northwest corner of Spain."

The intelligence officer spoke with a smooth southern accent and easily could have been a country singer. He had a hangdog face that made him look constantly unhappy. And he probably was. That short little bald man was hating life at that moment, giving a briefing before sunrise to a pair of bureaucrats fresh off a plane from Washington, DC. And this was amid another sensitive intelligence operation.

He continued. "Last night, Colonel Nicholas Allen met with Ms. Álvarez to inform her of her husband's kidnapping. As is standard protocol in a case of leaked state secrets, we wanted to find out everything about Martin Faber's private life. Anything that might confirm our suspicions."

"What's your theory, Mr. Hale? You don't trust your agent?" asked Tom Jenkins, a senior adviser to the president.

It was rare for a man like Jenkins to be involved in fieldwork. But his orders were clear. Half an hour after he got off the plane in Madrid, he wanted to see everything the embassy had on Martin Faber.

"Actually, sir, you should know that Faber hasn't worked for the US government since 2001," Hale said.

"No, he hasn't worked for the *NSA* since 2001," Jenkins corrected him.

Jenkins, a strapping blond with icy blue eyes, caught Hale off guard and used the opportunity to bring up another matter.

"Mr. Hale, when the Office of the President looked over agent Faber's file, we found something curious. No sooner had Faber accepted an assignment to the Kurdish-Armenian border than he put in a request for some confidential information from Langley."

"What kind of information?"

"Photographs, to be exact."

Richard Hale just shrugged his shoulders. "I'm all ears."

"Here's the rub: Just before he resigned from the NSA, Mr. Faber requested that a series of old photographs, aerial shots taken of the region he'd been studying, be sent to him by diplomatic pouch to Yerevan. These pictures were taken in 1960 and 1971 by U-2 and SR-71 spy planes and by our KH-4 satellites. And they were all of the Mount Ararat region, exactly where he is now. Sound like a coincidence to you?"

"Did you say KH-4?" Hale snickered and his southern twang rang out. "Man, that's nothin' but scrap metal left over from the Kennedy administration. Those things haven't been operational in years—"

"Never mind that," Jenkins said, hushing him. "The pictures that satellite took were classified and considered very sensitive at the time. Don't forget the mountains of Ararat marked the natural border between Turkey and the old Soviet Union. If that information had leaked, we would've had an international incident on our hands. Maybe even a war."

"So I hope you're going to tell me why Faber would've found those photos so interesting."

"In those shots, taken from about sixteen thousand feet, was something that's kept half the CIA's analysts baffled for years. They called it the Ararat Anomaly. At first, they thought this perfectly rectangular building was some kind of Soviet spy base or transmission station, built right on the edge of one of the glaciers near the summit. But they never managed to identify its purpose."

Jenkins pointed a remote at his laptop, which was connected to the overhead projector. The image flashed to a black-and-white photo of a mountaintop. A red circle had been superimposed over something about the size of a nuclear submarine, with straight, even sides and tapered edges, under a blanket of snow.

"Isn't that a Soviet bunker?" Hale guessed.

"You know as well as I do that it's not, Mr. Hale," Jenkins said flatly. "C'mon, a veteran like you? You know this story. And you know that after years of studying it, Langley concluded it could only be one thing atop the Parrot Glacier: Noah's Ark. Am I wrong?"

"Look, Mr. Jenkins, I'm an atheist. And I don't believe in children's stories."

"Well, this is an Old Testament story, Mr. Hale. And you better start believing," said a voice from the back of the room, where a young woman was leaning against the door frame.

"Okay, so it's an *Old Testament* fairy tale."

"Actually, if I may, gentlemen," the beautiful brunette said, striding forward with the telltale gait of a lifelong soldier, "it's Sumerian, to be exact."

"Sumerian?" Hale asked.

"The story of the Great Flood is originally Sumerian, Mr. Hale. And any student of ancient history knows the Sumerians were the first ones to tell a story of a ship that saved humanity from a rising tide."

"I'm sorry, miss. And you are . . . ?"

"Ellen Watson," she said, reaching out to greet him with a slender, well-manicured hand. "I work for the Office of the President. And let me cut right to the chase."

"Well, I'd appreciate it," Hale said, flipping on the lights and disconnecting the projector.

"Tell me about this Operation Elijah that Faber was working on."

Hale's stomach immediately tensed up. "How the hell did you . . . ? Look, I can't discuss classified information without knowing your clearance level. This is a matter of national security."

"I have White House–level clearance, Mr. Hale."

"Sorry. Not good enough, ma'am. Not for this kind of information."

The woman's mood darkened.

"Listen, I'm not authorized to discuss it," Hale said, "not without a written letter from NSA director Michael Owen. You know him, don't you?"

"That's a shame." She sighed. "Well, I suppose you could at least tell us about what Faber's wife had to say to the NSA's field agent. Do you know whether they discussed the ark? Did she tell him about her husband's secret obsession with that biblical relic?"

Hale knew she wasn't joking. And he knew he had to be diplomatic with his answers. "I'm afraid the conversation wasn't nearly that exciting, Miss Watson," he said.

"What do you mean?"

"Well, it turns out our agent didn't get to finish interviewing her. He had a minor . . . setback."

"What kind of a setback?"

Jenkins's eyes widened. "Look, I don't have all the details," he admitted. "But just before you got here, I got a call from the agent, Colonel Nicholas Allen, and the news wasn't good."

"I don't understand . . ."

"That's because what you don't know is that Colonel Allen was in a gunfight tonight with someone trying to shoot Ms. Álvarez."

"Someone tried to kill her?"

"Don't worry. No one was hurt. And she was under our protection until our agent . . . well . . . all I can say for sure is that while he was interviewing her, they were ambushed with an EM attack. Allen was out of commission for an hour and when he came to, the woman was gone. There's an all-points bulletin out on her right now . . ."

"An EM attack? Electromagnetics?" Tom Jenkins couldn't believe it. "In a civilian setting like Spain? That can't be right. That's like accusing the Russians of using a dirty bomb to hold up a supermarket in New Hampshire."

"I know it sounds crazy. The Department of Defense restricts EM blasts to testing ranges, but there are a bunch of hostile countries that are dabbling in rudimentary electromagnetics. Shoot, if you Googled it, you'd probably find an instruction manual."

"What are you getting at, Mr. Hale?" Ellen Watson said.

"The NSA believes an enemy of the state is cookin' up a plot behind our backs," he said. "A big one."

"And would you be divulging some big state secret by telling us exactly who this phantom enemy might be, Mr. Hale?" Watson said.

Hale rubbed his scalp nervously. "What I'm going to tell you doesn't leave this office, understand?" he said.

"Of course," Watson said with a sly smile.

"This is as plain as I can put it, miss. The agency believes some group with the capabilities to build an EM weapon took an interest in Faber. The theory we're bouncing around is that first they wanted to get him and then his wife."

"And you think this has something to do with the Ararat Anomaly?" Jenkins said, pressing him.

"We don't know."

"And, according to the NSA, this dangerous enemy is . . . the PKK? Who? Who, goddamn it?"

Richard Hale, now sweating profusely, nodded toward the file on the desk with the CIA emblem on the cover.

"That's all I can give you," he said. "If you take a look through that, you'll know everything we know about Agent Faber's disappearance. Even though it's highly unlikely they would have discovered Faber was one of ours, the PKK looks like the culprit."

"You want us to believe that some extremist group of Kurds, who don't even have enough money to buy cartridges for their AK-47s, have a weapon of this caliber at their disposal?"

Jenkins's question hemmed him in further. "We shouldn't underestimate them."

"What are you trying to say, Hale?"

"Maybe behind the PKK is someone who does have the technical and tactical knowledge."

"Maybe? Are you guessing or do you have some kind of proof?"

"Just take a look at the file," Hale said insistently. "I think you'll find something that . . . supports that theory. Martin Faber was grabbed during some huge traffic jam on the road that leads from Bazargan, in Armenia, to the settlement of Gurbulak on the border. It's a tough mountain passage peppered with tiny villages along the way, and the border's been closed—officially, anyway—since 1994."

"And . . . ?"

"Our sources tell us that on the day he disappeared, a sudden and total blackout settled over that entire area."

"A total blackout?" Jenkins's blue eyes flashed.

"Now, I'm not just talking about a power outage, no, sir. That traffic jam? Something killed the engine of every car within twenty-five miles. Same thing happened with every cell tower in the area. And even stranger, it even affected all satellite communications: phones, police and fire radios, even the tower over the airfield in Igdir, in Turkish territory. It's like a big electromagnetic bomb went off, sucking the power out of everything for hours."

"Sounds like the Rachele Effect. Ever heard of it?" Watson asked.

Hale stepped back and looked stunned. This agent clearly knew more than he had imagined.

"You've . . . heard of the Rachele Effect?" he muttered.

Hale was an expert on it. Years ago, he had published an article on it in an internal intelligence magazine. In June 1936, Rachele Mussolini, the wife of the Italian dictator, had planned to spend a weekend in Ostia, near Rome, when her state car broke down, sapped completely of its power during an electrical blackout. Her husband had warned her, only half kidding, as she left the palace: "I wouldn't be surprised if you had a big shock during your outing today, my love." And she certainly did. The power outage lasted almost an hour and then, just as suddenly, all of the nearby cars that had also stopped working started up again.

Mussolini later wrote that the blackout had also something to do with an experiment that Guglielmo Marconi was carrying out. The father of radio had stumbled upon a long-range, low-wave frequency—later called the Death Ray—that first caught the attention of Mussolini, and later of the Truman administration, as a potential military weapon. The sound wave could be used to disable any engine, civilian or military, in the air or on the ground. The Allied forces later speculated that that "ray" was responsible for the death of hundreds of small- and medium-sized animals near Marconi's farm. Animals whose hearing was many times more sensitive than humans' felt the vibration and suffered fatal brain hemorrhages. The event made such an impression on Marconi that he never experimented with those sound waves again.

"The Rachele Effect . . ." Hale nodded. "It's been years since I've heard those words. But now that you mention it, the power outages in Santiago and Bazargan might be related."

"Might be?" Watson said. "It's too bad you haven't been more helpful, Mr. Hale. You leave us no choice but to conduct our own investigation. And you can believe the president of the United States won't stop at the NSA."

"Or with Operation Elijah," Jenkins added.

41

Morning's first light broke across the verdant pasture at the foot of the Tambre River, golden beams refracting over the dewy field. From the window of Artemi Dujok's helicopter—an experimental craft he said was called the Sikorsky X4—I could see a pair of hydroelectric power plants at the edge of a pine and oak forest. I recognized it all, the bridges over the river, the oyster beds, the stone houses dotting the hilly land-scape, the belfries of the church I'd attended as a girl. San Martiño. Santa María. San Juan. Their stone walls, covered in moss under an overcast gray sky, gave this countryside the unique feel of a place where the past and the present managed to coexist peacefully, something I'd always loved about my hometown.

"Are you all right?"

Dujok's voice over my headphones brought me back from my nostalgia.

"Yes . . . of course. It's just that I've never seen my little town from this vantage point."

"Can you guess where in Noia we're headed?"

"Well . . . You're the expert in solving riddles. Colonel Allen thought Martin's video had some kind of hidden message, too. A reference to the place where he'd hidden my adamant."

"*Nicholas Allen* figured this out?" Dujok almost spat out his name.

"I guess he knows the way Martin thinks, too," I said, provoking him.

"Yes . . ."

"Have you managed to decipher Martin's message? Do you know what he was trying to tell me in the video?" I asked.

"You'll find out in a minute."

Dujok sat up in his seat eagerly when he felt the helicopter slowing down, as if it were looking for a place to land.

"Here's what's going to happen, Ms. Álvarez," he said flatly. "We'll stop in Noia to find the adamant Martin hid here. When we have it, I'll need you to help me activate it. Do you understand me?"

Goose bumps ran down my back. I wasn't so sure about bringing the adamant to life without Martin or Sheila around. I knew that once I'd reanimated it, its effects could be unpredictable.

But Artemi Dujok had set his mind on it.

"There's a reason for it, Ms. Álvarez. The adamant will tell us where its sister is, the one Martin showed us in the video. The stones work on high-frequency sound waves and they can find each other even thousands of miles apart."

"That's exactly what Colonel Allen said."

"You have nothing to worry about. Not from him, not from the stone."

Still, my stomach cramped into a knot.

"And, of course, I know the story of how Noia was founded," Dujok said, obviously sensing my apprehension and changing the subject while the pilot maneuvered for a landing.

"You mean the one legend that claims this is where Noah landed after the Flood? Oh, come on . . . ," I said, laughing nervously, as the helicopter descended. "I figured you for an intellectual. You don't really believe that fairy tale, do you?"

Dujok's hefty mustache bounced up and down as the helicopter reached the ground. It landed by the river, near a boatyard, and away from any trees or high-tension wires.

"Well, it's not so much a fairy tale as it is a legend," I said, looking out at the scenery. "One of those stories made up during the Middle Ages to lend this humble little town some nobility. To make it interesting."

The other men, including the pilot, jumped out of the airship with the rotors still spinning, as if they were military men hitting the deck and heading out on a mission.

"You know," I said as Dujok extended his arm to help me off the helicopter, "I study stories too. They influence art and the imaginations of people. But I'd never take them as fact."

"Don't underestimate legends, Ms. Álvarez," he said. "Think of them as Russian nesting dolls. Once you open one up, you find more truth encapsulated inside. Studying legends is like being on a treasure hunt. With each clue you decipher, you get one step closer to the truth. They all disguise something real. Something that, if not for the myth, might have been forgotten eons ago. That's why when you discover a legend's earliest telling, you are the closest to real knowledge."

"And what knowledge do you want to uncover, Mr. Dujok?"

"Martin and I became friends arguing over these very topics. Do you remember how the two of you met?"

"Well, he came to Noia on the Way of St. James."

"Yes, but not just as another pilgrim. He was looking for traces of early stories about Noah."

"The Way was the path pilgrims took to reach the tomb of the apostle St. James. It had nothing to do with Noah," I said, interrupting him.

"Really? Then why is the ark on your town's seal? Why is the highest mountain visible from here called Mount Aro? Why do you wear a symbol of Noah around your neck?"

He seemed to be amusing himself. Just then, he grabbed his weapon, gave his men an order to put on black coats like the one I'd seen the young "monk" wear in the cathedral, and added: "You have to understand that the Way is much older than this charade about finding the tomb of some apostle. Men have been traveling this path for more than four thousand years."

"A charade . . ."

"Haven't you noticed? The route to Santiago is littered with references to Noah. Not just the city of Noia, but also the Noain in Navarra, Noja in Santander, Noenlles in La Coruña, the Noallo River . . . You'll find references to Noah in northern Spain and up into Great Britain and France. Today, almost no one pays attention to this obvious connection."

I was absolutely floored. I had never thought of it either.

"But *I* do," he said, motioning for me to follow him. "And so did Martin. He was following the Way of Noah—not St. James—when he met you. He knew those places named after Noah actually demarcate a secret path of their own, one that leads to a specific location."

"A spot here? In Noia?"

"Exactly. And if the Way of St. James leads to the tomb of the apostle, then the Way of Noah must lead to . . ."

"The tomb of Noah!"

42

Ellen Watson found the best place she could to make a discreet call. She had hurried out of the US embassy in Madrid and found a quiet niche down the street. The city was still asleep at that early hour. A rare taxi and a couple of delivery trucks rumbled through the quiet business district. But that wasn't good enough for the president's adviser. She needed to make a call on her secured satellite phone without drawing any attention. She looked around and figured the dilapidated Jesuit church across the street, where the faithful were free to worship at all times of day, would be the perfect refuge.

The church was empty, just as she'd imagined. The sound of her clip-clopping heels reverberated throughout as she found a corner, looked over her shoulder and punched in the sixteen-digit number to an encrypted line in Washington, DC.

"This is Ellen. The code word is 'Belzoni,'" she whispered.

The man on the other end of the line recognized her immediately and could not hide the worry in his voice. "My code word is 'Jadoo' . . . I've been waiting for your call. Any news?"

She instantly relaxed at hearing his voice. "More or less, sir," she said. "You were right: Something strange is going on here. Last night, the NSA set off to find their ex-agent's wife, and their man was supposedly attacked with an electromagnetic weapon."

"Can that be?"

"From what I've been told today, yes."

The line went silent for a second as a computer program checked for bugs on the line. It found none.

"Do you think that has anything to do with Operation Elijah?"

"I'm sure of it, sir. You should have seen his face when I showed up armed with questions."

"Though he probably didn't say much."

"Like always. He hemmed and hawed about us not having a high enough security clearance."

"As usual . . ."

Ellen Watson wondered whether it was the right time to mention what she'd been thinking since she first heard about Martin Faber's kidnapping. It could be a grave misstep with her boss, but she risked it anyway.

"We do have one other option, sir."

"What's that?"

"You could ask for it yourself."

"How do you mean?"

"You could ask for access to the Elijah files, sir. You're the only one they can't say no to," she said, taking a deep breath before continuing. "Maybe this is the right time to risk it. Someone has reactivated Operation Elijah to find the stones and, for the first time in years, has run up against a problem. If Faber hadn't been captured, we never even would have known about it. That's why I think the time is right for us to intervene, to show them we know what's going on."

Watson exhaled and crossed her fingers. On the other end of the phone, the man chewed on her words.

"I'll consider it," he said finally. "And what does Tom think?"

"He finds it strange that the NSA in Madrid hasn't even mentioned the stones—because that's clearly what they were after from Faber's wife."

The man on the other end of the line remained silent before handing out his orders.

"Listen to me very carefully, Ellen," he said in a voice that was used to commanding. "If you and Tom manage to get your hands on that stone before the NSA does, then we'll have the leverage we need to make them tell us everything they know. Think you can handle that?"

"Of course, sir. We're on it."

"In the meantime, I'll consider your other request. Keep me posted."

Ellen Watson's face lit up. "Yes, sir."

"And, Ellen," he said, his voice solemn this time, "I know you'll do your country proud."

He knew just how to make her swell with pride and patriotism; she would run through a brick wall for this man. And she knew exactly what he meant: Get it done, by any means necessary. Only a handful of people on Earth knew what it was like to stand in that glow, to be urged forward by the president of the United States himself. And Ellen Elizabeth Watson was one of them.

"Thank you, Mr. President. If the woman has the stone in her possession, you can consider it the property of the United States of America."

43

It was six thirty in the morning when Artemi Dujok, a submachine gun hidden under his special black cloak, finally gave me a clue about where we were headed. Dujok hadn't explained how he had managed to deduce from Martin's cryptic message where my adamant had been hidden. But when they led me past the San Martiño church, I stopped doubting that Dujok and Martin had understood each other. At first, I couldn't believe it.

We passed the theater and as we headed down one of three streets that bisect the town, I could hear the cries of seagulls. Theirs was a familiar sound in this ocean-side spot where I'd spent a halcyon youth.

"Martin told me the two of you met in a very special church," Dujok said, his voice breaking the country spell.

This time, I wasn't surprised. I had accepted that this man knew things about my private life that I had never discussed with anyone else. So I just nodded.

"It was at the church of Santa María. The one they call A Nova here, right?"

"That's correct," I whispered.

God. We're headed for that *church.*

He went on. "Martin told me a lot about it. It's the one that impressed him the most along the Way. Even more so than the cathedral in Santiago."

"Is that where Noah's tomb is?"

Dujok held back, but only for a moment.

"Don't be coy, Ms. Álvarez. I know that's where you and Martin saw each other for the first time. That you were restoring the church and that you served as his guide. If Noah's tomb were in that church, you'd know about it. I hope, for your sake and for Martin's, that you'll be straight with me. We don't have much time left."

"But I don't know about any special tomb in Santa María."

"We'll see about that. Let's keep moving."

I immediately felt my stomach tighten. And whatever joy I'd first felt at being back in Noia had now left a bitter taste in my mouth. I followed closely, quietly, behind Dujok and his three young henchmen, but just as we made the turn toward Santa María a Nova, I decided I needed to know more.

"I'm sorry, Mr. Dujok," I said, and stopped dead in my tracks. "But I need you to clear up something for me before I set foot in that church."

"Oh," Dujok said, surprised, walking back toward me. "What do you want to know?"

"How did you figure out from Martin's video where we had to come? That part was shot in Spanish and you don't even speak Spanish."

Touché, I thought.

Dujok's expression changed. That look of determination in his eyes, that ruggedness, all slipped away as he was no longer able to hold back from bursting out in laughter.

"That's your question?" he said, laughing harder.

"Yes."

He gave an order in Armenian to one of his men, the one from the church who he called Waasfi, and the young man with the tattoo on his cheek pulled something out of the small backpack he was carrying. It was an iPad, just like Colonel Allen's. Maybe the same one.

"I know you've already seen this video," he said with a grin, setting a video into motion. "But look at it again."

Martin was again dressed in orange, surrounded by his captors, as he spoke directly to me in Spanish.

"Julia," it began. "We may never see each other again . . . And if I don't get out of this alive, I want you to remember me as a happy man, a man who found his other half at your side . . . If you squander your remaining time, all will be lost. The discoveries we made together. The world that opened up to us. All of it. Fight for me. Use your gift. And though others may strive to steal what was ours, keep envisioning a way for these two halves to be made whole again . . ."

I stared blankly at the screen.

"What, you didn't notice anything peculiar?" Dujok asked.

"Notice? What's to notice?"

Dujok handed me a pair of headphones so I could listen more closely and asked me to listen to Martin's words.

"Forget the image," he said, but I didn't know whether that was possible. "Try to distance yourself as much as you can from it, and try to hear whether you notice anything strange in Martin's words. Anything. A word out of place. An inflection. Everything is important."

I put on the earphones and listened to the video again, this time with my eyes shut.

"Now, did you notice anything?" he asked, as if this were a simple child's riddle.

"I don't know whether this is what you mean but . . . there seems to be a problem with the sound. There are two times when the volume spikes slightly, as if Martin is raising his voice."

"Exactly."

"Exactly? So what does that mean?"

Dujok stowed the iPad back in the young man's backpack and studied me like a teacher studies a student.

"What are the two phrases your husband seems to be saying louder than the rest?"

"Well one of them is 'If you squander your remaining time,' '*si el tiempo dilapidas.*' The other, near the end, is 'keep envisioning a way,' '*se te da visionada.*'"

"Perfect. Well, there you have it . . . Do you see what I mean?"

I still didn't understand what he was getting at. Nowhere was there any reference to Santa María a Nova.

"Okay, let me walk you through it," he said. "Just as John Dee did centuries earlier, your husband is a master at hiding messages in plain language. They trained him to do this at the NSA, and believe me, he was the best of the bunch at it. So when he was ordered to make this video, Martin tapped into that skill and delivered a message as clear as it is veiled. In the Middle Ages, they used to call this 'phonetic cabala.' Ever heard of it?"

I shook my head, still confused.

"It's very simple and easy to detect—if you're looking out for it. It goes back to an old French linguistic trick, where it's not as important what you say as how you say it, leaving a phrase open to double entendres—double meanings. If you were to say, out loud, *'par la Savoie,'* or 'by the Savoy,' you might mistakenly understand *'parla sa voix,'* or 'his voice spoke.' The two are pronounced exactly the same. Like homonyms—words that sound the same but have very different meanings. Dee used those linguistic tricks when he wanted to slip a message to Queen Elizabeth right under the noses of an entire listening audience. Martin was fascinated by it, and he studied it throughout his time at the NSA, playing with language, in Spanish and in English."

"I . . . had no idea," I muttered.

"These homophone phrases, as we call them today, sometimes work even better if the person listening doesn't speak the language. So if a Spanish-speaking person heard *'el tiempo dilapidas,'* he might actually just be listening for the literal translation. Not the *real* meaning."

"So what do you think *'el tiempo dilapidas'* actually means?"

"Why, the very place we're headed."

I sighed. "I'm sorry, I just don't hear it."

"Isn't the church of Santa María a Nova also called 'the temple of tombstones'? Or, in Spanish, *el templo de lápidas*? Now do you hear it? *'El tiempo dilapidas'* and *'el templo de lápidas'*?"

Was it just that simple? I wondered. Could Martin's message be hidden in something as simple as a pun, as a child's word game, like "I scream for ice cream" or "visualize whirled peas"? After all, Dujok was right about Santa María a Nova. The fourteenth-century church was known for housing Europe's largest collection of ancient gravesites and was dubbed the temple of tombstones, *"el templo de lápidas."*

"Okay, Mr. Dujok. Let's say you're right about this. So what can 'keep envisioning a way,' or *'se te da visionada,'* mean?"

A knowing smile crossed his face.

"Patience, Ms. Álvarez," he said. "But I will tell you this: That very phrase will lead us to the right tomb."

44

Roger Castle was sure someone at the all-knowing NSA had been giving him the runaround ever since he took the oath of office. Not that he had ever thought much of these covert operations. In fact, in the last election, he promised to slash the billion-dollar budget this spy game was costing the American taxpayers, and that earned him enemies in high places. But by this point, and over the course of his last two years as president of the United States, he learned he had underestimated them. There were some doors he had not yet managed to open. And especially not the ones to the Big Secret.

The Big Secret, he thought, shaking his head. It sounded like something right out of a Hollywood script. Some awful B-movie about aliens cryogenically frozen at Area 51. But behind that ridiculous moniker was something serious after all. And every now and then, it would come up in conversation, putting President Castle in an awkward spot. "Never heard of it," he would lie. And it hurt to have to lie about it. He held the highest office in the land and he hated not knowing the status of the NSA's investigation into the Big Secret, or as they'd code-named it, Operation Elijah. For a long time, he just ignored it, figuring it was some kind of inside joke at the CIA: *The Big Secret is that there* is *no secret,* he would think. But deep down he knew, ignoring it did not mean forgetting it.

He had first heard the term when he was still the governor of New Mexico, during an official visit with the Hopi Indians at the capitol in Santa Fe. The native tribe from upstate had been worried about recent meteorological changes. There had been a long drought and the Rio Grande had receded 15 percent. "All of it presages the coming of the Great Catastrophe, Mr. Governor," they had told him. "Knowing when it will arrive and how and when to be ready, that is the big secret," said the tribe's spokesman, a Native American almost ninety years old whom everyone called White Bear. "For many years, the white man has kept us in the dark about the details of the great and terrible day."

"Great and terrible day?" the then-governor Castle shot back. "My friend, I think you're mistaking that for a day that's already passed, the bombing of Hiroshima."

Roger Castle had forgotten about the exchange until a month later. The day his father, William Castle II, died. His father had given him everything: his wealth and intelligence, his John Wayne good looks, and, above all, his skepticism. Believing in something that he couldn't weigh, measure or turn into dividends was a hopeless waste of time.

During World War II, William Castle II was one of the mathematicians and physicists at the Institute for Advanced Study at Princeton who worked on the Manhattan Project. What few people knew was that after the war, after atomic weapons had been unleashed on humanity, a group of them continued to meet clandestinely, calling themselves the Jasons. This secret group of independent thinkers continued to advise the NSA, leading them to find solutions in Cambodia and Vietnam. And despite how they may have been loathed by pacifists, some of them, like Castle's father, had managed to salvage their academic reputations.

As a boy, over the course of three or four summers, Castle would dart between the legs of those genius minds while they discussed the boring topic of war. During those interminable discussions that the boy found hopelessly dull, the men discussed everything from missile defense systems to electronic warfare to the Internet—though, of course, that's not what they called it those many years ago—and they even predicted the advent of spy satellites. So when his father mentioned a "great and terrible day" as he spoke to his son from his deathbed, Roger Castle knew he would never forget those words.

"I can't believe this. Just a month ago a delegation of tribal Indians told me that a group of thinkers had been keeping this deep, dark secret from the rest of the public," he said, still shocked.

"It's true, Son. That was us."

"But, Dad, how can you believe in these wild stories?"

"I don't *believe*, son. I'm a scientist, remember?"

Roger Castle nodded.

"I *know*, Son. I know."

Now, consumed by terminal pancreatic cancer, the patriarch of the Castle family added something else: The NSA, working under the code name Operation Elijah, was trying to determine the exact date of that impending apocalypse. It had been years since his father met with the Jasons, but he was sure that a D-day had already been set for mankind. The NSA could monitor communications from all intelligence agencies—from NASA to NOAA, the National Oceanic and Atmospheric Administration. They had spent decades studying everything from cosmic rays to tectonic shifts, from radioactive earth forces to electrical charges in the atmosphere, and William Castle II was certain they had determined the day of the cataclysmic event.

"But, Roger, these bastards only answer to the weapons industry," his father told him. "They couldn't care less about democracy. They know if they have confidential information about the future of the world, they have ultimate control. They'll keep this secret from everyone. Even the president of the United States. When chaos finally breaks out, they'll have no use for the democracy that he's sworn to uphold."

"You mean no president in history has known about this?"

His father grimaced in pain. "This project has been kept so secret that very few have ever known about it. Presidents come and go, Son. It's all politics. But these men, they endure. And since no president has ever asked about it, as far as I know, they've had no reason to talk about it. Do you understand what I'm telling you? If you ever rise to that position, you will be the one who'll have to take the first step and ask about it."

Years later, Ellen Watson had told him the same thing. It was good advice. And it was exactly what he had to do. Now he was sure of it.

Roger Castle, the forty-fifth successor to George Washington, was ready to finally get to the bottom of the country's deep, dark secret.

It's now or never, he decided.

45

There was a hollow, metallic clang.

Under the fading shadows of darkness, the second of Dujok's men—the one he called Janos—wedged something that looked like a small soldering iron into the lock of the wrought iron gate at Santa María a Nova. It popped open with a metallic *thunk*. I was the only one who jumped.

The five of us sprang through the gate, dashed through the garden and up the small pathway that leads to the church. Gravel crunched under our feet and I was aware of even the smallest noise we were making. That's when I noticed how tense Dujok and his men had become. Dujok's relaxed smile was gone, replaced by an intense animal-like focus as we made our way in the darkness. Janos grumbled something inaudible in Armenian and I could tell they were arguing about the black nylon bag they were carrying or something in it. Dujok won out and they marched ahead. But it was clear these men were truly afraid of something. They had unsheathed their Uzi submachine guns, each with a scope sight, and one of them carried a Sig Sauer pistol in his waistband. They looked all around them as they moved, as if anticipating something or someone lunging at us from the dark.

But who would even do such a thing in my quiet little town?

I knew Santa María a Nova like the back of my hand. It was a peaceful chapel at the center of a town where nothing ever happens. The church is surrounded by apartment buildings and its grounds are still used as a cemetery. The most ancient souls rested out to the left and those tombs were covered in climbing vines and brush. To the right, on the other hand, the headstones were resplendent in white with filled flower vases at their bases. What unified the two very different sides were the granite slabs that covered each tomb. Beneath them were the bones of artisans, experts in canon law, even transients, all of which earned this ancient church the nickname *Templo de Lápidas*. I'd never been afraid in this place, despite the endles tombs. On the contrary, it felt like a place where thousands had finally managed to rest in peace.

"Why are you armed, Mr. Dujok?" I whispered.

"Have you forgotten what happened in Santiago?" he said tersely, his eyes scanning our surroundings for impending trouble as we skulked ahead.

We stopped at the entrance to the church. Above us were statues of the Magi, the very ones I had restored years ago. Their Romanesque forms hovered over us, as did a depiction of the bishop Berenguel de Landoira, on his knees, his eyes staring out to nowhere in particular. Janos quickly moved toward the door to work on his next lock. This one was much larger and ensconced in the massive oak door, so it took him longer to open it with his strange device, which I later learned was a small but potent ionized-gas laser.

"Let's go!" Dujok ordered under his breath. "We have to hurry."

He and I rushed inside while Janos, Waasfi and Haci—the pilot— waited outside to guard the door. Inside, his solemn voice reverberated throughout.

"All right, Ms. Álvarez, where is the oldest tomb?"

"There are hundreds of tombs. No one knows which is the oldest," I said, looking down at the endless granite slabs at my feet.

Dujok found a switch on the wall and flipped it. Halogen lamps illuminated the courtyard obliquely, bathing the tombs in light. All of them had images engraved on them. Some of the stone structures had staffs and clamshells etched into granite. Others had inscrutable symbols, eyes and claws. And others still had scissors, sewing instruments, arrows and hats. But not a single one had any kind of written inscription.

"Well, you're the expert," Dujok said, looking at the expanse of graves around us. "Martin met you here five years ago and returned to this very place a month ago to conceal your marital talisman. Where would he have hidden it?"

I looked over the church carefully. It had changed a lot since I'd last been there. Though everything was still in its place, the ancient ruins had become more of a modern tourist attraction. The floor was covered in tiles now, which were decorated with carvings of hammers, anchors, shoes and the tools of the trade that were once used by those who are buried there. There was no trace of the pews, confessionals or altars that once lined the church.

"So where do we start?"

"Mr. Dujok, it makes no sense to be looking for a tomb that's thousands of years old. The oldest ones are no more than seven hundred years old," I said.

"Let's try it another way. Why don't you try thinking back and remembering if anything in particular caught Martin's attention?"

"I . . . I don't know . . ."

"You have to try. We can't leave here without that adamant. We need it to find Martin."

"Agreed." I sighed. "When I first met Martin, he was one of those guys who came in knowing everything. I can almost see him standing here. He came in through that door," I said, pointing to the side of the church. "He had walked from Santiago, because he said no pilgrimage was complete until you left behind the cathedral at Compostela and set foot in this place."

"Did he say why he thought that?"

"Well . . . he wasn't the first one I heard say that. Many of the pilgrims who travel the Way say they do not consider the pilgrimage over until they make the day's walk to Noia. That, they say, is for the truly initiated. Actually, the roots of this part of the trek are pre-Christian. Ancient, actually. Tradition says you have to reach the coast and watch the sun melt into the west to understand that this is the land at the end of the world. The *terra dos mortos*. The place where solid ground ends and the sinister sea begins."

"Which is the adamant's very reason for being."

"Right," I agreed. "But I didn't know anything about that at the time. Plus, Martin had his own ideas. He was always busy copying the masons' marks along the walls of the church into his little notebook."

"Marks? Which ones?"

"Well . . . like that one," I said, pointing to one of the archways that held up the roof of the church. "Can you see it?"

It was a small, simple square carefully chiseled into the stone.

"There are hundreds of them around the church," I said.

"Hmm. Well, did he notice anything else?"

"Oh, lots of things. That's why he asked to speak to an expert. And that's when we met," I said, smiling at the memory. "Actually, I think he was fascinated by the fact that the soil on which the church is built was brought in from Jerusalem. I told him the Crusaders had carted it over by the ton and spread it throughout Santa María's foundation—and out there, in the cemetery."

Dujok's eyes suddenly widened.

"Is that right . . . ?"

"Well, there's a reason for it, Mr. Dujok. The Noians believe that when Jesus Christ returns to Earth during the apocalypse, he will first set foot on the holy soil of Jerusalem. And it was said that whoever was buried under that holy ground would be guaranteed a place in heaven during the resurrection of the dead."

"This all makes sense . . . ," Dujok mumbled to himself.

"What does?" I asked. "What makes sense?"

"The soil from Jerusalem contains a unique mineral composition," he said, nodding, "particularly around the Dome of the Rock on the Temple Mount. The earth there has a higher-than-normal iron content, which makes the ground an excellent electrical conductor. Come to think of it, that would explain why the people were so set on removing their shoes when walking on 'sacred ground' during ancient times. Somehow, they understood that it was important not to interfere with the ambient electrical currents. To do otherwise might mean they'd be electrocuted."

"You mean, you think there's a scientific explanation for this?"

"Absolutely. Remember what happened to those who touched the Ark of the Covenant?"

They were struck down by lightning, I thought, remembering my conversation with Sheila. "But wait. That would mean they knew about electricity centuries before Alessandro Volta."

"Oh, but they did. The ancient Egyptians used to galvanize metal by setting off low-level electrical charges. The archaeological museum in Baghdad displayed a two-thousand-year-old container they used to produce these electrical charges, like an ancient battery. And just consider the adamants themselves, which absorb electricity to serve their function. What we have to do is look past religious metaphors to discover the hidden science."

"And you think that's what Martin was doing here? Reading into the stories, looking for the scientific explanations?"

"Exactly," he said, smiling. "The deeper you look into human history, the more of those kinds of surprises you'll find. The Sumerians, for instance, paved their streets in asphalt. But for most of us, that was unheard-of until the twentieth century. Those are the kinds of things that fascinated Martin, so I'm not surprised he was intrigued by the holy soil around Santa María a Nova. He believed the best place to open communication with the gods was in a place such as this one, where energy courses just under our feet. Unfortunately, so much knowledge was lost on how to open those lines of communication. All we're left with are relics that we barely know how to use. Like the adamants, which should be able to be used in prime locations such as this one."

Dujok took several steps toward the center of the courtyard, thinking. "What else? What else caught Martin's attention?" he said.

"Well, let's see . . . He spent a good long while just walking alone inside the church. You know, he immediately struck me as good person, and since it was lunchtime, I let him look around by himself while I grabbed a bite . . . And if I remember correctly," I added, "when I returned, I found him sketching a picture of our most famous tomb."

"Your most famous?"

"Yes. That one right over there," I said, pointing to a well-restored mausoleum about ten feet away. "It's a stone sarcophagus with a life-size sculpture carved on the lid. It's one of the few pieces that we know everything about. And I can promise you Noah's not inside."

Dujok walked over for a closer look. It was a magnificent monument, probably from the Renaissance era, shielded over the centuries under the arched recesses of these catacombs. The sarcophagus had been meticulously decorated with angels, a family coat of arms, and a large medallion showing a bull and cow walking side-by-side along a row of cypress trees.

"What period is this from?" Dujok asked, caressing the surface with his hands. "It looks much more modern that the others."

"You're right about that. The character carved on the cover looks to be dressed in sixteenth-century garb. His tall hat, his long, pleated ceremonial robes, they're all typical of a Renaissance businessman."

"Do we know who he was?"

"We know his name and a little bit about his history. If you look right there, at the top, you can see his name carved into that scroll. It says Ioan d'Estivadas. Juan de Estivadas . . . The only strange thing is that the name is carved backward. See here?"

"Sad-av-itse-d-na-oi . . . Io-an-d-Esti-va-das . . . ," Dujok said out loud, tracing the name with his fingertips, and then remaining silent for a moment.

I could almost see the wheels turning in his head. He drummed his fingers over the name. He looked at the inscription up and down, backward and forward. He even blew a thin layer of dust from the letters. And when he was finished, he had this incredibly satisfied look on his face.

"Ms. Álvarez," he said, clearing his throat. "I felt I knew what your husband was trying to tell you in the last part of his message. Now I'm sure of it."

46

The president made his decision just before midnight.

Out of view of the press, under the cover of night, he had his car take him to the NSA's headquarters at Fort Meade, just a few miles north of the White House.

"Good evening, Mr. President."

An NSA staff member opened the door to his limousine. Four of his Secret Service men went inside first. One of his aides and his chief of staff followed the president inside when he got the all-clear. After having spoken with his agents in Madrid, Castle knew trouble lay ahead.

"Director Owen is waiting for you inside, Mr. President."

"It's an honor to have you here, Mr. President."

"Welcome to the NSA, Mr. President."

The farther he walked into of that labyrinth of offices and conference rooms, the sweeter the greetings became. Only Michael Owen, head of the NSA, with an inscrutable gaze and exquisite manners, seemed worried to see him.

Owen was the three-headed dragon that guarded the country's secrets. He was rarely—make that never—in a good mood. Most of his employees thought it was because he hated hobbling around the halls of the agency with his prosthetic leg, but that wasn't the real reason. Not on that night, anyway. He had been up all night because of one of his agents in Spain. The last thing he needed was to stare down the president of the United States at this hour. "Jesus Christ, when it rains it pours," he grumbled as he straightened up his desk.

When President Castle knocked at his door, Owen offered him a seat on the couch and a cup of hot coffee, and prepared himself for more bad news.

"The Big Secret."

Three words. It was all the president said.

Owen swallowed hard.

"Michael, I hope you've got that file ready for me," the president said, launching right in without so much as a sip of his coffee.

"Mr. President, it's only been an hour—"

"More than enough time," Castle said with his own hawkish glare, one *The New York Times* had made famous on its front page in times of crisis. "I want to know the Big Secret—or shall I say the status of Operation Elijah? Is it so hard for you to follow a direct order from your commander in chief? I thought after the attacks in Chechnya, you were clear on the kind of response I expect from this office."

"Sir, in that amount of time I can barely—"

"Listen here, Michael," he interrupted with feigned kindness. "I've been reading your goddamn reports for the last twenty-five months from inside the White House. They've all been meticulous. And they're at my desk first thing in the morning, right on time. Oh, and they're very informational. You've told me about world finances and nuclear weapons, biological terrorism and even manned missions to the moon. But I seemed to have missed any reference whatsoever to this operation."

"But I—"

"And, Mr. Director," he said, stopping him, "before you lie to the president of the United States, I want you to know the White House has done its due diligence. Yesterday, I sent two agents to Spain to investigate the disappearance of one of your former agents. According to my reports, this man *was* involved in Operation Elijah," the president said as he saw puzzlement wash over Owen's face. "But now he's been kidnapped in Turkey, so I figured that his wife, who lives in Europe, might have some pertinent information. But guess what? Your agents were already on the trail, like thirsty bloodhounds. And what's worse, apparently the NSA has *not* informed me of the kidnapping of an American citizen overseas. I had to find that out on my own, through back channels. And less than an hour ago, I just got word that the ex-agent's wife has disappeared, as well.

"What the hell's going on here, Michael? What are you not telling me?"

Michael Owen's face suddenly hardened. He shot a look at the president's chief of staff and his aide, one that left no doubt that he needed to speak to the leader of the free world in private.

"Right. Just you and me, then," Castle said, picking up on Owen's thought.

"Thank you, sir."

"But I just want to let you know I don't like having to keep secrets from my people, Michael."

"Believe it or not, neither do I, Mr. President. But this matter requires . . . discretion," Owen said.

A minute later, the two men were alone. Owen got up from the sofa to grab a book off his desk, a thick red-leather-bound Bible that he walked back to Roger Castle.

"I have to ask you one more thing, sir."

Owen placed the Bible on the coffee table in front of President Roger Castle.

"Mr. President, I need you to swear an oath that you will not discuss with any other person what is said in this conversation."

The president of the United States looked down at the book, stunned.

"What is this, Michael? I've already taken the oath of office."

"I'm sorry, Mr. President. This might seem out of place to you, but if we're to talk about Operation Elijah, you have to abide by the requirements of the operation's protocol. I know this seems antiquated, I'll give you that. But protocol is protocol."

Castle looked down at the leather-bound Bible and Owen seemed to read his mind.

"This operation is very old, sir. It was created during President Chester Arthur's administration. And before we speak of it, it's required that you take a special oath."

"Chester Arthur? Michael, you're talking about something that happened a hundred and thirty years ago."

Michael Owen nodded. "Few men in your position have ever asked for access to Operation Elijah, sir. This might seem an outdated ritual, but Elijah is what gave birth to all of our large-scale covert operations. It exists under a separate statute, one outside the confines of the Freedom of Information Act. Few men even know of its existence. Only Presidents Eisenhower in 1953 and George H. W. Bush in 1991 have asked for access to Elijah. And each of them followed procedure."

Owen waited for Roger Castle's decision, his unflinching gaze focused on the Bible.

"It's necessary, sir."

"Will this make me complicit in a crime, Michael?"

"Of course not, sir."

Roger Castle reached out his left hand, hesitated, then placed it on the Bible and swore to keep whatever information he received confidential. That done, Owen handed Castle a form that outlined the punishment for perjury, and the president signed it.

"I hope this is all worth it," Castle said as he tucked his pen into his coat pocket.

"You can judge for yourself, Mr. President. First, what can you tell me about President Arthur?"

Owen changed the subject as a way to lighten the tension, an invitation for the president to talk. And Castle appreciated the truce.

"Well . . . ," Castle said, trying to remember. "I guess I know what everybody knows about President Arthur. You can't say he was one of our most popular presidents, though they called him 'Elegant Arthur' in Washington. And I guess I owe him for the lavish accommodations at the White House. Tiffany designed my bedroom to his specifications. And I guess he's to thank for instituting a budget for 'official parties.'"

"Well, Mr. President, I can tell you that there was, in fact, a very serious man behind that frivolous façade. Chester Arthur was the fifth son of an Irish Baptist minister, who taught him his love for the Bible. But he kept his religious beliefs and those fundamental ideas very close to the vest. Not even his wife knew the depths of his obsession with the details in the Bible. You might not know that the National Archives have only three rolls of microfilm that preserve his notes. And he didn't mention his religious convictions in them . . ."

"Only three rolls? That's it?"

"He burned the rest of his papers before leaving office."

"Those were other times," Castle said, shaking his head. "Could you imagine what the press would say if I did the same thing? I'm sorry . . . Please, go on."

"But there's one thing President Arthur did that gives tremendous insight into his beliefs: He created the Office of Naval Intelligence, the country's first branch of secret service. And there was one topic that he constantly discussed with his admirals, something he was obsessed with finding proof of. Can you imagine what it was?"

The president, intrigued, shook his head slowly.

"The Great Flood."

"Go on . . ."

"You have to try to understand it within the context of the times, Mr. President. During the president's second year in office, a contemporary of his, Minnesota governor and fellow party member Ignatius Donnelly, published a highly acclaimed book titled *Atlantis: The Antediluvian World*. Donnelly had spent months in the Library of Congress, trying to prove that the Atlantis that Plato spoke of was an actual place and that it was, in fact, destroyed in the Great Flood. Even today, Donnelly is considered one of the most learned men ever to sit in the House of Representatives. It's no wonder that Arthur, an equally erudite man, was worried after reading Donnelly's work. And those worries grew exponentially when word of the eruption of the Krakatoa volcano reached the White House. Just imagine: That volcano wiped out an entire archipelago with the force of ten thousand atomic explosions. It created tidal waves forty feet tall that swept entire populations off the face of the earth."

"And this all happened during Arthur's presidency."

"You can see why a man like Arthur might have ordered the navy to look into a catastrophic event such as the Great Flood. He was worried it would happen again."

Castle couldn't manage to continue looking at Owen with a straight face. "I hope everything you're telling me is the truth, Michael."

"It is, sir."

"So then, if the object of that presidential order was to study the Great Flood," Castle said, "why did he call it Operation Elijah, and not Operation Noah?"

Owen smiled. Castle knew how to look for holes in an argument, and there was no doubt that sharp mind was what had landed him in the Oval Office.

"There's one thing I haven't explained yet, sir," Owen said. "See, Chester Arthur wasn't looking for proof of the Great Flood. By that point, he wholeheartedly believed it had happened. What he wanted to know is whether something like it could happen during his presidency."

"And did he have a good reason to think it would?"

"In the Bible, the prophet Malachi closes the Old Testament by alluding to a second Great Flood, a second great disaster, one after the time of Noah. Look, here."

Owen flipped open the red-covered Bible and flipped to the end of Malachi, chapter 3:

> And I will send thee my messenger, the prophet Elijah
> Before the arrival of Yahweh on that great and terrible day

"You see? A 'great and terrible day' is associated with the return of Elijah. It's a belief still honored by the Jewish faith, by those who honor him with a place at the table during every Passover. Chester Arthur was obsessed with determining when this new day of apocalypse would be. It became the priority of his administration. Yes, he ordered the navy to look into it, but also some of the country's top scientists from all different backgrounds, and to this day, no one has dared put an end to Operation Elijah."

"So . . . have they figured it out?" Castle said, still stunned that his father's reference to that 'great and terrible day' had come from the Bible. "Have they figured out the day of the apocalypse?"

"Well, I can tell you that that wealth of great minds did agree on one thing . . ."

"Tell me, Michael."

"After reading the biblical texts, they realized that information about the catastrophe—in the case of Noah and Elijah—didn't come from observing Mother Nature. In fact, the information came directly from . . . a higher power," Owen said nervously. "From a supreme intelligence. The Great Architect. God himself. Do you understand what I'm telling you?"

"God. Naturally," Castle said, shaking his head.

"I think you missed my point, Mr. President. The object of Operation Elijah was to find a way to open a direct line of communication with Him, so that He might have a way to warn us—as he did with Noah—should another global extinction be headed our way. An insurance policy, just like the one Noah had. Simple as that."

"What . . . ?" Castle couldn't wrap his mind around what he was hearing.

"Operation Elijah is about talking directly to God, Mr. President. That's why the NSA is involved. After all, isn't it our job to monitor *all* communications that might affect our country?"

"You're kidding, right? This is a joke. Oh, I can just imagine it: a nightly prayer group at the NSA headquarters, the pinnacle of the country's military intelligence."

"It's not a prayer group, Mr. President," Owen said flatly. "It's a communications task force."

Roger Castle's eyes were now bulging.

"You mean to tell me that for the last hundred years, the Office of Naval Intelligence and then the National Security Administration has spent time, energy and resources trying to *literally* speak to God!"

"It's actually more rational than you think, sir. President Arthur came from a very spiritual time in world history. Everyone thought it was possible to communicate with the 'other side.' And if telecommunications were to keep advancing—as they were at the time, exponentially—people could envision a time when we would indeed manage to communicate with whatever was on the other side. It wasn't beyond logic."

Fury settled into a dark shadow falling across the president's face. "Then tell me, Mr. Owen, how much has this cost the American taxpayer?"

"Elijah doesn't have a budget assigned to it, sir. Whatever time or resources Elijah needs, Elijah gets."

"So why hasn't anyone put an end to this madness, Michael? Because that's what this is: utter and complete madness."

Owen looked stoically at the president, lifted himself from his chair and limped with his prosthetic leg over to the window. "I'll remind you, Mr. President, that the *Apollo* program was considered madness at one time, too. And yet, we managed to put twelve men on the moon. If Elijah is still operational, it's because it's yielded some . . . interesting results."

"You're joking again."

For the third time that night, the president couldn't believe what he was hearing.

"Operation Elijah has evolved since Chester Arthur's administration, sir. We have satellites that cover every corner of the earth, a level of military intelligence never before dreamed of."

"Well, sure, they didn't exactly have radio telescopes in 1882 . . ."

"We also have a team dedicated to finding and trying to use the radios used in the ancient world, ones that were supposedly used to communicate with God. We've got some of the country's best minds working on these ideas. And their work is pure science. But the science and their results are so advanced that if they were ever made public, it might look like modern-day witchcraft."

"Wait, back up. Did you say ancient radios?" Castle said, still stunned.

"Remember the old crystal radios, sir?"

"Sure, my grandfather had one."

"Well, these primitive radios didn't use a battery. Instead, they relied on a galena crystal, a stone that had lead sulfide veining inside. The radio runs when the mineral reacts to electromagnetic signals or radio waves in the air. They're so simple but so effective. With an adequate stone and antenna, it could easily receive medium-wave signals."

"And they knew about this technology in Noah's time?"

"We believe they did, sir. In fact, we believe our ancestors used these stones to communicate with God. They were electromagnetically modified minerals that were capable of picking up on very specific frequencies. The power of these minerals wasn't kept secret for long. All of our holy books mention these stones: the stone tablets of the Ten Commandments, the Kaaba, the Stone of Jacob, the Scottish Stone of Scone, the "whispering" Oracle of Delphi, the Irish Lia Fáil . . . Even the Australian aborigines have revered stones they call 'soul stones,' or *churingas*."

A memory flashed like a bolt of lightning inside the president's mind. He was reminded of the promise he had made to Ellen Watson. "Okay, Michael, now I need you to listen to me. I want to know everything about this project. The timeline. The people involved. What steps they're taking next to reach this ultimate goal. And, also," he said, looking out the director's office window, "why two people connected to these stones have suddenly disappeared."

"Not a problem, sir. Though I have to tell you that your request comes at a very delicate moment for Operation Elijah."

"What do you mean?"

"For the first time in a hundred years, we have competition . . . Someone is using their knowledge of this ancient technology to try to establish that communication link before us. And we think that that 'someone' is who's responsible for the disappearance of those two people. But we're on it, sir."

"So tell me this, Michael: Who's in charge of this operation?"

Owen stepped away from his office window overlooking the glowing Washington Monument in the distance and fixed his gaze on the president.

"To answer that question, sir, we need to leave this building. I suppose your limo is still waiting outside?"

"Of course."

"If you order the route cleared, we can be at the NRO in forty minutes."

"You want to go to the National Reconnaissance Office? At this time of night?"

Owen nodded. "You need to see this for yourself, sir."

47

"Keep envisioning a way . . ."

"'*Se te da visionada.*' Juan de Estivadas. '*Sadavitsed Naoi.*'"

"Can't you see it, Julia?"

I shook my head, completely at a loss. Artemi Dujok's eyes were twinkling in amazement that two minds could work so differently.

"It's an anagram!" Dujok said. "It's so clear!"

"Are you sure?"

"Absolutely. The phrase Martin said in Spanish in the video is an anagram for the name on this sarcophagus. He used all the same letters but mixed up their order. Martin couldn't come out and tell you in the video where to find the stone, but he sent you a coded message to bring you to this church, to this very tomb. Your adamant is here."

"How can you be so sure?"

"Ms. Álvarez, Martin is using one of the oldest forms of encryption known to man. Remember the last part of the phrase from the video?"

"Yes. 'Keep envisioning a way' . . . '*se te da visionada*' in Spanish."

"Right. And if you reorder the letters in that phrase you get the name "Ioan de Estivadas" exactly, not a single letter left over."

I scratched my head, trying to see the pattern. "What I don't understand, Mr. Dujok," I said, "is what Estivadas has to do with Noah."

"I should be asking you. A minute ago you said you'd managed to learn everything about Estivadas, right?"

"Well, just about," I said. "Let's see: There's a street in town named after him. He was the oldest winemaker in Noia. He was born during the period of the Catholic kings, just before the discovery of America. And he was married to a woman of noble birth, María Oanes. That's what stands out to me the most. And, of course, he *was* born during the sixteenth century, which doesn't make him much of a threat to be *the* Noah."

"You think so, huh?" Dujok said. "It's all there in the details you just gave me, Ms. Álvarez."

"I'm sorry, I don't seem to understand anything you tell me . . ."

"It's simple: Juan de Estivadas never existed. He's a symbol, a marker. Look, Noah himself was a wine grower. And, his wife's last name has an antediluvian connection. The Babylonians used the name Oannes to refer to the god Enki. You do remember the story of Gilgamesh . . ."

"Of course!" I said, stunned.

"Then I don't have to tell you that Enki warned the Mesopotamian version of Noah about the impending flood. Plus, take a look at Estivadas's first name, written right here," Dujok said, tapping the tomb. "Juan, *Ioan*. Backward? Naoi. *Noah*. This is definitely the tomb we're looking for."

I was still astonished.

"Well? So what's inside the tomb, Ms. Álvarez?" Dujok asked.

"Noth . . . nothing. Not that I know of. When they moved it from its original place in the church of San Martiño, it was already empty."

"Well, I'm guessing it's not empty anymore. C'mon, Ms. Álvarez, give me a hand with the lid."

48

Being an atheist, Antonio Figueiras had never wished for magical powers. But just this one time, he wished he could be in two places at once. That way, he wouldn't have to make the difficult choice of whether to chase the helicopter that had taken off under his nose or head to Marcelo Muñiz's house to see what the jeweler had discovered about Martin Faber's precious stones.

The police station had already contacted the military about using their radar to figure out the helicopter's flight path. So he decided to visit his friend.

Just behind the Santa María Salomé parish, down a narrow alley away from the tourist-trap restaurants and hotels, was Marcelo's home. He had refurbished one of the oldest historical buildings in Santiago and turned it into his own sort of museum. It was a dream house filled with antiques and books and scrapbooks from trips around the world. On his bookshelves you could find the answer to just about any question. And that's what Figueiras needed: answers. The initial forensic evidence was right—the shell casings he found next to his murdered officers were the same as the ones found inside the cathedral. If he had only arrived at the plaza a minute earlier, *just one minute,* he would have caught the killer and saved his officers' lives.

"And you say they got away in a helicopter?"

Muñiz had just set out coffee and tea cakes on his dining room table. He sat at one end in a dress shirt but wearing his trademark bow tie, his head freshly shaven. He was rapt at the inspector's story.

"Saw it with my own eyes, Marcelo. Something big—and I mean *big*—is going on here, man."

Figueiras looked out of sorts. Compared to Muñiz's fastidious attire, he looked a mess, disheveled. His glasses barely hid the toll of a very long night. His lips were chapped, his shirt a sea of wrinkles and his hair greasy and matted.

"Well, maybe I can turn your night around," Marcelo said, serving him a cup of coffee. Marcelo took a sip of his coffee, keeping Figueiras in suspense before saying, "I know why those stones the Fabers brought into the country are so valuable."

Figueiras froze with the coffee in his hands. "Well . . . out with it, man!"

"You gave me the first clue when you said they'd declared them at customs. I ran a couple of Internet searches and found something . . . curious. Those stones, my friend, are extraterrestrial."

"Oh, come on!"

"Antonio, I'm serious," Muñiz said. "I used their registration number and traced their origin. Before the Fabers brought the stones to Spain, they spent some time at the mineralogical research lab at the British Museum. But there's no information about the findings. Damn shame. But when I looked at the museum's database, I found the dates the stones went in and out and came up with something interesting."

"C'mon, Marcelo, I don't have all day . . ."

Muñiz, very pleased with himself, adjusted his bow tie and gave his widest smile yet.

"The log says it wasn't Martin Faber but a company that took the stones to the British Museum. A corporation named the Betilum Company. TBC. Ring a bell?"

Figueiras, still dizzy from lack of sleep, shook his head.

"I looked all over the Internet for any sign of it without any luck. It's some kind of phantom corporation. I was just about to give up when something occurred to me . . ."

"What?"

Muñiz was a renowned computer whiz, but now he was raising Figueiras's already-high expectations.

"Last night, I ran that name through some of the most common sites for buying antiquities. I got nothing. But when I checked the VIP client lists—bingo! I found the company on a list of people who have purchased antique books in auctions."

"And . . . what did you find?" Figueiras was growing impatient with Marcelo.

"The Betilum Company has been quietly buying up antique books all over the Internet, for years. Expensive books. All of them having to do with magic, astrology, apocryphal gospels, that type of thing. The last one I saw they bought was *Monas hieroglyphica,* a textbook published in Holland in 1564, in Latin, by one John Dee of London."

"And what's that book about?"

"That's the most interesting part. It's a treatise about a symbol that the author says, if used correctly, can help you control the world. This Dee character maintained that that glyph held the principal elements of all creation. A sort of master key to control all of Mother Nature. In a word, to be like God."

"A symbol is supposed to do all this?"

Muñiz was now the second person since that morning to mention symbols.

"Supposedly. Here, take a look."

Figueiras pulled out his notebook and drew the symbol as best he could. Still, it didn't look like the key to world domination.

"So does this symbol mean anything to you?" Marcelo asked.

"Uh . . . no."

"There is something else you might be interested in. This John Dee became famous for manipulating magical stones during the Elizabethan era—which is how customs described Faber and Álvarez's stones. They were a sort of oracle, used to predict the future and to speak with spirits, things like that. And most of them were meteorites, which is why I said they're extraterrestrial. What I think," he added, sitting up in his chair, "is that those very stones are the ones Faber and Álvarez brought into Spain."

"Are you sure?"

Marcelo moved the coffee cups and tea cakes off the table and spread out several photocopies that looked to have been taken out of an antique book. All of the writing was in Latin. But it was all gibberish to Figueiras.

"Now, take a look at this. These are copies of pages from the *Monas hieroglyphica*. A friend of mine in Los Angeles scanned and emailed them to me earlier today. Look. Right here. In the prologue, Dee references the Holy Roman Emperor Maximilian of Habsburg, a man of science who also was devoted to magic, and explains that his symbol is actually a mathematical key for establishing contact with the heavens. He goes on to say—in some pretty complex language—that whoever discovers these rare and forgotten symbols and pairs them with heaven-sent 'stones of Adam' will be able to speak directly to God."

"Stones of Adam? What the hell is all this about, Marcelo?"

"Stones of Adam. Adamants. They've had many names throughout the centuries, Antonio. But they're always described as a mineral sent to Earth from paradise itself. Sacred stones, fallen to earth, which are supposed to allow us to see the future, if used correctly . . . It's obvious they're talking about some kind of meteorite that you have to 'activate' with some kind of religious ritual. Look here," Marcelo said, putting another photocopied page in front of Figueiras. "It says it right here, clearly: Whoever possesses these stones, '*aeream omnem et igneam regionem explorabit,*' will come to know all of heaven and earth."

Figueiras ran his index finger over the words.

PRAEFATIO AD REGEM

Primus Ipse abibit: Rarißimeque, pòst, Mortalium conspicietur oculis. Hæc, O Rex Optime, Vera est, toties decantata (& sine Scelere) MAGORVM INVISIBILITAS: Quæ (vt Posteri omnes fatebuntur Magi) nostræ est MONADIS concessa Theorijs. Expertißimus

11. *MEDICVS, etiam ex eisdem, facillimè Hippocratis Mysticam assequetur voluntatem. Sciet enim, QVID, CVI,*

Lib. de Fluxibus. ADDENDVM ET AVFERENDVM *sit : vt , ipsam Artem sub maximo MONADIS nostræ Compendio, & MEDICINAM ipsam contineri , Lubens deinde fateri*

12. *Velit. BERYLLISTICVS, hic, in Lamina Chrystallina, omnia quæ sub Cœlo LVNÆ, in Terra vel Aquis versantur, exactißimè videre potest : & in Carbunculo siue Lapide , Aëream omnem & Igneam Regionem ex-*

13. *plorabit. Et, si VOARCHADVMICO, nostræ Hieroglyphicæ MONADIS, Theoria vigesima prima, satis faciat; Ipsique, VOARH BETH ADVMOTH, Speculandum ministret: Ad Indos vel Americos , non illi esse Philosophandi gratia, peregrinandum, fatebitur.*

14. *Deinque de ADEPTIVO genere (quicquid vel ARIOTON Ars subministrare, vel polliceri poßit; vel viginti Annorum maximi Hermetis labores sunt assecuti)*

An. 1562. licet ad Parisienses, sua MONADE peculiari (Anagogica Apodixi illustratum) aliàs scripserimus: Vestræ tamen Maiestati Regiæ constanter asserimus, ID OMNE, Analogico nostræ MONADIS Hieroglyphicæ Opere, ita ad viuū exprimi; vt Similius aliud Exemplum, humano generi non

poßet

"Now, look at what comes just before that phrase," Muñiz said. "Three Hebrew letters right before the word *'lapide,'* or 'stone.'"

"What, you think I can read Hebrew, Marcelo?"

"They're the letters *aleph, daleth,* and *mem.* אדם The consonants in the word 'Adam.' *Adam lapide,* or Adam's stones, adamants—stones from paradise."

"And you think Faber and Álvarez have these kinds of stones?"

"No, not those *kinds* of stones. The very stones themselves. As a matter of fact, do you know what 'betilum' means?"

Figueiras shook his head as he felt his cell phone vibrating in his pocket.

"I didn't think so," Muñiz added with a smile. "It comes from the Bible, Antonio. Bet-El was the place where Jacob had the vision of a ladder that connected heaven and earth. And he had this vision when he fell asleep with a smooth, black stone for a pillow. That was one of these very same adamants. The place name means 'house of God' and in the Middle Ages, the term 'betilum', or betyls, came to mean a meteorite with a certain kind of mineral property."

"So what do you think one of these stones costs?" Figueiras said as he checked to see who had texted him.

Muñiz was taken aback at how little his friend seemed to appreciate the matter. "Well, I guess that depends . . ."

"On what?"

"On the stone's properties, its age, its documentation . . . Antonio, a stone that can be traced back to John Dee could be worth a fortune. And if they could actually open a gateway to heaven, I couldn't even venture a guess . . ."

"Oh, you think there are doors in heaven?"

"I'm a man of faith. Not like you . . ."

Antonio Figueiras had stopped paying attention. The text message he'd gotten was from his captain. He'd failed to reach him by phone yet again and instead sent Figueiras his orders in a text. He was supposed to go to the Lavacolla airport to pick up some "very special" reinforcements—right away.

49

The figure on the lid of Juan de Estivadas's sarcophagus was covered in scars. Its face had been disfigured by some careless or unscrupulous idiot with a chisel. And a repair to a hole on the side had been slathered over slapdash with cement.

Artemi Dujok wordlessly traced his fingers over the damage. He said nothing even after noticing that two of the seven coats of arms had been chiseled away to the point where the entire sarcophagus might be structurally unstable.

"Careful! Don't stand there," he told me, mirroring my concerns. "We'll only move it a couple centimeters, take a peek inside and leave it be."

"But it's five hundred years old . . . ," I murmured.

"I promise you no one will notice."

We set up at Juan de Estivadas's feet, grabbed the sides of the lid and steadied ourselves. Our first push did nothing. Either the stone cover was heavier than it looked or the cement repair job had inadvertently sealed it shut. But on our second push, the lid began to give way. It slid open with a deep, hollow scraping that echoed throughout the church.

I turned my head as a pungent, acidic smell emanated from it. But I was stunned when I finally looked inside.

The tomb was empty.

"Nothing," I said, and Dujok could feel how disappointed I felt.

"Are you sure?" he said, poking his flashlight around the inside of the crypt, finding nothing but dust and cobwebs. The walls of the inside looked even worse than the outside. They were covered in uneven holes, as if they had been eaten by concrete-eating worms. An inch of grime covered the bottom of the tomb. But then the light flashed against something that immediately caught our attention. Drag marks along the grimy bottom led to the corner of the crypt where I stood.

"There! That's it!" he said.

I reached down to find a small bundle of black fabric tied with a golden string. Someone had tied it neatly and placed it in a small hole in the corner.

My hands began to tremble as I pictured my husband carefully preparing this little package with his large, manly hands and placing it carefully just so. Maybe that's why I hesitated to open it right away.

"Open it!" Dujok urged.

I untied the string, my hands shaking as I stepped away from the tomb, looking for better light. The fabric unfolded and there it was. Perfectly unharmed. The adamant was set in a pendant with a silver chain so that it could be worn around the neck.

A rush of memories and emotions began to wash over me when Artemi Dujok's rough voice boomed from behind me.

"Well, what are you waiting for? We have to activate it right away!"

50

Roger Castle could recall every detail of the first time he was allowed to speak openly about the National Reconnaissance Office. It was September of 1992. He had just been elected New Mexico's governor and this military installation was still one of the country's most closely guarded secrets. But that year, on the heels of the Gulf War and with the country needing to show its military strength, President George Herbert Walker Bush acknowledged the NRO's existence—and inadvertently opened Pandora's box, sending the news to televisions across the world. Until that historic decision, insiders like Castle joked only that NRO stood for "Not Referred to Openly," frustrated that they had no clear answers for where its six-billion-dollar annual budget was going.

Castle had dreamed of one day visiting the installation and putting its cutting-edge technology to work for the taxpayers. The "eyes and ears watching and listening from space" would one day work for all of America—not just for its military interests, he had said. Given that, as his motorcade made its way to the offices of the NRO, President Castle knew he was about to step foot in a place where he was persona non grata.

It wasn't long before Roger Castle and Michael Owen reached the NRO headquarters in Chantilly, Virginia—a nondescript, inoffensive-looking salmon-colored building. The motorcade pulled in at the back entrance just before one in the morning, and soon, they were standing in an expansive control room that monitored every satellite the world over, twenty-four hours a day, three hundred sixty-five days a year.

"My name's Doctor Edgar Scott, Mr. President. It's a pleasure to have you with us."

Scott was in his fifties, dressed neatly in a dark blue suit, but clearly had been woken up no more than twenty minutes ago and certainly hadn't had time to shave. He was a small man with thinning silver hair, yellowed teeth and deep wrinkles across his forehead. And he most certainly never thought he'd find himself in a situation such as this: standing in front of the leader of the free world, without any idea why a minor incident had brought the president to his office in the middle of the night.

Maybe it wasn't so minor after all, Scott thought, trying to glean any information from the expression on Michael Owen's face.

"Dr. Scott is the NRO director," Owen said, "and he runs the scientific unit of Operation Elijah. He's up-to-date with all its happenings and can answer any of your questions, sir."

Castle took a moment to size up Scott. He could tell right away that Scott was confused by being asked to openly talk about a usually taboo subject. And then, Owen went a step further.

"Dr. Scott, why don't you show the president what our 'eyes in the sky' caught happening just two hours ago, at oh-five twenty-three local time in Spain?"

"Sure . . . sure. Of course, Mr. Owen," Scott said. "I'm not sure how much you know about our global scanning technology, Mr. President."

"Why don't you give me the tutorial, Edgar?" Castle said, smiling and trying to put him at ease.

"We have about fifty satellites with high-resolution radiometers at our disposal," he said with obvious pride. "The NSA; the CIA; the Air Force Intelligence, Surveillance and Reconnaissance Agency; NASA and the US Navy all use our information daily because our satellites can measure electromagnetic energy emissions. We can detect even the slightest EM fluctuations the world over. How accurate is it? We could determine the temperature of a bowl of soup being served at the White House—and tell you what's in it by just measuring the heat signature and the EM fluctuations it causes."

"And here I thought our spy satellites were for reading what Vladimir Putin writes in his journal every morning," Castle joked.

"Oh, we can do that too, sir. But with all due respect, that's kind of the least of our worries."

"All right, all right, Edgar. From now on, I'll only have vichyssoise at the White House," Castle said. "Now tell me, what was it that our satellites discovered in Spain?"

"I've never seen anything like it, sir. We had a warning go off from a state-of-the-art satellite, an HMBB, designed to pick up any unusual energy readings coming out of Iran, Iraq and India. It was making its usual sweep from an altitude of two hundred fifty miles above the Middle East when it picked up something by accident as it swept over the western part of the Iberian Peninsula."

Edgar Scott pulled out several documents from a black plastic tube and unrolled them on the table in front of them.

"Let me explain what you're looking at, sir," Scott said. "This is a picture taken from a hundred thousand feet above sea level just forty-eight hours ago. These explosions of light you see *here* and *here*," he said, pointing to two areas north of Portugal, "came from the cities of La Coruña and Vigo, on Spain's western coast. Now look at this darker area. About twenty-five miles inland is the city of Santiago de Compostela. It's just two little specs of light amid the darkness."

The president nodded, following along.

"Now look at this next aerial photograph, taken by the same satellite today, just before dawn local time."

He unfurled a second image. It still smelled of developer.

"So why does the city of Santiago now appear flooded in a bright light?" the president asked, noticing the area that was once pitch-black.

"I'm glad you asked, sir. That's why the HMBB's alarm went off. The phenomenon lasted just fifteen minutes, but the intensity of the EM field was like nothing we've ever seen."

"Has anyone else detected it? The Chinese? The Russians?"

"I don't think so, sir. If it were a magnetic pulse bomb, all of the city's energy would have been absorbed and the radiation would have lasted longer and would have been unavoidably seen. It would have caught the attention of every satellite in the sky. But this was a very small, concentrated pulse in an urban area. You can see it clearly on this photo where we've zoomed in," Scott said, unrolling another shot, this one close and detailed enough to see the roads and streetlights. "The

EM pulse drained all of the power in about a one-mile radius from this big building here."

Castle leaned in closer. He could make out a gray, crucifix-shaped building.

"What is that?"

"A church. A cathedral to be exact, sir. The emissions came from this area, though we haven't been able to determine if it came from inside the church or from one of the surrounding buildings."

The NRO's director loosened his tie as if he knew it was going to be hard to say what he needed to tell the president of the United States.

"It almost goes without saying, sir, but there aren't any research or science labs in the area. No military bases, no facilities that we suspect are housing an EM device. And, uh, what's worse . . ."

"Yes?"

"Well, we think someone deliberately fired the blast into the upper atmosphere."

"I don't understand."

"Sir, someone has just sent a high-energy signal into outer space from the northwest corner of Spain. We don't know who did it, or how, or certainly what a message within that signal might have contained. What's more, we don't know of anything capable of creating that kind of high-intensity burst. That is . . . nothing except one of the ancient stones that Operation Elijah was created to find."

"And the biggest clue," Owen said, cutting in, "is that we know that the wife of the former Elijah scientist you asked me about earlier was there when the EM pulse went off. After that, she disappeared."

"You're serious . . ."

"Now do you understand why I sent one of my best men to find her? And why we find ourselves in such a delicate situation?" Owen said, his mood darkening. "A device or stone or relic with that kind of power should be under our control."

Castle turned back to study the photograph.

"And your satellites didn't manage to photograph whoever it was that kidnapped her?" Castle asked Owen.

"No, sir. But we've determined that the EM emission happened at the same time she was taken. You know what that says to me, sir?"

Castle shook his head.

"You're a strategist, Mr. President. Now add up every part of this equation: an unknown subject has captured a former agent who worked on Elijah; they've taken one of his closest relatives and they've learned to use the stones to tap into an ancient technology unknown since biblical times . . . What could they possibly be after, if not the very thing that we also seek, sir?"

"To speak to God?" Castle murmured, stunned.

"Sir, with your permission, Operation Elijah is still poised to be the first to control this technology to open humanity's first line of communication. Please, sir. Leave it to us. There's still time . . ."

51

"And how the heck am I supposed to activate the adamant?"

Dujok stared at me for a moment, trying to decide if I was playing dumb.

"Well, the same way you always have, of course," he said. "Didn't they teach you that the crystals respond to vibration? Didn't your husband tell you that just humming or reciting an incantation at the right pitch is enough to change their atomic structure?"

Dujok was right. I did know that. At least in theory. But I was so nervous about everything that had happened in the last few hours that my mind had pushed that knowledge away. I'd been so occupied with trying to find the damn adamants and rescuing Martin that I'd forgotten the most important thing about them: Without the spells John Dee used, the seer stones would remain only useless rocks.

"The second that adamant comes to life," Dujok said, "Martin's will begin to resonate in unison. It's what the philosophers like Dee and Roger Bacon called *speculum unitatis*—the mirror of unity. Or, as modern physicists call it, quantum interlacing: Twin atomic particles born of the same 'mother' act exactly like one another despite the distance between them."

"And that's how we'll find Martin?" I asked.

"Exactly. We have the technology to detect the electromagnetic emission from your stone, no matter where on earth it may be. If Martin's adamant reacts the way yours does, we'll be able to lock onto its coordinates almost in real time. You do your job, I'll take care of the rest . . ."

"What if I don't manage to activate it?" I said, worried. "What if nothing happens?"

"You *have* the gift, Julia. Concentrate on your adamant and recite the spells that you remember. That's all you have to do."

There was no other choice . . .

I nervously took the adamant in my hands and removed it from its silver casing. Meanwhile, Artemi Dujok punched an address into the GPS of his cell phone. He said he was looking up the sun's recent magnetic readings from the National Oceanic and Atmospheric Administration. I knew from Martin's work as a climatologist that the NOAA kept up-to-the-minute information on the sun's X-ray emissions and did everything from tracking the aurora borealis to predicting possible radio outages from solar flares. Only recently did scientists begin to understand the effects these energy emissions had on everything from climate to seismology. But more scientists were now taking notice, and, apparently, Dujok was one of them.

At finding a recent image of the sun mottled with dark spots, Dujok smiled, satisfied.

"The time is right," he said. "The atmosphere is saturated with solar particles, Ms. Álvarez. It's all up to you now."

I tried not to think too much about what I was about to do. This strange combination of the high-tech and the occult sent shivers down my spine. I'd rather not have known what was going on and just concentrated on the stone in my hands. I caressed my adamant carefully with my eyes closed and I held it up to the heavens. Blocking out every anxious thought, I began reciting the first words I remembered from Dee's book of incantations.

"Ol sonf vors g, goho Iad Balt, lansh calz vonpho . . ."

I'd never done this alone. Not without my teachers nearby. Even though Sheila had urged me to memorize the words, telling me I would one day need to say them on a very important day, my fear was always greater than my curiosity. At least, it was until this day . . .

What I never imagined is that as those archaic words rolled off my tongue, everything around me—the church of Santa María a Nova, the graves beneath my feet, the ever-present Artemi Dujok—would begin to disappear.

Suddenly, my world went black—as if some unknown force had taken control.

52

Something's . . . very wrong here.

Nicholas Allen tried and failed to open his eyes, again and again. He couldn't remember where he was. His hearing was muffled, he couldn't keep his balance and the scar across his forehead was pounding violently. It felt like he was hanging upside-down. And it wasn't just his eyes that weren't following orders. His arms and legs were lifeless and it felt like there was an elephant on his chest every time he tried to breathe. The last thing he remembered, he was on the phone with Michael Owen telling him that Julia Álvarez had disappeared when the phone went dead.

He figured out he must have fainted . . . again.

These were symptoms that Colonel Allen knew all too well, unfortunately. The headaches, nausea, loss of consciousness, it all fit.

"Mr. Allen . . . Mr. Allen!" A voice brought him part of the way out of his stupor. He could hear the labored English accent through what sounded like an echo chamber. "I know you can hear me. You're in the intensive care unit at Our Lady of Hope. You're in a hospital, Mr. Allen. Today is November first. You don't seem to have any injuries, but you've had several epileptic seizures. You're secured to a gurney. Please don't try to move. We've already alerted your embassy to your condition."

Well, there's some good news, he thought.

"The medical staff thinks you're out of danger. But try to rest while we figure out what might have caused this."

I know what caused it! he wanted to yell out. *It was a high-frequency electromagnetic burst!*

But his vocal cords were among the body parts that still refused to respond.

There was no way the medical team could have known that Allen had been part of a secret army program experimenting with electromagnetic fields (known as EMFs), and he knew their effects better than anyone. He knew anyone blasted with an EMF would have his internal organs affected, as his, no doubt, were. The effects had been classified as highly as the Manhattan Project. And the published results concluded that "electromagnetic injuries" usually were concentrated in the eyes and ears. The NSA and the Defense Advanced Research Projects Agency had learned how to focus an EMF beam to affect a single person in a crowd. They had also devised "acoustic bullets" that vibrated at 145 decibels and could be "fired" from precise sound cannons. You could stun a man—or flat-out kill him—without the person next to him ever realizing what was going on. And, what's more, you could do it without leaving behind any evidence. If the subject didn't get out of the way of the beam in time, the sound wave would rattle his bones and skull, raise his blood pressure, and cause a stroke in a matter of seconds. And if you were lucky and the blast wasn't a lethal one, all you would remember was a loud humming, like the kind you'd hear standing near high-tension wires.

A loud humming . . . like the one Nicholas Allen was still hearing.

Now it was a matter of figuring out who else, besides his government, had access to this kind of weapon. And Allen already had an idea about that.

"Your old friends have been here," he had told Michael Owen.

But he knew those "old friends" himself. He'd crossed paths with them during a mission he wouldn't forget soon.

It happened in the Armenian mountains—in the boonies, if you will. And for some reason, those memories were bouncing around inside his head at that moment as he tried to regain the use of his body.

WESTERN ARMENIA
AUGUST 11, 1999

Standing in front of the Echmiadzin Cathedral, in the very seat of the so-called Armenian Vatican, Nick Allen thought he'd seen it all. It was noon in Paris when a total eclipse of the sun cast a shadow over half of

Europe. But at forty-four degrees longitude, on the other hand, the clock read four in the afternoon, the sun was shining brightly, and every radio and television station was broadcasting news of the celestial event. And all of them were squawking about an impending apocalypse: "The fashion designer and psychic Paco Rabanne has predicted that the Russian space station Mir will fall to Earth today, crushing the French capitol, killing more than a million people . . . ," one announcer said. "Nostradamus called this eclipse the 'King of Terror' in one of his predictions," another said. And on Narek TV, an empty-headed bleached blonde was interviewing a guest, with the Eiffel Tower in the background, asking, "So do you think this has anything to do with Y2K—you know, the glitch they say will paralyze our computers at eleven fifty-nine on New Year's Eve?" "Well, of course! It's *all* connected! What we're seeing in Paris is the beginning of the end!" her guest answered breathlessly.

Allen's new boss couldn't have chosen a better moment to carry out their operation. The cathedral and all the buildings around it were empty. Even the church's oldest patriarchs were glued to their television sets.

Allen calmly strode into the cathedral, dressed in black, with his trusty sixteen-shot pistol in his waistband, passing the iconic scenes from the ancient master artist Hovnatanian; this was the only corner of the world where you could see his famous paintings of Christ's apostles. All around him, votive candles flickered and the pungent smell of incense wafted in the air. But none of those sacred surroundings fazed him; he was a man used to all kinds of missions. His only concern was that security remain lax, as it was. There wasn't an armed guard in sight, a metal detector, not even a video camera to dodge. These were trusting people . . . and that, ironically, is what made him nervous.

"Everything going as planned, Nick?"

Martin Faber's voice in his ear told him his partner was keeping close tabs on him from the Russian Lada van parked two hundred yards outside the gate. This Faber character had arrived with a stack of detailed instructions under his arm and a reputation as the "human computer." Sure, Allen preferred men of action to the brainy types, but at least Allen knew Faber was keeping an eye on him and had his back.

"Everything looks good. The cathedral's empty," Allen responded.

"Excellent. I'm getting a clear picture of you from the satellite. The thermal sensors show you should be near the main altar, correct?"

"Correct."

"Judging from the colors on the thermal imaging scanner, I'd say you're a little nervous," Faber joked.

"Goddamn scanner," Allen muttered. "I'm not nervous. I'm hot in this black getup and this church is a friggin' icebox . . . I'm going to get goddamn pneumonia."

"Okay, okay. Listen, our eye in the sky shows the coast is clear."

"Besides . . . I hate churches."

Allen tried to lighten his footsteps as he headed toward the altar. He passed a painting of St. Gregory the Enlightener, the first official head of the Armenian Apostolic Church, as he reached his goal: the Episcopal museum.

"You know, this museum houses some of Christianity's oldest artifacts. It's a shame you're not into it, Nick. The Armenian Church is actually older than the Roman Catholic and has tons of priceless antiquities . . ."

"You don't say . . ."

"All right, I get it. You're not into this stuff." Faber sighed. "I just figured since you're going to spend some time in this country that you'd *like* to know some of these facts. Did you know that this country was the first to officially embrace Christianity, in the fourth century, and that—"

"Do you think you could shut up, brainiac?" Allen shot back. "I'm trying to concentrate here."

"Have your reached the site?"

"Yes. What, can't you see that from your fancy satellite?"

Faber had been fiddling with the equipment for half a minute after losing the thermal signal from the KH-11. Even though the NSA had positioned the satellite directly above them for this mission, both screens went black.

"I don't know. There must be something wrong with the antenna. I can't see you."

"Doesn't matter. Everything's quiet on this end. As long as you can hear me, we should be all right."

"Okay, describe what's around you."

"I've reached the museum," he whispered. "Doesn't look like this place gets a lot of visitors. Everything's gray and old and ugly . . ."

Two seconds of silence passed.

"Okay, now I'm standing in front of a glass showcase. It's in the middle of the room. It's got several open books and some coins inside. On the walls there are several . . . I don't know how to describe them. They're like small medicine cabinets."

"Ah, yes, those are reliquaries, Nick. For storing . . . never mind. Head to the right. What we're looking for should be in the middle of that wall."

"Is it hanging?"

"You should see it right away. It should be right in front of you."

"Just in front of me, in the center of the wall, I have two of those little cabinets. They look old."

"Get closer."

"One looks like it's made of gold. Rectangular. About the size of a large book. It's got etched glass on the lower part and angels painted all around it.

"Ah, right. It's the reliquary for Christ's thorn," Martin said knowingly. "And the other one?"

"Christ's thorn . . . ?"

"Please, Nick. The other one?" Martin urged him.

"Wait, if you've been here before why aren't you doing the dirty work?"

Martin ignored him. He couldn't tell him, not now, that he'd been there three times for this very mission and failed each time. That's why he wanted a professional to handle it.

"Let's stay focused, Nick. If you're looking at a small, scallop-shaped shrine with a golden cross and precious stones studding the wood, then you're in the right place."

"Well, that's exactly what's in front of me, Martin. What the hell is it?"

"It's petrified wood from Noah's Ark."

"*Hmph.* Looks brand-new to me . . ."

"Well, it's not. It's believed that St. Jacob found it AD 678 during a pilgrimage to Mount Ararat."

"There's a pilgrimage to Ararat? That's almost fifteen thousand feet!"

"Well, there used to be. Though back in the old days, most people never made it to the summit. It's not exactly the most hospitable mountain terrain. St. Jacob fell asleep during the journey, though it's said that to encourage him, God himself put a plank of Noah's Ark in his path for him to find."

"Damn, Martin, you're a goddamn encyclopedia."

"Just thorough . . ."

"Well, I'm sorry to break it to you, but this is no plank; it's a small wooden tablet."

"You have it in your hands?"

"Affirmative."

"O-okay . . . ," he stammered. "Well, maybe they broke it up to spread the pieces around. Anyway, get your tools out and get ready to extract the object. We don't need the wood, just the stone that makes up the corner."

"You don't want the piece of the ark?"

"No. Just the stone."

"The black one?"

"Right. Just the *heliogabalus,* the 'sun stone.' Carefully remove it and replace it with the replica."

Allen ran his fingers over the wood and the stone, looking for some kind of trip wire or alarm. When he was sure it was safe, he carefully pried the stone loose with a watchmaker's knife, and it fell gently into his hands. He dabbed a couple of drops of adhesive into the concave opening, and when he placed the imposter stone inside, he smiled at how perfectly it fit, down to the millimeter. He figured it would be months before anyone noticed the difference.

"Done."

"Great. Hang it back up and get out of there."

"So . . ." Allen's voice was emitted through a speaker inside the van. "Are you going to tell me why you didn't do this yourself? You really didn't need my help."

Faber didn't respond.

He couldn't.

The door to Martin Faber's mobile lab had slid open and a monk with a long beard was aiming a machine gun at him. Wordlessly, he ordered Martin to switch off the radio, step back from the computer and walk toward the deserted plaza with his hands above his head. Three other shadows rushed across the plaza and headed toward the main entrance—toward an unwitting Nick Allen. They ducked behind the tomb of the patriarch Teg Aghexander and waited for the unsuspecting colonel to come out. They may have been wearing black cassocks down to their feet and large golden crosses around their necks, but make no mistake: They were soldiers.

Before Allen ever saw them, they had him in their gun sights.

"You're not welcome here, Colonel Allen," the man who looked to be in charge said in perfect English. He smiled slyly beneath his straw-colored mustache. "Though . . . we've been expecting you."

"Really?" Allen said, feigning amusement.

"Oh, yes, Colonel Nicholas J. Allen. Born August 1951 in Lubbock, Texas. Graduated magna cum laude. Agent of the National Security Agency and stationed in Armenia. And, apparently, you've come looking for something that doesn't belong to you, does it, Colonel? Something that's really none of your business."

Allen's eyes flashed with fury. "And who the hell are you?"

"An old enemy of the state, Colonel."

Nick Allen stood very still, silently.

"Americans love to think they know our country. They read about Armenia in the CIA's *World Factbook* and conclude they have us all figured out. It's a shame, really. You ignore the fact that our culture was flourishing four thousand years before yours began."

"What the hell do you want?"

Allen kept his hands above his head, but as he looked out on the wide plaza, he could feel his body heat rising, the icy cold from inside the church now just a memory.

"What have you done to my partner? Do you even know what you're getting yourself into?"

"Oh, come on now, Colonel. Your partner's just fine." He smiled. "If you're in such a hurry to see him again, all you have to do is hand over what's rightfully ours. Seem like a fair trade?"

"I don't know what you're talking about."

"Now's not the time to play dumb, Colonel," the man said, his eyes now sparking. "You've come to steal one of our national treasures. You don't think others have tried—and paid with their lives? Fool with sacred forces that you don't understand, and you could find yourself . . . struck down. Hadn't anyone warned you about that, Colonel?"

"If you're talking about the reliquaries, I haven't touched them. They're inside right where—"

The man with the mustache *tsk-tsked* Allen.

"We want the stone you've taken from inside of it, Colonel. It was part of the ark's original cargo, and it's very, very valuable to us."

"You really believe in this ark crap?" Allen snickered.

"Woe to him who believes in nothing, as Victor Hugo said . . . Let me give you a little history lesson, Colonel. Maybe then you'll understand. Do you know why Armenians still call our homeland Hayastan? Well, I'll tell you: It means 'the land of Hay,' or Haik, son of Togarma, grandson of Gomer, great-grandson of Jafet and great-great-grandson of Noah. They and their progeny repopulated these lands after the Great Flood and they swore an oath to guard this land's holy heirlooms. Mount Ararat, where the ark ran aground, is less than fifty miles from here. My town was charged with protecting not only the ark, but also its valuable cargo. We have absolute *faith* in it."

He added, "And you should have been warned that in Armenia, attempting to steal one of Noah's sacred relics is an offense punishable . . . by death."

"Now, wait a minute. I'm an American citizen. You can't just—"

The man burst into laughter. The two men with him nervously pointed the barrels of their rifles at Allen's chest as they led him down a corridor.

"So who the hell are you people? Do you work for the Armenian Church?"

"My name is Artemi Dujok, Colonel. And God has granted me unlimited resources to protect what is His. Now, if you will, hand over the stone."

As they walked, Allen realized where they were headed. Just ahead was a small, hidden alley. A dead end, in every sense. He watched as two other men forced Martin Faber to kneel, facing the wall. *They're going to kill us, right here . . .*

"What's it going to be, Colonel? Do I have to take it from you by force?"

Allen figured this was his best chance to distract Dujok and make a run for it. As he lowered his arms to pull the stone from his pocket, Allen spun around and landed a solid blow right on Dujok's face with a hollow thud. Dujok dropped like a rock, blood gushing from his nose. A hail of gunfire whizzed past Allen as he dropped to the ground and kicked up at one of the gunmen, breaking his knee.

The soldier fell down in a screaming lump as his partner fired a fresh volley, but the gunfire only splintered a nearby door and chipped the stone archway to one of the church's entrances.

"Don't let him get away!" Allen heard Dujok yell.

Allen leveled a punch at the soldier with the broken knee, picked him up by the armpits and hurled him into the soldier trying to line Allen up in his sights.

But Dujok had regained his senses. He pulled a dagger from his waistband and leaped at Allen, the knife's razor-sharp blade slicing into his face. It was so sharp, Allen barely felt the blade split his forehead open to the bone, unleashing a blinding waterfall of blood.

Just as Allen reached up instinctively to stanch the bleeding, he saw something he'd never forget: Dujok reached for a small black box hanging from his neck and pointed it directly at Allen's head.

"You're dumber than I thought, Colonel," he said, swallowing his own blood.

That's when Allen heard a buzzing that sounded like a thousand angry hornets swirling around his head and overwhelming him with a deathly fear. It was the first time he'd felt it, but he never would forget his first electromagnetic blast.

53

It all came at once, the head-splitting migraine and the nausea from the very pit of my stomach.

"Are you all right, Ms. Álvarez?"

Dujok was standing over me. And that's when I realized I had fainted again, this time inside the church of Santa María a Nova.

"Wha . . . what happened?" I asked.

"Congratulations. You've managed to activate the adamant," he said with a smile.

"Really?"

"Yes, really."

"Everything went black all of a sudden. I tried to focus my mind, but—"

"Don't worry. It's just that being exposed to the electromagnetic forces knocked you out. It happens. As soon as you sit up and drink some water, you'll be fine," he said flatly.

But I could tell my health wasn't the most important thing on his mind.

"So what happens next?"

"Simple. Your adamant is going to help us achieve what any true believer hopes for when he steps into a church: to speak to God."

He must have noticed the surprise on my face. "Wait, I thought we were going to use the adamant to find Martin," I shot back.

"God is everything, Ms. Álvarez, and that includes your husband. That's why, thanks to the holy gift inside of you, we've managed to send a signal to Him."

"A signal? To God?"

"Well, and also to Martin's adamant."

54

"Dr. Scott! You have to see this! *Argh,* these stupid goons out here won't let me in to see you!"

Edgar Scott's desk videophone blinked to life as he and the others studied the aerial photographs from the north of Spain. The Secret Service had made security at the National Reconnaissance Office extra tight with the president of the United States in the building. But they hadn't had a chance to restrict communications to Scott's office.

"The HMBB just detected a new X emission!" the man yelled.

Michael Owen looked over at Scott, whose round red face filled the video screen.

"Okay, Mills. I'll be right out," Scott answered.

"Wait a minute. What the hell's an X emission? And where do you think you're going?" Owen said.

"That's what we call the kind of EM field that we detected a few hours ago in Santiago. If we've just detected another, and so soon after the first, then we'd better get to the control room right away. You can follow me or wait here, whatever you prefer."

"Well, if the president doesn't mind . . . ," Owen said.

Roger Castle was already on his feet and following Dr. Scott.

The three of them clanked down the metal catwalk that separated the administrative offices from the technical operations area. Scott stood in front of a bulletproof metal door and stated his name as he stared into a retinal scanner to open the door. Soon, they found themselves in a room with the lights dimmed, redolent of fresh coffee and facing an enormous flat-panel monitor. About ten people shifted around the control room, and the president felt at ease, as if perhaps he might not even be recognized. But no such luck.

The chubby man from the videophone rushed to introduce himself.

"M-Mr. President?" he stammered.

"Uh, this is Jack Mills, sir. Our monitoring chief," Scott said.

"It's an honor, sir!" Mills said.

"Keep your voice down, will you, Mills?" Castle told him.

"Yes, sir, Mr. President!" he said, still too loudly.

The enormous screen showed a map of Earth with the trajectory and global position of different satellites shown in different colors.

"Okay, show me the X emission," Castle told Mills.

"We detected the first signal about six minutes ago. Here, you can see it clearer on one of these smaller screens."

The four of them leaned in to see a real-time map of the Iberian Peninsula on Mills's desk as he cleared away the remnants of his dinner. He punched in a couple of commands on his keyboard and the image zoomed in on the map until they had a detailed picture.

"Santiago again?" Castle said as the image closed in.

"Actually . . . no, Mr. President," Mills whispered, trying to get his bearings. "Now it looks like we're getting two signals. The HMBB detected the first one in northern Spain, in a town called Noia, at five forty-seven in the morning, our time."

"Noia?"

"It's about twenty-five miles west of the earlier signal, sir."

"And the second signal?"

"It started about twenty seconds later. Another one of our satellites, the KH-19, traced it to a position near Mount Ararat. The coordinates put it on the border between Iran and Turkey."

"Isn't that near where—"

"Yes, very close to that, sir," Owen said, stopping him. Castle got the hint and bit his tongue.

"Do you have any idea who might be responsible for these emissions?"

Jack Mills just shrugged his shoulders and grimaced as if asking for forgiveness.

"I'm sorry, sir. We don't have any idea."

"The Russians? The Iranians?"

"We just don't know, sir."

"What are the chances the stones you're looking for caused those signals, Michael?" Castle said.

"They're high, sir."

"So is there a plan for getting our hands on them?"

"Of course, sir. The NRO is already in touch with the navy's fast-intervention division. As we speak, if everything is going according to protocol, the closest units already have orders to comb the area."

Castle turned from the monitor and caught Owen's eye, beckoning for him to meet him by the door. He needed to ask Owen something else, something that had been on his mind since he spoke to his adviser Ellen Watson.

"Michael, because of these stones, two people are missing, including a US citizen. I hope you have a plan that includes more than shifting around satellites and taking pictures of my soup at the Oval Office."

"Understood, sir."

"Keep me informed. As for the rest of you," he said, raising his voice loud enough to be heard throughout the small office, "I don't have to tell you to keep this little visit a secret.

"Now," he said, turning back to Owens, "I need to make a few calls."

55

"You've done a good job, here, Ms. Álvarez," Artemi Dujok said while taking off his backpack and opening his laptop to look for a wireless signal.

Dujok was positively beaming. He'd leaned his rifle against Juan de Estivadas's sarcophagus and left the adamant sitting on the lid.

"Your husband's a genius, you know that? Came up with just the right phrase to lead us to your adamant. He counted on your gift. No one he's ever met has made the adamants react like you do. Something happened to the stones' previous owner—"

"You mean John Dee . . ."

Dujok had been furiously pecking commands into his laptop when he stopped to look at me quizzically.

"Dee? No, of course not . . ."

"Someone else?" I said, confused.

"The last historical record we have of these stones being used was in 1827," Dujok said. "A young man from Vermont came across them in Virginia. Both of them. Though his story is very similar to Dee's. Just like Dee, he claims it was an angel who gave them to him. He received them along with a book with golden pages. And the words were written in a strange language that he had to use the stones to translate."

"I've never heard that story."

"That's odd. It's a famous story, after all. Especially in the United States, your husband's country. Maybe you'll recognize the young man's name. Ever heard of Joseph Smith?"

"Smith?"

"The founder of the Mormon religion," Dujok said, smiling, without lifting his eyes from the computer screen. "Or, rather, the founder of the Church of Jesus Christ of Latter-day Saints. Smith was the founder and the prophet. As a matter of fact, before that golden book disappeared, there were several witnesses who swore under oath that they saw it."

"So the Mormons have something to do with the adamants?"

Actually, I knew very little about Mormonism. I'd been born and raised in a Catholic country, so any other Christian faith was foreign to me. But from my work restoring sacred art around Galicia, I'd learned that Mormons had been recording their ancient texts on microfilm for years, from baptismal to death records, and storing them at their head-quarters in Utah in preparation for the "end of days." As far as I'd been told, they believed that only those whose family trees were documented and stored at a special bunker in Salt Lake City would be granted ever-lasting life.

"Not only was Smith able to use the adamants, Ms. Álvarez," Dujok said, "he also called them by their ancient name.

"Among the revelations he received while using the adamants was that the Hebrew patriarch Abraham was one of their best-known own-ers. And that he inherited them from Noah himself. So he named them Urim and Thummim."

"What do those names mean?"

"It means 'lights' and 'vessels' in ancient Hebrew. Abraham, the fa-ther of Judaism, used them for divination and communication in the town of Ur, near the modern city of Nasiriya, in Iraq, where they found clay tablets with fragments of the epic of Gilgamesh dating back to six-teen hundred years before the birth of Christ."

"So Abraham was a keeper of these stones too?"

"You'd be amazed at the names throughout history who have been linked to the stones before they reappeared in 1827. From Moses to King Solomon, who stored them among the treasures in his Temple and passed them down to Roman emperors, popes, kings, politicians, financiers . . ."

"And what ever happened to Smith?"

"He was obsessed," Dujok said gravely, now staring intently at the figures on his screen. "He was so serious about his role as redeemer, as the last prophet of Jesus Christ, that he was lynched by his enemies one day in Illinois. Urim and Thummim disappeared in the melee. And the adamants were never spoken of again . . . well, at least not publicly . . ."

Dujok looked up and raised an eyebrow, as if trying to add suspense to the story.

"What do you mean?" I asked.

"After being lost for more than four decades, they were rediscovered in the American Southwest during the administration of President Chester Arthur," Dujok said. "The Hopi Indians had been their keepers until Arthur's people got their hands on them. That's when the navy ran tests on them and discovered, conclusively, they were made up of unknown materials. They would change their mass and color, even their temperature, as if they were responding to some unknown force. And now the emission of this adamant will lead us to Martin. It's already happening. Look!"

56

Beep. Beep. Beeeeep.

Three new messages appeared on Ellen Watson's BlackBerry. The plane descended toward Lavacolla, about ten miles east of Santiago de Compostela. And the second her phone could receive cell service, the president's assistant had to decide which message to open first. They were all marked "urgent."

The first one was from Richard Hale, who'd left such a bad taste in her mouth in Madrid. It included a pair of attachments: a picture of Julia Álvarez—"This is your target. Married five years to ex–NSA agent Martin Faber"—and a recap of Nick Allen's conversation with Álvarez up until the point she was kidnapped. "Inspector Antonio Figueiras will help you with whatever you need. He's handling the case for local police," the note read, and included his cell number.

Watson memorized the information and Álvarez's picture and closed the document with a press of her thumb. *And I'll have to have a little chat with Colonel Allen, as well,* she thought.

The second message was cryptic. It came from her office in Washington, whose last orders were for her to catch the first flight to Galicia. "The stone you're looking for has been detected in that region," she'd been told. "Another signal was detected 2,085 miles to the east in Turkish territory." But now, this new message was instructing her to examine the latest HMBB satellite images taken over the town of Noia regarding the stone closest to her. Watson thumbed a few keys, got on the web, and soon gained access to the NRO's restricted database. That's when she realized why the White House's message was marked "urgent." "Be careful. Elijah is on the trail," it read. "These images were sent this morning to the USS *Texas*. Don't let your guard down."

The USS Texas? she thought, startled. *How the hell did they get a submarine there so quickly?*

The third message was the most specific of all. It came from one of the president's scientific advisers and contained an analysis of two images, one from the HMBB and another from a seven-year-old private satellite, a relic in terms of space exploration, called GRACE (Gravity Recovery and Climate Experiment). And the analysis drew a strange conclusion: The gravitational field in the area where they were headed had been reduced by 2 percent. And the only anomaly was the electromagnetic emission recorded by HMBB.

"Tom, did you see this?"

Thomas Jenkins was flipping through a newspaper. The man in the striped Saks tie peeked over from behind the sports page to look at Watson's BlackBerry.

"Looks like we're going to have to split up," he said. "When we land, rent a car and get yourself to Noia. That's where you'll find Julia Álvarez's adamant."

"And what are you going to do?"

"I'll get together with Colonel Allen and we'll make our way to Turkey. We'll find Martin Faber and recover his adamant. I'll meet you back in Washington in three days. Four, if things get hairy."

"Are you sure?"

"It's the only way."

Jenkins started to put on his blazer as the plane finished its descent, and he caught Watson with another one of his unexpected questions.

"So, did you know Faber's a climatologist?" he said, looking at her out of the corner of his eye.

"Yes," she said. "I studied his file when the president asked us to investigate him."

"You know, Ellen, a climatologist and a meteorologist are two very different jobs. From a national defense standpoint, it makes sense for the NSA to have a meteorologist on staff, in case they need to decide if the weather's right to launch a ballistic missile or if they're testing something in the upper atmosphere. But a climatologist doesn't serve any kind of short-term function. They study the climate as a whole and if they make projections, it's usually for something years down the road and sure as hell not with any kind of certainty," he told her, waiting for the information to sink in before he finished his thought. "So, why do you think they need this kind of person on staff?"

Tom Jenkins never spoke just to hear himself speak. Traveling with him was like playing a game of chess. You had to stay on your toes, listening for the meaning behind everything he said, and carefully think over your answers before he caught you off guard. Ellen Watson knew this.

"Maybe the Elijah project has something to do with climate change," she said. "It wouldn't be the first time the NSA studied how to change the climate of a region to destabilize it politically. Remember the High Frequency Active Auroral Research Program, HAARP, which studied the ionosphere? They wanted to see whether they could control Earth's and the sun's natural magnetic forces to change atmospheric conditions at will. Some military intelligence agencies think those are the weapons of the future, more so than thermonuclear bombs . . ."

"Sure, that makes sense. But tell me this, Ellen," he said, rushing to finish his coffee and hand it to the flight attendant. "If the NSA needs atmospheric information, it could just reach out to the National Weather Service and get whatever data it needs. But it's clear the Elijah project is somehow beyond that. And what, pray tell, does any of it have to do with a couple of old stones? Why do you think they're so interested in them? Think maybe they could be used to affect the climate?"

"Well, let's see: So far, we know they're capable of producing EM radiation strong enough to send a signal into space," she said. "And now it looks like they can change the Earth's gravitational force when they're activated. So, no, I don't think we're talking about just any old rocks."

"Maybe you're right . . . Maybe they're not 'stones' in the traditional sense at all. Maybe they're made up of some kind of ancient artificial compound. A crystal from the city of Atlantis. A chunk of kryptonite . . . How the hell should I know?" Watson said, chuckling.

"But what would they have to do with the climate?" Jenkins said, pressing her.

Ellen was getting tired of this game of twenty questions. She knew Jenkins loved to squeeze information out of people and that had earned him a bad reputation in Washington. Others in Castle's office said he could get into the heads of a whole team, turning one agent against another. Behind his back, they called him "the Serpent."

"Stones and climate . . ."

Still, despite all that, Ellen tried to take up his challenge. "Maybe . . . maybe the radiation the crystals emit can break up thunderstorms. Or cause them. Or maybe they affect the ozone layer. You know, since the adamants can affect gravitational forces, they might be useful in areas of heavy seismic activity—"

"Wait! I think I got it . . ."

Jenkins's interruption caught Watson off guard.

"I think the president thinks Elijah is some kind of program to forecast a global catastrophe," he said, his face lighting up as if something had just dawned on him. "But all of this centering around some stone? It makes no sense. Still . . ."

"Still what?"

"If the program is designed to predict a global catastrophe, they'd need a climatologist."

"So why would Faber leave such a choice assignment?"

Jenkins was about to respond when he felt the thud of the plane's landing gear touching down.

He continued when the noise had settled down. "According to the NSA, Faber left his job just after being sent to Armenia, toward the end of 1999."

"Do we know why?"

"He wrote an obscure resignation letter that said he'd found his true faith there. At first, I didn't pay much attention to it. Believe it or not, when most intelligence agents resign, it's over a woman or because they've had a religious awakening. In either case, the pressure's too much to stay with the job. But now that I've had a chance to really look into Faber's file, I think there's something very different going on. There's no moral quandary. Actually, quite the opposite. He said the followers of the world's oldest religion had given him the answers to all of his questions. And that's why he left the NSA."

"The world's . . . *oldest* religion?"

"They still talk about that resignation letter at the NSA. It was particularly bizarre. He dated it with the year 6748, from the calendar year of his new religion. He said that's how many years it had been since the Great Flood that ended life on Earth."

"What . . . ?" Watson just stared at him wide-eyed and instinctively clutched the Star of David hanging from her neck. "A religion older than Judaism?"

"You got it. Ever hear of the Yezidi, Ellen?"

57

A colorful world map flashed across Artemi Dujok's laptop screen. A multitude of colorful figures scrolled down the right side, while a cursor danced around the screen, spitting out geographical coordinates and acronyms I didn't understand.

"This program tracks a network of low-orbit satellites that take electromagnetic readings around the world," Dujok said without looking up. "Any reading above point-seven gausses of magnetic energy sets off an alarm and registers on-screen with this red graphic. See it here?"

I peered around for a look, but none of the cryptic figures made any sense to me.

"If we zoom over the Iberian Peninsula," he said, quickly tapping commands into the computer, "you can see that the area of Noia will show up in red. See? There you go . . ."

"So, the adamant did that?"

"Not 'did.' It's *still* doing it," Dujok said. "The adamant is still sending out a signal."

"So were you able to find Martin?"

"The program is processing that information as we speak, Ms. Álvarez. A twin signal has shown up just a few miles from the border between Turkey and Iran, near Mount Ararat."

"Is that where my husband is?" I said, swallowing hard.

"More than likely."

"And this information . . ." I hesitated to finish my thought. "Can others see it as well? Someone like, say, Colonel Allen?"

"Ms. Álvarez, Colonel Allen is probably dead."

"Dead?"

"When we rescued you in Santiago, we unleashed a one-tesla geo-plasmic blast with a force of more than ten thousand gausses, which is what knocked you unconscious. It's not the first time in his life he's been hit with one. And let me tell you, there's no living thing that can withstand several blasts without being incapacitated—or killed."

58

The patient in room 616 remained unresponsive even though his vitals—body temperature, pulse, breathing and blood pressure—said he was out of danger. But the shots of adrenaline still hadn't managed to rouse him. The movement of Nicholas Allen's eyes indicated he was still in REM sleep, lost in an endless dream. Maybe that's why the doctors at Our Lady of Hope hospital couldn't venture a guess at how long he'd be that way.

"He could wake up at any minute," the chief of the emergency room had said during a meeting with other physicians at six in the morning, "but it's also possible that his central nervous system could be compromised, and he might never recover."

"Is there anything we can do for him?" another doctor asked.

"Not much. In my opinion, it's best to withhold any treatment until we know exactly what happened to him."

"But he's been unconscious for hours, Doctor," a nurse said.

"Look, that's my medical opinion. As long as he's stable, we won't intervene. It's better that we wait until he wakes up and we can ask him what might have caused this."

None of them could have imagined that Allen's brain was working on that very problem as they spoke. His neurons fired rapidly, bringing to mind the last time such an irresistible force felled him.

SOMEWHERE BETWEEN ARMENIA AND TURKEY
AUGUST 11, 1999

Everything seemed to happen in the hours following their foiled robbery in the St. Echmiadzin Cathedral.

Unarmed, beaten into semiconsciousness by Artemi Dujok's goons and bleeding from the gash in his forehead, Nick Allen had been thrown in the back of an air-conditioned van, which secretly crossed the Turkish border. Next to him, Martin Faber rode with his hands tied behind his back. Allen was sick with the thought of how differently things might have turned out if Faber had been more alert and not been discovered in the van. Well, what was the use of regrets now, anyway? The young bureaucrat sat nearly unharmed next to him. Allen couldn't see so much as a scrape on him, and even though he was only tied up with duct tape, Faber looked too scared to move. Allen, though, was in much worse shape. He had lost a lot of blood. He was too weak to try to escape and the muscles in his arms and legs seemed drained of all strength. If he was going to survive this, he had to conserve his strength until they got him to a hospital—if he was lucky.

Over the course of seven interminable hours, they sat next to each other without so much as an attempt to communicate.

If the cathedral's vigilante group was trying to make it hard for the NSA to find them, they certainly were doing a good job of it. For starters, they had been carted off to the middle of nowhere, to some inhospitable plain. They were no longer in mountainous Armenia but in some expansive plateau where the Armenian peaks cast their shadows in the setting sun.

He and Faber noticed a large, squarish building a couple of hundred yards in the distance. It was on the other side of a chasm, and next to it was a sort of tall, slender tower, wider at the base and tapering to a peak, like a finger pointing to heaven. It had been partially obscured by a tower of adobe blocks, as if someone had tried to camouflage it from prying eyes.

"Where . . . where are we?" Allen stammered. His wound had started to clot.

"This is the free part of Kurdistan, Colonel," Artemi Dujok said, spreading his arms out toward the abyss that separated them from the buildings. "This is the holy land of Noah's heirs. And over there, on the edge of the horizon, is Urartu. Or Agri Dagi.

Martin Faber gasped.

Dujok wasn't lying. They had traveled almost two hundred and fifty miles. He could see the snowy peaks of the Ararat mountain range in the fading light. Faber figured they were somewhere near Mount Ararat's southern face, probably right in between Armenia, Turkey and Iran.

"Well, what are we doing here?" Allen asked, kicking his legs as if he was trying to get the feeling back in them. "You can't hold two American citizens hostage."

Dujok and his men just smiled at each other. "You don't understand the significance of this place, do you, Colonel?"

"I do," Martin said. " 'Agri Dagi' means 'the mountain of pain' in Turkish. Or 'Urartu,' 'the door to the heavens' in Armenian."

"Very good, Mr. Faber. And today, you're going to find out why the Turks call it that."

"So that's your plan? You're going to leave us to die on the mountain?" Faber said. "Or are you going to toss us over the side of a cliff?"

"No, no, nothing like that," Dujok said with that disquieting grin. "That would be too light a penalty, Mr. Faber. And we *do* want you to suffer. We Yezidi are very deliberate in our actions."

"Yezidi?"

Nick Allen wondered why Martin Faber looked frozen after hearing that term. The young NSA agent kept staring at Dujok with open-mouthed amazement, and Dujok seemed pleased to inspire such respect—or fear. Even though it was the middle of August, a cold northern wind had whipped up once the sun went down.

"You know who they are?" Allen whispered to Faber when Dujok was distracted by one of his men.

Martin nodded, answering low and quickly. "Of course," he whispered. "My father talked a lot about them. He explored this region years ago and he told incredible stories about the Yezidi. Some people think they're devil worshippers, but in reality, they're the world's last known cult dedicated to worshipping angels. They have all kinds of strange rituals: The Yezidi never shave their mustaches. See? They believe in reincarnation. They don't eat lettuce. They never dress in blue. They believe they are the true descendants of the survivors of several world-ending floods, and, as such, they consider themselves the only loyal protectors of the ancient relics like the ones in St. Echmiadzin."

"Great. Religious fanatics . . . ," Allen said.

"But not murderers."

"Yeah? Well, they almost killed me back at the cathedral!"

Martin Faber didn't know how to respond. It would have been useless to try to explain to someone sliced open with a Yezidi blade the fascination his own family had with that tribe. Martin's parents had spent years studying the Yezidi's strange theology and they had considered them pacifists. But maybe his parents had been blinded by the Yezidi's subtle ties to John Dee. Both the Yezidi and Dee's followers claimed to have established communication with higher beings and to have seen "holy books" and dealt with "celestial tablets" that gave them access to the Creator.

And that's exactly why Martin Faber had come to Armenia, driven by his father's stories and working under the guise of a top-secret project.

"You know . . . ," Artemi Dujok said, quickly turning around, interrupting the agents' whispers and staring directly at Martin. "It shouldn't surprise me that you inherited your father's ambition."

"My father? You . . . you know my father?"

"Mr. Faber, your innocence is touching. I know every single thing about every person involved with the Elijah project. As a matter of fact, I myself used to work on Elijah. While you were still in diapers. But I left as soon as I learned the real reason behind your government's interest in it."

"Wait, you used to work for Elijah?"

Both of the agents' eyes flashed.

"That's right. And from what I can see, they're still bent on being the ones to control the adamants at all costs."

Nicholas Allen was confused, and not just from the blood loss. Did this Yezidi know his partner's parents? What the hell was the Elijah project? And why the devil had his bosses sent him into this hornets' nest without telling him any of this?

"But I don't understand," Martin said. "Why have you brought us here, to one of your famous towers?"

Dujok leaned in close to Martin, his hands clutched behind his back. "I'm impressed you know about this place, Mr. Faber. Then again, I'd expect nothing less from you."

"I've read about it in William Seabrook's books. And in Gurdjieff's."

Towers? Gurdjieff? Seabrook? Allen was getting more worried by the minute.

"So I assume you've read what Pushkin and Lovecraft had to say about us," Dujok said with a malevolent smile. "Maybe you've already figured this out for yourself, but I can tell you they're all lies. Gurdjieff, our country's so-called famous mystic, never even saw these towers. But that didn't stop him from publishing his little pamphlets in French and becoming famous in Europe."

"But, wait, William Seabrook did discover your secret, didn't he?"

"Well, yes, Seabrook did," Dujok muttered.

"He was a mystic-slash-reporter who worked for *The New York Times* in the early twentieth century—"

"I know who William Seabrook was, Mr. Faber. The first outsider ever to write about these sacred buildings," Dujok said, pointing toward the stone spire outside the van window. "The idiot called them the 'towers of evil' because he thought they radiated energy that Satan used to control the world. But when he wrote about the towers, he couldn't even prove their existence. Most have been destroyed or hidden beneath other structures."

"I read his *Adventures in Arabia*," Martin said, nodding, happy to at least be distracting his captor, "and I thought it was odd that he never gave the towers' exact locations."

"That's because he never knew them. None of the Yezidi sheikhs he spoke to would ever have revealed their locations. He had to settle for assuming that they were hidden throughout the region and that we visited them from time to time."

"And this is one of those sacred structures . . ."

"That's right," Dujok said. "My family had to find a way to conceal it after Seabrook published his work. He stigmatized us when he called us devil worshippers and wrote that these buildings were tools of the devil."

"Well, aren't they—tools of the devil? And aren't you devil worshippers, all of you?" Nick Allen said, interrupting. His legs were growing weaker and his breathing had become even more labored. He was starting to wish that whatever was going to happen to them would just be over.

"Of course not!"

"Then why are you going to sacrifice us?" He coughed. The colonel was getting worse by the minute. He was running a high fever. His sliced forehead was pounding. And the cold sweat told him the end was drawing near. "Isn't that what devil worshippers do—sacrifice people?"

Dujok leaned in close to the strapping Texan. "That's where you're wrong, Colonel," Dujok murmured. "I'm not the one who is going to execute you. I don't want the stain of your blood on my hands. But as it turns out, when you stole a sacred object, you opened yourself to *ordalia*. Do you know what that is, Colonel?"

Nick Allen had no idea, and Dujok knew this.

"I'll tell you what it is: It's a judgment from God, Colonel," Dujok hissed. "Justice imparted by the All-Powerful One. An implacable sentence. Instant and exact. He will be the One to decide your fate. Does that sound fair to you?"

"You're insane . . ."

An icy blast of wind from Ararat's lower peak whipped through the van and suddenly ended their conversation.

"There's no time to waste," Dujok said, ignoring his prisoner's jeer.

He gave the signal and two of his men grabbed Faber and Allen and dragged them to the edge of a giant precipice, the lip of an enormous crater. As they moved their feet over the rough terrain, they could feel a heat rising up from the ground, which was parched and cracked. Was

Dujok planning to hurl them into that chasm? Was this his idea of an *ordalia*?

Faber had heard the term before. It was coined during the Inquisition when they tried accused witches and heretics by tying them to a burning stake or throwing them from a precipice; if they were innocent, they would pass the test. But Martin didn't think the Yezidi would simply toss them into the void. By its nature, an *ordalia* gave the accused the opportunity to save himself.

"What are you going to do to us, Dujok?" Martin asked when his feet had run out of room.

"We are going to test your faith, gentlemen."

Dujok had taken the stone from the cathedral, turned it over in his hands and held it above his head. That kidney-shaped oracle began to glow like a star in the night sky, as if it had its own power source.

"Now do you understand why they call these 'sun stones,' Mr. Faber?" Dujok said, holding the stone aloft. "These *heliogabali* are made of a specific material that reacts to the sun's energy. Just a few hours ago, a total eclipse of the sun cast its shadow over this entire area, revealing the sun's corona. And although probably no one noticed it, that solar energy has powered the remaining seven angelic towers on earth for several hours. If one of these stones comes in contact with that energy it can trigger an . . . *interesting* reaction."

"What kind of reaction?"

"We call it the Glory of God, Mr. Faber," Dujok said, smiling. "The Hebrew Torah calls it *kabod*. It's the glow of the Eternal Father, the same fire that Moses encountered on Mount Sinai. The flame that engulfed the Burning Bush without consuming it and allowed man to speak to God . . . It is our oldest mode of communicating with the Lord. But for mortal men like you, who do not have the gift to receive God's light, it will surely kill you."

"John Dee stood before that fire and didn't die," Martin yelled defiantly.

"He was an exception. He used the gifts of his seers, who passed on the holy incantations that protected him."

"In that case," Martin Faber said, smiling at the memory of studying Dee's books of spells, "I am ready to see the Glory of God."

Dujok held up the glowing stone. Its light cast hard shadows on Dujok's face, giving him an ominous visage.

"Then, gentlemen, let His will be done . . ."

59

39° 25' 34" N.

44° 24' 19" E.

The coordinates flashed on one corner of the screen, illuminating Dujok's face.

"We got it!" he yelled, and all of a sudden it didn't matter how long they'd been sitting on the cold, hard ground at Santa María a Nova.

Dujok's mind was too preoccupied with other things, like hiding his true plan from me. How could I have known what lay ahead?

He quickly punched those coordinates into Google Earth, and we watched as a virtual earth spun on its axis, closing in on the location. Both of us held our breath. We hoped these figures would finally tell us where Martin and the second adamant were.

The map moved past Europe and continued east, past the Balkans, past Greece, and started to focus on a point between the borders of Armenia, Iran and Turkey. At 39° latitude north, the map started to zoom closer to the ground.

It finally came to a stop on an image that was bleak in more ways than one.

"Is that it?" I asked. Dujok nodded.

The terrain was desolate, ochre yellow, without a single tree anywhere in sight, an endless rocky earth with a handful of dilapidated houses scattered over the hilly terrain.

"This program won't give us an exact location," Dujok said, clicking and dragging the map. "We'll have to explore the surrounding area."

He moved the map around with his cursor, each time revealing bleaker terrain. Only the border post of Gurbulak had a handful of large, all-terrain trucks dotting the only road. He kept moving the image around the barren lands, looking for something distinctive. And that's when we saw it, less than a mile from the shoddy little town of Hallaç, behind a fenced military zone. It was the only feature that looked out of place: the perfect new roof of a sprawling mansion and a smooth strip of earth that could serve as a landing strip for a small aircraft. A word that could only be read from high above had been scrawled across the terrain. "Turkey." And at the other end of the airfield, something that resembled the shape of a building had been digitally erased from the satellite image.

I knew from past experience that those blurred images were common in Google Earth. When I had tried to study several Christian churches in Jerusalem, I found a few had been marked as "classified because of national security." The same thing happens with military installations over China and Cuba. But what could someone want to conceal in Hallaç?

When he moved the cursor to the other end of the airfield, we found something else surprising, something even stranger than the censored satellite picture. It was an enormous, perfectly round gap in the earth, a chasm some one hundred thirty feet across.

Dujok zoomed in on the image.

"What is *that*?" I asked.

But he wasn't paying attention to me. I saw him jotting down the details of the location: altitude—4,746 feet above sea level; 39°25'14" North; 44°24'06" East. And then he calculated the distance to Ararat's twin peaks. It was close, less than eighteen miles as the crow flies.

He spun the image around to get a good look at it from all sides.

"What? *What* is it?"

Dujok wouldn't take his eyes off that gaping wound in the earth. It looked as if a missile had struck that very spot and left a perfectly symmetrical gaping hole in the ground. He finally turned and smiled.

"That," he said, "is where your husband is."

60

For years, Nick Allen had tried to describe exactly what happened to him that summer of 1999 near the Ararat mountains. The best he could do in his report to the agency was to detail what he saw: When the Yezidi held up his glowing stone, some kind of whirlwind, a sphere about the size of a six-story building, rose weightlessly from the bottom of a crater and hovered in midair just several yards from the tower and the group of men.

The windstorm swirling around that . . . *whatever it was* was so intense that at first he thought it might be some kind of vertical-takeoff jet. But it wasn't shaped like anything he had ever seen. He lacked the vocabulary to even describe it, especially when he got an up-close look and realized that it wasn't made of any kind of metal he had ever seen. That spherical *thing* looked like some kind of umbilical cord, lights dazzling beneath a transparent membrane. And if that wasn't enough, it gave off a wide spectrum of sounds and colors that overwhelmed his senses.

His vision was the first sense to deceive him. He looked over at the Yezidi who held him at gunpoint and saw that their bodies were becoming transfigured, shapeless. He felt the features of his own face losing their form, like melting butter.

This isn't real, he said to himself over and over. *This isn't happening. It's some kind of hallucination.* But his mouth suddenly went dry, as if his tongue had fused itself to the roof of his mouth.

He could hear his captors speaking, but their voices were like a far-off echo.

"Behold, the Glory of God!" he heard them say over the pulsing chirps coming from the spherical thing.

"Glory be to God!" he heard others answer in the echo.

Allen tried to let himself fall to the ground. But his enormous body was now weightless, defying gravity. He knew he was at the edge of the abyss and feared one false step might send him over the precipice. Meanwhile, the spherical thing was floating just a few feet overhead. It had shifted and moved toward him and Martin, spinning at an incredible speed and sucking in nearby rocks and tumbleweed like a luminous twister. If they didn't do something fast, it would surely devour the two of them.

That's when he saw one of Dujok's men collapse. And Dujok suddenly became just a fine vertical line in his peripheral vision.

Allen's world began to evaporate as the spinning mass engulfed him, illuminating the world around him as if night had turned to day.

But somehow, the Glory of God did not devour him. He was still alive . . .

It moved past him and now he could hear Martin shouting back at the irresistible light. He spoke in a language Allen couldn't understand, his words resounding all around them as the glowing, spinning sphere engulfed his companion, casting Allen aside.

He would not see Martin Faber again.

And that's why now, years later, when the US government's satellites located Martin at the other end of the continent, Nicholas Allen found a powerful reason to live again: He needed to speak to Faber one more time. He needed to know what the hell happened to him when he disappeared inside the belly of that monster.

61

"Are you serious? My husband is there . . . right now?"

Artemi Dujok wasn't fazed by the despair in my voice. He continued to focus on the barren soil of northeastern Turkey on his computer screen, as if the images could tell him something that no one else on earth could understand.

"There's something I should probably tell you, Ms. Álvarez . . ."

The tone of his voice made me fear the worst; his eyes were fixed on the screen. So I was so relieved to hear him finish his sentence.

"I know that place," he said as if deep in thought. "I was there with your husband many years ago."

"Really?"

"Yes," he whispered, his lips trembling for just a moment. "That was the day I became his sheikh, his teacher. His captors have taken him to that place because they know more about the adamants than we imagined."

"How much more?"

"Too much," he said flatly. "Get your things. It's time to go."

62

Three miles off the coast of Noia, the fifty-six-foot fishing boat *Lalín's Siren* bobbed motionlessly in the ocean, trying to get its battered four-hundred-horsepower engine working again. The high seas had overcome its main engine and flooded the auxiliary one, stranding the crew of eleven men and leaving their cargo of cod and eel to spoil within sight of the coastline. Power was completely shut off. The chief engineer, a chubby Galician who liked to polish his bald head to a shine with olive oil, had the crew cut off the power to the engines, and with it went the sonar, the radar, the radio and even the microwave so he could work safely in the bowels of the ship.

So he was the first one to notice the disturbance in the silence.

He was lying just above the *Siren*'s keel, his ear to the ship's wooden frame as he tried to listen to whether the propeller was turning, when he heard three hollow thuds, one after the other. And they were close. Too close.

Thump. Thump. Thump.

Tito—that's what his shipmates called him—had no time to react. A massive thud now rocked the ship and he could barely believe his eyes: Less than two feet away, a giant needle of some kind was splitting the hull open, a gash that let the Atlantic Ocean spill into the *Siren*'s bowels. It tore through the ship with a monstrous sound, like a butcher's knife tearing through a bedsheet, and Tito's ruddy face paled in fear. The gash widened and the foamy sea spilled inside as Tito tried to run for the stairs. But the force of the hungry ocean pulled him down, down into the blackness, forever out of sight.

The ship buckled. Three of the crew members, who had been sharing beers with the captain upstairs, felt the wooden deck move beneath them, their chairs crashing to the deck. As the ship listed to one side, all of the crew's closets in the cabins down below swung open, tossing their possessions to the floor. Tristan, who mended the fishing nets, tripped over a sliding trunk as he tried to run out of his cabin and fell head-over-heels against the doorjamb—instantly breaking his neck. He never felt a thing. Unfortunately, his shipmates weren't spared the brutality of their deaths. Others were trapped in the cargo hold as hundreds of wooden pallets toppled over and crushed their bodies while the ocean swirled their blood out to sea.

Four men were killed and seven others injured in six and a half seconds.

Not until hours later, after the coast guard had given the survivors a clean bill of health, did they learn what had destroyed their ship. And even then, when they heard all the unbelievable details, they were sworn to secrecy after signing a confidentiality agreement—that is, if they indeed wanted to claim their cash settlement and a brand-new metal ship, courtesy of the United States government.

"Either you all sign or none of you sees a single euro," a man said, as if the unsuspecting sailors had been the guilty party.

As it turned out, their ship had been gutted like a fish by the top-secret photonic mast of a three-hundred-and-eighty-foot undersea titan with a fitting name: the USS *Texas.* The United States' Department of Defense had sent the state-of-the-art Virginia-class nuclear submarine to the western coast of Spain, into NATO territory, on a rescue mission—the details of which even the ship's admiral would never fully know.

Inside the *Texas,* red warning lights went off the second it scraped against the doomed *Lalín's Siren,* but it was far too late.

"I can't explain it, sir," the sailor in charge of the three-dimensional sonar said as he blessed himself with the sign of the cross. "Our sensors didn't pick up a single thing. We must have been hit with some kind of electronic countermeasures."

"Will this affect our operation on land?"

The ship's captain needed an answer.

"Negative, sir. We can send in the team right from here. All our computers and communications seem to be operational."

"Excellent." The captain sighed. "Commence operations."

Exactly eight minutes later, the surviving crew of *Lalín's Siren* watched in amazement from their listing ship as the side of the USS *Texas* opened with a hum, and a team of six men armed with M4A1 rifles and grenade launchers and wearing high-tech helmets hopped aboard a speed boat and shot from the submarine's belly as they headed for the Spanish coast, the fishermen swearing at them in a language none of them would have understood.

63

Artemi Dujok walked out of the Santa María a Nova church to give orders to his men standing guard outside. I didn't have to understand their language to know what he was telling them: Grab your gear, double-time it to the helicopter and prepare for takeoff. Our work in Noia is done.

Fortunately, our mission had been quick, clean and fruitful. We hadn't damaged the historical site—aside from a pair of locks that could easily be repaired—and it was clear to Dujok that it had been overkill to come loaded up with weapons. Especially considering the grim prognosis of the only enemy who might have stood in our way: Colonel Nicholas Allen.

I know this will sound strange, but I felt at ease for the first time since this whole fiasco began. I was exhausted from the tension. The racing around, my nerves, not knowing anything about Martin—all of it had sapped my strength. And now that my world started to clear a bit, my brain started to release the necessary endorphins to bring me a modicum of peace.

During that momentary respite, I thought back on Dujok calling himself Martin's teacher, and it reminded me of something that happened years ago, back in London, just after our wedding, a time filled with such excitement—and so many secrets. One of the few Martin shared with me happened to him on an esplanade in northern Turkey, not too far from the site where we were now headed. And it happened the day he met his "sheikh," an Arab word that means "teacher" or "wise man"—a word whose depth I was only now beginning to grasp.

Their friendship was forged during the one and only time Martin had ever been captured, and on the very day he lost a companion. His colleague, he told me, was a stubborn, hardened soldier who disappeared before his very eyes during a mountain storm. "You know, one of those powerful squalls you only see at high altitudes—and that always end badly," he told me. Whether his colleague had died or not that day had always been a mystery to him. "That storm, Julia, was like nothing I've ever seen before." He said it came without warning, a wall of grayness that seemed to rise out of the earth and overwhelm them in mere seconds. The terror on his face as he recounted the story said it all. It had been years since that day, but he still had nightmares about that whirlwind of sand and stone that consumed them. He started to shake just at the memory. Something about that day rattled his understanding of the world, "like one of those magnetic storms in science fiction movies," he told me.

And that's when he told me his deepest secret.

He said that amid that chaos, a force that felt like a pair of steel arms grabbed him and tossed him violently. He hadn't seen any machines nearby that could have been responsible for it; it made no sense. But he swears it wasn't a dream or a hallucination. And, moreover, he thought he caught a glimpse of whose arms they were: At the center of that swirling storm he thought he saw an inhuman angular face with glowing red expressionless eyes, and he felt he needed to fight for his life. "Like Jacob and the angel, remember?" he had said. But Martin didn't have the energy left to resist. Dizzy and disoriented, he tried to crawl away from that monster, but instead he only managed to move toward it in his stupor. When he realized his mistake, it was too late. He had crawled into some kind of electrical storm and found himself floating in midair with sparks and flashes zigzagging all around him.

That was as much as he could ever bring himself to say. I think he was too scared to get into the details. Or maybe he just couldn't remember. In fact, the few times I ever asked him about that day again, he said what had saved him had been the familiar theme in his life: John Dee. Needless to say, he was obsessed with the man. And after hearing the rest of the story, I understood why.

While he was inside the whirlwind, one detail made him think of Dee. Before Martin fell unconscious, the whirlwind blew him toward a rocky ledge, to which he held on with all his might. And carved into the stone, he swore he saw a familiar symbol: ⅂

Seeing that glyph emblazoned on a stone so close to Ararat reminded him of a spell he had learned from his aunt Sheila, one used to conjure storms.

Martin had practiced the incantation so many times that now, even exhausted, he could muster the strength to recite it once again:

"Dooaip Qaal, zacar, od zamram obelisong," he cried out.

His words drowned in the swirling tempest. And just as he was about to say them again, something changed.

It's as if the sparks flying all around him paused to hear more.

"Dooaip Qaal, zacar, od zamram obelisong!" he yelled.

And he yelled it again.

After the third time, he could sense that his words were having some kind of effect. It's as if he had called out "Open sesame!" and it had triggered an end to the nightmare. Everything came to a standstill. His body was bruised and burned in places, and he barely had enough strength remaining to breathe. But he was alive. And in a second, the electrical field that had held him in midair evaporated, and he crashed to the ground, losing consciousness.

When he awoke, he found himself in the home of the man who went on to care for him for eight long weeks. The man had been so impressed to see a foreigner survive an attack from the "Guardian of the Earth" that he concluded it must have been divine providence. "If you defeated the monster the way Gilgamesh defeated the steel lions, it is because your heart is pure," he told Martin.

It turned out that this humble and generous man was the same one who had taken him there to die; Martin's enemy had become his friend. He told Martin about those mysterious guardians, how they appear different to each person and how they had been placed there—dormant and invisible—to protect an ancient treasure. He taught my husband how to control the forces of nature and overcome his fears—to be "like

Enoch, who was consumed by a whirlwind and yet managed to overcome it to return home."

Martin always spoke warmly of this man, as if he were part of the family. He called him only "my sheikh."

But now, I realized his true identity: Artemi Dujok.

64

Antonio Figueiras arrived at the Lavacolla airport just as his unwanted reinforcements hit the tarmac. And he was nervous about it. Now there were *two more* Americans interested in his case, and they were important enough that the chief ordered Figueiras himself to attend to them. He hadn't managed to shut his eyes the entire night, especially after hearing that the army didn't have any luck finding the rogue helicopter. They said something had been interfering with the radar throughout the night.

He nervously paced the terminal with a well-worn copy of the morning's *La Voz de Galicia* under his arm.

"Inspector Figueiras?"

A woman's voice snapped him back to reality and he was stunned when he turned around to see her. She was a curvy young brunette dressed in tight pants and a black Armani blazer, one hand on a leather briefcase, the other extending a hand in greeting. And God, what a lovely hand it was. Her long, slender fingers, with perfectly manicured nails, slipped like silk into his large, rough paw.

"M-Me? I mean, yeah, that's me," he stammered in only passable English. "And you must be . . ."

"Ellen Watson, from the Office of the President of the United States."

"The Office of the President . . . ?"

Ellen smiled. She loved how announcing her title unnerved others. Especially men.

"And this is my partner, Tom Jenkins, intelligence adviser," she said. "I hope you'll get along famously because you're going to be working together."

With the pleasantries out of the way, Figueiras led them out to the parking lot. Ellen Watson headed for the rental counter to get herself the fastest vehicle in the fleet, while Figueiras was left with her stiff counterpart.

Just my luck, Figueiras thought.

The American wasn't going to be much of a talker, Figueiras figured. He sat shotgun in Figueiras's Peugeot, snapped on his seat belt and said nothing other than telling Figueiras to take him to see Colonel Allen. He didn't have to hear another word to realize he wasn't going to be able to squeeze this guy for any information on the case. Just like it was any time he worked with a secret service agency, the relationship was going to be one-sided: They would ask for everything and leak nothing in return.

"This is shaping up to be a pretty complicated case, huh?" Figueiras said, trying to spark some kind of conversation as he weaved his way out of the airport and sped back toward the city. Daybreak was upon them and it looked like it would be clear in Santiago, not like the day before. "Two of my men were murdered last night while they were investigating some kind of aircraft that landed in the plaza outside the cathedral. Some kind of . . . *foreign* aircraft. You wouldn't happen to know anything about that, would you?"

"Was that what they used to kidnap Julia Álvarez?"

"That's what we think."

The American smiled enigmatically but said nothing.

"Something funny, Mr. Jenkins?"

"Today's your lucky day, Inspector," he said, reaching in his pocket for his cell phone. "At this very moment, the helicopter you're looking for is near these coordinates: forty-two degrees, forty-seven minutes latitude north, eight degrees, fifty-three minutes longitude west."

Figueiras shrugged his shoulders. "I don't know much about maps."

"They correspond to the little town of Noia, Inspector," Jenkins said. "Our satellites have located Julia Álvarez there. But don't worry, we won't let them get her out of the country."

"And how do you intend to stop them? You're just two . . ."

Jenkins again broke in with that smug, self-satisfied smirk. "And where do you think my partner is racing to at this very moment?"

"To . . . Noia?"

Jenkins nodded. "Once she's there, if she needs backup, she'll know to call for it. That's why we've got you, isn't that right, Inspector?"

Figueiras immediately tensed up and began gesticulating frantically with his hands. "We're dealing with murderers, Mr. Jenkins! We should contact the station and have them send reinforcements right away. You can't leave these killers to a woman!"

Jenkins grabbed Figueiras's hand and planted it on the steering wheel. "You worry about driving and not getting us killed, Figueiras," Jenkins said. "This is above your pay grade, boss. Let us take care of this our way and I'll personally hand over your suspects."

"Your way?" Figueiras's voice cracked. He pressed down on the gas pedal.

"We have more resources dedicated to this case than you can imagine, Inspector. We're just as interested in Julia Álvarez's and her husband's safety as you are, believe me."

"In that case, I'm going to be following your every move," Figueiras said, pounding the steering wheel. "Goddamn it, those dead cops weren't just my men. They were my friends!"

"I'm on your side, Inspector. But right now, I need you to get me to Nicholas Allen—alive! Watch the road!"

Figueiras adjusted his glasses and gunned the accelerator. "Okay. We'll be there in five minutes."

65

Outside Santa María a Nova, things took an unexpected turn.

A split second before he saw his partner Janos fall to the ground face-first in a heap, Waasfi—Dujok's right-hand man—felt a puff of air on his cheek and a buzz by his ear as if a rocket-powered mosquito had shot past him.

"Gun!" he yelled, adrenaline immediately surging.

The wall of marble tombs at his back chipped, and there was no doubt they were under attack.

Crack, crack, crack!

Three silent shots whizzed past him as he ducked for cover and a red laser hopped from tomb to tomb, looking for a living victim.

Janos was fifteen feet away; his nose was broken, and blood dripped down his face and left arm as he writhed in pain, their so-called *Amrak* just inches away. The men had sworn a blood oath to protect what was inside that chessboard-sized box.

Just before entering Santa María a Nova, Dujok had ordered his men to position the *Amrak* outside the temple entrance. If the adamant they were searching for was inside, the *Amrak* would likely activate it. Their sheikh knew that one of the Yezidi's secret towers had been built in this very spot centuries ago—what the ancients called the *finis terrae,* the end of the earth—and he trusted his men to handle the *Amrak's* mysterious power. They were to awaken and place it on the northern wall, just below the catacomb of one Pedro Alonso de Pont. But Janos doubted Dujok's plan. He was a mercenary, an expert in chemical and biological weapons who trained at Saddam's death camps until they discovered his mother was a Kurd and his father a Yezidi priest. And he had thought all along that Dujok's plan was madness. He worried that if the *Amrak* reacted the way it had that night in Santiago, anyone within thirty feet of it could be killed. And that might mean none of them would get out alive.

Waasfi watched dispassionately as Janos writhed in agony. Providence, Waasfi figured, had punished him for his sinful insolence.

He calmly switched the safety off on his machine gun and adjusted the high-tech infrared scope. Waasfi knew his sheikh was finishing important work inside the church and that the mission's success now depended on him. So without turning to shoot wildly, he sized up the situation.

When he saw Janos leaving a bloody trail as he dragged himself for cover, Waasfi knew he wouldn't be of any help. Judging from the position of Janos's wound, Waasfi figured he must have a punctured lung. Dujok was still inside, and Waasfi couldn't see where his other partner, Haci, was. He had originally set up on a balcony just outside the cemetery.

Maybe he was already dead.

What else could go wrong?

Of course. The *Amrak*.

Just before they were ambushed, the *Amrak* had done something unexpected. Janos had reluctantly removed the leaden top, allowing the cool night air to flow inside. He peeked in and couldn't believe what he was seeing. The object's surface was rough and black and scarred and looked as if some ancient unintelligible language had been scored into its surface. But when Noia's humid air washed over it, it began to change colors. The "slate" pulsed red and began emitting a rhythmic chirping, like an alarm.

"What the . . . ?"

But Waasfi's voice crackled over the walkie-talkie and told him to hurry up and put it next to the tomb where their teacher had ordered them to, without complaining or second-guessing.

Before Janos could comply with the order, a thirty-caliber bullet plunged into his back and sent him face-first to the ground. Janos felt his heart stop for a full three seconds, leaving him breathless.

Waasfi then saw their attacker dash along the cemetery's perimeter. He was carrying an assault rifle, and from the way he moved, he looked well-trained. He moved in a zigzag pattern that Waasfi recognized. *A SEAL? Here?* Waasfi wouldn't move a muscle as he waited to get a clear look at his target. Unfortunately, they saw each other at exactly the same moment.

Waasfi had no choice. He squeezed the trigger, firing off six rounds a second and knocking his enemy against a wall of tombs. He was dead before he hit the ground.

There was barely time to let it sink in. The unmistakable sounds of footsteps crunching over gravel were at his back, and he turned just in time to unload another barrage of gunfire and see another heavily armed navy SEAL fall to the ground in a motionless lump.

Two.

The adrenaline from nearly being ambushed shook his entire body. And that's when he remembered Haci. Although their enemies were using silencers, Haci should have heard his gunfire. The sound seemed to come from everywhere; Santa María a Nova was encircled by apartment buildings and thus the cemetery was surrounded by walls, forming a virtual soundstage. *They must have killed Haci* . . . And that's when he remembered something else: SEAL assault teams never operate in pairs. They are always in teams of six or more.

"Lower your weapons and come out with your hands up," he heard an American voice say. "We've got you surrounded."

Waasfi lay flat against the ground, silent. He slithered across the dirt until he reached a large stone crucifix and a stone wall he could use for cover. He wasn't about to give up. He knew if he could make out where the voices were coming from, he still had a chance.

He saw a third soldier headed for the main entrance to the church, where Dujok and Julia Álvarez were oblivious to everything outside. His sheikh and the seer were helpless. And that's why Waasfi didn't hesitate. He fixed the crosshairs of his night-vision scope on the soldier's left temple.

"Give yourself up and abandon your position!" the American voice said just as Waasfi squeezed the trigger. "Otherwise we will open fire—"

The third soldier went down, and the Armenian crossed himself, thanking God—and his uncle for having provided him with armor-piercing bullets.

Waasfi narrowed his vision. *Are they carrying heavy artillery?*

He'd barely finished the thought when five bullets splintered the stone an inch above his head, destroying the Latin inscription. *They're shooting to kill.* He grabbed the Uzi and hit the ground as a fresh barrage of gunfire covered him in marble dust from overhead. Falling backward, Wassfi looked up to find his executioner standing above him.

He was huge, dressed in black and had Waasfi dead in his sights.

A bullet buried itself next to Waasfi's knee. And then another. And another. That bastard in the ski mask had Waasfi at his mercy and was toying with him like a lion with its prey.

"Pray . . . ," the voice said, muffled behind the black ski mask.

"What?"

"Pray to whatever God you believe in, motherfucker."

Waasfi's mind immediately went to Melek Taus, the angel that was sworn to protect their clan, and he clung to his rifle, hoping at least to be remembered as a hero. His last thought was for his uncle. The man who had converted him. Sheikh Artemi Dujok.

And then came the shot.

It came somewhere from the east and smashed the soldier's Adam's apple. He gurgled his last breath as Waasfi looked around, confused.

Praise be to God!

Haci had stealthily crawled across the cemetery and saved his life.

That's four . . .

"You all right, kid?"

"Yeah. Yeah!"

Waasfi hopped up, fueled by adrenaline, and signaled for his partner to meet him at the cathedral's north wall to regroup. They first had to secure the *Amrak*. Haci, a wiry man with bulging eyes who had grown up fighting on the border between Armenia and Turkey, calculated the distance and danger to the meeting spot. There, Janos was struggling to pull himself together. He held the "box" tight against his chest and tried to wriggle his way toward the north wall. Lying between others' final resting places helped to keep him focused on staying alive.

The American's voice came over the megaphone. "This is your last chance!" But this time, the voice seemed farther off. "Turn over the transmitter and we'll spare your life."

Transmitter? Janos shook his head. *That's what they call this thing?*

"Five . . . four . . ."

The American voice counted down.

"Three . . ."

Waasfi and Haci pointed their rifles left, then right, unable to determine where the voice was coming from.

"Two . . ."

There was a pause.

"One."

Janos felt a pull, like a vacuum sucking him backward. A puff of smoke. Something huge and hot sailed overhead, destroying a wall of Santa María a Nova. Janos instinctively tried to cover his ears. But the blast had already blown his eardrums. *Wait, didn't they want the* Amrak? he thought as a flurry of machine-gun fire exploded. He figured his partners had opened fire. As he felt along the ground with his good arm, trying to find the box containing the *Amrak* in the shower of dust and smoke, a pair of large, powerful hands grabbed him under the arms and dragged him inside the church.

"We've got to get out of here!" he heard Waasfi yell. "Now!"

66

First came the explosion.

Then the noise and the rumbling and the smell of hundred-year-old dust and scorched earth.

And if you had asked me then, I'd have said I thought the angel of the apocalypse himself had batted me across the back with his golden trumpet, launching me into Dujok's laptop and against Juan de Estivadas's sarcophagus. *Oh, Jesus . . . !* My knees crashed onto the floor, my forearms and face fell against the cold, hard ground, and I finally came to rest somewhere near the middle of the church.

When I had stopped bouncing from stone to stone, it felt like I was broken deep inside. The pain throughout my body and the metallic taste of blood in my mouth made me wish I had lost consciousness. I should have been woozy, disoriented. But instead, I felt all of my senses heightened; a shock wave was bringing me back from the brink. The room started spinning. I lay on my back, my clothes in charred tatters, and one of my boots had been knocked clear across the floor.

For a minute, I lay perfectly still as my body and mind regained their composure. A dust cloud floated throughout Santa María a Nova and settled over me, and I began coughing violently and painfully.

"Are you okay?"

Artemi Dujok staggered toward me in the settling mist, coughing and trying to wave the dust cloud from his face.

"Julia! Say something!"

He inched his soot-covered face close to mine. He shook me, then tried unsuccessfully to lift me.

"C'mon, Julia, we've got to get out of here."

"What's happened?"

"No time to explain. Come on, get up. Here, this way . . ."

He finally managed to help me to my feet and we stumbled toward the wall where Juan de Estivadas's crypt had rested. It had been blown to smithereens.

"Here. This way. Follow me."

I wasn't sure what he was thinking. I knew there was another twenty-foot wall in the direction we were headed, but I was too weak and dizzy to argue. I followed him. I didn't expect to trip over a mass on the ground. I looked down and saw that it was one of Dujok's men, and I started to realize the severity of the situation. It was Janos, slumped over and grabbing at a bleeding wound in his side.

"Keep moving, Julia."

"But your man—"

"Janos knows what he has to do. We need to get out of here."

As I watched Dujok disappear into the swirling smoke, I started to realize what had happened. A bomb—or some kind of explosive—had gone off outside the church, blasting shards of marble and stone in all directions. The enemy Dujok was so reticent to talk about had finally caught up to us. And the damage they had caused to the centuries-old church was inconceivable. The blast had blown a hole in the eastern wall, the oldest part of the church, turning centuries-old relics into dust—among them the base of an ancient monument. Where stone had once stood, there was now a dust-covered set of narrow stairs leading down into the basement.

At first, I thought I was seeing things, still shaken from the blast. But it was no illusion. Dujok hurried down the stairs, and I followed him.

At the bottom of the stairs, we came to a wall and found a small crawl space about three feet high that Dujok quickly began to squirm through.

"What are you waiting for?" I heard him yell from the other side.

I hesitated—until I heard footsteps rushing up from behind me. They resounded throughout the cavernous church. And I knew that whoever had caused this kind of destruction—and likely had kidnapped Martin as well—meant business.

I dove into the tunnel just as a single thunderclap of gunfire exploded somewhere upstairs in the church.

Janos! Oh, God . . . !

Sure that Janos had been killed, I quickly wriggled through the small tunnel and out of the church. The ancient drainpipe went on for about a hundred feet east beneath Calle Escultor Ferreiro and joined what was undoubtedly part of the city's sewer system. Daylight from the drains above us lit our path through the ancient sewers, which stank of urine and rotten eggs, but at least they were leading us farther away from the church.

"What's going on?" I said, pulling myself out of the other end of the pipe and into a newer section where we could stand upright. I tried to take inventory of my situation: I was missing my boot, and my clothes were infused with such a wretched stench that I fought not to gag.

"They found us, that's what's happened."

"Colonel Allen?"

"Him or his people, who knows?" he said, grabbing me by the arm and rushing up the tunnel. "One thing's for sure. They're after you . . . and this."

Dujok held my adamant in his left hand as we rushed ahead. It was still emitting a soft glow.

"Just promise me one thing," I said. "Promise me we'll find him."

"Martin? Of course we will! And now we know exactly where he is. He's a stone's throw from Ararat. Right now, we've got to get out of here—"

"No! No, you can't leave me hanging by a thread like this, Mr. Dujok! I'm just supposed to keep following you around on blind faith? How do I even know the adamant sent that signal to find Martin?"

I'd stopped thinking straight. My head was spinning as I found myself shoeless and disoriented, limping along the sticky and slippery bowels of the city of Noia. My heart was pounding, my breathing labored, and I felt like I might pass out or throw up at any minute.

"Keep your voice down!" he hissed. "And keep moving!"

"No, I won't shut up!" I said, my voice now rebounding through the drain system, bordering on hysterics. "They're trying to kill us. *They're trying to kill us!*"

"Shut your mouth!"

"No, no, I won't! *I won't!*"

Dujok squeezed my hand to the point where I winced. "Don't you understand the kind of people who are after us?"

"I don't care! I want to get out of here. *Let me out of here!*" I yelled, blind with fear, and wrenched my arm free, making Dujok lose his balance at the edge of a small ramp leading down. He slipped and fell hard to his knees against the stone ground where a river of filth flowed.

His Uzi crashed down with a splash and disappeared down the slope. His eyes flashed with an incandescent rage that shook me out of my histrionics. And for a few brief seconds, I thought Artemi Dujok was going to tear me limb from limb. He picked himself up, rubbing his aching knees, and turned his attention toward the street above us, listening, standing perfectly still. I was trembling . . .

"You hear that?" he said.

I was still waiting for his retribution. But he just calmly looked down the tunnel behind us.

"Notice anything?"

"No . . ."

"I think they've stopped following us."

We froze and listened, hearing only the sound of water lapping gently across the ground. A few minutes passed. Dujok was right. And that respite was all I needed for my heart to slow. Although my body still ached and my head was pounding, I was starting to think clearly again.

"We should keep going . . . ," Dujok said calmly, breaking the silence.

I exhaled.

"You have nothing to worry about, Ms. Álvarez. I promise you everything will be all right."

Somewhere on the street above us, I heard the distant wail of police sirens, and I knew we couldn't stay here for long.

"You know, you remind me of Jacob," he said as we made our way down the tunnel.

"Which Jacob is that?"

"From the Bible. He lived an amazing life. He bought his family's birthright from his brother Esau. He fought and defeated an angel, even injured its leg. But most important, thanks to an adamant just like yours, he had a vision on his way to the promised land."

"He had an adamant?" I asked, while also amazed that Dujok could think of the Bible at a time like this.

"He rested his head against a stone—an adamant—and fell asleep during the journey, and what a dream he had! The skies opened up and he saw these heavenly creatures going up and down a fiery staircase—Jacob's ladder—oblivious to him. Without knowing exactly how he had done it, he had attracted the messengers of God and had used the adamant to open a portal for them to come to earth."

"And what does Jacob's story have to do with me, Mr. Dujok?" I said, sighing. "Is that what you did with my adamant? You used it to open a stairway to heaven?"

Artemi Dujok smiled for the first time in hours. "You're the one who said it . . ."

A sharp, far-off noise, as if another wall had just come crumbling down at the church behind us, made us hasten our step.

"And who do you hope will come down that staircase?"

"Angels. Beings of light. The messengers who are mentioned in all forms of religion, Ms. Álvarez. They're the only ones who can help us overcome the impending apocalypse."

"You really believe this?"

"I'm not the only one, Ms. Álvarez," he said, leading me to a clearing up ahead where the tunnel forked. "Martin believes it, too."

My thoughts went to my husband as we trudged along the dank underground cavern.

"Now that you mention him, I still haven't asked you why they've kidnapped him."

"Same reason they're after us. They want the adamants so they can be the first—and maybe the only ones—to open that passageway to the other side to speak directly to God."

"And they can do that with the adamants?"

"No. They also need the tablet to make them work."

Dujok climbed a set of corroded stairs that led up through the roof of the tunnel and into a round clearing—where Waasfi was waiting for us.

"Tablet? What kind of tablet?" I asked, following him up.

"Come up. Quickly," he said, helping me through. "I'll ask my men to show it to you. Today, you've earned at least that much."

67

The door to room 616 in the intensive-care wing of Our Lady of Hope swung open. Nicholas Allen had been starving for breakfast all morning and looked up hungrily. But he immediately lost his appetite. *Not this guy again . . .* he thought, rolling his eyes at the sight of Antonio Figueiras. A man he didn't recognize followed him in.

"Mr. Allen," Figueiras said in his muddled English, his trench coat a wrinkled mess, "one of your fellow countrymen has come to visit you."

An IV bag was dripping into his arm as Allen nodded at the new visitor. "If he's from the funeral home, tell them this one's still breathing," Allen grumbled.

Tom Jenkins feigned a smile. "Well, it's good to see you still have your sense of humor, Colonel."

"Do I know you?"

"Tom Jenkins. I work for the Office of the President of the United States. I've come here personally on his behalf."

"*Hmph.* The Office of the President? Well, that was fast."

"Our embassy in Madrid tells us you and Julia Álvarez were attacked with some sort of electromagnetic weapon about eight hours ago, is that right?"

"Who told you that?"

"The embassy's director of intelligence, Richard Hale."

"Oh, right. Rick," he said, letting his guard down a bit. "I guess Director Owen's got you up to speed on my mission."

Jenkins noticed the look of surprise on Inspector Figueiras's face. His English might not have been good enough to catch every detail of the conversation, but he understood enough. He still hadn't put two and two together, between the electromagnetic weapon and the blackout in Santiago the night before, but he was starting to get the idea.

"So tell me, Colonel. Any idea who got the drop on you?" Jenkins asked.

"Of course. I've already told Owen all about it. But if you want to know anything else"—he coughed—"you're going to have to wait for my final report."

"A report we'll never see because it belongs to Operation Elijah, isn't that right?"

Allen didn't answer.

"Listen to me, Colonel. It's urgent that we find the woman," Jenkins said. "We can't waste time with this bureaucratic nonsense."

"Why does the president of the United States care about Julia Álvarez?"

Tom leaned in to whisper something that Figueiras overhead—and that immediately made him perk his ears up.

"You know as well as I do, Allen. We need the stone. The president wants to be out in front of this whole situation."

Whatever weakness Allen felt was immediately gone as he sat himself straight up in his hospital bed.

"Listen, I don't know what you think you know about Elijah, but this operation has maximum priority. And you can't order me to tell you a damn thing. You hear me? Not a damn thing! You want answers? Talk to my boss."

Tom Jenkins snickered. "You'll have to play ball sooner or later, Colonel . . . ," Jenkins whispered, eyeing Figueiras, whose eyes were as wide as saucers.

Figueiras remembered his jeweler friend's information about the stones and now hearing the word in English confirmed there was a connection.

Jenkins continued. "Have it your way. We'll eventually find the woman and you and your men will go down as the unpatriotic rogue agents who ignored a direct order from your commander in chief."

Nick Allen tried to contain himself.

"May . . . I . . . ask a question, Colonel?" Figueiras ventured suddenly, feeling this might be his only chance to get some answers. "Do the initials 'TBC' mean anything to you? What do you know about the Betilum Company?"

Jenkins was even more surprised than Allen at the question.

"Where the hell did you hear about that?"

"Please, answer . . ."

Allen hesitated for a moment. "It's a phantom company owned by the agency, Inspector. That's all I can tell you. It's top-secret."

"Can you at least tell me why that company has been buying old manuscripts and first-edition books by one"—Figueiras flipped through his notebook—"John Dee?"

Allen was backed into a corner. That information wasn't easy to come by. The cop had done his homework. Everyone associated with Elijah knew Dee was Martin Faber's obsession. As it was his father's. Faber had worked for his father as a climatologist at the NSA until they started to distance themselves from the project and the agency took it over—putting Allen in charge of operations. Most recently, the agency had been trying to get its hands on as many of Dee's works as possible to try to understand what insights Faber and his father thought Dee might have.

"We needed . . ." Allen hesitated. "We wanted to decipher a symbol we found in some old photographs. Top-secret material. I can't say anything else."

Tom cut in. "Photos? When we were in Madrid, they told us about some old photos of Mount Ararat that Martin Faber had requested from the CIA before he resigned. Are we talking about the same ones?"

"Could be," Allen admitted reluctantly. So much for leading Figueiras down a dead end.

"And the symbol you were trying to decipher," the inspector said. "Could it be this one?"

Figueiras handed him the drawing in his notebook.

Nicholas Allen furrowed his brow at seeing the symbol. He took the notebook from the cop and wondered how much he could say. The symbol was from the cover of one of Dee's books, printed in 1564. That was no big secret. He figured Figueiras already knew that.

"Yes . . . That's the one," Allen said, handing him back the notebook.

"So what does this symbol have to do with the stones?" Jenkins asked. Figueiras was starting to get ticked off at Jenkins's butting in on his own investigation.

But Allen just turned away to face the window.

"It's okay, Colonel. You don't have to answer anything now," Jenkins said, patting Allen's leg. "You will soon enough, though. Because we know where the two adamants are at this very moment. Our satellites have pinpointed their location. And we also know where Julia Álvarez and her kidnapper are headed. And you know what else? You're coming with me to find them. To Turkey. Right now."

"Turkey?" Allen looked back at Jenkins. "I'm in the goddamn hospital!"

"I could go with you too," Figueiras said. But Jenkins ignored him.

"Colonel, you already know the country where the adamants are to be reunited, you speak the language, and you know both of the people who've been kidnapped. I'm asking you to help your president. Your country."

"And if I refuse?"

"Then I'll make sure you don't leave this hospital, Colonel. Ever."

68

"What is that tablet, exactly?"

Waasfi smiled and the snake tattooed on his cheek recoiled. I don't think he understood a word I said, but from my pantomime he knew I was talking about the object he was carrying in his black nylon backpack. The explosion at the church had left barely a scratch on him. His clothes weren't torn or charred, and he looked no worse for the wear.

"Ta-blet?" he repeated, pointing at his treasured possession. *"Amrak?"*

I nodded.

"It's a relic from John Dee's era, Ms. Álvarez," Dujok said from behind me. "He called it his 'table of practice' or 'invocation tablet.'"

As Dujok came up out of the tunnel and dusted off his clothes and boots, Waasfi opened the bag and let me peek inside.

At first, I thought it was empty. The bottom of the bag was dark and wrinkled, and I never imagined *that* could be John Dee's famous relic. But as I could see by the approaching daylight, I was wrong. There was indeed something in the bag, a coarse, square tablet that looked like it was made of coal, covered in bumps and pits. Inscrutable inscriptions were scrawled all over it. It clearly had been weathered over the years . . . or eons.

"Not since the disappearance of the Ark of the Covenant—about a thousand years before the birth of Christ—had God given us instructions on how to build another sacred object. That is, until he gave us what you are looking at," Dujok said, standing over the tablet.

"And you think it was God who . . ."

"It was the archangel Uriel." Dujok smiled. "Rather, that's what John Dee explains in his book *De heptarchia mystica.* Uriel, a being whose head shone as bright as the sun, with long, flowing hair and a dazzling light gleaming from his left hand, appeared to Dee. He handed him two stones and went on to give him instructions on how to build this tablet, this 'invocation tablet.'"

"And that's what you dug up in Biddlestone."

"Precisely. Martin found it and wanted to activate it on your wedding day. And since that day, it hasn't stopped emitting signs of life."

"What kinds of signs?"

"Well, for starters, it maintains a constant temperature of sixty-four degrees Fahrenheit. No other mineral on Earth does that."

"Doesn't seem like such an important detail."

"Oh, but it is. Every detail is important."

"Okay, well, do you have an idea why the angels would give John Dee this object?"

Dujok placed his hand on my shoulder the way a father would a daughter. "That's a very good question. Martin and I ask each other that all the time and we always come to the same conclusion. Here's how I see it: Dee spent the last few years of his life obsessed with writing what he called the Book of Nature. He believed the universe could be read the way you read a grimoire, a book of spells. Moreover, he believed you could manipulate the universe if you changed around the words that were used to create the universe—that is, if you understood the language God used in the creation. But the fact is the angels seemed anxious about entrusting him with this tablet. So they told Dee that it was imperative that he learn this secret language, the foreign tongue that would allow him to modify the work of God. Imagine: It must have been like trying to teach genetics to an eleven-year-old—there was no way. They warned him that the survival of the human race depended on him, that cataclysmic climate changes and unrivaled destruction would happen if he couldn't master the language and use the tablet. But he died before they ever finished their lessons."

"So what ever happened with these natural disasters?"

"They came to pass, Ms. Álvarez." Dujok sighed. "They certainly did."

"Really?"

"A few years after his death, around 1650, Europe suffered one of the worst climate shifts in the last nine thousand years. Temperatures dropped and entire crops were lost. Thousands of families died of famine and sickness. And using today's technology, we know why. It was all because of the sun. The sun's magnetic activity reached historic lows. Astronomy books would come to refer to those times as the Maunder Minimum, when sunspots were exceedingly rare. And the effects lasted well into the eighteenth century. We think that's what the angels wanted to warn Dee about, but he was never able to understand."

"And you think you can do a better job?"

"Well . . ." He smiled. "If his holy messengers reestablished communication with us now, I think we'd be able to do a much better job. Unlike the time of Dee and Moses, we live in an age where we have access to the language of science, not just story and metaphor. And we can interpret the messages more accurately. That's why it's important for us to be the ones to establish communication and not someone who might use the knowledge for some other, dark purpose."

"So, you're not in this for religion or power or wishful thinking."

"No, miss. We're in this for the sheer survival of the human race. And we know that the angels only speak by way of the tablet and the adamants when they have something vital to communicate to us. And this time is no different. Of that, I'm sure."

69

A full silvery moon hung over the National Mall as the president's bulletproof Cadillac pulled up to the White House. The Washington Monument cast a long, swordlike shadow toward the Reflecting Pool and the Lincoln Memorial. Roger Castle took that as an ominous sign as he paced the carpet of the Oval Office, calculating what his next move would be if Owen's men got their hands on the stones before his people did. Could he trust the NSA director? Who could he even talk to, given that he'd signed a confidentiality agreement not to discuss the Elijah project?

He'd never felt so alone.

He was sure no one else in his administration could ever understand something that, from the outside, might look like a bizarre eccentricity. Only he understood that it was much more than that.

Well, at least I know Elijah exists. Dad was right . . .

And just like that, his mind flashed to dinner the night after the reception with the Hopi Indians. It's funny how memory works. A single musical note, the scent of perfume, anything can take you back to a far-off time you thought you had forgotten . . . This time, it was the mention of a name while visiting with Michael Owen that had taken him back: Chester Arthur. It was White Bear, the barrel-chested elder with a lifetime's worth of worries wrinkled into his forehead, who recalled Chester Arthur signing the executive order that gave the Hopi two and a half million acres in the heart of Arizona in 1882.

"But it was a cursed gift," White Bear had told him. "Until that day, our tribe had been hounded by colonists who despised us and missionaries who wanted to convert us. Having our own land was like rain for a people in a terrible drought."

"So where's the curse?" Castle had asked. He knew that Arthur was sensitive to America's ethnic tribes of New Mexico and Nevada and wanted to grant them their own space away from pillagers and invaders. He couldn't convince White Bear to concede the point.

The eighty-five-year-old tribesman had gone to Santa Fe that day to tell something important to a white man with power, with influence. He chose Castle.

"You know, Mr. Governor, it amazes me the lengths to which politicians will go to get votes."

"Why do you say that? The reception isn't to your liking?"

"No, it's wonderful," White Bear said, smiling. "It's just that . . . I wonder, if you knew what our ancestors said about humanity's future, whether you wouldn't spend more time with your family and less time at these parties."

"Oh, so you want me to retire? Is that it?" Castle joked.

"No, I want you to be prepared. The prophecy is very clear."

"Prophecy?" he said as a waiter refilled his coffee cup. "What does your prophecy predict?"

"That we are near the end of the fourth world, Mr. Governor. Our children, and perhaps even we, will live to see the end of our civilization."

"The fourth world? I'm only aware of this world, my friend . . ."

The old Indian smiled kindly. "We know very little about the first world. Man did not exist then to witness the volcanic eruptions and landslides that brought about its end. And fortunately, neither did he endure the freezing earth of the second. Now the third . . . we certainly suffered its destruction."

"The third . . . ?"

"The third world was destroyed by an apocalyptic flood."

"Ah, yes, the Great Flood!"

The old man nodded. "That is what you Christians call it. Though you all have tried to forget what happened just before the catastrophe. The Hopi do not. Our elders still tell the story of the capital of the last world—the Washington, DC, of its time, if you will: Kasskara. It was founded on an island in the middle of the ocean. But it sank below the seas as the waters rose."

"I know that myth, too . . ."

"Everybody knows it, Mr. Governor. But the question is, do people believe it? The ancient Kasskarans were the last ones who had the privilege of speaking directly to the gods. The "high and respected sages" called their gods the Kachinas, bestowed the knowledge of the ages on the citizens of that great land. For millennia, they were the true kings of Earth. They built flying machines, could communicate over long distances, controlled the forces of wind and rain and even had the power to destroy an entire country overnight. When President Arthur first heard the story of the Kasskarans and realized how much their story resembled that of the city of Atlantis, he acknowledged the Hopi as the keepers of an ancient truth he was interested in. And he went about trading US land for that knowledge. And that, Governor, is why I say his gift was cursed."

White Bear ignored Castle's incredulous stare. If Castle had known then what he came to know about Arthur's fascination with the "Big Secret" and the end of days, he might have paid closer attention.

"Despite all their science and their technological advances, the Kachinas weren't able to stop the great flood. When they realized that destruction was inevitable, they decided to save at least some of the human race. And they entrusted them with a gift to help humanity survive the next great catastrophe."

"A lifeboat?"

White Bear continued, unfazed. "A sacred stone, Governor. Or rather several stones, which were hidden throughout the four corners of the earth in sacred places."

"A rock doesn't sound like much of a gift."

"Do not be so quick to judge. One very powerful stone was brought here, to what is now New Mexico and Arizona. It was carved by the Kachinas and hidden in a secret place where only the chiefs of each tribe may visit it from time to time. They seek out the oracle to know whether it has anything to tell us, anything to warn us about. President Arthur learned of the oracle from one of my ancestors and he consulted it on various occasions. I visited it for the first time in 1990. And I can tell you, Governor, that it remains hidden in that very place."

"So did the stone have anything to say to you?" Castle said, holding back a smile.

"I feared I would leave this earth without it ever speaking to me. That is, until this week. And now, Governor, I wish it had spared me and spoken instead to my successor. Because something has happened . . ."

"What is it?"

"The recent drought and falling water levels of our major rivers convinced me it was time to visit the oracle again. And this time, after three thousand years of silence, the stone has spoken again. I know what you're thinking. And no, I'm not crazy." A darkness had overcome White Bear. "Believe me or don't, but the stone has foretold that the end of the fourth world is upon us. Possibly in as little as a few years. Our people swore an oath to the government of the United States when they signed the pact with President Arthur, and I've come to you on their behalf. You, as the governor, can speak to the White House before this chain of events begins to unfold. And you *must* do it, quickly. If you like, I could take you to consult the stone yourself, so that you can speak with authority before the nonbelievers."

70

Sergeant Major Jerome Odenwald shook with fury as he looked through the scope of his M72 grenade launcher at his target. The motherfuckers who killed four of his fellow soldiers—his brothers—and injured another were going to pay. He didn't care whether he'd be court-martialed and charged with war crimes for turning a small town in northern Spain—clearly a NATO territory—into a war zone or for risking the lives of civilians. Odenwald was blind with rage. Still, the adrenaline from coming across one of their enemies in the church and blowing his brains out had started to subside. The more he thought about it, he should have shot him in the stomach and let him die a slow death—the bastard. But that still wouldn't have given him the answers he wanted. Like how that son of a bitch ended up with a high-powered military rifle. Or where the hell he'd been trained to use it with such deadly accuracy.

But Odenwald *was* sure of one thing: The killers he was lining up in his scope weren't your garden-variety terrorists. Certainly not the low-level risks described back at headquarters.

The soldier switched off his radio and focused on the targets in his scope.

"I've got you now . . . ," he whispered.

Three men and one woman—Dujok, Waasfi, Haci and Julia Álvarez—had just emerged from an underground sewer near the entrance to the Noela Theater. The SEAL recognized them immediately. They were running from the chaos just down the road, where a swarm of cops and paramedics were trying to make sense of what had happened.

But just as he started to squeeze the trigger, he noticed the tired filthy group gather around something on the ground, some object they pulled out of a black bag.

The *Amrak*!

Odenwald froze. His eyes widened. That was his mission objective.

He took his finger off the trigger and felt around for the "whisper detector," a directional surveillance device built into his weapon. Through the earphones underneath his wool skullcap, he could hear any conversation up to five hundred feet away. He pointed his weapon, flipped the switch and listened.

". . . Ms. Álvarez . . ." Artemi Dujok's military-like voice sounded clear in Odenwald's earphones. "You're looking at the world's oldest radio. It's four thousand years old and works just as it did the first day."

Four thousand years . . . Odenwald adjusted the volume.

Dujok continued. "Martin and I spent years trying to find it. Finally, Martin discovered where it was hidden after deciphering a list of angelic names Dee wrote before he died."

"And the list said you could use this to . . . to speak to God?" the young woman stuttered while glancing at the *Amrak.* "How did it get to Biddlestone?"

"One legend has it that Saint Jeremiah used this very tablet to interpret the Word of God and write the Bible's Book of Jeremiah. Thanks to this stone, he was able to foresee the turbulent times that would lie ahead for Jerusalem, the coming of Nebuchadnezzar and the Babylonian Exile. So to keep such a precious artifact from falling into the wrong hands, Jeremiah took it as far away as he could, as far as the British Isles . . .

"We also know that this object only becomes active when it feels the electromagnetic force of an adamant on one of these 'special days,' and when there is someone special—like Jeremiah—to act as the catalyst. And you, Julia, have made this tablet come to life twice, without even knowing it. No other person we've met has ever done anything like it."

Odenwald had heard enough. He was sure that was the item his team had been ordered to secure. If his aim was true—and it always was—those bastards had exactly three seconds to live before he could get his hands on the *Amrak* and end this goddamn mission.

Maybe his permanent record wasn't completely screwed after all.

71

Despite the hand and seat warmers in her rented BMW K1200 motorcycle, Ellen Watson couldn't shake the freezing cold in her bones. So
she just cranked the throttle and zoomed ahead. She knew there was no
time to waste if she hoped to catch up to Julia Álvarez and her kidnappers before they left Noia, which is why she opted for a motorcycle. Although the little fishing village was only about twenty-five miles outside
of Santiago, it was beyond a wet and foggy valley that made the trip take
almost an hour. The road between the towns had been under construction for years, so unless she had a fast ride, the drive could take forever.

She made the right choice.

It was twenty minutes to nine when the motorcycle's one-hundred-
ten-horsepower engine rumbled onto Rua de Juan de Estivadas in the
town of Noia. She'd be at the center of town in no time. The GPS talking into her Bluetooth earphone counted down the meters to her destination. But she found it strange that none of the local businesses were
open yet.

Don't these people work for a living?

It wasn't until she turned the final corner toward her destination
that she saw the silhouette of a person. The young man was leaning
over the hood of a pickup truck. Resting, maybe? And that's when she
noticed he was wearing a pair of Eagle-1 polycarbonate sniper goggles,
the kind US sharpshooters wear—and only when they're lining up a
target. She looked closer. He was wearing a ski mask. And there was
some kind of black cable coming out of his shirt and going into some
kind of walkie-talkie.

What the hell . . . ?

Ellen slammed on the brakes, propped up her bike and reached for
something in one of the saddlebags, her heart pounding in her ears.

He's gonna shoot! I've got to stop him . . . !

She was right. She watched as the soldier in black aimed the green tube of his rocket launcher up the street—right about the place where the satellite coordinates had led her.

I've got to stop him . . . one way or the other . . .

Just as he fiddled with the sight on his rocket launcher, she drew her pistol and lined up her shot.

"Freeze! Hands in the air!" she yelled.

He was unfazed. He settled the launcher on its target and reached around for the trigger. Ellen didn't think twice. Two shots from her Beretta broke the small village's silence. *Cack! Cack!* Only then did she take off her helmet, breathing in the mixture of gunpowder and salty sea air, to realize who she'd just shot. Blood from the muscular young man gushed out of the black assault SEAL uniform and pooled on the centuries-old cobblestone road.

Holy shit! He's one of ours!

Her two shots were true. One punctured his neck, the other his kidney and lungs. Kill shots, both of them.

At the end of the street, where the young SEAL had been aiming, she saw four dark silhouettes scrambling to pack up a backpack and take defensive positions. Three of them were men, and they were armed. The fourth was a woman with carrot-colored hair—a woman she recognized from the pictures she'd seen in Madrid. It was Julia Álvarez. Watson's gunshots had tipped them off.

She'd been trained to make split-second, life-and-death decisions, and now she wondered what her next move should be. She was alone and up against men who, according to military intelligence, were heavily armed, carrying a sophisticated electromagnetic weapon and had managed to kidnap a US agent and his wife.

I was a wreck.

With the explosion at Santa María a Nova still fresh in my mind, now I was shaken by two nearby shots. I recognized their hollow cracks right away. And with them, a hidden figure dressed in black camouflage and squatting behind a truck fell to the ground in a heap.

"*Anvrep kragoj!*" Waasfi yelled.

"Shooter!" Dujok yelled, translating. "Hit the deck!"

But he wasn't referring to the motorcyclist standing in the middle of the road, a small pistol still smoking in her hand. He seemed more worried about the soldier they hadn't seen on the ground.

"Take cover!" Dujok yelled.

I dove behind a blue car, trembling. "Wha . . . what's happening?"

"I . . . I have no idea!" Dujok said, uncharacteristically nervous and clutching his rifle.

Some five thousand miles from the Spanish coast, a supercomputer in the National Reconnaissance Office whirred dutifully as it analyzed information from the HMBB satellite.

"Jesus Christ, they've shot S23!"

S23 was Sergeant Odenwald's code name. A single bead of nervous sweat ran down Michael Owen's brow as he followed the operation from a monitor in the control room. *Thank God the president didn't have to see this . . . ,* he thought. A second later, the icon just below Odenwald's name on-screen went from green to red. He was dead. The real-time news streaming in from Spain kept getting worse. The captain of the USS *Texas* had just slammed shut his computer after Owen told him via video conference that he wasn't authorized to send in another team. Owen just didn't want to risk it. *The less I have to explain to Castle, the better.*

Meanwhile, Edgar Scott took off his glasses to wipe a tear with a tissue.

"Sir," the director of the NRO sniffled. It hadn't been easy for him to keep his composure and lie to the president of the United States. "I really don't mean to be out of line, but shouldn't we have told the president *everything* we know?"

"What do you mean *everything?*"

"You *know* that magnetic discharge wasn't the only one we detected in the last few hours," he said, pointing at another signal on the giant monitor. "What all about all these minor ones? There have been discharges all over the world. Jerusalem. Arizona. The one in Noyon, France, last night was especially significant—"

"It's all under control, Dr. Scott. We don't want another Church Crisis of 1999, do we?"

Scott bit his lip. "That was a long time ago, sir . . ."

What Owen called the Church Crisis brought back bad memories. That year, right about the time Nicholas Allen and Martin Faber had tried to steal the stone from Echmiadzin, a scientist at the National Center for Space Studies in Toulouse, France, who was studying images from an ERS satellite, discovered X emissions emanating from under six Gothic churches in northern France.

The engineer, Michael Temoin, had a run-in with his bosses after they ignored his findings. So he decided to investigate on his own—and almost made a mess of things. No one had told him he'd stumbled across information that was being used by a top-secret program to study energy emissions. His search took him to Amiens—the site of one of the six early Gothic cathedrals that had shown up on his images—where he unearthed a stone that he should never have seen without the permission of the Elijah project. And it put everyone in a bind. No one wanted an artifact that could have such serious scientific, historical and political repercussions becoming public knowledge. Luckily for Elijah, "climate change" wasn't as much a buzz word in 1999, and the press largely ignored it.

But the situation was different now. If a new, independent scientist showed a connection between energy emissions from those ancient beacons and a severe geological event—a euphemism for the end of the world—well, suffice it to say there would be ramifications. Big ones.

"That *will not* happen again, do you understand me, Dr. Scott?" Owen said, putting the argument to rest. "The situation in 1999 caught us all by surprise. None of us imagined the August eclipse over France would have produced those kinds of anomalies . . . the ones Nostradamus predicted. What we did in Noyon is what we're going to do here: We detect the signal, send in a team and secure the stone from under the crypt. Case closed."

"And you think we can cover *this* up just as easily?" Scott said, pointing at fresh information coming in from the HMBB satellite over Spain.

Owen froze.

"Wait. No. That can't be . . ."

Edgar Scott was quick to contradict him. "It is, sir. It certainly is . . ."

The computer had triangulated the position of the shooter who'd killed agent S23 and taken a snapshot of the killer's profile. It ran the image of the person in gray-and-white biker leathers through the NSA's database and came up with a match. A picture, a name and a designation flashed on the screen.

Michael Owen fell back into his chair.

Ellen Elizabeth Watson.

Office of the President. White House. Washington, DC.

74

I was paralyzed with fear.

Still, somehow I gathered up the courage to peek around the car and look out into the street, where someone had clipped off two shots. Two minutes had passed without a third. And that, I figured, was at least a good sign.

And that's when I saw her.

The biker was a woman. She slowly paced up the sidewalk by the Noela Theater with her hands in the air. And she was alone.

"I've dropped my gun! Don't shoot!" she yelled in perfect English that reverberated throughout the surrounding buildings. "I work for the Office of the President of the United States. I only want to talk to Julia Álvarez."

Hearing her say my name made something leap inside me. *Did she say she worked for the president of the United States?*

"Just keep your hands in the air and don't make any sudden movements, you got that?" Dujok said, poking the barrel of his rifle over the car's hood.

The woman nodded.

He asked whether I knew this woman and I shook my head. She was an attractive brunette and I would have remembered seeing her before.

"I can help you!" she yelled. "I know where Martin Faber is. I have the coordinates. I just want to make sure that Ms. Álvarez is all right and that you still have the stone that the Operation Elijah agents are searching for."

"What do you want with the stones?" Dujok shouted back.

Ellen let a smile slip; the man confirmed it—they did have the adamants.

With her hands still in the air, Ellen said, "I'm an aide to the president. And I know he has not authorized this operation. We're on the same side here."

This time, Dujok was the one to smile. I could see something had just popped into his head. He left his cover and walked toward the woman with the barrel of his assault rifle pointed down.

"If I can fill in the gaps about the Elijah project for the president, will you guarantee our safety until our mission is complete?"

"Mission? What mission?" Watson said.

"To get to Turkey, free Martin Faber and secure the adamants. That's it."

"Only if I can go with you."

"It's a deal."

Ellen Watson stretched out her hand and shook his. It was her best chance to get close to the adamants.

"And you are . . . ?"

"Artemi Ivanovich Dujok, baba sheikh of the ancient Melek Taus faith. We are the Yezidi."

"I've heard of your people . . ."

"Well, now you'll get to know the *truth* about us. C'mon, we'd better get moving."

75

Who has any right to call God?

Roger Castle kept turning over the question in his mind as he dialed New Mexico. He'd asked his secretary for a secure line and fifteen uninterrupted minutes to take care of a personal issue.

And what in the world could any human say that would be even mildly interesting to God?

He turned his chair to look out at the gardens behind the White House as the line rang. Someone picked up on the third ring.

"Andrew? Is that you?"

Andrew Bollinger's name had been in the president's address book for more than two decades, listed under the heading of "astronomers." In fact, they'd been friends since college and even played college basketball together. Ever since they'd met in class in 1982, Castle was sure that the proud southern kid was going to be a genius in math and physics. And he was. Bollinger was one of those guys who, with a little luck and enough funding, could help his country put a man on Mars. Anyone who might have known the two men back in the day would have bet on Bollinger to be the next great "it" kid. And that's the way it was until Castle entered politics. Bollinger got his doctorate in astrophysics by twenty-three and was heading up the Very Large Array Telescope (VLA) in Socorro, New Mexico, by twenty-seven. He helped put the VLA on the map after the movie *Contact* with Jodie Foster (although the center didn't actually spend its days listening out for radio signals from extraterrestrials). Now it wasn't just the philanthropists and communications companies who were paying the bills; tourists from all over lined up for guided tours and T-shirts in their gift shop. People from all walks of life are drawn to the promise of the VLA: to hear the "sounds" from deep space, from quasars and supernovas, to listen to the intrinsic radio signals that suns emit, and even to hear the message still being sent out by *Voyager 2* from the other side of Neptune.

So Castle couldn't imagine a better person to talk to now that so many celestial questions were piling up in his head.

"Andrew . . . Andrew Bollinger?" the president asked again, excited. Making a regular phone call to a friend was something of a treat for the president.

"Oh my God, Roger? Roger! What's going on, man?"

"Hey, I'm just glad you remember an old teammate."

"How could I not? I get to see you on the news every night. How long has it been? Four, five years?"

"At least. But it's been too long, Andy."

"So tell me, what can I, a mere servant, do for the president of the United States? Don't tell me it's a national emergency."

Andrew spent too much time behind a computer not to joke around when he finally was able to sneak in some human contact.

"Actually, I need to ask you something that requires your expertise."

"At your service, Mr. President. I know it must be important to finally be getting a call from you."

"It is . . . Do you remember White Bear?"

The line went silent for a moment.

"White Bear? The Hopi chief?"

"That's the one."

"Sure I remember him. Who could forget after that surreal trip we made out to his reservation or wherever the hell it was we ended up. I heard he died a while ago, didn't he?"

"Yes, years ago. Actually, it's that trip I want to ask you about. I need you to go down memory lane with me for a minute . . ."

How could they forget? How could either of them forget that radiant spring afternoon south of Carlsbad, hunting for a stone that speaks?

White Bear had asked Castle and Bollinger to meet him at the crossroads of Routes 62 and 285, near the Mexican border, to show them his tribe's most sacred treasure. Then-governor Castle had agreed to the meeting on one condition: that his most trusted scientist be allowed to go as well, someone who could help him understand the phenomenon. If there's one thing Castle had learned in his political career it was to listen to his experts. They were his life insurance policy—they kept him from making mistakes in front of the voters and became the perfect scapegoats if he did screw up.

White Bear agreed, but with a condition of his own: Castle and his friend would have to travel to their final destination wearing a blindfold and must swear never to speak of that visit to anyone else.

Both sides agreed.

In March, as the state offices slowed down for Holy Week, Castle and Bollinger went out to meet the Hopi. On Monday the thirteenth, the governor scribbled a quick note on his agenda, leaving his assistant the directions to the meeting site and a joke to call the national guard if they didn't hear back from him in twenty-four hours.

Not that the note would have been of any help. They changed cars three times. During the trip, White Bear reminded them that they must never say a word to anyone else about what they would see, telling them, "This is a sacred place. The white man is not welcome here." Not that he needed to worry. After so many twists and turns, they'd never in a million years be able to find their way back.

When they took off their blindfolds, they found themselves in some kind of mine. It was a cool, dark cave wired for electricity—power ran off a generator—that opened up to a wide room.

"You have nothing to fear," White Bear said, reading their faces.

"Your stone . . . is *here*?" Castle whispered.

"Right over there."

One of the chief's men shined a light on something that twinkled about three feet away.

It was a crystal about the size of a quarter. The edges were smooth but uneven. It was opaque and glistened like obsidian and looked like it had been chiseled out of a larger stone, like a chip from a larger block. And it wasn't displayed in some kind of showcase, but rested in a small nest of dry leaves. As their eyes adjusted to the darkness, Castle and Bollinger noticed five young men lying in a semicircle around the stone, almost perfectly still, their heads a foot or so beneath the crystal. And they seemed to be mumbling an almost-inaudible, monotonous chant.

"What are they doing?" Bollinger asked.

White Bear beckoned them to move closer. And as they did so, Castle and Bollinger realized it was not the young men who were singing.

It was the stone.

The crystal's melody acted as a sort of carrier signal, the chief explained, reverberating at a constant pace by some unseen mechanism.

"These young men have a special gift. They are listening to its song. And they alert us if they detect even the slightest variation."

Andrew Bollinger couldn't speak. *Nature just doesn't act this way . . .*

"So now do you believe me, Governor?" White Bear was beaming. "The stone has been speaking to us for more than a week now."

It was . . . speaking to them?

Bollinger leaned in closer. He stepped around the listeners and slowly reached out to touch the stone with his index finger. With the chief's permission, he picked up the stone and carefully brought it to his lips. The crystal continued its singular song. The Hopi let them pick it up, measure it and size it up, for more than half an hour. Yet it continued its hypnotic hum the entire time. No matter how they poked and prodded it, it was clear it was some kind of natural mineral. It wasn't a machine or hooked up to speakers. It wasn't metal or manmade, nothing that could ever explain this sound. And yet, there it was, humming . . .

After visiting with the stone, Castle and Bollinger sat next to White Bear and carried on a two-hour conversation, trying to deduce exactly what they had seen, managing only to raise more questions than answers.

"That sound you hear is the stone's constant conversation with the land of the gods," White Bear finally said.

"Can you understand it?"

The old Hopi chief looked at Bollinger as if pitying his ignorance. "Of course. All of my people can understand it."

"So what does it say?"

"It speaks to us about the final day."

"It does? And it gives you an actual day?" Castle said.

"That's right. And it tells about it over and over again. But it doesn't refer to the calendar that you know. In the vastness of our universe, time is not measured by how often our tiny planet orbits around our infant star."

"So what does it measure?"

"The time of the sun."

"My God, Roger, has it been twenty years since that day?" Andrew Bollinger said from the other end of the line. "I almost wish I could forget it."

"Forget it? Andrew, what kind of scientist are you?"

But Bollinger still couldn't joke about that day.

"All I could figure is that it had something to do with the solar flares going on in those days. You might not remember this, but the date March 13, 1989, is etched into my mind; the Hurricane Katrina of solar storms was happening. That was the day that there were all sorts of electrical phenomena across the United States. In San Francisco, garage doors were opening and closing all over town like scenes out of *Poltergeist*. Half of our satellites had to be reprogrammed. And even the space shuttle *Discovery* had to delay its return from orbit when the gauges that measured its hydrogen fuel went haywire. And you know what the worst of it was?"

By this point, Castle was listening in stunned silence.

"Quebec's entire power grid went down—twenty-one thousand, five hundred megawatts went to hell in a matter of ninety seconds without any explanation! Half of Canada went dark for nine hours and it took months to completely repair the damage. When I heard about the disaster after getting home from our little excursion, it almost seemed normal to me to find a singing stone out in the middle of the desert."

"You never told me about that."

"You never asked. You went back to your busy life right after and we didn't talk again for years."

The president overlooked his friend's subtle barb.

"Well, here's the thing, Andrew. I've got people looking for a pair of stones just like White Bear's—stones that emit signals and could be used to help us predict another catastrophe just like that one," Castle said. "My team knows these signals can increase their strength and even send sound waves into deep space. But we have no idea what it means."

Bollinger said nothing.

"Look, I don't know what you think about all this, Andy, but I'll tell you what has occurred to me: What if that stone were some kind of . . ." He hesitated to finish his sentence. "Some kind of transmitter to alert an alien civilization of something going on here? It might have detected some kind of shift in the earth's magnetic field and sent out a signal . . . a distress signal. Does that make any sense?"

"You're joking, right? Roger, do you have any idea what it would take for a signal to escape our atmosphere and reach some distant point deep in the universe? Besides," he grumbled, "even if that did happen, if White Bear's or any other stone managed to send a signal into deep space, our network of antennas and satellites would have detected it."

"Our spy satellites did exactly that, Andy."

"What?"

"Some kind of signal is being sent out from our planet, Andy, and we're not the ones doing it. What I need to know is where that signal is headed. Can you help me figure that out?"

"Of . . . of course." Bollinger suddenly didn't sound so convincing. "But it won't be easy, Roger."

"I didn't expect that it would be."

"Even if we're able to figure out the trajectory and determine its destination, there are thousands of planets where it could be headed. We've cataloged immense planets bigger than Jupiter, some made up of all gas, some too close to their suns to sustain life, much less harbor a civilization advanced enough to receive a signal coming from Earth. Then again . . ."

Andrew Bollinger hesitated.

"Well . . . We've estimated, conservatively, that there are some forty thousand planetary systems within one hundred light years that have a 'sunlike' star at their center. You know, planets that orbit an M-class star, one that's not too big, not too small. And even though statistics say that only about five percent could have conditions that might support life similar to Earth's, that leaves in the neighborhood of some two thousand possible planets that could be listening out for your signal."

"That many."

"Maybe more," Bollinger admitted. "That's why your question is so complicated."

"Look, I'm going to send you all the data we have on these signals, Andy. Will you find out anything you can?"

"Of course, Mr. President."

76

The three sets of rotors on Artemi Dujok's metal flying insect screamed back to life, and I finally felt at ease. We'd found the helicopter just as we'd left it right on the shore. That was a good sign. Better yet, we hadn't come up against the military strike force that tried to kill us at the church. Now, reunited with my adamant, I was finally starting to see the light at the end of the tunnel. Dujok promised that in a matter of hours—a day at the latest—I'd be reunited with Martin. And this entire nightmare would finally be over.

"What if the kidnappers are better armed than we are?" I asked.

"That's why we've got her," Dujok said, nodding at Ellen Watson.

But she didn't look like any kind of secret weapon to me. As a matter of fact, she struck me as arrogant and reckless, someone set on winning at all costs. I didn't like our chances if we came up against a band of terrorists armed to the teeth.

"You must be Julia Álvarez."

Her eyes lit up at finally finding me. When I took my seat in the helicopter and put on my headphones, she made a point of sitting right across from me.

"That's right."

"I'm glad I found you."

"So is it true you know where my husband is?"

She nodded. "I'll check my coordinates with Dujok's once we're in the air, but I think we're working off the same information. Your husband is near Turkey's northeastern border. Do you have your adamant with you?"

"Of course."

"Can I . . . may I see it?"

I could see the eagerness in her eyes. I handed it to her just as the helicopter's landing gear left the ground.

"It's . . . beautiful," she whispered, caressing it. The crystal had turned dark again.

"Amazing, isn't it," Dujok said, clearly more at ease now that the craft had taken off without incident, "that so many people are willing to kill or die to get their hands on it?"

"People like you," Ellen said, quickly turning to meet his stare.

"Or like your president," Dujok said as he casually opened a refrigerated compartment and handed each of us sandwiches and bottles of water. I was dizzy from hunger. I'd been up all night and the stress after the attack at Santa María a Nova stirred up my appetite. As I tore into a crab and lettuce sandwich, I listened as Dujok and Watson dove into conversation.

"So how long have you known about the secret US operation?"

"Since Martin's father came to Armenia looking for the stones years ago," Dujok said, seeming surprised.

"Martin's father, Bill Faber?" I said, almost choking on my second bite.

"William L. Faber. Precisely. How well do you know your father-in-law, Ms. Álvarez?"

And with that, I lost my appetite. "Actually," I said, forcing down another bite, "I've never even seen him. The day I was supposed to meet him, at our wedding in Biddlestone, he never showed."

"Well, I would have been stunned to have seen him there," Dujok said. "Mr. Faber was an . . . elusive character. He came to our country in 1950, shortly after the Pentagon's spy planes chanced across pictures of Noah's Ark on Mount Ararat. He showed up in our community like a lost pilgrim. He told everyone that he was after a sacred stone called the *chintamani*. Everyone thought he was some kind of beatnik after he told us he'd crossed the Himalayas looking for a stone he thought might have ended up somewhere near our mountains. Everyone fell in love with him, though. But then he'd disappear for long stretches at a time and no one ever knew where he'd go or what he was up to."

"He crisscrossed Asia looking for a stone? Who paid for all that?"

"Well, now I know it was the Elijah project, Ms. Álvarez. But back then, no one had any idea that that project existed. Actually, Bill said he only learned about the stone from a Russian painter named Nicholas Roerich, who had painted a sacred object for communicating with heaven. Roerich said that the stone was the key to entering Shambhala."

"Shambhala?"

"It's an old Tibetan Buddhist myth, Ms. Álvarez. Shambhala supposedly is a hidden kingdom where a brotherhood of sages secretly plans out the fate of our species. It's a sort of heaven on earth that is inaccessible to all but the pure of heart."

"But Tibet is a long way from Ararat, Mr. Dujok," Ellen Watson said, cutting in.

"Not for a myth like this one, miss. That so-called *chintamani* stone had a lot in common with our adamants. Roerich's followers claimed that when the *chintamani* darkened, it drew rain clouds overhead. When it grew heavier, it foretold of bloodshed. And it was common for signs to appear on or inside the stone just before important events.

"And did he tell you about Elijah as well?"

Dujok smiled. "Eventually, we talked about everything. Bill and I became fast friends. He spent several years in Armenia and ended up inviting me to come back with him to study in the US and to become part of Elijah."

"So, did he find what he was looking for?"

"More or less. He eventually won over the sheikhs in my village, who told him that the mother of all of those stones was hidden somewhere in Mount Ararat. His *chintamani,* they told him, traveled inside Noah's Ark during the Great Flood . . . But then the Russians came. Armenia was a poor province, not exactly on Moscow's radar, but when they eventually found out there was a 'white capitalist' in the region, they sent their men for him. He managed to escape, but the Russians infected the region with their propaganda. They told all these simple people that Faber worked for a secret enemy project and that his only goal was to steal one of our natural treasures. And for good measure, they added that the father of your president was behind them."

"Roger Castle's father knew about the Elijah project? Are you sure?"

"Absolutely. William Castle II worked on the project with Bill Faber. And Martin inherited the task—which is when he met me. Curious little circle, don't you think?"

"I'll say."

"Ask yourself something: Why is your president so interested in Elijah? I think at this point you'd want some answers."

"Well, you can bet the next time I speak with him, I'll have some questions."

"No time like the present," he said, handing her a satellite phone with a half smirk. "And when you do, ask him who sent the men who tried to kill us. Was it him?"

"I can tell you that, sir," she said. "Those men were SEALs. They came ashore from a Virginia-class submarine cruising just a couple of miles off the coast."

"Please tell me you're joking . . ."

"No, sir. Elijah sent the sub. No doubt in my mind. And you can bet the president knows nothing about it."

The blood drained from Dujok's face at that last piece of information. "Well, then make that call, young lady!"

He slammed shut the cooler beneath the seat and sat up uncommonly straight. He fired off a couple of orders to his pilot in Armenian and fixed his glare on Ellen Watson.

"What are you waiting for?" he yelled. "If that sub is where you said it is, we're still within firing range! For God's sake, make that call!"

77

Things looked bad for Michael Owen.

If he didn't act fast, the president's men were going to get their hands on the adamants first, jeopardizing his entire mission. And now, thanks to that signal from Faber's stones, other crystals around the world were firing off similar X emissions. Something fundamental was changing in the planet's geomagnetism. Maybe it was some kind of warning. A harbinger of that "great and terrible day." But was the agency ready for that kind of event? Was the country?

The answer was no.

There was only one such precedent for such a cataclysmic event. For years, his only concern had been documenting the "great and terrible day" that all the ancient chronicles referred to. In that, he was as obsessed as his predecessors, dating back to Chester Arthur himself. Unfortunately, everything that had been learned about the event could fit easily inside of a single file. He had examined that folder countless times at his office in Fort Meade, Maryland, and it always led him to the same dead end. *To understand the end, you must first understand the beginning,* he would tell himself.

Despite all the brute force that he could command from that fortress of an office, Owen felt helpless.

"The news coming to us from Oise, France, is disconcerting . . ."

The flat-screen in his office had lit up suddenly and the volume came up gradually.

Owen tossed his suit jacket on his armchair and listened. His office was equipped with a system that scanned news across the globe, and when it detected something of interest, it began recording and played it back when it sensed his presence in the room. His secretary knew he had spent the night working at the National Reconnaissance Office and had set the system to record anything having to do with the region just north of Paris.

When the television flashed on, C-SPAN commentator Lisa Hartmann seemed more worried than usual.

"So tell us, what's happening in France, Jack?"

The screen switched to the network's chief correspondent in France, Jack Austin.

"It's just after nine in the morning here in the small town of Noyon, and its twenty thousand residents are still trying to figure out why they've been without power since last night. The power company, Electricité de France, hasn't given any reason for a massive power outage that is affecting not just all forms of transportation but even hospitals. And the people here are starting to worry, Lisa."

"Are people concerned this might be part of a terrorist attack?"

"Police are telling us no, Lisa. They say they're still trying to figure out the source of the power outage, but they insist it's unlike any technical malfunction they've ever seen. They spent the night examining every substation and they all seem to be in working order."

"So what do the experts think might have caused it?" Hartmann asked from the newsroom in Washington, DC.

"A group of researchers are putting their heads together as we speak. Everyone's hoping that whatever the cause, it won't spread to a larger city like Amiens . . ."

Owens checked his watch. The broadcast had been recorded just six minutes ago.

Has the "end" begun?

Owen shook the thought out of his head. *If it was a magnetic storm, our satellites would have been affected.* He flipped off the television and tried to concentrate on the entire reason he'd rushed back to his office. He needed to review the folder just sent over from the NSA archives, and he needed to do it with a clear head.

He poured himself a hot cup of coffee with plenty of sugar and set his mind to the task at hand.

He was almost comforted at knowing what he'd find inside: a handful of old photographs and handwritten documents, some of them nearly a hundred years old. He'd requested the folder again after his man in Spain, Richard Hale, told him Martin Faber had requested this very file just before he resigned from the agency.

What were you looking for, Mr. Faber?

Studying the file brought back mostly good memories. His old friend George Carver, a CIA security expert who had died of a heart attack in 1994, had dedicated the last few months of his life to studying the discovery of Noah's Ark. He had tried to convince Owen that it should be kept under constant surveillance. He insisted they had to learn everything they could about "that great and terrible day" if humanity was to survive it the way it did eons earlier.

Carver had been interested in the topic since he was a West Point cadet. He heard a professor from the University of Richmond discussing photos the CIA had taken of Noah's Ark by chance as a spy satellite flew over Mount Ararat. Carver made some inquiries at Langley and discovered, to his surprise, that the story was no fairy tale. In September of 1973, a series-KH-11 satellite indeed shot an image of something bizarre: At the edge of a melting glacier on the northeast face of Ararat's highest peak was the outline of three curved wooden beams that seemed to form the shape of an ancient ship. What other ship would anyone find atop a mountain if not Noah's Ark?

Carver discussed his findings with anyone who would listen. He asked questions, requested classified documents and even asked several senators about getting to the bottom of it. Unfortunately, his illness cut short his work. After Carver's death, his professor friend doubled his efforts to bring to light the secret dossier on the ark and the pictures of the "anomaly of Ararat." And it finally happened in 1995. Needless to say, it was on the cover of the *New York Times* the next day and set the intelligence community buzzing.

Among the declassified images were not just the KH-11 images but others from U-2 spy planes and Corona satellites. All the pictures were dated between 1959 and 1960 and they all seemed to indicate that an enormous wooden ark indeed existed. Still, it was only visible when snowy conditions allowed.

But this wasn't all Martin Faber had requested from Langley's archives.

He had asked to see a smaller, more exclusive dossier, one that had not been declassified, one that only a handful of Elijah's members had ever seen—the folder that was now on Michael Owen's desk.

Just holding it filled him with an indescribable nostalgia.

He now had an idea what Faber was looking for, why he had rushed off to Ararat before his kidnapping, and he also now understood what Dujok was after, as well—it was all one and the same. He just hoped whatever the government satellites were picking up didn't have anything to do with them.

"Is that it?"

Ellen Watson's phone conversation was so brief, so clinical, that I thought she hadn't managed to get through. I guess I thought it odd that such a young woman could simply dial up the most powerful man on the planet.

"Well, what did he have to say?" Dujok said impatiently.

"The president will personally ensure that the USS *Texas* won't be an issue," she said, her aquamarine eyes darkening.

"Is that all he said?"

"He asked where we were headed and whether we were going by helicopter."

"And what did you tell him?"

"That our objective was in Turkey, at the site where we detected the last adamant, and that I had no idea how we'd reach such a remote location. Do you?"

Dujok swelled with pride. "This vehicle can fly nonstop for eleven straight hours and reach a top speed of three hundred seventy miles an hour. We can be at our destination within seven or eight hours," Dujok said. "Can you get your president to clear our flight plan?"

"Sure. Do you need the coordinates for the type-X emission that Washington triangulated?"

"Not necessary," he said, tapping his laptop. "The signal that gave us our coordinates came from one of your satellites. I trust they're accurate."

Worry had reached the bridge of the most modern submarine in the US fleet. Two of the three giant monitors showed satellite images of their tactical team coming under enemy fire. Everyone aboard was on edge. The HMBB had caught the very moment when an unidentified vehicle entered the combat zone and neutralized Sergeant Odenwald—effectively rendering the mission a failure. Moreover, the captain of the boat cut off communications with the NSA director when he was ordered to stand by, sitting on his hands.

And now, something else to worry about.

"Captain, sonar ops here."

The image of the officer who was the underwater eyes and ears of the sub flashed on a third monitor. Captain Jack Foyle turned around to face him.

"Sonar, report."

"We've detected something, sir. An unidentified helicopter departed Noia several minutes ago heading north-northeast."

"And . . ."

"Sir, we just cross-referenced its heading with the coordinates of the anomaly we received from the satellite. It's a match. And, sir"—the young officer steadied himself—"the 'transmitter' is aboard. The electromagnetic signature is a match."

"How far are they, son?"

"Less than ten miles, sir."

The USS *Texas* was topside in the Atlantic. There was no way to intercept the bird given its current position.

"Should we take it down, sir?" said a young officer fresh out of the academy.

"Our orders are to recover the tablet intact, sailor. If we open fire now, we'll lose it. Plus, have you stopped to consider the implications of racking up more casualties on Allied soil? The ones from the fishing town this morning are more than enough for me, kid."

The subordinate didn't answer.

"Sonar, is the helicopter maintaining its heading?" Foyle asked.

"Right now, they're still headed along the coast toward La Coruña, Spain, sir."

"La Coruña?"

"It's a medium-sized city just north of our position, sir."

"Does it have an airport?"

The officer turned to his computer and punched in some information.

"Affirmative, sir."

"Com!" Captain Foyle said, turning on his heels to face a young brunette, an officer in charge of all ship's communications, who was, at the moment, carrying a wireless phone. "Call the NSA and tell them to freeze all activity at that airport and to contact local authorities to limit access by all trains and buses. We'll send a strike team immediately."

Instead of snapping into action, the young sailor stepped forward and handed the captain the phone.

"You have a call, sir."

"It'll have to wait!" he grumbled.

"I'm sorry, sir," the officer said stiffly. "This can't wait."

80

Haci was clearly a talented pilot.

To get out of Noia, he skillfully maneuvered around power lines and stayed low to avoid radar. He knew he was flying an unregistered craft in unauthorized airspace and was bound to draw attention, so he tried everything he could to go unnoticed. Before we knew it, he had stopped following the coast and had started northeast, over the homes and villages of Galicia, giving us our first taste of freedom. From the outside, my situation might not have seemed so promising: I hadn't slept all night, had been shot at twice, was bruised from head to toe and had been inches from death. And all because of the person who was now heading up this mission.

Still, knowing I was finally on my way to see Martin, I was grateful to Artemi Dujok and his men.

Typical Stockholm syndrome, I thought. *But what the hell . . .*

We were relaxed at last, enjoying the scenery. And then, a warning light on the instrument panel went on.

"Sheikh, we've been detected by radar," Haci said.

"Can you shake it?"

"I'll try . . ."

The Sikorsky X4 dove down low again, nearly grazing the tops of the eucalyptus trees passing by in a blur, but the warning light continued to flash.

"How far away are we from the coast?" Dujok asked.

"Maybe three kilometers, sir."

"Well, Miss Watson, we'll soon know whether it was worth it to bring you along," Dujok said. "If your boss gave the order in time, we're saved. Otherwise, we'll be dead in the next few minutes."

"I trust my president, Mr. Dujok," she said. "I know he won't let us down."

"I hope you're right."

81

"Is this Captain Jack Foyle?"

Foyle had transferred the call to his adjacent ready room. The voice on the other end of the line seemed familiar and authoritative.

"This is Captain Foyle. Who do I have the pleasure of—"

"This is President Castle."

Foyle held the phone, dumbstruck.

"I know you're off the coast of Spain, Captain," he said flatly. "And I know the NSA gave you one set of instructions. But I'm giving you a direct order to stand down."

"Sir, I—"

"You're a soldier, Captain Foyle, and you were just following orders; I understand completely. And you won't be chastised for it."

"It's not that, sir," Foyle said. "We launched a sortie earlier today. And we lost five men."

"You launched a raid on Spanish soil?"

"Yes, sir."

The phone went silent for several seconds. Castle needed to think.

"Did you recover the bodies?"

"No, sir. They're in the hands of local authorities. I assume our embassy is trying to repatriate them as we speak," Foyle said. "We encountered enemy fire during an urban gun battle."

"Enemy fire? Where?" The president's tone went from incredulous to worried.

"A small coastal village called Noia, sir."

Castle needed another minute. That was close to where Ellen Watson had been when she made her phone call from that helicopter.

"Were there any civilian casualties, Captain?"

"Not that I know of, sir. But we caused substantial damage to a historic building."

"All right, Captain," Castle said, sighing. "Your mission has officially changed. I need you to do three things for your country."

"Yes, sir?"

"First, I need you stand down and call off all combat and search-and-rescue operations. You are not authorized to fire one more round. Understood? I know an unidentified aircraft has just taken off from the city of Noia—you may already be tracking it. There's an official from my office aboard on a special mission. You are instructed to let them on their way."

"Sir, if I may . . . it's the subjects aboard that helicopter who killed our men."

"Captain, right now, I need you to simply follow orders," Castle said. "The next thing I need you to do is contact the admiral of the Sixth Fleet, fill him in on what's happened and ask for new orders. Notify the families of the soldiers killed in action, and leave the area."

"And your third order, sir?"

"I want you to listen to my next question and be completely honest with me, Captain."

"Of course, sir."

"What exactly were you ordered to do in Noia?"

Jack Foyle hesitated. The NSA's director had been explicit that he could not reveal the contents of the countersigned message he received to anyone under any circumstances. But he wasn't about to lie to his commander-in-chief.

"Sir," Foyle said, "our orders were to locate a powerful mobile electromagnetic weapon and secure it for study by US scientists."

"Is that all?"

"No, sir. We also were to capture a civilian, one Julia Álvarez, without bodily harm, and to neutralize her captors."

"Were you told why?"

"Yes, sir. Apparently, one of them is planning a global-scale attack. One that would cause immeasurable damage—using an electromagnetic weapon."

Three minutes later, the warning light on the Sikorsky's instrument panel went out.

"We lost them, sir," Haci said.

"Are you sure?" Artemi Dujok turned toward the cockpit with a raised eyebrow.

"Yes, sir. The radar has stopped tracking us."

Dujok turned around and looked, satisfied, at Ellen Watson.

"Thank you, Miss Watson. You've been a big help."

"So now that I've proven my worth, will you tell me everything you know about Operation Elijah?"

I watched Dujok carefully. She clearly had held up her end of the bargain. Would he confide in her with me looking on?

"Wouldn't you rather get some rest before we reach our destination?"

"There'll be time for that. Right now, I want to know everything about this mysterious operation."

"Suit yourself," Dujok said. "You've certainly earned it. And we have a couple hours ahead of us. I can't see why I shouldn't tell you everything I know."

Ellen sat up in her chair, in rapt attention as Dujok filled her in on a centuries-old mission.

The first picture was an old one. Almost ancient.

Michael Owen slipped it out of the envelope and held it carefully. It had been taken by Czar Nicholas II's troops in the summer of 1917 near the Turkish-Russian border. It showed a group of tired, filthy men, frozen to the bone in their threadbare uniforms, and clearly none had shaved in days. Three of them posed stiffly in front of the ruins of a house that had been destroyed by an avalanche or an earthquake. The image spoke to Owen across the valley of time.

He understood what it had taken to get that picture into his archives. American operatives had paid for it in blood. They had snatched it four decades after it had fallen into the Bolsheviks' hands. The Russians needed this picture as much as their revolution. And it wasn't hard to understand why.

If you looked closer, beyond the grainy image, you could see something strange about the house. It was three stories high and looked as if the façade had only recently been destroyed. The levels that were exposed to the elements did not reveal the typical items in a household. There was no furniture, no clothes, no broken bricks or splintered beams. Only a series of small, dark, empty rooms, stacked one next to the other.

When you pieced it together with the other photos in the dossier, it all made sense. Another photo taken some three hundred yards from the curious house appeared to hold the key. The odd "house" was really only the visible part of a long, rectangular structure that disappeared into a glacier, which, apparently, had split in half during some kind of earthquake or landslide, exposing the building's innards to the elements. Written on the back of the photo in Russian was the following:

Romanov expedition. July 1917
Noah's Ark

For years, experts had speculated as to the existence of these photos. All the books about Noah's Ark referred to these photos but none had ever published them. They only spoke about an exploration that Nicholas II commissioned to the Turkish border before he and his family were murdered, but there was never any physical proof. Yet here was the evidence, in black and white. The hundreds of soldiers, engineers, photographers and historians were captured on their way down the mountain by Nicholas II's enemies and accused of high treason. Most were summarily executed and the ones who managed to escape never spoke again of what they had found on that mountaintop. For a regime founded on atheism, the discovery of a biblical relic was pure dynamite. The very father of the revolution hid the photos among his private papers, resisting destroying them for the equal parts of fascination and disgust they stirred in him. But that didn't keep him from sending a team of combat engineers—who were more naïve and less resistant than imperial soldiers—to blow up the ark. But they were never able to find it again.

Or maybe it was just God's will.

But then, of course, came the theft.

In 1956, a double agent stumbled across the pictures when he gained access to Leon Trotsky's archives. He managed to slip them out of the country and sell them in Berlin to a representative of the US embassy. But on the day of the exchange, he and the buyer were discovered in the eastern part of the city and gunned down by the Stasi, East Germany's secret police. Two days later, though, a border captain—enticed by a million dollars—eventually got the photos to their ultimate buyer; the Elijah project had finally managed to get them, although it cost them one of their top spies.

Michael Owen was only a boy when all of that had gone down. Maybe that's why it didn't hurt to hold these pictures now.

The picture he was most interested in was the last of the series. It was a shot of one of the top floors of the "house," which looked to have been hermetically sealed. It was a picture of a Russian soldier whose eyebrows and mustache were covered in frost, leaning up against a wall stained with dark streaks. His icy stare, emboldened by vodka, seemed to say, "I dare you to come any closer, asshole." It was Owen's favorite picture from the moment he first saw it. The soldier pointed a gloved finger at several etchings on the wall. They looked like initials carved into stone. You could only make out four of them, but from the picture, it was clear there was room for more letters. Just below them were a series of scribbles that Michael Owen had come to know very well. In the sixteenth century, someone had called them *Monas hieroglyphica*. But interestingly, none of those characters were Hebrew. If this was Noah's Ark, then the biblical patriarch had not marked his ship with the alphabet of his people, but rather these inscrutable symbols:

$$ \daleth \; \mem \; \gimel \; \mem $$

These were the same characters that the project's best analyst—one William L. Faber—had studied years ago. He said they were part of a language called Enochian during the Renaissance and that was later used by a small group of mediums in England during the reign of Queen Elizabeth. Faber believed that whoever could correctly pronounce the words—and there was no way to learn other than to study Enochian—could bring the adamants to life and control their electromagnetic powers.

Every indication was that William L. Faber was close, very close, to cracking the code when he went missing.

In Turkey.

Probably searching for his son.

84

It was only a gut feeling.

Still, Andrew Bollinger had learned to trust it. All of a sudden, while surrounded by empty Coke cans and used Styrofoam coffee cups, he knew exactly where to begin answering the question his old friend Roger Castle had asked. After staring long and hard at the data from Spain and Turkey that the White House had sent him, it hit Bollinger like a bolt of lightning.

How did I not notice it before? These were not identical signals. The first one wasn't emanating from a fixed point; the second one was. Moreover, the first one seemed to be moving on a direct course toward the second one. Of course, the goal wasn't to try to figure out what message those stones were sending but rather where the signals were being sent. And at the moment, it didn't look like they were being aimed at a planet in outer space.

That's what gave him the idea.

From his office in the operations center, he quickly telephoned the VLA telescope's satellite chief and asked him to concentrate his surveillance on a specific range of radio waves. He knew this should only take about a half hour, an hour at most. He needed to isolate any natural electromagnetic signal that might be crossing the ionosphere at that moment with a frequency of 1,420 megahertz and a wavelength of twenty-one centimeters.

"Let's start with"—he peeked down at his monitor—"as close as you can get to thirty-nine degrees, twenty-five minutes north, forty-four degrees, twenty-four minutes east."

Bollinger had to repeat the coordinates.

"And remember, I'm only interested in signals that might be broadcast *from* that location and at that exact frequency."

"Broadcasting at *that* frequency?"

The skepticism in Lawrence Gómez's voice irked Bollinger. But Gómez, a fifty-six-year-old engineer, had seen and heard just about everything in his career, and he had never heard of anything or anyone being able to broadcast at a powerful 1,420 MHz. Nor could he imagine why his boss would have any interest in chasing LGMs—little green men.

"Keep the commentary to a minimum and get me results, Mr. Gómez," Bollinger said.

Nine minutes later, all twenty-eight of the VLA's two-hundred-thirty-ton satellite dishes turned eastward in unison, like sunflowers chasing sun. Then the computerized network honed in on the area the National Security Administration's satellite had detected the signal. To his amazement, Gómez found what he was looking for almost immediately. Over the next nineteen minutes, his spectral analyzer captured data from a powerful singular emission, just as he'd been told. And when the computer took the next step and calculated the direction of the signal, Gómez couldn't believe his eyes.

"It can't be . . ."

Gómez ran the numbers again and got the same result. He recalibrated the computer, taking into account the signal's residual rebound in the Heaviside layer of the ionosphere, and reanalyzed the course. He did it twice. There was no denying it. The powerful unexplained electromagnetic stream was pointing directly at . . .

"The sun? You're sure?" Bollinger's usually tan complexion paled.

"I'm sure of it, Dr. Bollinger. It's sending out a signal at the exact frequency of the element hydrogen. And what's even more unbelievable . . . the sun seems to be responding with a similar emission. If I didn't know any better, I'd say they were communicating."

Bollinger felt a shiver run down his spine.

"Have you been able to determine whether it's a sequenced signal?"

"You mean whether it could be the result of . . . intelligent life?"

"Yes," Bollinger stammered.

"Not yet, sir. That'll take a little more time."

Bollinger turned around in his chair, staring at the poster of the solar system in his office. A fiery giant took up most of the left side of the image. The artist had shown the sun's flares licking the tiny planet of Mercury. *The sun contains 98 percent of all matter in the solar system,* the poster's tagline read. To Bollinger, the phrase now read like a threat.

Outside the New Mexico Institute of Mining and Technology, winter was on its way. It had rained more than usual this fall, and Bollinger had longed for the sun to show its face and stave off the impending cold.

Now he wished he'd never even thought it.

He turned to face his computer and composed an e-mail to two recipients. *God, I hope I'm wrong.* The Air Force's Fiftieth Weather Reconnaissance Squadron in Colorado Springs had a division dedicated to space weather prediction. And so did the Goddard Space Flight Center in Greenbelt, Maryland, not far from the White House. If the sun had displayed any unusual activity in the last few hours, both of them should have picked up on it. Only those scientists could help ease his mind. The only other time he'd ever seen a stone "speak" was just before the great solar storms of 1989, the ones that caused the massive blackout in Quebec and billions of dollars in damage to satellites and power grids. Some even speculated that the solar flares might have been responsible for damaging the navigation system of the *Exxon Valdez*, which struck a reef and spilled thirty-seven thousand tons of crude oil in Alaska. If the president was right and other crystals were now "speaking," it was a threat worth taking seriously.

He knew each time the sun pulsed unexpectedly, it unleashed billions of tons of plasma into space. Traveling at more than nine hundred miles a second—about two million miles an hour—the burst would reach Earth in two to three days. They couldn't take any chances.

"Urgent," the message began. "Have you detected a CME in the last few hours?"

Just typing those three initials was enough to worry him. A coronal mass ejection was about the worst thing our nearby star could do to our tiny planet.

He hit the send button, and off it went.

Now, all he could do was wait.

85

My head felt like it was going to explode.

After seven hours and forty minutes of flight—hearing the high-pitched whistling of the helicopter blades and the warning bells every time we tripped a radar signal or received permission to cross into French, Italian or Greek airspace—I felt like I'd spent all day on a roller coaster. I'd barely been able to sleep. And I wondered how much more twisting, turning and turbulence my body and mind could take. Fortunately, I didn't have to find out, as we approached our destination in northeastern Turkey. The helicopter touched down gingerly, and I barely noticed it. My back was in knots, my mind couldn't process another bit of information and all I dreamed of was a soft bed to lay my head on.

Maybe that's why Dujok unexpectedly clapped me on the shoulder, jolting me out of my stupor.

"C'mon, we're almost there!" he said, trying to hearten me.

It was already nighttime in Turkey and the air was cold and crisp, the moonless night studded with stars. The Sikorsky X4 had landed in stealth mode just three hundred yards from our destination, and under the cover of stillness and darkness, we moved in. I trudged like a zombie at the back of our group, dragging my feet, buffeted by the icy dry wind.

I didn't feel like taking another step, much less taking one toward that vast crater that Dujok had located using his laptop. I was out of breath as we reached the edge of the precipice.

But this is the place where Martin's adamant had signaled it was, at the bottom of what Dujok called the Hallaç crater. Still, standing at its edge in the dead of an icy night—despite our night-vision goggles and the warm clothes Dujok had given us—I was overcome with anxiety.

The crater was easily forty yards deep and its walls had been baked to a glassy hardness by the pounding Middle Eastern sun. I had no idea how we were going to get down.

"If we're going to go down inside the crater, I don't think I—"

"We're not going into the crater, Ms. Álvarez," Dujok said. "We're headed toward the building next to it. That's where Martin's signal was coming from."

"You mean . . . *that* building?"

About a hundred yards away, down a slight slope, was a sizable fortress that looked to have been abandoned years ago. Despite the darkness, I could see its walls were covered in bullet holes. I was no ballistics expert, but I'd restored enough Galician churches damaged during the civil war.

"But what if Martin's captors are still inside?" I whispered, hurrying to keep up.

"You leave that to us. They won't be a problem," Dujok said flatly.

Dujok, his two armed men, Ellen Watson and I soon reached the perimeter. The main building was attached to three other smaller buildings, which also looked abandoned. But the principal two-story had a gabled roof and a small tower, like a minaret. A courtyard stretched out toward another building—the one that was blacked out in satellite images—that looked unlike any building I had ever seen.

Steel plates unevenly covered the tower, which rose out of the ground like the fang of some gigantic underground creature. It was spartan, with no windows or any other unnecessary architectural features. And although it appeared ancient, it also had a sort of avant-garde design.

"Keep moving," Dujok said, snapping me back to the task at hand.

"What is this place?"

"An antenna."

"A . . . what?"

"An antenna, for high-frequency signals . . . Come on, keep moving."

"But . . . it looks ancient."

"It is."

We walked quickly and quietly toward the larger building's main entrance and stood on either side of the door, waiting for Dujok's instructions. The front door, of massive wood reinforced with steel plates, was wide open, and it was quiet inside. Ellen Watson, who was the only one besides me not armed, piped up.

"We're just going to waltz in?" she asked.

Dujok nodded. "That's right. And you two are going to lead the way," he told us.

"Us?" Watson said. "Oh, I don't think so . . ."

"Well I *do*," Dujok said. And with that, he pointed the business end of his Uzi right at my chest. "Move. That's an order."

86

Not even Dante could have imagined such an inferno.

A wave of plasma more than sixty thousand miles long, burning at more than 100,000 degrees Fahrenheit, burst from the sun's outer crust. The two STEREO-class space probes—nicknamed *Ahead* and *Behind*—that NASA had placed in orbit around the sun were the first to detect the eruption. Together, they help construct a three-dimensional image of the sun and its surface. However, since they weren't positioned to detect any radiation *going to* the sun—why would anyone ever do such a thing?—they did not detect the powerful magnetic beam that struck near Sunspot 13057.

Sunspot 13057 had been no bigger than the size of Earth—tiny in comparison to the massive sun. But thirty seconds after the signal from Earth began, the spot's intense magnetic field began to fluctuate—and grow. It soon swallowed up Sunspots 12966 and 13102. And that amount of turbulence was enough to trigger the STEREO probes to begin recording automatically, without any input from the Goddard Space Flight Center in Maryland, and to begin transmitting data back to Earth. The multimillion-dollar instrumentation soon determined that Sunspot 13057 had exploded. The dark spot was soon replaced by a roiling tower of plasma shooting up at nearly two hundred miles a second.

What came next was off the charts for any activity ever recorded from our sun.

The plasma burst came crashing back down onto the star's surface of liquid fire the way an old oak tree might as it tumbled into a placid lake: The shock wave sent ripples out as far as six hundred thousand miles, producing a tsunami of magnetic energy and blazing gas of unimaginable temperatures. A quintillion of high-energy particles—primarily protons—shot out from the sun's surface into space, followed by the most intense spiral of solar radioactivity that the STEREO space probes would ever detect.

That alone would be enough to put the Solar Terrestrial Relations Observatory into the history books.

But then the *Ahead* probe's ultraviolet cameras picked up something else.

Like twisted cosmic fingers, a magnetic current nearly twenty-five thousand miles across reached into space. Meanwhile, fissures five times the size of Earth opened and closed on the surface of the sun, like hungry mouths eager to feast.

In just eight short minutes, that radiation would engulf our tiny blue planet—and that would be just the beginning.

Between eighteen and thirty-six hours later—if the calculations were correct—the plasma would reach Earth and rain down like liquid fire. The space probe calculations would soon predict where the hellfire would strike the planet. Humanity was facing the largest coronal mass ejection this planet had ever known, a class X23 event whose consequences no one could predict.

Just as the space probe *Behind* relayed its calculations for where the magnetic tsunami would make landfall, a message popped in from the director of the radio telescope in Socorro, New Mexico: "Urgent. Have you detected a CME in the last few hours?"

But the Goddard Space Flight Center had more pressing concerns at the moment. They had just calculated where the plasma would meet Earth.

And they needed to notify the Turkish authorities immediately.

87

We took our first uneasy steps into the building by the crater.

There was no light, the ground was covered in debris and my legs were shaking from utter terror. I couldn't understand why Artemi Dujok—Martin's friend, the man who'd risked his life to find me and bring me here—would now force me inside at gunpoint and glare at me as if I were his worst enemy. Ellen Watson didn't know what to make of it, either. Haci stood behind her with his machine gun poking into her back, dutifully following his sheikh's orders. But what was Dujok's plan? He was no fanatic—or didn't look like one, anyway. I felt there must be some logical explanation, something I was missing. So when I noticed a look of delight, not tension, in his face, I couldn't imagine he would put me in harm's way.

Dujok led us through a labyrinth of hallways and empty rooms in complete silence and down a flight of stairs to the bottom floor, which did have power. When the light first came on from a single bulb hanging from the ceiling, I shielded my eyes and kept my hands there for a second. Haci prodded me with the barrel of his machine gun.

"Yu-lia Al-vrz!" he said rudely.

Then I opened my eyes.

And the shock washed over me in an instant. Despite being halfway across the world in a place so far from anything I'd ever known, I recognized this room.

So did Ellen Watson.

I spun on my heels and glared at Dujok for an explanation, but with nothing but a threatening stare he ordered me to turn back around. "You still have a lot more to see," he grumbled.

There was no doubt about it: The filthy, crumbling walls and peeling paint, graffiti on the plaster that hadn't crumbled, the rickety table beneath the single hanging lightbulb—it was the room in Martin's kidnapping video. His plea had been recorded in this very place.

A thousand questions rushed to my mind.

"Well, well, well . . . You finally made it. I do hate to be kept waiting," said a voice I recognized from the doorway behind me. His was a perfect queen's English, measured and seemingly happy to see old friends. "We've *all* been expecting you, love."

That voice, that haughty pompous tone. I spun around again to prove what my memory already suspected.

My God . . .

"Daniel . . . ? Daniel Knight?"

He stood in the doorway in a thick parka and heavy mountain boots, his unmistakable ruddy face and bushy red beard cutting more of a menacing figure than he deserved.

"I'm happy to see you remember me. It's been, what, five years since the last time we saw each other, love? Five years and not a single phone call. I'm hurt . . ."

"You know this man?" Watson said.

I nodded. "He was at my wedding. An old friend of my husband's."

"Oh, I'm much more than that, love."

"It's true. He also taught me how to use my adamant."

Daniel Knight wasn't armed, but it was clear he was the one in charge. Still, I couldn't understand what a bookworm like him was doing there or, more important, why he hadn't ordered Dujok to lower his weapon.

"Where's Martin?" I asked sharply.

"Come on now, love," he said, stepping closer and putting his index finger to my lips, "you should be a little happier to see me. After all, I'm going to give you the answers to all your questions."

"I want to know where Martin is."

"Your husband is in perfect health. As a matter of fact, he's been waiting for you, too . . . Would you like a spot of tea?"

"T- . . . tea? At a time like this? What the hell is wrong with you?"

"You need to stay hydrated, love. And your friend, too," he said, turning his attention to Ellen. "You'll need to save your strength for all the work ahead of you."

"Work? What are you talking about, Daniel?"

"Oh, Julia, come on, now," he said, shaking his head, as if I should already have known the answer to my own question. "The work that is your destiny—like it or not."

"I have no idea what you're talking about."

"No? Let me refresh your memory," he said, smiling. "When Martin last saw you before leaving for Turkey, you told him you wouldn't help him with his 'witchcraft' anymore. Remember? That you never wanted to hear him talk about adamants or John Dee or an apocalypse ever again. You insisted on ignoring your destiny, the very reason for your existence. But luckily for you, these old friends and I are going to help you get back onto your path."

"I told him to do whatever the hell he wanted with the adamants!" I said. "As long as he didn't drag me into his obsession anymore. Wait a minute . . . is Martin behind all this? Tell me, right now!"

"This is no obsession, love . . ."

"Besides, what does any of this have to do with Martin's kidnapping?" I said, unable to stop a rising fire inside my chest. "I don't understand . . . I don't understand anything anymore!"

"Kidnapping? Please . . ." Daniel's cherubic face lit up. "Julia, you're an intelligent woman. Think about what's happened to you these last few weeks. First, Martin hid the adamant in a secure location because you refused to continue. But he continued his work, which brought him here. And you, love, knew as well as he did that sooner or later, you would come to Turkey to be at his side. Am I right?"

I felt the heat rush up into my face until I almost couldn't speak. "What are you getting at, Daniel?"

"Julia, Julia . . . ," he said, shaking his head, "you married a man who *needed* a woman like you to answer a higher calling, to finish a mission greater than your marriage. Martin spent years searching for a woman with the gift of sight. Someone who could help him—help *us*—take his work to the next level—to open a pathway to the angels."

"Just like John Dee and his mediums . . . same old story," I said.

"Exactly."

Daniel's hand shook almost imperceptibly as he poured me a cup of tea from the hot kettle on the table. But I was too tied up in knots to care, still wrestling with everything that had happened the last few weeks.

"So . . . you . . . faked the kidnapping," Ellen Watson added, "just to lure Julia here?"

Daniel Knight tried to contain a smile. "That's one way to look at it, Miss Watson."

"But . . . why?" I said.

"If Martin simply had asked you to come with him to Mount Ararat and to bring your adamant for one last ceremony, would you have done it?"

That question was all I needed to finally realize that Martin really was behind all of this. But where was he? Why hadn't he shown his face? I felt my pulse quicken, my lungs struggle to breathe the cold, humid air.

Daniel continued. "We needed to give you a strong enough reason for *you* to come to *us*. You have no idea of the cosmic forces at work even as we speak. The time to activate the adamants is upon us. We had to devise a plan to get you here, fast, in the least threatening way possible—"

"The *least* threatening? And this is what you came up with?"

"I know you love Martin, and love is a very human weakness. I counted on it, actually. And, look, here you are! Just in the nick of time."

"Damn you! I was almost killed because of you!"

Daniel just sipped his tea, exchanging a scornful look with Ellen Watson. "I miscalculated. I had no idea the people from the Elijah project might intercept our video and go for the stone as well," he said, holding his glare on Ellen. "But no matter. That's why we sent guardian angels of our own to ensure your safety," he said, patting Dujok on the back. He was still holding us at gunpoint.

"So now what? You're going to force me to play your little game again?"

Daniel finished his tea before answering.

"The time for games is over, love," he said, setting down the cup. "Every so often, this world's earth and sky are bombarded with solar magnetism, changing our planet into a kind of cosmic beacon for several hours. I've spent years studying these events at the Greenwich Observatory, and I can tell you they are exceedingly rare. There might be one or two every century. And they are brief. But while my colleagues are content with making statistical charts, I have compared these data with monumental moments in history. I realized if we learned to channel these forces, we could open a pathway to realms we have never thought possible."

Daniel's eyes narrowed.

"As I mentioned, John Dee managed to establish his angelic communication because his first tries took place during one of the greatest solar storms in history. The sun went wild that May of 1581. By the twenty-fifth of that month, the aurora borealis could be seen as far south as the Tropic of Cancer. Earth had never seen anything like it. We know now that, as all this was going on outside, Dee was inside his small chapel in Mortlake when a noise made him come to the window. Maybe it was the crackle of the aurora; we'll never really know. But what he saw outside dumbfounded him. It was a sort of child-angel with a luminous complexion, floating several feet off the ground. He opened the window, reached out and touched the heavenly figure with his fingertips. And the angel in turn gave Dee the powerful stones he would use in later years to communicate with the other world.

"Dee was fifty-four, elderly by the day's standards, and he would not waste his remaining years with childish fairy tales. Instead, he hired a medium to use the adamants to open a connection to the other plane, one that had not been established for more than four thousand years. And now," he said, clearing his throat, "those cosmic conditions are repeating themselves. A new solar storm is on its way toward Earth . . . and you have the gift to help open that portal once again. What more could we ever ask for?"

Emotion welled up inside me as Daniel reached his crescendo. I wanted to cry, to scream in his face that I wanted no part of his insane experiments, that I'd had enough of his cat-and-mouse games in London. But I managed to maintain my composure. If Daniel, who until this moment, I had considered a harmless bookworm, was capable of bringing all of this to bear, it was better not to draw his anger.

"What I still don't understand," I finally managed to say, choking back my rage, "is why you and they"—I motioned to Dujok and Haci—"are so obsessed with establishing this connection with angels."

"That's because there's something you don't know about us, love. My family and the Yezidi are the descendants of an ancient dynasty: We are the sons and daughters of angels."

My mouth must have dropped open. Because from the expression on Daniel's face, I could tell that he delighted in my stunned silence. He stroked his beard and leaned his towering figure close to me, his crystal-blue eyes flashing. I'd never been that close to him, and I'd never felt such fear.

"We are descended from a lineage of fallen beings and desperately want to reconnect with our origins and leave this forsaken world," he said, and I could hear the honest desire in his voice. "My family has been trapped on this world for more than a thousand years. And here we mated and lived side-by-side with man, just as it says in the Book of Enoch. But regardless of the many generations that have passed, we do not forget who we are or where we came from . . .

"So you see, to us, this is no obsession, love. It is the fulfillment of an ancient dream."

I couldn't speak. I didn't dare say anything. Neither did Ellen.

"And, as you've probably figured out, Dee was one of us. Quite possibly the one who has done the most to bring us home. But since his death in 1608, we have not been able to build on his work."

"You *have* to be joking," Ellen finally said.

"You think so? Why don't you ask the Yezidi here, Miss Watson?" Daniel said, and Dujok stood up straighter. "It was only a few years ago that we determined they were also descended from the angels that populated Earth some ten thousand years ago. They survived the Great Flood just

as our ancestors did. The only difference is that they were more successful at preserving their history. We were amazed to learn they still knew
how to control forces that we had long forgotten how to manipulate. And
they are able to do it because they keep sacred the very land where it all
began. Here, in these mountains, is the remaining vestige of a forgotten
antediluvian world. The only surviving piece of angelic technology that
will help us to reestablish the connection to our native world."

"Noah's Ark, I suppose. . . ."

"Precisely. God may have given Noah the instructions on how to
build the ark, but our ancestors were the ones who supervised its entire
construction."

Ellen cut in. "Right. And I'll bet that huge crater out there is also a
result of your technology."

Daniel smiled. He seemed to delight in her sarcasm. "The Hallaç
crater is the source of these blessed crystals. That's why the Yezidi have
guarded it for generations, to keep these sacred stones with their trans-
mitter-like properties out of the wrong hands."

"Angels, Yezidi . . . what kind of craziness is this? You don't believe
this bullshit, do you, Julia?" Ellen said. "This is the most ridiculous pile
of garbage I've ever heard."

"I can assure you that it's all true, Ms. Watson," Daniel muttered dis-
missively. He seemed bent on convincing me. "Believe what you will,
but humanity is, in fact, descended from a hybrid of man and divine angels. We are flesh and bone. And we share your DNA, though we aren't
entirely human in the strictest sense . . ."

"I'll say," Watson muttered. "How could you people manipulate
Julia like this? How could her own husband—"

"I already told you this mission is more important that his wedding
vows. Maybe your inferior mind can't comprehend it, but our species
has a different, more pragmatic view of ethics. Maybe that makes us
colder—that logic should supersede emotion. But it also makes us more
efficient. And stronger."

"Your *species*? You're a different *species* now? Well, I've never heard
of you," Watson scoffed.

"But I'll bet you have, Agent," Daniel said flatly. "Every religion has a fable for how our species came to mix with yours and was doomed to this planet. We are the sons of exiles. Cursed. Even man condemned us, blaming us for all the evils of the world. You wove the folly into your myths and called us Lucifer, Thoth, Hermes, Enki, Prometheus. On one hand you worshipped us, these beings who brought knowledge from the heavens. But you also feared us for what we might want in return. You demonized us in every myth. We've been your heretics, your witches and warlocks, even your vampires. And if some of our ancestors were affiliated with the occult, it's only because that is how they could disguise their knowledge about our true origins. And that's why our ancestors appear only intermittently in your history. We are sworn to protect this information until we can decipher it, so that one day we might call to ask for permission to return home . . ."

"And you think now you've finally got it figured out?" I asked, disbelieving.

"We do," he said. "Thanks to Martin. To his father. To Dee. Thanks to mystics such as Emanuel Swedenborg, William Blake and so many others who sought to study the ancient science that will allow us to finally reconnect with our home."

"And who do you suppose is going to come take you 'home'? A squadron of winged cherubs? Little green men aboard a flying saucer?" Ellen said.

Daniel raised his hand to stop her. "No, Miss Watson. Contrary to what people might think, we angels do not have wings. It says it clearly in the Bible. Abraham, Tobias, Jacob, all of them met us face-to-face and each time they described us as what we really are: creatures from a far-away place who are more attuned to our surroundings. We can communicate with and understand all manner of life without having to speak or to put it under a microscope. We can see part of the electromagnetic spectrum that you are not able to. But aside from that, we are virtually identical to you . . ."

Daniel didn't seem to notice as I shook my head in disbelief.

"And that's why we admire humans like you, Julia," he said, turning

to me. "You possess a gift that we have lost over time. A gene that disappeared from the angel lineage after our DNA mixed with humans'—but
one that still remains in you. And that sublime gene, which appears in
just one in a million humans, is the reason you can communicate with
the heavens."

"So the 'angels' forgot how to talk to God, is that it?" Ellen shot back
acerbically.

"Frankly, yes. Many generations ago. But fortunately we passed on
that ability to you when the sons of God mated with the daughters
of man. That's why some of you have this gift," he said, staring at me
with his icy blue eyes, "and why we are so drawn to you. As it turns out,
you're our only hope of ever reconnecting with our origins."

"What a convoluted history . . ."

"I know it is. But now do you understand why Martin was so overjoyed when he found you, Julia? He felt he'd discovered the key that
would unlock the passageway back to the heavens."

"Where's Martin now?" I asked.

Daniel looked at Dujok out of the corner of his eye. Dujok was still
standing beside me, his Uzi at the ready, and his eyes seemed to ask the
same question.

"He's on the mountain," Daniel said finally. "He's preparing to open
the line of communication. And he's waiting for you."

88

The role of the Executive Office of the President is often underestimated. In fact, it's made up of some of the smartest and finest people in their fields, who are divided into teams to advise the president on everything from climate change to the Treasury to internal security matters. However, only rarely does the president give orders directly to one of these subordinates without his assistant knowing about it. But when he does, it's considered one of the highest honors—an honor Tom Jenkins had come to know well in the last year and a half. He was one of the few people who had the president's personal encrypted phone number and the authorization to use it at any time of day or night. No more than a dozen people—the president's wife and children and Ellen Watson included—had this privilege. So Tom tried not to abuse it.

But just after meeting with Colonel Allen in his hospital room, Jenkins decided it was time to use his direct access to Roger Castle and report to him about the lack of cooperation from the NSA agent.

"I'm sorry to disturb you with the details of the operation, Mr. President," he said, "but I need you to put pressure on the NSA so this agent will tell us what he knows."

The phone call caught President Castle in the middle of a state dinner, surrounded by European ambassadors. He'd already jumped in to save Ellen Watson—who, thankfully, was now keeping a close watch on Julia Álvarez and her kidnappers, as far as he knew. But he realized that if he wanted to stay ahead of the game, he'd have to do as Tom asked.

"Don't worry, Mr. Jenkins. I'll take care of it. I was only waiting for your report. Owen needs to cooperate with us."

"Thank you, Mr. President," Jenkins said. "Maybe this goes without saying, sir, but Ellen and I think you've taken a major step here. The Elijah project's days are numbered."

Castle hung up without responding. Minutes later, he ducked out of the dinner to call Michael Owen.

"I suppose you know what's happened to your agent in Spain."

Owen knew Castle was getting closer to the truth. Owen had just read the preliminary report that Nicholas Allen had sent via encrypted email. And he'd heard about the mess aboard the USS *Texas,* where the president had stepped in. Things were *not* looking good . . .

"I'm up-to-date on everything, sir. We've been hit with the second electromagnetic attack in a civilian area since they kidnapped Martin Faber. The situation is . . . worrisome . . ."

"I want to propose something to you, Michael. And I want you to really think about it. Maybe you already know my people have located the stones and the terrorists you're looking for. I've got information about where they're headed and I'd be glad to share it with your people—if you're willing to work together."

"I already have that information, Mr. President. The satellites your people are relying on report to my office."

"Open your eyes, Michael. We have a common enemy. I want those stones as much as you do, and I'm aware the Elijah project knows more about them than anyone else. I'm suggesting we unite our forces to get them. You help me, I help you."

"United against a common enemy? Like Reagan and Gorbachev in Geneva?"

"Right. Just like Reagan and Gorbachev," Castle said.

"Very well, Mr. President. As of this morning when you first stepped foot in Elijah, I consider you 'in.' There's no reason we shouldn't work together. What would you like us to do, sir?"

"Get in touch with Colonel Allen in Spain and ask him to work with our people on the ground. I want them to go after those damn stones and get them under our control."

"Do you want me to take care of the logistics? My men have a private aircraft at the ready, which could take them all to Turkey."

"That's more than I could have hoped for. Thank you, Michael."

"Good," Owen said. "And just so you have no doubt about my willingness to work with you, let me give you the latest news."

The president shifted the phone from one ear to the other. "News? What news?"

"It's not good, sir."

"None of it ever is . . ."

"We've just received word that there has been a colossal electromagnetic explosion on the surface of the sun. We still can't say for sure whether it's related to the class-X emissions we've been reading on Earth. But we have confirmed that the solar shock wave is headed our way. Sir, it's going to be bad. Like a massive electromagnetic bomb going off right in our faces."

"A bomb?"

Just then, he remembered what the submarine captain had said to him about an attack of global proportions. That was Owen's biggest fear, too.

"Yes, sir. That's why Elijah is so bent on getting the stones under our control. Aside from being a supernatural communications device, in the wrong hands they could cause a worldwide catastrophe."

89

"Angels? Can you believe these guys? What a crock . . ."

Ellen really let loose after Daniel ordered us taken to a small windowless room to spend the night. Her eyes were red and puffy. She looked exhausted.

"Honestly . . . I don't know what to believe anymore," I mumbled as I contemplated our makeshift beds: a pair of filthy mattresses wedged into rusted metal frames.

"What's to believe? *Hello*? Angels aren't real!" Ellen shot back. "Can't you see what's happening? These people stumbled upon some kind of powerful technology here and they're trying to cover it up with all this angel mumbo jumbo. If you let yourself believe even one iota of their lies, they'll just go on wrapping you up tighter in their ghost stories. What's worse, it'll let them keep all this knowledge to themselves."

"What do you mean?"

"You ever heard Arthur C. Clarke's famous quote 'Any sufficiently advanced technology is indistinguishable from magic'? That's what's going on here."

"Okay, now I understand," I said. "The United States is interested in the stones because they think it's some kind of superior technology. Is that it?"

"Look, if Artemi Dujok was telling the truth, then some secret US project has been studying this technology for more than a century. The president has just learned about it and he's trying to blow the roof off the thing, to bring all this secrecy to light. Julia, we're on the same side here."

"Except that my husband and I are pawns in all this."

"Nobody's saying that, Julia. Martin Faber is a US citizen."

"Okay, okay . . . Let's get ahold of ourselves. We're just under too much stress."

Ellen plopped down on the cot.

"Tomorrow morning we'll set off to find Martin. Then everything will be cleared up." I sighed. "Just tell me one thing: Why are some old stones with some kind of electrical properties so important to the US government?"

"You know they're a lot more than that. They could be part of some kind of prehistoric technology that was lost after a global catastrophe. Could be a fragment of a meteorite. Or some machinery from the future that ended up in our time by accident . . ."

"Oh, but you don't believe in angels . . ."

"Angels, ghosts, gods, spirits . . . those are just terms we use to disguise our ignorance. If we took that lightbulb"—she pointed at the roof—"back in time to the fifteenth century, they'd burn us at the stake for witchcraft because we created a glowing rock."

"Well, John Dee did go through that," I mumbled. "Maybe there's something to it."

"You ever hear of 'cargo cults,' Ms. Álvarez?"

I shook my head.

"It was this bizarre thing that happened after World War II on the islands off New Guinea, which had been totally isolated from the outside world. When the US Army was getting ready for a confrontation with Japan, they set up military outposts on these islands to use them as tactical bases and to cut off supplies. Now, just imagine the kind of impact all of this must have had on these aboriginal tribes. All of a sudden, thousands of white-faced men came out of nowhere—from the sky and from the sea—carrying 'fire sticks' and coming out of the bellies of metal birds, and leveling the forests near their villages to set up barracks. They thought we were gods, that we had complete control over the forces of nature."

"Why did they call them cargo cults?"

"Well, they kept seeing these boxes fall from the sky with the word 'cargo' written on the sides. They figured the gods were sharing their heavenly riches with them. So they started praying to those gods. Those interactions gave birth to tribal religions that still exist today."

"This is fascinating . . ."

"And it's all because they came in contact with superior technology, which they called magic. You see what I mean?"

"All I see is that you prefer to have a nice, clean secular explanation over a religious one."

"You got that right. And you can bet it's that belief that's going to get us out of here. Not trusting in angels."

"What do you mean?"

"I mean that we've been in Hallaç for several hours now. More than enough time for our satellites to triangulate the position for Dee's adamants. We're going to have company real soon."

It wasn't yet dusk four thousand miles to the west in Santiago de Compostela when Inspector Antonio Figueiras finally figured out he'd been duped. The American who'd promised him information about his two murdered police officers had disappeared into thin air. Naïvely, Figueiras had believed Tom Jenkins when he said he was taking the spy who'd started the church gunfight just to finish up his investigation. And he'd believed Jenkins—had been suckered, that is, by his fancy credentials and his expensive suit and aftershave—when he swore that neither he nor Julia Álvarez would leave Spain without telling him first.

He'd definitely been had.

A phone call from the national police at the Lavacolla airport confirmed his suspicions: His North American friends had boarded a brand-new Learjet 45—the same one Nicholas Allen had flown to Santiago on—and left the country just an hour after Jenkins had made his promises. They had gotten a priority flight plan with a stop in Istanbul and permission to land and refuel at the airport in Kars, all courtesy of the Spanish Ministry of Defense.

But by the time Figueiras got all the details, it was too late. If the airport officials were right, Jenkins and his buddies would have been in the air for more than three hours. And Figueiras hadn't even gotten so much as a text.

So Figueiras wearily sized up his situation. His key witness had disappeared in Noia and so had his American "reinforcements." The news coming out of the small fishing village of about fifteen thousand was all bad, too. The killers' helicopter had landed just outside of town and took off after leaving more bodies in its wake.

It was the only thing people were talking about in Noia: The confrontation with American soldiers that had left four dead and a fortune in damages to a historic building.

With no one left to interview, Figueiras decided to return to the scene of the crime—where his nightmare had begun. He figured that with the old dean's help, he could get inside the cathedral and maybe find some other evidence to keep him busy until Jenkins decided to call.

So at a quarter to nine that night, the two men met outside La Puerta Santa—the Holy Door—of the cathedral. By this point, neither had anything to hide.

"Tell me about that symbol that showed up inside the church again, Father," Figueiras asked under the wan light of streetlamps. The rain had stopped and the temperature had started to fall. He had almost felt sorry for the hunched-over old priest when he saw Benigno Fornés shivering as he came to the door. Almost. He and Figueiras never had much occasion to exchange a kind word. Despite himself, when he saw Fornés, he tore right into his line of questioning. "So you still think this is some kind of symbol for the end of the world, Father? What'd you call it last night—the mark of the angel of the Apocalypse?"

Fornés let out a sigh of resignation and stretched out his hand for a reluctant handshake. "It's late," he said.

The dean looked tired, and to be honest, he was in no mood to argue angelic theory with a communist.

"Inspector, you're an atheist who doesn't believe in a damn thing. A man without hope. Why should I waste my breath talking with you?"

"I'm not looking to be saved, Father," he said. "I'd be content to figure out why Julia Álvarez was kidnapped just after the gunfight last night when that symbol appeared."

"Julia was kidnapped?" The old priest's mood darkened.

"That's what I said, Father."

"I . . . I hadn't heard anything about that," he stammered. "I figured she hadn't come to work today because you were still interviewing her."

Figueiras didn't offer any details. Instead, he got right to the point. "Remember that helicopter we saw last night?"

"How could I forget?"

"We believe it belongs to a terrorist group."

Fornés looked worried. The ETA, the Basque terrorist organization, had bombed parts of Santiago in the past, but they'd never had these kinds of resources.

"They're some kind of fanatics with international ties. They've taken her to Turkey," Figueiras said, mainly trying to keep the old priest in the dark about the details of the situation. "They're probably the same ones who kidnapped her husband."

"They've kidnapped Martin, too?"

Figueiras thought the priest sounded genuinely surprised.

"That's right, Father. Do you have any idea why they might have done that?"

The hard-edged old Galician thought hard before answering. He knew this sly cop would use anything he said against him. "Well . . . what do you think happened?" Fornés said finally. "Do you think her kidnapping has something to do with the symbol?"

"Or maybe with her work on the Pórtico. Who knows? Maybe you've seen something suspicious in the last few days? Was she acting strange? Anything that might stand out could be useful to us." He smiled. "Well, at least useful to help find her."

The men hurried out of the cold and into the church through a side door that Fornés opened with an old iron key. Their footsteps reverberated throughout an old stone passageway as the priest opened door after door, each decorated with images of St. James the apostle.

"What can you tell me about the men who kidnapped Julia, Inspector? You know I'm very fond of the young woman . . ."

"Can't say much, Father. Just that half the world is looking for them."

"Is that right?"

"The US government has agents all over this thing."

"Well, that makes sense . . . ," Fornés said as he opened the last door into the office, one with a depiction of St. James swinging a broadsword at the Battle of Clavijo. "Martin was an American, after all." Fornés felt around the dark wall for the light switch, then went inside and sat at a large oak table. "Is that it? You don't know anything else about these kidnappers?"

Now it was Figueiras's turn to measure his words. The old priest sat at his desk with his hands folded, as if waiting for something.

"Well, sure, we know some things," Figueiras said. "Looks like they're after some kind of stones. Not gems, exactly, but I guess they're valuable. I guess they have something to do with another kind of strange symbol."

"Another symbol, Inspector?"

"That's right, Father. And I figured since you were an expert in these kinds of things, maybe you could take a look and give me an idea for where to look next."

"May I see it?"

"Of course." Figueiras dug around his coat and pulled out his notebook. He flipped to the page where he had drawn the symbol at the jeweler Muñiz's house and handed it to Fornés.

"Any idea what it means, Father?"

Fornés just continued to examine the drawing. "Hmm. Looks like a stonemason's mark," he muttered, turning the symbol at different angles.

"A mason's mark. Great," Figueiras said, not hiding his disappointment. But Fornés didn't notice. He was engrossed in the symbol.

Fornés continued. "Mason's marks are ancient symbols, Inspector, and many of them are of unknown origins. Some of them are between four and ten thousand years old. They're all over Galicia. I don't think any other region in Europe has as many as we do. These engravings are called petroglyphs when they're found in ruins. But when you find them in churches they're called mason's marks. The most famous ones are in Noia—"

"Noia?" Figueiras couldn't hide his surprise. And Fornés noticed.

"Some of the world's most important medieval tombstones are there. And many of them have symbols similar to this one. Here, let me show you."

Fornés reached over to a bookcase with a pair of wooden doors, and unlocked them with a small key hanging from his waist. He pulled out a tome filled with ancient engravings and flipped through it on his desk.

"No one knows whether these are letters or symbols or some kind of coded directions, but one thing they do know: You never find them on secular buildings," Fornés said as he flipped through the book. "That tells me these are sacred icons of some kind. And the church of Santa María a Nova in Noia is loaded with them. Here, look at this."

He flipped to a series of strange characters. They looked like some kind of stick figures made up of crosses and circles. Just like the one Figueiras had copied from Dee's book. Figueiras studied them intently, trying to make out the meaning of the inscrutable figures.

"Did they ever figure out what these symbols were used for?" Figueiras mumbled as he flipped through the pages.

"No. No one's come up with a good explanation. Every historian who's looked at them has his own theory. And, of course, I have my own."

"So what's your theory, Father?"

"Well, these symbols, the ones with the dot inside the circle, seem to have something to do with families. They could be some kind of primitive coat of arms. A sort of branding iron for identifying property."

"Hmm. That seems pretty vague, Father."

"Well, I don't deny it. But we don't have much else to go on."

"So what do you think about the symbol I showed you?" Figueiras asked. "Any idea what family that might belong to? Or at least from what period?"

Fornés held Figueiras's gaze anxiously as he closed the book.

"I have my suspicions . . . but I'm afraid it leads to a dead end."

"So, you do recognize it?"

The old dean put the book away and remained silent for a moment before answering.

"That symbol you're so interested in is a version of one of the oldest of its kind in Noia. As a matter of fact, it resembles the one symbol that we know the least about. If it means anything to you, in Noia they think it represents the patriarch Noah."

"Noah? As in the ark?"

The wrinkles around Fornés's forehead intensified his scrutinizing stare.

"You know, come to think of it, that symbol you've got there may be the very reason they dragged the Fabers to Turkey."

"*This* is the reason?" he said, holding up the notebook. "I don't understand."

Fornés sighed and rolled his eyes. *How could this man be so dense?* "Didn't you learn in school that Noah's Ark was said to have run aground atop the tallest mountain in Turkey? Haven't you ever heard of Mount Ararat?"

"Honestly, Father . . . I never managed to stay awake in religion class."

Daniel Knight made good on his promise.

Just as he said he would, he woke us up at the crack of dawn. As if we were guests in his home, and not simply his prisoners, he kindly asked us to dress in the hiking gear he'd set out for us and said he would return a half hour later to tell us breakfast was served. Ellen and I dressed wordlessly. We were still groggy from staying up late talking about angels and cargo cults. We clumsily put on the heavy thermals—made with lead fibers, one of the tags said—wool pants and heavy climbing boots, and followed him out the door.

Ellen and I served ourselves from a selection of fruit, cheese, yogurt, honey and dried fruit. Fed and more alert from the food and the blasts of cold mountain air, we were escorted outside toward the Sikorsky X4, where a group of men we had never seen awaited us. They were a rough-looking bunch—wind-cracked, leathery faces, their heads wrapped in frost-covered turbans, wearing well-worn tunics. Each carried an AK-47 on his shoulder, and from what we could tell, none spoke a word of English.

"Let's get a move on, ladies!" Artemi Dujok yelled from the door of the helicopter. "Today is going to be unforgettable!"

It was hard to look at him. I still couldn't believe that Martin's mentor could have lied to me in that way just to get me here.

But Dujok looked positively overjoyed. In his world, everything was as it should be. They had the adamants, the invocation tablet . . . and me, at their mercy, hundreds of miles from anyone who could help.

It was a short flight.

The last base camp before the peak of Mount Ararat was less than thirty miles from the Hallaç crater. It was at nearly fourteen thousand feet, buried under a blanket of freshly fallen snow that covered all but the tops of several volcanic rocks. Dujok happily explained that the helicopter saved us a two-day hike up the mountain—the bitter cold, the cumbersome climbing gear, the rain and sleet that would have made our trip a nightmare.

"From here, the hike up to the Ark isn't so bad," he said, trying and failing to calm our nerves.

Built on one of Ararat's relatively flat hillsides, the base camp was the picture of solitude. By the first rays of morning, you could see several small igloo-type structures and a sort of teepee that were used to store food and water. Snow and wind twisted in all directions as the helicopter blades neared the ground.

"You know, most Kurds think it's impossible to climb this mountain," Daniel said over the headphones, smiling and chatty.

"I can see why," I said, trying to make poor conversation. But he was undeterred.

"See, they believe Ararat was touched by the finger of God and that no man may desecrate the sacred treasure it keeps," he said as he handed each of us Diamox pills for altitude sickness. "It's good to keep that in mind: Never offend the mountain . . . We're going to be summiting on the south face, the most hospitable part. The north face is an impassible canyon. They call it the Ahora Gorge or the Gorge of Arghuri, which means 'the planting of the vine,' even though nothing has grown there in thousands of years. It's steeper than the Grand Canyon and was once a volcano . . ."

I'd been absentmindedly watching the helicopter blow eddies of snow down below when Daniel's history lesson made me look up at ominous clouds surrounding the mountain's peak.

"Is . . . is it still active?"

"Oh, no, no, no . . . ," Daniel said, shaking his head. "It's been quiet for centuries. It was probably dormant by the time Noah arrived."

"It better be . . ." Ellen joked.

"As delicate as it is, any kind of volcanic activity would have destroyed the Ark. What a travesty that would have been . . ."

"Although there was an earthquake up here in 1840 that almost did the job," Dujok yelled from the cockpit.

"Earthquake? Wait, so it *is* a seismic area?"

"Well, it was. That quake was as powerful as the eruption of Mount St. Helens. It destroyed several mountain villages. Killed more than two thousand people. Leveled St. Jacob's Cathedral, which housed the Ark's most valuable relics. Believe it or not, there used to be pilgrimages to visit the Ark before the quake. We still have some of the worshippers' journals."

"Really?"

"Sure, everyone around here has heard about the Ark and the holy stones it carried," Daniel added. "You can hear story after story of all the groups who sent expeditions to recover the stones in the years following the earthquake. Napoleon III. Nicholas II. Viscount James Bryce. The CIA. The list goes on and on. Actually, any of the stones you hear about out in the world, including Solomon's Urim and Thummim, only left here with our people's blessings."

"The stones all came from the Ark?"

"The one and only, Ms. Álvarez."

It amazed me that there was no doubt in their minds that buried under the permafrost was a ship thousands of years old. An enormous vessel built to the Bible's specifications: three hundred cubits long by fifty cubits wide; forty-two thousand cubic feet of space. It was like a giant box floating on the high seas. As hard as I tried, I just couldn't imagine a ship the size of the *Titanic* marooned on a mountaintop fifteen thousand feet above sea level.

I'd always had a hard time believing the story, whether the protagonist was Noah, Utnapishtim or Atrahasis. Like so many other Western kids, I'd grown up with the story of the Ark. I'd colored pictures of it in kindergarten class. And I daydreamed about it when a story about it appeared in the press in the 1980s. That's when an explorer named Jim Irwin had set off to Ararat to find the Ark. The nuns at my Catholic school kept us up-to-date with his travels and even encouraged us to pray for that astronaut-turned-archaeologist and his expedition. Irwin gave everyone hope; he was, after all, one of only twelve men ever to set foot on the moon during the *Apollo* missions. And if he believed in the

Ark, he would not be deterred. My rational mind was developing only then, and I remember hearing over the radio that his mission was more mythology than science. And that it was important for Irwin to prove God had once walked on this earth as surely as he, Irwin, had walked on the moon.

But, alas, Irwin failed in his mission. He never found the Ark. And his failure planted the seeds of my skepticism.

As a matter of fact, every so-called Ark discovery that made news ended up being debunked shortly thereafter. If there was, in fact, an Ark buried atop Mount Ararat, no one had been able to find it.

Or had they?

Something told me I was about to find out.

It was nine thirty in the morning when Daniel Knight and Artemi Dujok decided it was time to begin our climb.

From the outset, though, I had a feeling that the mountain itself wasn't going to be our biggest hurdle. It was the fog and icy snow underfoot, not to mention our inexperience at this altitude. Any experienced mountain climber will tell you it takes time to acclimate to the thin air and the atmospheric pressure at high altitudes—time we didn't have. It was never more apparent than when I hooked myself up to the tethering cable that connected all of us.

Dujok shot ahead at a pace I knew I wouldn't be able to match.

He hiked confidently, poking his walking stick into the powder to check the depth with the assuredness of someone who knew this path well. Watching him trek ahead so confidently reminded me how stupid I'd been when he made me believe we had discovered my husband's location together. How goddamn naïve I'd been! What's worse, I felt betrayed knowing Martin had put my life in danger just to satisfy his insane obsession.

Martin.

How will I react when I see him? How will he try to explain all this madness?

Ellen Watson panted as she followed behind Dujok. She'd been complaining for a while now about a headache, but no one had paid much attention to her. Waasfi followed behind her. And, just behind me, Daniel and Haci brought up the rear, pulling along an aluminum sled stocked with supplies and provisions. We walked at a moderate clip, literally following in Dujok's footsteps. I was surprised to find that, despite the tension last night and my growing doubts, our troupe was not in bad spirits. Behind me, for example, Daniel huffed along but was as chatty as ever.

". . . and the etymology of the place names in this region confirms this mountain was where Noah disembarked," he was saying, panting because of the altitude. "On the north face, just before the ravine, there's a little village called Masher, which means 'Judgment Day.'" A blast of cold air made him clear his throat. "On the Armenian side of the mountain, the capital city is Yerevan, which is said to be the first word Noah said when he saw solid ground—'*Erevats!* There it is!' And over yonder is the village of Sharnakh, which means 'Noah's settlement.' Oh, and over there's the town of Tabriz—'the boat.' It's all like that for a hundred miles around . . ."

I was more worried about watching my step than listening to his litany of worthless information.

With each passing mile, we moved more sluggishly as we tracked around slopes and snowdrifts. Daniel Knight and Ellen Watson proved to have a harder time than any of us had expected, and they slowed us down as well. Which is why, after three straight hours of climbing, I breathed a heavy sigh of relief when we finally stopped to rest at the foot of a giant stone wall. It was an impressive structure covered in deep, vertical gouges that sometimes intersected like crosses, and the wind howled as it rushed over the scars. The wall rose up, up until it disappeared behind the low-lying clouds, making us feel like ants next to a skyscraper. Dujok explained that we were standing at one end of an enormous glacier.

"We're here," Dujok said.

"Really . . . finally?" Ellen panted.

Dujok staked his walking stick into the snow and turned to his GPS.

"Yes," he said, offering nothing more. Their voices echoed in the mountain silence.

"So, where is he? Where's Martin?" I said, impatient, looking at what clearly seemed like a dead end.

Dujok didn't say anything. He just brushed the frost out of his mustache, unlatched himself from the tethering line and headed toward a stone outcropping with a flashlight.

"Where's he going?" Ellen muttered behind me.

"To get you the answers you're looking for," he shouted, and disappeared into the foggy base of the stone.

Little did I know we were not alone. Somewhere in the distance, an unseen set of eyes watched our group through a pair of infrared military binoculars.

92

"It's the entrance to some kind of ice cave," Nicholas Allen said as he watched the group through his binoculars.

The thought of an ice cave only made Tom Jenkins feel worse. Despite being wrapped in layers of thermal clothing, his face and body felt frozen through and through. Although they'd rented all the best gear in Dogubayazit—North Face clothing, ultraviolet goggles, Marmot gloves—the climb had left Jenkins exhausted. What was worse, their cell phones weren't working. They couldn't seem to get a signal—actually, all their electrical equipment seemed to be malfunctioning—anywhere on Mount Ararat. But what worried Allen was that the local authorities had confiscated their weapons and assigned a pair of trackers to follow them. "Understand our point of view, Colonel," the Turkish police had told him. "Ararat is still a very sensitive area for us. If something happens during your climb, our men will be there to take care of it before you know it."

"What's that? A cave? Wonderful," Jenkins grumbled.

"And it looks like they're going inside."

"How many men?"

"I can make out five. Maybe six. Some of them are armed. I count one . . . two submachine guns. I hope they're not stupid enough to use them. They'll cause a damn avalanche."

"Recognize anybody?"

Allen steadied the infrared binoculars. But looking at simply their heat signatures wasn't enough to identify them.

"No. But I'll bet the one who just went into the cave is Julia Álvarez. It's them, no doubt. No one else would be crazy enough to climb all the way up here in November."

He silently continued to scan the mountainside.

"Notice the shape at the top of the mountain? Looks like some kind of structure, doesn't it?"

"What are you getting at, Colonel?"

"That maybe we're looking at the actual Ark. It looks a lot like the classified photos I've seen in the Elijah archives. A geometric shape jutting out of a frozen block of ice . . . one that's visible only when the ice melts during really hot summers. Makes sense they'd have to go *into* the glacier to reach it."

"Wait, wait . . . you mean *Noah's* Ark? They think they've found Noah's Ark?"

"It's the only thing that makes sense," Allen said, shrugging his shoulders and handing the binoculars to Jenkins. "What else would they be looking for up here?"

Jenkins looked through the lenses and zoomed in. "Well, the damn boat must be a hell of an attraction, Colonel, because they've all gone inside."

"Perfect. Time to move in. You coming, Jenkins?"

93

My heart was pounding as I approached the crevice in the stone, my breath freezing in nervous puffs. It must've been close to midday because my stomach was starting to grumble from hunger.

It wasn't until I reached the rock face, past the looming fog, that I got a better look at it. The fissure was just wide and high enough for a person to slip through, ducking under the hanging icicles, as Dujok had done. I dug my hiking cleats into the icy ground and carefully made my way through.

I was surprised to find any kind of light inside such a narrow space. But soon I saw why. That crack into the very heart of the glacier was slowly melting and the ice acted like a prism, refracting and reflecting light all around me. It was beautiful, yet I couldn't stop thinking about how dangerous this was. The walls were brittle, not the kind of solid ice you'd expect to see inside a glacier thousands of years old. But I pressed on, moving forward toward a faint murmur coming from inside the mountain until I reached an opening.

Three dark outlines were waiting for me at the end of the tunnel. The first was Artemi Dujok, who'd taken off his rucksack and was reaching out to help me down a steep step at the end of the pass. The other two faces I didn't make out right away.

"Hello, love!" I heard a familiar woman's voice say. She was holding a lantern, and it took a second for my eyes to adjust to the dark.

But I could've picked out her British accent from a mile away. I should have known that wherever Daniel Knight was, Sheila Graham would be close behind.

"Sheila!"

"Well, of course it's me, love. Who else would you expect?" she said, lowering the lantern.

Sheila looked as splendid as usual. Forget that her perfectly coiffed hair was under a thick wool hat. Her lips were perfectly made up in a carmine red and her eyelashes were curled. It's as if the cold only managed to make her more beautiful.

"I suppose," she said, after stamping a pair of kisses on my cheeks, "that you haven't met William, have you?"

The third shadow stepped into the light. He walked with a cane and a slight limp, although he tried to stand up straight, gentlemanly. He had a snowy white face with a carefully manicured beard and rosy red cheeks. No, I'd never seen this man before in my life. And yet, when our eyes met, he smiled as if my face brought back fond memories.

"You look lovely, Julia," he whispered.

I couldn't get over seeing a man almost in his eighties deep inside a mountaintop glacier. Although Mount Ararat was no Everest, it still wasn't hospitable for a man of his advanced age. Yet he didn't seem out of place. On the contrary. He was dressed in warm thermals like the rest of us with a flashy Granny Smith–green scarf that hung around his neck neatly, giving him a lofty air. He spoke and moved gracefully, as if the thin mountain air had no effect on him.

"I can see everything I've heard about you is true," he added, his eyes smiling. "True in every way."

"This is William Faber, love," Sheila said.

It took a second for all the information to register.

Bill Faber?

The man who refused to attend my wedding?

A flood of images and memories flashed in my mind, the blood pounding in my temples.

The father who never called his son? The man who ran off to the United States and left Sheila and Daniel to do his work with John Dee's crystals?

The elder Faber grabbed my hands with such strength and caring warmth that it caught me by surprise. He radiated a presence. I had to admit, despite all my prejudices, that he simply exuded something special. A sort of majesty. He was almost a foot taller than I was. Though age had wrinkled his skin and made him hunch a bit, his face glowed. This was a handsome man. And absolutely magnetic.

"So you must be another one of those angels," I muttered.

William Faber gave a hearty laugh. "I want you to see something, Julia. I've been waiting for this moment for years . . ."

William Faber limped toward the deepest part of the glacier, opposite the mouth of the icy passageway. The walls of the cavern were thirty feet high with an opening to the sky above us. Only one of the walls wasn't frozen. Actually, it was more like a perfectly geometric slab of dark stone jutting out into the room, and it was surrounded by several metal folding tables covered with electrical equipment.

A lab at fifteen thousand feet?

It was warmer in this part of the cavern. I could see several devices—which explained the humming sound—including a digital barometer, a thermograph, a seismic sensor and another to measure gravity. There was a data-storage tower, some kind of satellite communication device connected to a tubular antenna and a mixing board connected to a network of speakers that were, for some reason, aimed at the rock face. PVC and metal pipes pumped warm air over the equipment while a generator the size of a refrigerator powered them.

I looked at Bill Faber, stunned.

"This is what Martin's been working on since he arrived in Turkey," he said.

"Wha . . . what exactly is this?"

"That wall," he said, tapping his cane against the rock, "is part of the bridge of Noah's famous ship. It's been waiting for us here for the last four thousand years, buried under layers of ice forty degrees below zero."

Bill Faber let his words hang in the air so that the information could wash over me. And then he continued.

"It's amazing, really, that it's in such good condition. The constant snow and ice have been petrifying it over the millennia, transforming the cellulose in the wood into what we have here today: wood as hard as stone. Or, rather, a stone that vaguely resembles wood."

"The . . . Ark . . . ," I said, still in denial. He kept speaking, but I couldn't get my mind around it.

"The inside is sealed off, unfortunately," he said. "There's no way to get to it without using explosives. But that would be suicide. The blast would bury us under tons of ice and snow."

I tried to imagine the dimensions of the ship. But it was hard to, given that I could only see a segment eighteen to twenty feet long.

"We've spent decades trying to find it," Bill Faber said. "The last ones ever to see this were the Russians. They found it in the summer of 1917, when the abnormally high temperatures melted part of the glacier in which we're standing. And then the soldiers made an even bigger discovery, something vital to our quest: an inscription."

I could feel myself tensing.

"What kind of inscription, Mr. Faber?"

He twirled his cane in the air, walked five steps toward the ship and pointed at the most eroded part of the ship's hull. There, over what looked like the frame of a sealed doorway, I could make out the outline of four symbols carved into the stone. They would have been easy to miss if you weren't looking for them.

I stepped closer for a better look and ran my fingers over each character.

$$\daleth \mem \gimel \mem$$

"Recognize them?" he said.

I just stared at the cryptic squiggles.

"It's said that those characters spell out the true name of God," he said, smiling. "And that pronouncing it correctly reveals its power. Martin thinks this is some kind of passkey, which, if we say it correctly, could open a doorway inside."

"What do you expect to find in there?"

"A metaphor."

I turned from the wall and looked at Bill Faber questioningly.

"A symbol, Julia. We're looking for the stairway that Jacob saw in his dream, the means that will allow us to return to the place where we belong. Nothing more, nothing less."

"And what do you think Jacob's ladder actually is?"

"Well, we think it's probably some kind of electromagnetic singularity that activates when these letters are pronounced correctly. The right harmonic frequency should work just like a light switch. But all of it depends on pronouncing the letters precisely and having the adamants to enhance the signal."

"And that's why we need you."

The voice came from somewhere above us. It reverberated throughout the cave and almost knocked the wind out of me. I spun around and looked to the top of the wall and there I saw him, suspended near the opening atop the glacier.

"Martin!"

I instantly got a knot in my throat. Martin, dressed in a red overcoat and white turtleneck, tried to smile as he rappelled down the opening.

"Julia! You're here!"

Before I could catch my breath, his arms were wrapped around me, and he was spinning me around in a dizzying, loving whirlwind.

"Martin . . . I . . ." I loosened his grip on me. "I need to know what's going on."

"Oh, you will, my love, you will!"

This Martin didn't look anything like the one from the supposed kidnapping video. He was elated, strong and bursting with life. There was no sign that he'd ever been held captive.

"My love, I hope you can forgive me for all this," he said, whispering into my ear as he gently placed me back on the ground. "Just when I needed you, here you are."

A flood of emotions rushed to my chest, like an eruption of molten lava that made my eyes sting. I tried to breathe, to hold back the tears. But it wasn't easy, not after finally seeing the man to whom I'd pledged my love and devotion, his eyes twinkling from beyond his strong square jaw and that wavy blond hair. *Oh, God . . .* This man, this man who I loved . . . This man who deceived me . . . This man who now, even at this moment, was asking me to help him.

"I . . . I don't even know who you are, Martin," I stammered. "Don't you understand? I have no idea *who* you are!" I sobbed, the pressure in my chest building.

Martin leaned in close to me. "I've tried to tell you since the day we met, but I was always afraid to tell you everything."

"I don't believe you."

"I know you don't. Not right now you don't. But you will, my love. Even though you might not trust me right now, I promise you'll understand everything."

Martin reached out and stroked my hair, gently resting his hand on the crook of my neck.

"After all the incredible things we've seen together, all the things that defy reason, you still have this internal conflict, this battle between logic and faith. And I'm telling you that it's time to let go of all your doubt, my love. Right now, more than ever, Julia, I need you to believe in yourself—and to help save us all."

"To . . . save us?"

Martin's deep blue eyes stared into mine. They glowed with an emotion I'd never seen there before. I'd have sworn it was fear. And for a moment, I was able to sense his terror. Truly feel it.

"Julia, as we speak, a massive explosion of solar plasma is headed our way. In just a few hours, it'll smash into Earth and cause the kind of global catastrophe our world hasn't seen since the time of Noah. Except this time, there'll be no escape. There's no ark, no gods coming to our rescue . . ."

I could see Martin struggling to find the words to continue.

"When that invisible solar cloud punctures our atmosphere and makes landfall, it'll affect the very balance of Earth's core. It will cause earthquakes across the globe, destroy all of the planet's electrical networks, disrupt the very DNA of every species on Earth and cause even inactive volcanoes, such as this one, to erupt again, darkening the sky for decades to come. It is, without a doubt, that great and terrible day described in the Bible, Julia."

The terror in his voice shook me to the core, and I grabbed his arms. I felt my nails dig into his coat desperately. "And . . . there's . . . nothing we can do about it?"

Bill Faber pounded his cane on the floor. The crack made Ellen Watson jump. Sheila, Daniel and Dujok hung their heads silently.

"There's only one hope, young lady. *You* must activate the adamants to help us communicate with God."

"You think God will stop the solar storm?"

"God is just a metaphor, Julia," Martin said. "A symbol for the underlying force in the universe, the energy that—if we can control it—could help us counter the rain of solar plasma headed our way."

"But how am I supposed to talk to God?"

The elder Faber gave me a serious look—and a tall order. "It's just like praying, Julia. You haven't forgotten how to pray, have you?"

94

One of the Oval Office's emergency lines rang just as Roger Castle was reaching for the phone.

The president was about to call the director of the NSA. The first wave of data from the STEREO space probes was on his desk, urging him to take action. "STEREO has calculated that the first wave—two billion tons of high-energy protons—will impact Earth's Northern Hemisphere," read the e-mail from the Goddard Space Flight Center's control room. "Ground Zero will be the thirty-seven million acres between Turkey and the Caucasus republics. Impact should take place within forty-eight to seventy-two hours." The e-mail added: "We recommend alerting the United Nations and NATO's Supreme Allied Command to take all electrical and communications systems in this region offline until the storm has passed. We also recommend moving our satellites as far as possible from the impact zone."

"Yes?" Roger Castle abruptly answered the phone.

"It's Bollinger, Mr. President."

"Andy! Have you seen the news from Goddard?"

"That's actually why I'm calling. This storm isn't like any of the others. Someone caused it, Mr. President."

The line went silent.

"I'm sure about this, Roger," Bollinger said. "Our equipment tracked the electromagnetic signature of those stones you're looking for and traced where it was sending those category-X emissions: the sun."

"Andy . . . are you sure?"

"Positive. They weren't aimed at some far-off planet. And they weren't just aimed at the sun in general, either. They specifically targeted Sunspot 13057. And that's the very spot that's just erupted."

The president waited for another moment of silence to pass. He knew his friend had more to say.

"But I'm also calling to tell you," he finally said, "that I think Goddard's calculations about the intensity of this storm are wrong."

"What do you mean?"

"The STEREO probes classified the eruption as a class X23. Class X23, Roger! There's no precedent for that."

"X23? Help me out here, Andy."

"Mr. President, solar flares are classified as C for minor eruptions, M for moderate ones and X for the strongest ones. The one that plunged half of Canada into darkness in 1989 was a Class X19 emission, and it was the highest one we've ever recorded to date. This one is four orders of magnitude higher! We're not talking about some pretty aurora borealis over Florida or even a few million new cases of skin cancer . . ."

"What's this mean, Andy?"

"I've made a couple of inquiries, Roger. I've searched the archives of the Air Force Weather Reconnaissance Squadron in Colorado Springs, and I spoke with several climatologists I trust. And it all points to the same thing," Bollinger said, and this time, his tone was even graver. "The last time solar activity hit a peak, in 2005, we caught only a glancing blow from the solar storms and still it was enough to warm the Gulf Stream and bring about the worst hurricane season in more than a century. Remember Katrina?"

The president held the phone to his ear and said nothing.

"That solar eruption came from a single sunspot, number 720, we believe. Well, I've taken another look at that data, and, Roger, the news isn't good. That eruption was only a class X7, about the size of the planet Jupiter."

"So what does that mean for us?"

"How long did Goddard say it would take the proton storm to hit Earth?"

"Between two and three days."

Andrew Bollinger sighed into the receiver. "That's the standard amount of time we use. But in 2005, for some reason we haven't been able to determine, the blast from number 720 hit us . . . after just thirty minutes. Thirty minutes, Roger! Instead of traveling somewhere between six hundred and twelve hundred miles per second, that thing moved at forty-six thousand miles a second. We're talking about a quarter of the speed of light! My God, Roger. That mass might be on top of us any minute!"

"As far as we know, it's not supposed to hit the United States," Castle said, no less worried. "But it is going to hit one of the Allied countries—"

"Let me guess: Turkey."

"Right."

"That's because the coronal mass ejection is following the signal from the stones. They're acting like a homing beacon. God only knows what'll happen when the two meet . . ."

"Andy, what do we do?"

But that unexpected question from the leader of the free world was beyond Bollinger's knowledge. "There's not much we can do, Mr. President. Just watch. And pray."

95

"So what do we know about the symbols?" I asked.

We'd all huddled around the warm lab to figure out our next step. At fifteen thousand feet, with the icy wind pounding the glacier outside and finding its way through the cracks until it hummed like a pipe organ, I figured it was better to work together. Even with Martin. The loquacious Daniel Knight, who'd found a warm spot next to the generator, was the first to offer what he knew.

"You mean the symbols on the Ark? We think they're part of our ancestors' angelic language," he said.

"And do you know the meaning of the symbols, Daniel?"

"Unfortunately, we've lost whatever their meaning is over the millennia. In fact, until John Dee came along, no one had been able to interpret or even order them. Thanks to the stones and those on the 'other side,' he was able to receive the complete alphabet."

"Back to John Dee?"

"It was Dee who classified the symbols and named the language Enochian. Enoch only learned how to speak a rudimentary form of this language after being taken to the heavens in a kind of magnetic windstorm that occurs in this region, something we call the Glory of God. The epicenter of the phenomenon is in the Hallaç crater, although the storm has been known to occur in a thirty-mile radius. And that includes where we are now."

"As Enoch and Dee discovered, activating the adamants is all based on hitting the frequency that will resonate with their atomic structure," Bill Faber said.

"How are you all so sure they'll actually work?" I asked, looking at each of them.

"Because I've seen that force in action, Julia," Martin said. "I was with Artemi in these very mountains. And when the Glory of God decides to awaken, it can be a frightening experience."

"And yet, it's not powerful enough for what we need," Bill Faber said, shaking his head. "That ship was in constant contact with God during its voyage. Somehow, it managed a continuous connection with the other side and held it at a time when Earth's magnetic field was hit by an enormous energy strike similar to the one that's on the way."

"I can't speak Eno—whatever it's called. Not even a word! But all of you seem to know everything about it . . . ," I said, exasperated.

Bill Faber tapped the ground a couple of times with his cane. "There's no need to lose our temper . . . What we need from you is very simple: Just stand in front of the Ark holding the adamants and pronounce the name of God. Actually, you won't even have to speak it . . ."

"And how's that going to work?"

"We've got a sophisticated piece of equipment that can read the electrical impulses in the language centers of your brain and turn them into sound. It works like a neural scanner. Of course, it won't work while you're in your normal state of consciousness. Still, if we manage to get your brain waves to reach the delta frequency, between one and forty hertz—which only manifest during a trance—we should be able to achieve the results we need."

I couldn't help feeling like a lab rat again.

"So what makes you think this is going to work, Mr. Faber?"

"Simple," he said. "The medium John Dee used to communicate with the angels in the sixteenth century, Edward Kelly was able to pronounce words perfectly in Enochian countless times. And each time he did it with the help of the three items we have here today: the two adamants and the invocation tablet. The combination of their electromagnetic fields is what will amplify your gift. The adamants and the neural sounds your mind will make will play as a single instrument."

"I'll be like the *Amrak*."

"In a basic sense, yes." He nodded. "That's why we feel it'll work."

"Will it hurt me?"

"Dee's mediums always came away unharmed—"

"But they never tried what you want to try, did they?"

Bill Faber looked at me tenderly. "You have no reason to fear, my dear. You're surrounded by angels."

"Oh, right. I almost forgot . . ."

"Julia, the time is now. We need to get started right away."

96

Tom Jenkins dug his fingers into the snow and lugged his body forward to the edge of the precipice.

He knew just one wrong move could do more than endanger the mission—it could send him hurtling thirty feet to the bottom of the cavern. Out of habit, he checked his satellite phone once more and again he found it without a signal.

That's it. We're on our own now . . .

From this vantage point, he had a perfect view of everything inside the ice cave. He felt like he was a dove, looking down through the oculus in Rome's Pantheon. So he carefully settled himself as best he could, set his binoculars on a small tripod and got ready to watch the show. There was no need to rush now. He knew Nick Allen had his back, and most important, they had the element of surprise. If he played his cards right, he'd be out of there soon with his coworker, the Fabers and the two stones that the president himself had ordered secured.

Now he just had to find a way to let Ellen Watson know that the cavalry had arrived. But how to do it?

Watson looked petrified. He could spot that figure anywhere, despite her being bundled in thermals. She was watching Artemi Dujok and a young man in a red jumpsuit help Julia Álvarez onto a gurney and wheel her toward the lab. Ellen didn't look like she was getting ready to make a move.

"See that?" Allen whispered, pointing to a metal locker some eight to ten feet left of Ellen Watson. "I think that's the weapons locker."

Tom nodded but was distracted. There was something off about Ellen's body language, but he couldn't put his finger on it.

"If we could get our hands on some weapons, we could take control of the situation. It's six against two, but they're distracted."

Jenkins absentmindedly bit his lip.

While the two soldiers plotted their next step, things were taking shape down in the lab. A timer displayed on a fifty-inch flat-screen counted down the time remaining before the first wave of plasma blasted Earth. NASA had recalculated the speed of the tsunami several times thanks to Andrew Bollinger's findings—and Faber's equipment had intercepted the figures thanks to an antenna he'd placed just outside the roof of the glacier.

Twenty minutes, forty seconds . . .

The clock counted down the time until the high-energy protons made contact with the ionosphere, when all radio communications in the Northern Hemisphere would be lost.

My goddamn satphone got an early start, Jenkins lamented. The Iridium satellites must already have been affected.

The timer continued to count down. Dujok and the older Faber kept a close eye on it. Meanwhile, Sheila, Daniel and Martin surrounded Julia. They held her hands while one of the Armenian henchmen strapped her down and placed a helmet with all sorts of cables coming out of it on her head. He went around, checking all the connections.

"What the hell are they doing?" Jenkins mumbled, trying to zoom the binoculars in farther.

He watched as they wheeled Julia toward one of the glacier's walls. There, on some kind of platform, the invocation tablet and the adamants were waiting.

"There they are!" Jenkins said in a loud whisper.

The adamants had begun to glow ever so slightly, a pulsating shimmer that Allen watched nervously.

"Julia, try to relax," Allen and Jenkins heard the older man say clearly. Thanks to the acoustics of the icy cavern below, their voices rebounded and could be heard with crystal clarity.

"Relax? With these harnesses all over me?" Julia shot back.

"It's for your own safety, Julia," Martin said, trying to calm her. "We don't know just how powerful your mind will be under the circumstances. You know we'd never let anything happen to you."

"Remember what happened to you in Noia when the *Amrak* surrounded you in its magnetic field?" Dujok said. "You could've broken your neck when you fainted . . ."

The older Faber rushed toward them. "The impact will happen in exactly eighteen minutes," he said. "We should get started."

"But how do you *know*? That this is the moment? That this is the 'great and terrible day'?" Julia asked.

Daniel Knight stepped close to Julia. He carried a pen and a briefcase under his arm as if he were ready for just such a question. He pointed at something on the wall.

"John Dee predicted it all in *Monas hieroglyphica*, love," he said, blinking beneath the floodlights in the lab. "He drew a symbol in the book that, as a matter of fact, is also engraved on the Ark."

"You mean John Dee was here?"

"No. Well, at least we don't think so," he answered. "We know Dee traveled throughout Europe. But there's no evidence that he ever came to Turkey, much less a place as remote as this one."

"So how did he know about this symbol?"

"Until the 1840 earthquake that demolished most of the mountain's north face, pilgrimages to the Ark were common among the locals. Probably one of the pilgrims who journeyed to Ararat showed it to him. We do know that this is the oldest representation of the symbol."

"And you think the symbol contains some kind of prophecy, Daniel?"

"Without a doubt. Dee deciphered it, but for reasons that are quite easy to understand, he never published it. The Inquisition was full-on, and they scrutinized every publication. Disguising a message within a symbol has proven the safest way to transmit such information for millennia."

"So you think the symbol came from the Ark?"

"Right. Noah, who descended from angels just as we have, engraved it on the bridge of his ship in case future generations came up against a similar catastrophe. I think he knew that if it happened again, no god was coming to our rescue . . . so he left us this warning. It's like one of those road signs that signals 'dangerous curves ahead.' You might not be able to avoid it, but you can slow down enough to survive . . . Just look right here."

Julia and Ellen nodded. Jenkins focused in on the symbol and asked Nick Allen to have a look.

"So that's the big mystery," Jenkins whispered. "That's the symbol in the pictures Elijah poached from the Russians, right?"

Allen handed the binoculars back, nodding.

"At first glance," Daniel Knight said, his voice echoing throughout the cavern, "you might think this symbol is a cross between astrological and occult symbols. The sphere with the horns hints at the astrological sign of Taurus. And the horizontal line beneath it could easily be some symbol of femininity. Venus, maybe. But don't be fooled . . . We have to realize we're making assumptions based on Western culture, which is loaded with images of astrology and alchemy. None of that existed in the time of Noah. So we have to rely on much simpler terms to read it. This symbol is a universal warning."

"Get to the point, Daniel," Bill Faber said, eyeing the counter, which now read fourteen minutes, thirty-two seconds . . . thirty-one . . . thirty . . .

"The circle with the dot in the center was a symbol the ancient Egyptians used to represent the sun. Even modern astronomy uses this icon to denote the sun. The dot in the center is the key. It represents a sunspot. And in ancient times, when you could see a sunspot with the naked eye, it was considered a terrible omen. Some of the more than two hundred legends of the Great Flood make a reference to the sun 'falling ill' just before the flood began. These were allusions to the surging sunspots. And that's where the half-moon shape on top comes into play; it's a reference to the plasma waves that the sunspot produces. In prehistoric times, people had no idea what they were. They were invisible, after all. But they nevertheless felt the effects—on their skin, with internal bleeding, blindness . . . as if they'd been invaded by some invisible force. Infected by it."

"And what about the cross?"

"It's no cross at all, Julia." Knight smiled. "It's a sort of sword suspended over a pair of twin peaks . . . peaks that are identical to the twin summits of Ararat. Taken together, the symbol is both a warning and a sign of hope for mankind: The very moment when the sun focuses its power on this place will also be our opportunity to open our connection to the other side, to drink from the fountain of knowledge that allowed Dee to communicate with God. With his messengers. Our incorruptible ancestors."

"It's mankind's most ancient symbol," Martin added, taking Julia's hand and checking to make sure the helmet was snug against her temples. "Noah's earliest descendants spread the symbol far and wide, engraving it on important landmarks across the world as a warning to future generations."

"So . . . what I am supposed to do with all this information?" Julia asked.

"Concentrate on the invocation tablet, my love. Just remember the symbols and what each means. Let them combine in your mind. Hold the adamants and try to focus on what you're feeling. Let the desires in your soul come to the forefront," Martin said. "The electrodes you're connected to have been designed to pick up on even the slightest electrical activity in the left hemisphere of your brain. If any of those electrical signals correspond to a sound of speech, the computers will synthesize it into sound waves and transmit them to these speakers. There's no purer way of tapping into that information. The acoustic vibrations your mind produces will open the stairway to heaven."

Daniel interrupted. "Do not doubt, because the ability is within you. It's something programmed into the human genetic code. Before mankind was expelled from paradise, God taught humans his perfect language. Humans spoke it until he confounded their speech during the building of the Tower of Babel. We angels never had the ability to speak it. When we were pure, we didn't need it to communicate. So our only hope of communicating with our homeland is to use these ancient stones and entrust them to someone with your gift."

Julia sighed deeply, knowing she had no way to escape her captors. "Okay . . . Tell me how to start," she said.

"Take a deep breath," Martin said. "Try to relax. Find your center. And remember what your gift is capable of."

97

Remember what your gift is capable of . . .

That phrase somehow resonated deep within me. The sound of the words reverberated in my mind, even as I was strapped to the stretcher, which was tilted so I was nearly vertical. The sensation traveled over my skin, down my back, tickling as it coursed through me. My muscles gave way and all the tension from the past few days—the sleepless night in Hallaç, the climb up Ararat, seeing Martin again—seemed to simply slip away as I slid into a dream state.

A feeling of euphoria, sudden and unexpected, washed over me. I was overcome with a sense of calm. And having Martin near me, despite everything, infused me with a newfound confidence. I was awash in endorphins that filled me with an overwhelming sense of well-being, a sensation unlike anything I'd ever felt. And that's when I realized that this indescribable feeling of peace only began the second I took the adamants in my hands.

If there's one thing I'd learned about the psychic realm in my thirty short years on Earth, it's that nothing happens unless we open ourselves to possibility. So when Martin asked me to remember all that my gift made me capable of, I'd accepted his invitation and opened myself to him. All he had to do was place the adamants in my hands and my mind was ready and willing to accept them.

I could have clenched my fists shut.

I could have dropped the adamants to the floor.

But I didn't. I took them from him and made my choice . . .

"Now . . . ," he whispered softly into my ear, "let the crystals guide you. Don't force it, my love. Gaze into the invocation tablet. You already know the *Amrak* and its forces. Focus on the symbols etched into the Ark. Inside your soul is the key to pronouncing them appropriately. Let the symbols float together in your mind. Visualize them. Let your mind put them in order . . . Let your mind sing their sounds. Let them reverberate throughout this ancient place and call out to the Creator just as they did more than nine thousand years ago. You have the gift . . ."

"I . . . don't know if I can," I said. "It's been so long . . ."

"You can," he whispered. "Believe in yourself. Believe in us . . ."

And at that moment, I turned myself over completely to the forces inside of me. I squeezed the adamants and closed my eyes.

At first, I felt nothing but the adamants' smooth, warm surfaces. But then, as I took one last peek at the symbols etched on the Ark, I thought I saw the adamants glimmer a second before I closed my eyes again. It was a pale glow, much like the way they had pulsed on my wedding day those many years ago. It comforted me and encouraged me to give myself over to their power once more.

Just one more time.

And for the very last time.

"Feel how they palpitate in your hands," I heard Sheila say, though her voice seemed muffled, far-off, as if she were speaking to me from the bottom of the ocean.

"Find the essence that you share with the stones," Daniel said, also from somewhere far away. "That pure vibration is the holy language of the celestial beings."

"You've come all this way to help us communicate with them. Help us, now, Julia." Sheila said.

Help us . . .

Their plea echoed in my mind.

Help us, Julia . . .

It was a desperate plea. Intense.

Help us . . . , they repeated again.

It became a mantra. An ancient plea. A supplication that I'd heard once before, many years ago. It brought back a forgotten memory of my youth.

I closed my eyes and let it carry me to the day my grandma Carmen told me about my gift. I was nine years old. She was the one who taught me to see the auras around people, to judge their health and attitude—their life force—by gazing at the colorful clouds around them. Grandma, with her eyes fixed on mine, said, "You're like the jackals the Egyptians used to rely on as guides to the spirit world. Among us, there are angels whose auras glow the color of pure gold. They search for girls just like you. The day they come to you, they will say, 'Help us,' and that will be your signal."

She held a gnarled finger up to her lips and smiled—this would be our secret. I noticed the aura around her flicker, then dim.

Two days later, my beloved grandma Carmen died peacefully in her sleep.

And on that day, the day I learned my visions presaged her death, my gift felt like a curse.

98

Zero minutes, zero seconds.

A hush fell over the icy cavern below where Jenkins and Allen hid. Down below, William Faber held his breath. Jenkins had been so enraptured with the beauty that Julia Álvarez radiated that he didn't even notice when the countdown on the flat-screen hit zero. He watched her sleeping peacefully, her head resting on a small pillow, even as she lay dangled at a nearly ninety-degree angle and electrodes came from her head. She looked like a fairy tale princess just waiting for Prince Charming's kiss. He wondered what she was dreaming about at that very moment.

But when the counter went to zero, she didn't open her eyes.

As a matter of fact, no one around her—not even Ellen Watson, who was still eyeing the Ark in a stunned stupor—seemed to expect it. Everyone was simply focused on Julia, waiting for that invisible gift of hers to combine with the crystals to activate that mysterious communication device.

"It's time," William Faber finally said. "The hail of plasma should just be coming into contact with the ionosphere. We're about to find out whether these high-energy particles are going to do their part. It should be only a matter of seconds before—"

A loud *crack!* interrupted him. It sounded like it came from the diesel generator, as if something had shorted out.

Artemi Dujok looked but saw nothing. His henchmen pointed their trusty Uzis in the general direction of the sound, looking for an intruder. After all, someone might have followed them up there. Before they could turn their attention back to Julia, an arc of electric-blue light shone down from the sky just a few feet away from them. And then another. And another. In a matter of seconds, a crackling flood of blinding blue light rained down around them, sparking like a welder's torch.

"What is this?" Ellen yelled.

All of the angels immediately froze.

The sparks of blue light didn't fizzle once they hit the ground. Instead, they crawled along the icy floor, headed for the gurney where Julia was strapped. They were like a million flickers of light, twisting and intertwining—and moving with a purpose, like some kind of intelligent life form.

Martin took a step back. Haci and Waasfi followed his lead.

These electric spiders crawled their way up the bed onto the helmet on Julia's head, then began spreading out, doubling and tripling in number until they completely covered her body. Most of them gathered around her fists; the adamants seemed to draw them like magnets. Julia, still unconscious, shuddered for a moment. Then again. And again. Then, she began to shake wildly and violently, popping several of the straps. Then, just as suddenly, she straightened against the bed, stiff as a board.

"What is it? What's going on?" Ellen yelled hysterically.

But this time, they could barely hear her voice.

The loudspeakers had begun to emit a sound, a high-pitched squeal that seemed far off, almost inaudible at first. Then, as the electric spiders multiplied and spread all over the lab, the electrical equipment sparking as the charge tested their circuits, the sound coming out of the speakers became a constant hum. Meanwhile, the invocation tablet, which Sheila and Daniel watched dutifully, began smoking, sending a column of greenish fog to the ceiling. A second later, as if meticulously choreographed, the loudspeakers began pulsating and emitting a rhythmic tune. The Armenians looked spellbound. Martin and his father seemed positively in ecstasy.

Iossssummmm . . . Oemaaaa . . .

"It works!" Ellen said, laughing nervously, looking over at the angels.

Hasdaaaaeeee . . . Oemaaa . . .

"It works!"

Twenty feet overhead, Tom Jenkins and Nick Allen knew right away this was their chance.

Careful not to disrupt the column of thick, green smoke, they scaled down unnoticed. Jenkins's pulse was pounding even before he set foot on the icy ground. If he was lucky, he thought, he'd be inside the weapons locker in less than sixty seconds. Meanwhile, Allen made his way around the perimeter of the cave and hid behind a pair of metal containers. He was within striking distance of Haci and just seven or eight steps from the weapons. If those sparking spiders continued to keep them entranced, this was going to be easy, he thought.

But just as he was about to make his move, a flash of light made him stop dead in his tracks.

It was a spark, a flash against a wall that made him remember something from years ago that he'd rather have forgotten. The air seemed rarefied, just as it was on that day in 1999 as he stood on the edge of the Hallaç crater.

The colonel couldn't help the shiver down his spine.

Just then, there were four flashes, like lightning, against the wall of the Ark.

The symbols!

That forgotten terror he'd felt those many years ago, while standing next to Martin Faber and Artemi Dujok, came rushing to the forefront of his mind and all but paralyzed him.

The Glory of God . . . Not again!

But he was a soldier with a mission to accomplish, so he steeled himself. He gathered up his courage and broke for the weapons locker. He whipped it open and found several M16 assault rifles. Quickly, he grabbed two and loaded a clip in each, slinging one over his shoulder and holding the other at the ready.

This time, he thought, *that thing won't catch me unarmed and off guard.*

Meanwhile, the sounds coming from the speakers connected to Julia's electrode helmet got exponentially louder. The four notes—*Iossssummmm . . . Oemaaaa . . . Hasdaaaaeeee . . . Oemaaa*—became higher in pitch. And soon, the sound synchronized into a terrifying rhythm with the glyphs on the Ark—᧚, ᝫ, 2, and ᝰ—which began to light up, on and off, in perfect sequence with the sound.

Allen either was too busy to notice any of it or didn't want to. But that didn't spare him the sight when he spun around to find the people near the Ark transfigured.

The electric spiders had crawled all over them, too. And their web of lightning made them shine like copper in the sun.

Allen noticed that the old man had reached his arms up toward the Ark, while the ones who'd been armed had let their weapons drop. He thought he saw Waasfi look over at him, but he didn't seem at all fazed by Allen's presence.

Allen broke toward Ellen Watson and pushed her out of the way just as a bolt of electricity struck the very spot where she'd been standing. She went flying into the arms of Tom Jenkins, and they rolled across the icy floor before coming to rest at the other end of the cavern.

"Tom, it's you!"

His deep blue eyes widened. "My God, Ellen, I thought they'd done something to you."

"Where . . . where's Julia Álvarez?" she stammered. "She's got the adamants! You've got to get them away from her!"

Jenkins thought his partner was in shock. Between the electromagnetic field she'd just been exposed to, plus the solar energy hailing down on them at fifteen thousand feet, she'd clearly been affected.

"Wait . . . Where is Martin Faber? He masterminded this trap!" she said, her eyes lost.

Tom looked around for Martin. Even though he'd only seen him in the kidnapping video, he quickly picked him out. He was about fifteen feet away, as motionless as a statue, covered from head to toe in crawling blue electricity. He needed to get him out of there, but Jenkins didn't dare touch him. He was trapped in some kind of high-voltage network that kept him alive but unconscious to his surroundings. Only the four notes playing over the loudspeakers seemed to matter to these zombies. They repeated rhythmically as if someone had set the tune on an infinite loop. *Iosssssummmm . . . Oemaaaa . . . Hasdaaaaeeee . . . Oemaaa.* And each time a note played, a bolt of electricity struck a different part of the cavern. Every lightbulb in the room had been blown out. The computers were fried. And their satellite link was gone.

Jenkins was surprised to find only three people unaffected by the connection: himself, Colonel Allen, and Ellen Watson.

He couldn't make out Julia Álvarez within the electrical storm. She was covered in a glowing electric current like the rest of them. From the outside, it looked like she'd been swallowed by a giant insect whose tentacles enveloped the others, at once immobilizing them and connecting them via a high-voltage umbilical cord.

"What the hell is going on here?" Nick Allen yelled, breaking Jenkins's stupor.

"Something . . . something's happening to the angels!" Ellen Watson yelled, just barely above the resounding buzz. Tom was worried about his partner. She was weak and looked ready to fall over.

"Angels? Ellen, are you okay?"

"That's what they told Julia, Tom," she said, her eyes half-closed. "These people . . . they're all descended from fallen angels. And they're doing all this to try to get back into heaven. They're using the energy from the solar storms to . . . to . . ."

"Ellen, relax. You need to rest," Jenkins said, worried. "Don't worry, we'll get you out of here."

"No . . . wait . . . ," she said, shaking her head, her eyes focusing for the first time. "We can't leave without the adamants. We swore to the president we'd bring them back."

"The adamants! We've got to get them," Allen said.

But before he could make a move toward Julia, a powerful blast of wind—as strong as steel—knocked the three of them against the glacier wall.

Stunned and bruised, the three of them nevertheless noticed that the remaining electrical equipment was finally powering down. The room plunged into darkness save for the rhythmic pulsating glow enveloping the Ark, the invocation tablet and the group covered in the electric spiders.

And then, just like that, the sound stopped.

The room fell silent.

But the calm didn't last for long.

Before Allen and Jenkins could decide what to do next, the ground began to tremble and the walls of the cave began to crumble overhead.

"Oh, God!" Allen said, crouching over his rifles.

It was as if the whole world was shaking now. The ground cracked under their boots, along with the glacier walls around the Ark, as if the entire mountain was trying to shake loose these intruders. A shower of icicles and chunks of ice rained down on them.

It's an earthquake! Allen thought.

But the first tremor was just a warning. Three or four other quakes jostled the cave. Allen fell and slid down the icy floor, coming to rest against one wall. Ellen fell hard out of Tom's arms and tumbled dangerously toward the electrified outline of William Faber. The old man, oblivious to the goings-on, remained frozen, his hands stretched toward the Ark, his feet planted firmly on the floor.

But it was Tom who bore the brunt of it.

He lost his balance and slammed his head against the corner of a metal lab table. The metallic taste of blood immediately filled his mouth. Flat on his back, he saw the cave's icy dome shatter overhead, shards flying in all directions.

And that's when he saw it.

It. He had no words for what it was.

Some kind of phosphorescent wave flowed over the cave like cascading water. It was shapeless and floated down toward them like a silk scarf, like a beam of soft light from heaven itself. Despite its delicate translucence, it appeared solid in places, and it swayed delicately in the wind.

Before Allen and the president's men could move, the veil began sweeping over the room, moving over the angels still encased in electrical light. It was a singular sight, watching it sweep over them. Looking through this translucent membrane, you could make out the outline of the Ark, the invocation tablet and even the darkened flat-screen monitor that had shown the countdown. But strangely—and this is what most frightened Jenkins—it engulfed each person as it swept over them.

William Faber was the first to disappear.

Then his son.

After that, the young man with the tattoo on his cheek disappeared, followed by the pilot, the towering man with long hair and then his companion. Then Sheila and Daniel.

Finally, as if saving the best for last, the wave swept deliberately toward Julia Álvarez.

"The adamants!" Tom yelled as he watched the wave move toward her. "We have to get them!"

Allen jumped up, aimed his M16 toward the luminescent mass and sprayed a wave of bullets toward it.

Bad move.

The veil shuddered at the contact with the white-hot metal. It pulsed, immediately sending a fierce and powerful wave of energy in all directions, violently shaking the glacier. Chunks of icy wall crumbled down all around them.

"The whole cave's coming apart!" Allen yelled.

"We gotta get out of here, now!" Tom said, dragging Ellen with him. "You have to get Julia, Colonel! For God's sake!"

Julia Álvarez was still unconscious and strapped to the gurney. Before her, the Ark had opened, revealing its cold, dark insides. But Allen couldn't bother looking inside as the floor continued to shake. If the hull of the petrified ship came apart, it would crush the only person who had ever managed to control the adamants. Michael Owen would never forgive him.

Allen broke toward Julia Álvarez at a full sprint.

He had to save her.

99

It was the cold that made me come to. A dry, biting cold I felt deep in my bones. What a bitter awakening from such a sound and beautiful sleep. As I awoke to violent shivers and wet hair, I was sure that if I didn't get somewhere warm soon, I was going to freeze to death.

When I finally was able to open my eyes, I felt the sudden sting of daylight.

"Where . . . where am I?"

The last thing I remembered was being strapped to a gurney as Martin looked down on me warmly, peacefully, telling me to relax. I must have lost consciousness when I took the adamants in my hands.

The adamants!

I squeezed my fists, hoping to feel them. But they were gone. Instead, I got a handful of powdery snow.

I was lying face-up, out in the open, under a thin gray fog, and I wasn't sure whether I should try to move or just lie still. For some reason, I couldn't think straight. My brain was numb. All I could think about was some strange dream where I had seen Jacob's ladder come down to earth. *What a crazy dream . . .* Yet this pang in my gut told me this wasn't just a dream; maybe I really *had* seen it.

The Jacob's ladder.

And even the angels traveling up and down.

"Look! Her eyes are open!"

A friendly voice nearby perked up when I finally blinked.

Ellen Watson was soon leaning over me, studying me. I barely recognized her under a wool cap and a scarf that covered all but her eyes.

We were outside the cave. And there was a stranger standing behind Ellen. His nose and cheeks were rosy from the cold and his lips were cracked from the frigid wind. He looked young. He gave off a distinctive air right up to the point when he put a cell phone to his ear and turned away, no longer interested in me.

"That's Tom Jenkins, my partner," Ellen said. "He works for the president, too. He's trying to figure out our coordinates so they can get us out of here. The solar storm knocked out several satellites and it's been almost impossible to get a signal . . ."

"Solar storm?" I stammered as I tried to sit up. I couldn't think straight.

"Please, Julia, don't try to move," she said, placing her hand on my chest. "We still don't know whether you were hurt."

"Why would I be hurt?" I said, lying back down.

"You don't remember any of it, do you?"

I shook my head.

"Nick Allen. You remember him?" she asked.

"Of course . . . I met him in Santiago. He was talking to me when Artemi Dujok and his men kidnapped me."

"He was the one who got you out of the glacier in time. About an hour ago, a tremor brought down the whole cavern. He managed to shove you toward the mouth of the entrance just before. You're lucky he's not afraid to die . . ."

"An . . . earthquake? Here?"

"A big one," Ellen said. "We think the magnetic field from your adamants combined with the proton shower to cause it. Damn storm knocked out all the satellite communications, too . . ."

"What about the adamants?"

"Lost inside the glacier."

"And the Ark?"

"Same fate."

I lay my head back for a second, unsure if I was brave enough to ask my next question.

"What about Martin?"

Ellen turned away. She looked like she was searching for the right words. "Just before the avalanche, something bizarre happened inside the cave . . . ," she said, as if still trying to convince herself of what she had seen. "The adamants attracted some kind of strange *force*. Like a cloud of light of some kind. It came sweeping down from the sky, right to where all of you were standing . . ."

"So what happened to Martin?" I asked insistently.

"Martin . . . was swallowed up by that thing, Julia. He disappeared."

I could feel my heart in my throat. Tom and Ellen stood still, watching for my reaction. But I managed to keep it together. "How's Colonel Allen?"

"He has some bruises and burns from when he jumped in to save you. But otherwise, he's fine."

"And . . . the others?"

"All the angels disappeared."

"I don't understand. What do you mean?"

"Dujok. Daniel Knight. Sheila . . . all of them. Whatever that cloud was, it took all of them."

"The ladder!"

"The *what*?"

"Jacob's ladder," I whispered, more to myself, the words sticking in my throat. "The stairway to heaven. Oh, God, it took them all . . . They were right. Don't you see? They did it. They did exactly what they set out to do."

"Did it? Did what?" Jenkins asked, shrugging his shoulders, looking to each of us for answers.

"Julia's right. They went home, Tom," Ellen said.

Tom Jenkins looked at Ellen, then back at me, and shook his head. "Oh, brother . . . Both of you are nuts," he said, turning back to his phone, looking for a signal. "I think that earthquake jogged something loose inside your heads."

100

The Oval Office was still buzzing.

From the moment he'd hung up the phone with Andrew Bollinger, he hadn't wasted a single second. In a matter of minutes, the staff had moved the comfortable Chester couches out of the way to make room for a table with several flat-screens so the president could teleconference with four strategic centers at once. *Watch and pray.* Castle had given strict orders to hold off saying anything to the National Security Council and had even bypassed watching this all play out from the Situation Room in the basement.

He needed to concentrate. And he could do it better in the Oval Office.

Now, from his desk, he could see what was happening at all the important locations: the Goddard Space Flight Center, the radio telescope in Socorro, the National Reconnaissance Office and even the NSA. They'd all spent the last half hour scrutinizing any and every change in the ionosphere. They'd each been made aware, to some extent, of the existence of the stones and Operation Elijah. And so had the secretary of defense and the vice president, who stood next to their commander in chief, watching the monitors in stunned silence.

Until we know just how big the crisis is, we should act with discretion, Castle thought.

Andrew Bollinger had been the only one who guessed right. That's why his was one of the faces on the screens. And it's why everyone else waited to hear his opinion. The proton storm that he'd predicted would make landfall hours ahead of time was now, in fact, pounding the skies over Mount Ararat.

"All right, Doctor," Castle said, purposely not calling his friend by his first name. "There's your storm, just as you said. What do you think's going to happen next?"

Bollinger cleared his throat. "There's no precedent for a radiation storm of this category, Mr. President. This storm's sixteen times more powerful than the last one, in 1989. And this one's going to be worse. A lot worse, sir."

"Damage report," Roger Castle said to the screens in front of him.

"Dr. Bollinger's right, Mr. President," answered a female scientist at Goddard, on the center screen. "The first wave of protons has knocked out thirteen percent of our communications satellites. Just as he predicted."

"What other damage can we expect, Dr. Scott?"

Edgar Scott straightened his glasses back at the National Reconnaissance Office. "Uh . . . it's actually off the charts, Mr. President. If these emissions last m-much longer . . . ," he stammered, "well, the next thing to go will be all shortwave radio transmissions. It's still too early to know what kind of effect it will have on Earth's magnetic field. So far, we're seeing aurora borealis far south of the North Pole. And if you're asking for my opinion, Mr. President, we're going to see widespread radiation poisoning: eye damage, skin cancers, crop mutations, a breakdown in the food chain . . ."

"It's the Third Fall from Grace, just as the prophet Enoch predicted, Mr. President," Michael Owen said from behind his mahogany desk at the NSA. "A biblical curse."

"The Third Fall, Michael?"

"Well, at the risk of being the doomsayer of the group . . . Enoch predicted that after the Fall from Grace and the Great Flood, the next 'end of the world' would come by fire. And his metaphor seems pretty apt right now, don't you think?"

Castle's face tensed up.

"You know anything about Hopi Indian prophesies, Mr. Owen?"

Owen looked back at him with a serious expression. On the screen next to him, Andrew Bollinger shifted uncomfortably.

"Right, well, I was the governor of New Mexico and I did learn about them," he said. "They believe Earth, and humanity, is sentenced to go through cycles of global catastrophes—unless their gods have mercy on them. They believe we're living in the fourth world, and that the previous ones were destroyed by fire, ice and flood. So you see, it looks like your destruction by fire has already happened at least once . . ."

"And the last time," said the woman from the Goddard lab, "the Bible says we survived only because of divine intervention."

"The same story in the Bible is told the world over, on all five continents, in as many as two hundred seventeen different stories about the Great Flood. But more to the point, none of them say anything about divine intervention getting us out of this mess this time. We're going to have to assume we're on our own here, people. Let's act accordingly."

Michael Owen's eyes dropped, defeated. And Castle could imagine just what was going through his head: Operation Elijah, whose goal it had been for more than a hundred years to find some way to communicate with a superior being before the next apocalypse, had failed. Someone else had beaten them to it, and he hadn't been able to do anything to stop it.

"If this storm keeps up for another twelve hours," the scientist from Goddard added, "the United States is going to get pummeled. And there's nothing we can do about it."

"Did somebody say something about divine intervention?" Edgar Scott said, squinting toward the camera. It sounded like he either wasn't paying attention or his satellite signal was on a delay. "You mean like some kind of Noah's Ark . . . or like the ship from the Gilgamesh epic?"

"Yes . . . something like that," Owen grumbled, distracted. "But we don't have anything like that to help us this time . . ."

"Uh . . . well . . . maybe we do," Scott said nervously.

The president focused in on Scott's screen. He appeared to be having an offline conversation while the video conference was going on.

"Let's have it, Mr. Scott. What do you mean?"

"Take a look at this . . . The HMBB is sending us new information about the category-X emissions from Mount Ararat. All this happened so quickly that we didn't have time to move the satellite from northern Turkey, out of the way of the solar shower. And it was still tracking the frequency from the stones at the time. It should've been fried in the storm, but somehow it's still working, so . . ."

"So . . . what, Mr. Scott? Save the explanations and get to it!"

"The satellite's still up and running, sir, and we're still getting live readings from Ararat."

"Are you sure?" Goddard's director turned to her own assistants and ordered them to double-check the information.

Scott set his glasses on his head and rubbed his eyes. "Confirmed. Data's just coming in, Mr. President . . . Looks like a six-point-eight-magnitude earthquake just struck near the very peak of that mountain range. Wait, there's something else: The signal from the adamants has . . . disappeared . . . and so has the plasma storm!"

For a second, everyone fell silent.

"The solar storm is over? Mr. Scott, are you sure?"

"Yes, sir. Yes, sir, Mr. President!"

Before Roger Castle could even breathe a sigh of relief, his secured cell phone started vibrating on his desk. At any other time, he would've ignored the call as cheers went up all around them. But the number that came up made him leap for it. Just reading the caller ID told him it was more good news.

Incoming call: Thomas Jenkins.

101

The call lasted all of three minutes. One hundred and eighty seconds of sheer joy and celebration that soon spread to the rest of the group. Even before hearing all the details, Nick Allen and Ellen Watson hugged like old friends. The president of the United States had just promised Tom he'd be sending a special search-and-rescue team to get them off that mountain posthaste. Apparently, there was a NATO outpost in the nearby valley of Yenidogan that could have a team there in less than four hours. We'd be back to civilization before we knew it. That was the best news Tom had gotten since he'd seen his cell phone turn back on and he cheered like a schoolboy.

They all celebrated.

I was just trying to get my bearings. Maybe this will sound crazy, but I think I was the only one in our group who wasn't eager to leave Mount Ararat. My eyes searched the landscape for the glacier where I had seen Martin for the last time.

But it was nowhere to be found.

My senses were still hazy. Images and sensations flashed in my mind, a patchwork of memories that I couldn't manage to fit together: William Faber inside a radiant cocoon. Martin floating toward a whirlwind of pastel colors, his body wrapped in a soft, serene glow. His eyes smiled with joy and thankfulness—and when he turned his gaze toward me, seconds before disappearing into that shimmering veil, I was overcome with such a feeling of indescribable gratitude. I never felt afraid or anguished to see him disappear into the ether; I simply knew that it was our destiny. "Your gift has sent them home," I heard a voice say.

"Your husband was a special guy, Julia . . ."

Nick Allen caught me off guard, bringing me back from my daydreams. It was the first time he'd ever called me by my first name.

I know he was trying to console me, as if Martin had been killed inside that glacier and he were offering his condolences. But that's not what I believed. On the contrary. I looked back at the colonel serenely, because strangely enough, I felt no pain or loss at being without my husband. I didn't have the words to express how deeply being submerged in that exquisite light had affected me. That whatever ill will I'd felt over the way Martin and his companions had used me had turned into something different, a feeling of acceptance and joy. Even gratitude.

I understood so much more now: That our call to the heavens had been answered. That the destruction that had threatened to rain down on us had been channeled away just in the nick of time, thanks to that celestial connection. And that for the first time in four thousand years, the heavens had lowered Jacob's ladder to take Martin and his people home. The exiled descendants of traitorous angels had redeemed their ancestors' misdeeds through this one act—and saved mankind.

Maybe this won't make sense—I admit it's hard to fathom. After all, my mind was still cloudy from everything I'd lived through. But at that moment, all I felt was peace.

"Julia!" Ellen shook me as if I'd forgotten something. "Don't you think you should thank the colonel? He saved your life!"

"It was nothing. Really." Allen seemed uncomfortable at the attention.

"Nothing?" Ellen said. "You should've seen what he did. He tucked a pair of fiberglass skis under your gurney and slid you out like a toboggan."

"I just figured if I put some kind of insulator between you and the ground, it'd be enough to break you free of the electricity. Really. It was no big deal . . ."

Ellen bragged for him: "You wouldn't be alive if it weren't for him."

"I'm just sorry I couldn't help Martin," Allen said, dropping his gaze to the snowy ground. "I'm really sorry. I had a lot of things I wanted to ask him, like I'm sure you did."

"You, help Martin?" I smiled from ear to ear and that seemed to rattle him. "Why would you try to 'help' him?"

"Doesn't . . . doesn't it bother you that he's dead?"

"Colonel, don't you know the story of Enoch and Elijah?" I asked him.

"Of course . . . *of course.*" The veteran military man immediately saw where I was headed with this. "They were both ascended into heaven . . . without having to die . . . Wait. You don't think he and those people did the same—"

"Yes, Colonel. That's exactly what I believe."

102

SANTIAGO DE COMPOSTELA, SPAIN

THREE DAYS LATER

"God, you're gullible, Antonio! You're completely blind."

Marcelo Muñiz's cheeks had reddened after his third beer. He picked at a plate of Galician-style octopus with his friend Inspector Figueiras. Figueiras's jeweler friend was maybe the only person Figueiras felt he could vent to about the Faber case.

Muñiz pressed on. "Don't you see what's going on here? You come in and tell me how upset you are that Julia Álvarez got back from her little adventure and met with the old priest, Fornés, before meeting with you."

"Right. So what?"

"So . . . that woman's taking orders right from the authorities, that's what!"

"What are you talking about? I *am* the 'authorities.'"

"You're missing my point. She's a restorer at the cathedral," Muñiz said. "Her loyalty is to them, not the cops. God knows what she saw during her kidnapping. But you can bet she'll never tell you about it unless her 'bosses' give her approval first. And, honestly, I can't blame her," Muñiz said with a chuckle. "If you looked any scruffier, I wouldn't trust you either."

"Hey! What's wrong with the way I look?"

"Look in a mirror, my friend. You haven't shaved in days, you've got bags under your eyes and even your skin color is off. This case is going to kill you . . ."

"*Pfff!* There *is* no case anymore, Marcelo," Figueiras said, taking a swig of beer.

"Oh, come on, you can't give up now. That lady's got a story to tell. Just give it a couple days, then take another run at her."

"I did. I tried again this morning—the fourth time I've talked to her. That's when she told me about the meeting with the dean . . . ," Figueiras said, glancing at his watch, "which should be going on right now."

"Well, then, you're going to have to *make* her talk," Muñiz said, munching on another tentacle. "Little Miss Innocent is a witness to the murder of five men in Noia. Four American soldiers. Navy SEALs! Just put out an arrest warrant on her, and that's that."

"I wish it were that simple. NATO's taken over the investigation and kept us completely in the dark."

"So that's it? You're just going to lie down and take it?"

"They told me to keep my nose out of it. Order came straight from the Ministry of Foreign Affairs. I can't do a damn thing about it, Marcelo."

"Damn it . . ."

"The US government is going to pay for the restoration of the Santa María da Nova church and make a 'generous donation' to the town. They even offered a settlement to the widows of the two young cops who were killed. In exchange, they say they can't tell us anything about the case until it's resolved. It's all 'top-secret,' Bastards . . ."

"And you don't find all of this odd?"

"It is what it is, Marcelo. I've got no case. But that's not even the strangest part of this whole mess."

"So what is?"

Figueiras chugged the rest of his beer as if trying to drown all the worries on his mind—and burped loudly. "You know the first thing Julia Álvarez did the second she returned to Spain? Went to the police station inside the airport and canceled the missing-person report on her husband."

The jeweler tapped his fingers nervously on the table. "Did she say why?"

"The report said she found her husband in Turkey, and they agreed to part ways."

Muñiz tugged absentmindedly on his bow tie, as if trying to figure out what it all meant. "So . . . do you believe her?"

"Man, I don't know what to believe," Figueiras grumbled. "I can't figure women out. They're a bigger mystery than all your stories about symbols and talismans."

"Hey, now that you mention it, what ever happened to the stones?"

"He kept them, I guess. Who knows? Apparently, that's another taboo subject with the Americans. Nobody's saying anything . . ."

"Did she at least tell why they took her to Turkey?"

"Oh, you're going to love this one. Now she's saying they didn't kidnap her at all. That she went of her own accord. And the ministry agrees! And get this, the US embassy asked for all our files on the Fabers—and we're handing them over!"

"Well, she must have at least told you what she did in Turkey. No?"

"She had a story for that, too: looking for Noah's Ark. Can you believe this woman?" Figueiras said, shaking his head. "She could've had the decency to come up with a better lie."

103

I'd never known I meant so much to him.

Father Benigno Fornés's clear blue eyes filled with tears as I recounted all the details of the last couple of days. But his was not a sad, desperate cry. These were different kinds of tears, as if, through my story, he had found a kind of comfort he'd been searching for, for years.

It was easy to say yes when he asked to meet with me. He was, after all, the only person who'd been interested in me—and not my adamants—from the moment I set foot back in Santiago. He'd left a kind note in my mailbox and I was immediately thankful for that tender gesture. Especially after the odyssey I'd endured just trying to get home. I had to convince the officials at NATO Air Dispatch No. 6 that I didn't have any kind of ancient technological treasure to hand over to them. And don't even get me started on the three separate flights it had taken to finally get back to Spain.

And then there was that sensation—that I'd left everything important to me back in Ararat. Including my husband.

Fornés had asked me to meet him outside the cathedral entrance a few minutes before eight, just before it closed to the public. Clearly, he wanted to know all the details of my adventure, but he never pressured me. I could tell he empathized with all I'd been through and I appreciated that he respected my feelings enough not to pry further than I could bear. Talking about it felt good. It helped me sort through all of the feelings I'd had from the night of the shooting at the church to my final moments inside the glacier. It seemed like no matter what I said, none of it was too far-fetched for him to believe. Not even when I broached the subject of the descendants of angels and their obsession with returning home. He even agreed with me that the force I'd felt inside the cavern sounded a lot like Jacob's famous ladder.

What I really didn't expect was for Father Fornés to make a confession of his own.

"I'm an old man, Julia, not long for this world. And I don't think I can afford to keep this secret to myself any longer," he said.

The stillness of the old cathedral imparted a sense of awe.

"What secret, Father?"

"It's not so much knowing what it is," he began, "but how to use it. Do you know why I've always been such a big proponent of yours during the restoration of the Pórtico de la Gloria?" he asked as we headed toward the spot where I'd left my scaffolding and computers five days ago. Everything was just the same, as if time had stood still and all I'd lived through had just been a horrible dream.

"You've always been one to stick up for what you believe in, my child. You always insisted some kind of telluric force was to blame for the Pórtico's deterioration, some kind of invisible Earth energy that—like faith itself—can be felt but not seen. Every time I saw you take on the Barrié Foundation's scientific committee, I'd ask myself when would be the right time to tell you what I know. To help you show them that all discoveries can't always be weighed and measured . . . And I think *now* is that time."

Father Benigno labored as he walked down the hallway, holding my hand. The cathedral had emptied out and only the private security guards remained as they began making their rounds before turning on the motion sensors.

"See that marvel?" he said, gesturing toward the Pórtico. "It should have never been there, Julia."

"But, Father—"

"Never, Julia. Master Mateo was commissioned to build it in 1188, as you know, as a way to draw even more pilgrims to Santiago. The diocese was so motivated by money then that it allowed the true meaning of the Way of St. James to be distorted. There was a backlash, Julia. The city was divided. So a group of priests who were against the trivialization of the Way secretly decided to preserve this place's entire reason for existing. Amazingly, it has a lot to do with what you just lived through. And I think it's time you know about it."

"They're connected?"

"Yes. Back in the twelfth century, those who traveled the Way—also known as the Jacobean route—were well aware that their journey was a metaphor for life. And if you ask me, it's still the most brilliant one ever conceived. They began their journey at the base of the French Pyrenees, surrounded by lush vegetation and fresh springwater, perfect symbols for the beginning of life. Over the course of a few days, they came to the fertile open fields of La Rioja or Aragon, images that evoked the abundance and promise of adolescence. And as they reached Castilla, they saw the world literally turn to dust. The dry and rough terrain of Burgos and León was a reminder of old age and, eventually, death. But all the pilgrims knew the journey did not end in León, Julia. The road to paradise still awaited them. With renewed energy, they forged ahead, crossing through O Cebreiro and coming to the lush trees and flowing streams of Galicia. Their eyes wide at all the new life, they pressed on to Santiago, and finally, after nearly five hundred miles on foot, they came to this church. To this very place where . . . the final miracle awaited."

I felt the chills as Father told his tale.

"It all happened at this Pórtico, this very spot, my child," he said, tapping the floor with the heel of his shoe. "Except that back in those days, before the master Mateo built his pórtico, there stood another designed by the pilgrims who made this trek. And it had nothing to do with the apocalypse or the Second Coming. No, this was a commemoration of something much more . . . transcendental: the Lord Jesus's transfiguration and ascension into heaven from the last place where his disciples saw him on earth, Mount Tabor. It was a replica of the place where the risen Jesus left behind his earthly body, transformed into pure, divine light, and returned to the home of God the Father. The pilgrims completed their trek, from birth to death, and continued on to this place, where they were reminded that one day they, too, would become pure light . . . and live on."

"Father . . . what ever happened to the original Pórtico?"

"It was broken up and the stones were scattered all over Galicia. And that relates to the secret I want to share with you, Julia. A secret the deans of this sacred cathedral have passed down over the centuries for one very important reason. A reason that I think will help you understand why you had to endure everything you did the last few days, only to return to this place where it all began."

Father Fornés smoothed his cassock and stepped toward the center of the sculpted figures.

"Long before the birth of Our Lord and Savior, long before a single Christian church was ever built, this place was already long considered sacred land. The Celts—and actually, even before them, the seafaring peoples of the world—were drawn to energy that emanated from this hillside. Their legends tell of a giant named Tubal who claimed to be the father of Noah. And he declared that he would make these hills a holy ground. He built a tower over the very holiest of earth and told the nearby townspeople to honor this place, warning them to come here only when they sought to pray to God. Others built similar structures around the world. In Jerusalem. Rome. In the plains of Wiltshire. Paris. And they were built long before we gave any of those cities their modern names. But the goal was always the same. People from around the world believed if they climbed to the top of the towers, they could communicate with God. Later, humanity dared to build a taller tower, the Tower of Babel. And that incurred the wrath of God, the Great Flood and the destruction of the ancient world. Humanity lost its way. It forgot about that golden era when the children of God shared their wisdom with us. And soon, all that remained of that knowledge were myths and stories in ancient books."

Father Fornés turned toward the center column of the Pórtico de la Gloria.

"People didn't build those towers around the world on a whim. They truly believed they could send messages from Earth to a supreme being. However, they could only establish that communication with two equally important keys: a 'physical' key, a celestial stone or *lapsis exillis,* which, during the Middle Ages, they called the Holy Grail; and a 'spiritual' key, a sacred invocation, a name that must be uttered precisely. The secret to using those stones in Santiago was written in an ancient tome that the church of the Inquisition chased tirelessly: the grimoire of San Cipriano, which, legend says, would somehow be connected to this church. But those are just symbols that the ancients used for lack of a proper vocabulary to describe all the treasures of the Golden Age, the time before the Great Flood."

"Father, why are you telling me all this?"

Father Fornés stood up as straight as he could. "Because, Julia, for you, those are no longer just symbols. Your mind has managed to see beyond the confines of the secular world. You have seen stones that speak. Stairways descending from heaven. Heavenly creatures to guide your path. But still, there is one more symbol left for you to learn. The very last one. One that, I guess, it is my responsibility to show you, here, in the very place where your adventure began . . ."

"Which one, Father? The one the Armenians discovered the night of the shooting? The mark over the Platerías door?"

"No, no, my child. After hearing your story, it's clear to me that was just part of the Yezidi and the Faber clan's research. They'd spent half their lives searching for hidden symbols at these ancient towers, trying to learn which symbols made up part of the spiritual keys. The ones that had to be pronounced correctly to tap into its energy. No, there's another symbol I'm referring to."

"Which one, Father?"

"How long have you been working on the Pórtico, Julia?" he said, his eyes twinkling. "Six months? Maybe more?"

I nodded.

"And yet, you've never asked yourself who the mysterious figure is at the base of the column that holds up the Pórtico de la Gloria?"

"Well, of course I have, Father. Every historian who's studied the Pórtico has written about it. Well, for starters, it's no one from the New Testament, that's for sure," I said, bending down and reexamining the sculpture.

I knew this figure well. I'd wondered about it every time I walked into the cathedral.

"Curious, isn't it?" he said, caressing it.

At the base of the central marble column that held up the Pórtico was the carving of a man with a thick, curly beard subduing two roaring lions with his bare hands. The sculpture was a completely different style from the rest of the art there. And yet, this sculpture held up the entire Pórtico.

"It's a very important symbol, Julia. The first thing you notice is that the sculpture is made of a material you just don't find anywhere else in Galicia. Second, the column is a depiction of the family tree of Jesus Christ, tracing all the way from Adam to our Lord and Savior. For eight centuries, everyone who has made the pilgrimage here has placed his hand on the column and said a prayer of thanks. And even today, it's the symbolic gesture that signifies the end of the religious trek—the moment the traveler is born again into a more spiritual life. But I want you to take another look at the base, my child. The Christian religion is, quite literally, based on a perfect stranger . . . Would you like to know who he is?"

"Of course!"

"This is a sculpture of Gilgamesh. The protagonist of the epic who conquered two lions on his way to the Garden of Eden."

"No. No, Father, that's impossible," I said, trying not to be disrespectful. "Gilgamesh isn't a biblical character. And his story wasn't even known in the Western world until the twelfth century . . . Those clay tablets weren't discovered until the nineteenth century . . ."

"Well, it's him, Julia. And as strange as it may seem here, it fit perfectly on the now-defunct Pórtico of the Transfiguration, where, obviously, it made more sense. As you already know, the king Gilgamesh failed in his obsessive quest for eternal life, but he didn't stop until he found Utnapishtim, the survivor of the Flood. Maybe a pilgrim overheard his story and brought it here, seeing as how it applies to the basic tenet of our faith."

"How do you mean, Father?"

"Very simply, Gilgamesh failed in his attempt to overcome death. But thousands of years later, another man, one who was part human, part divine, did achieve that very goal. His name was Jesus of Nazareth. And he did it in a very curious way: He managed to transform his physical body into one made of light. And he ascended into Heaven."

"And this is the secret you've been guarding, Father?"

"Part of it, Julia. You see, light is everything. It's the perfect symbol of all the mysteries around us. Something invisible that allows us to see. Just an infinitesimal part of the electromagnetic spectrum, which includes everything that is audible, tangible, and visible—our ancestors before the Great Flood understood that. That light is what your husband was after. And he found it—the first person to do so in more than two thousand years. And what that tells me, Julia, is that something is changing in our world . . ."

"Maybe he just managed to alter the gravity or the molecular structure in that cave—who knows? He only did it for a matter of seconds. And, you know, there was an intense solar storm going on and the mountain absorbed an incredible amount of energy just as Martin ascended . . ."

"Now do you see what I mean about symbols, Julia? What I describe as transfiguration into heaven, you describe in scientific terms."

"But why does that matter? What matters is that it happened. Martin realized his dream. And I know that, wherever he is, he's safe."

Father Benigno sighed, taking my hands and patting them gently. "Julia, do you know why you brought me to tears earlier?"

I looked tenderly into the old priest's eyes.

"Because fifty years ago, my predecessor told me the secret of this place and I didn't understand him. His descriptions were, of course, shrouded in symbolism and, naturally, open to interpretation. He told me all about the statue of Gilgamesh, about the significance of the Great Flood, about the lost towers of the old world, even about the method Utnapishtim and Jesus of Nazareth used to cross over. And he was the one who told me that right here, beneath our feet, is one of those antediluvian antennas. At the time, I thought it was just another one of his symbols. But after hearing your story tonight, I finally understand the metaphor."

"So what does it mean?"

"Simple. That only angels can summon God."

I slumped my shoulders. It wasn't exactly the great revelation I was hoping for. But he quickly added, "Don't look so disappointed, my child. After all, you, me . . . we're all one and the same. Or have you already forgotten that we are the children of angels, the progeny of the sons of God and the daughters of man?"

"You and me? Angels?" I chuckled.

"Now, *that's* a pretty great secret. Don't you think?"

Author's Note

I have to admit, my writing method is a little unorthodox. For years, I've tried to set my stories against real, historical backdrops and to ground them in verifiable facts, sharing with the reader the fascinating discoveries I make along the way. In writing *The Lost Angel*, I was so obsessed with exact dates and painting accurate scenes that it nearly cost me my life.

But now I think it was worth the trouble.

Perfect example: I couldn't bring myself to finish this novel until October of 2010, when I finally received the necessary approvals from the Turkish government to climb to the top of Mount Ararat. Three times, I tried and failed to scale the 16,945-foot peak. Every morning, I'd wake to the towering peak inviting me to conquer it. But by the time I'd gotten ready for the climb, it veiled itself again and again in frost and clouds. Of course, that only made me want to surmount it more, so that I could accurately describe it in these pages.

Near the top, on the auspicious day of 10/10/10 and standing more than 16,400 feet above sea level, I understood the grip this place has on man, especially in times of crisis. In that solitude and majesty, among the many twists and turns on my trek, the limits of my personal and literary search were tested. If any place on earth deserves to guard the secrets of Noah's Ark, or at least the dream of salvation in the face of adversity, it's Mount Ararat.

But the sanctity of this mountain isn't all that's real in this story. So are the CIA and Keyhole satellite photos, which have started to be declassified in the last fifteen years, thanks to the brave efforts of George Carver and Porcher L. Taylor III of the University of Richmond in Virginia. The Hallaç crater, one of the world's great wonders, is hidden behind a military zone, just steps from a Turkish army outpost near the border. Showing up with video camera in hand almost cost me a serious confrontation with the military. The St. Echmiadzin and Santiago de Compostela cathedrals and the old church in Noia are exactly where I write they are and are open to visitors. The old church is at the very end of the Way of St. James in Spain's northwestern corner. My fascination with its ties to Noah was born when I learned that legend has it that Noia got its name when Noah's ship landed at the nearby Mount Aro. I'm sure no one missed the similarities between the names Noia and Noah and Aro and Ararat, and the slew of other place names that refer to the "myth" of the Great Flood. These places are, in fact, not figments of my imagination but of the creative minds who named so many places in southern Europe after that event, for whatever reason.

Suffice it to say that all the references cited in this book—from the works of John Dee to those of Ignatius Donnelly, from the Book of Enoch to the epic of Gilgamesh—are quoted exactly. So, too, are any allusions to the lives and works of Joseph Smith, the founder of the Church of Jesus Christ of Latter-Day Saints; the mystic George Ivanovich Gurdjieff; the painter Nicholas Roerich; even the Yezidi and the Hopi Indians.

My intent was to show all the ways these cultures and their beliefs are tied together—sometimes closely, sometimes loosely—in the notion that our species was, at some point, doomed by God—or the gods. And that in each of those myths, we were given the opportunity—the gift, if you will—to survive extinction, individually and collectively. All we have to do is believe.

And I, of course, have come to believe—even in angels.

Acknowledgments

I've lost count of all the people who offered me their unconditional help in the making of this book. At one point or another, all of them were crucial to its success, and I cannot close without leaving a written record here of the critical roles they played.

Aside from the incalculable support of my family—always loving, unrelenting and endlessly generous with their faith in me—I have felt the constant angelic presence of my editors in Spain and in the United States: Ana d'Atri, Diana Collado and Johanna Castillo. Thanks also to my agents, Antonia Kerrigan and Tom and Elaine Colchie, and to Atria's Judith Curr and Carolyn Reidy, not to mention Carlos Reves, Marcela Serras and the formidable team from Editorial Planeta in Madrid and Barcelona. From Marc Rocamora and Paco Barrera to Laura Franch, Lola Sanz, Eva Armengo and Laura Verdura—thank you all. And thanks to the innumerable people along the way whose enthusiasm and professionalism helped me maintain my faith in this novel.

Thanks also for the invaluable help of several writer friends and researchers, such as Juan Martorell, Alan Alford, David Zurdo, Enrique de Vicente, Julio Peradejordi, Iker Jiménez and Carmen Porter, and my webmaster David Gombau. Thanks to experts such as José Luis Ramos—the guru of electromagnetism at the Universidad de Alcalá de Henares, Spain; geologist Luis Miguel Domenech of the Universidad Politécnica de Cataluña and Pablo Torijano from the Department of Hebrew Studies at the Universidad Complutense de Madrid. I pray I have not inadvertently twisted their information as I tried to add tension to the plot.

I'll never forget the good times with my own guardians, Carmen Cafranga, Ana Rejano and Maite Bolaños, or the well-wishes from Cagla Cakici of Pasión Turca and the assistance from Turkey's Office of Public Relations in Spain, which facilitated the cumbersome permits to allow me to scale Mount Ararat. And there, I met several people to whom I'm indebted, including Mustafa Arsin, Cesar and Bruno Perez de Tudela and Alvaro Trigueros. They, and other guides and sources I was fortunate enough to meet along the way, made this entire endeavor all the more worthwhile.

Thank you, all.

About the Author

Javier Sierra, whose works have been translated into thirty-five languages, is the author of *The Lady in Blue* and the *New York Times* bestseller *The Secret Supper*. A native of Teruel, Spain, he currently lives in Madrid. Please visit javiersierra.com and thelostangelbook.com.

About the Translator

Carlos Frías is an award-winning journalist and author of the memoir *Take Me with You: A Secret Search for Family in a Forbidden Cuba*. The son of Cuban exiles, Frías was raised bilingual and bicultural in South Florida and floats easily between the Spanish-speaking and English-speaking worlds. For more about his writing, please visit cfrias.com.

The Lost Angel
From A to Z

adamants: Literally "stones of Adam." Those who possess two of these stones can use them to communicate with God and other higher beings, a theme that runs throughout *The Lost Angel*. In the book, it is written that the stones are of a "celestial origin," as rare as any stone NASA brought back from the moon. Later on, we learn the stones become activated during solar storms. Julia Álvarez learns that they are first described in the ancient epic poem *Gilgamesh*, though it is the sixteenth-century mystic John Dee who gives them this name, which you will find reference to in an actual fragment of his work *Monas hieroglyphica* included in the novel.

Agri Dagi: From Turkish, meaning "mountain of pain." This is another name for Mount Ararat, located in Turkish territory but disputed for decades with neighboring Armenia. This is the sleeping protagonist of the novel. The mountain is, in fact, a dormant volcano with two major openings: Buyuk Agri (Greater Ararat) and Kuçuk Agri (Lesser Ararat). The greater peak is covered in permafrost and stands nearly fifteen thousand feet above sea level, and it is the site of the critical phase of Sierra's novel. Ice caverns are common on this peak and it is the place where CIA spy planes discovered "the Ararat Anomaly" in the 1940s, which some have identified as Noah's Ark.

Glossary of Javier Sierra's Research

Introduction
How to use this glossary

This exclusive glossary is a tool for our early readers to use while reading *The Lost Angel*. Javier Sierra's latest novel is so rich with his research that we believe this material will interest those who want to learn more about it. Javier pulls back the curtain to give us an inside look into hidden worlds, those that seem accessible only to the intellectual elite and secret societies closed to the outside world.

You'll find the terms here organized as you find them in the novel. That is, when we refer to a person, say Chester Arthur, he is not listed as "Arthur, Chester." This book is intended to be a light reference guide rather than a strict academic document. It should also be noted that any person listed with a date of birth and passing refers to an actual person, not a fictional character. This, too, is a feature of Sierra's writing, drawing from actual historical persons to build his fictional worlds. He did it with Leonardo da Vinci before, publishing the *New York Times* bestseller *The Secret Supper*. But this is the first time he has accompanied his work with a helpful tool such as this one.

The Lost Angel
From A to Z

adamants: Literally "stones of Adam." Those who possess two of these stones can use them to communicate with God and other higher beings, a theme that runs throughout *The Lost Angel*. In the book, it is written that the stones are of a "celestial origin," as rare as any stone NASA brought back from the moon. Later on, we learn the stones become activated during solar storms. Julia Álvarez learns that they are first described in the ancient epic poem *Gilgamesh*, though it is the sixteenth-century mystic John Dee who gives them this name, which you will find reference to in an actual fragment of his work *Monas hieroglyphica* included in the novel.

Agri Dagi: From Turkish, meaning "mountain of pain." This is another name for Mount Ararat, located in Turkish territory but disputed for decades with neighboring Armenia. This is the sleeping protagonist of the novel. The mountain is, in fact, a dormant volcano with two major openings: Buyuk Agri (Greater Ararat) and Kuçuk Agri (Lesser Ararat). The greater peak is covered in permafrost and stands nearly fifteen thousand feet above sea level, and it is the site of the critical phase of Sierra's novel. Ice caverns are common on this peak and it is the place where CIA spy planes discovered "the Ararat Anomaly" in the 1940s, which some have identified as Noah's Ark.

Javier Sierra standing next to Mount Ararat (Agri Dagi), Turkey

Amrak: Armenian for "the box." But in reality, it is a stone tablet that, according to *The Lost Angel,* can activate the stone adamants, allowing them to emit high-frequency signals and alter nearby electromagnetic fields. The *Amrak* is very similar to the invocation tablets built by John Dee, of which we have very few actual examples.

Ararat: *See* Agri Dagi.

Armenia: This small, mountainous country, where part of *The Lost Angel*'s climax takes place, has deep and enduring ties with Noah and the myth of the Great Flood. Its ancient name of Hayastan comes from Haik, the son of Togarma, great-grandson of Noah and descendant of Jafet, another of the Ark's passengers, who, along with Noah, Sem and Ham, set foot on Ararat once the waters receded. Armenia gets its name in part from Aram, sixth descendant in the lineage of Haik. It was first used by the Greeks more than three thousand years ago.

It is also interesting to note that one of Armenia's major exports is diamonds (which are mined and sent in their rough form to be cut overseas) and that the word "adamant" is thought by many to be the precursor to the word *"diamante"* or "diamond."

betilum: The word is derived from the Hebrew word "Bet-El" (house of God) and appears in the biblical description of the ladder described by the prophet Jacob (Genesis 28:11–19). Today, "betilum," or "betyls," is used to refer to all stones of an extraterrestrial nature, fallen to Earth in meteorites. The term appears within the name of the mysterious organization the Betilum Company, which is rounding up works by John Dee and is a front for the United States' secret services in *The Lost Angel.* (See chapter 48.)

Biddlestone: Small town in the English county of Wiltshire, in the southeast part of Great Britain, where Julia Álvarez and Martin Faber were married in 2005. Its name comes from the term "Bible of Stone." This is the place that John Dee uses—according to Javier Sierra's tale—to hide one of his mysterious "invocation tablets" to summon angels. (See chapter 39.)

Book of Enoch: Written in the second century BC, it is attributed to Enoch, potentially the first biblical prophet who did not have to die in order for Yahweh to take him to Heaven. The book goes into great detail about the fall of the angels and the reasons God was so determined to destroy mankind with the Great Flood. This book was almost unknown in Europe until the nineteenth century, when copies were introduced from Ethiopia. But there is substantial evidence to suggest John Dee had privileged access to the book's contents as early as the sixteenth century. (See chapter 27.)

Campus Stellae: *The Lost Angel* makes several references to this modern monument built into an interior wall of the cathedral at Santiago, near the door leading to Platerías. It is a metal sculpture fashioned in 1999 by the artist Jesús León Vázquez and it is said to represent the medieval idea that to reach Santiago, one must follow the field of stars, or the Milky Way. It so happens that many place names along the Way of St. James have names that refer to stars, establishing a tie between the terrestrial and the celestial like nothing seen in any other place on earth.

Cargo cults: The subject of Ellen Watson and Julia Álvarez's conversation while in captivity, this topic has been one of the most fascinating anthropological phenomena of our time. The term comes from a time when Allied forces during World War II set up bases on islands in the

Campus Stellae

South Pacific where the natives were still living in the Stone Age and had not had any contact with Western cultures. Contact with such an advanced culture led the natives to deify the soldiers and pray for them to share the treasures inside their cargo crates. Many of these cults have disappeared over the decades. But there is still an active cult devoted to a random US serviceman, John Frum, on the island of Tanna, Vanuatu. Its followers construct straw models of the "birds of the gods"—the airplanes they first saw during the military conflicts in Tanna.

This—according to the discussion between Watson and Álvarez—could help explain how ancient religions might have sprouted after contact with an advanced, prehistoric race.

Cathedral of Santiago de Compostela: For more than eight centuries, this temple located in the heart of the city by the same name has been one of Christianity's most important pilgrimage sites. Supposedly buried here are the remains of the apostle St. James, one of three disciples of Jesus Christ said to have witnessed His transfiguration at Mount Tabor. As such, the journey to this holy place is symbolic of a person's transformation into a more spiritual being who becomes closer to God. This trek was depicted in the original portico at the main entrance to the church. The portico was replaced centuries later by the now world famous Pórtico de la Gloria. The first church was built on this site in the year AD 829, although it was remodeled several times until, in the eighteenth century, it earned its characteristic baroque style and became the cathedral it is today. There is a longstanding controversy over the name Compostela, which many experts believe is derived from the word *campus stellae*, or "field of the star," because, according to tradition, a pilgrim discovered the apostle's tomb there in AD 814 when a miraculous star appeared at the site, indicating where to dig. This discovery prompted an endless stream of pilgrimages from all over Europe, earning this pilgrimage the name by which it is still known today: El Camino de Santiago de Compostela—the Way of St. James.

Chester Arthur (1829–86): Twenty-first president of the United States. Under his administration, the Office of Naval Intelligence was created and became the precursor of US secret services such as the FBI and CIA. His administration also oversaw the creation of the Hopi Indian reservation in Arizona in 1882. In the novel, Arthur also prompts the creation of Operation Elias, born of the era's obsession with the Great Flood. Its purpose was to study the end of civilizations such as Atlantis and to communicate with "higher planes." (See chapter 69.)

**A Tibetan engraving on the *chintamani* stone
on the mount of *Lung-ta***

chintamani: One of the many "communication stones" to which traditions throughout human history refer. The term comes from a Sanskrit word. The *chintamani* stone in particular is associated with Nicholas Roerich, who named one of his famous series of paintings after it. This glowing stone served as a key to the underground utopia of Shambhala, a hidden paradise where scholars oversaw the evolution of our species. Andrew Tomas described the *chintamani* in detail in his book *Shambhala: Oasis of Light*.

The *chintamani* stone is surrounded in rich lore the world over, such as in Tibet during the reign of Tho-tho-ri Nyanstan, around AD 331. There, it was prized as a talisman fallen from the sky, coming to Earth on the back of a "wind horse" named Lung-ta. It was considered such a sacred object—it was called the "Treasure of the World"—that it was only brought out into public to mark spiritual changes or changes in consciousness in humanity. Perhaps that is why it so often shows up in Tibetan folklore. (See chapter 76.)

coronal mass ejection—CME: Once every eleven years or so, the sun cycles through a period of pronounced activity when its surface erupts and sends waves of radiation and solar winds out into the cosmos. It has been well documented that if one of these waves of radiation strikes Earth, it can affect the planet's magnetic field and electrical networks. These solar storms are categorized according to their strength. The Class X storms referenced in this novel are the most severe. They can seriously affect the climate, telecommunications, even human health. The Class M storms are more brief but can also cause small blackouts and affect geomagnetic activity in the polar regions. Class C storms are the mildest and often go unnoticed.

Enochian: A language that John Dee supposedly received from divine communication with angels in the sixteenth century. It is made up of twenty-one letters, nineteen invocations and more than one hundred inscrutable tables of composite letters, whose combinations would allow humans to establish contact with a "higher plane." However, the Enochian language was all but forgotten until the early nineteenth century, when occult groups such as Golden Dawn studied it, and they have preserved it to this day. Symbols taken from this language are peppered throughout *The Lost Angel* at pivotal points. They include the strange psalms that the character Artemi Dujok recites, which are part of John Dee's original invocation phrases. (See chapter 98.)

epic of Gilgamesh: Written four thousand years before the birth of Christ, this story found etched on clay tablets and unearthed in modern-day Iraq is the oldest literary text known to man. It tells the story of Gilgamesh, a Sumerian king determined to seek out the gods in paradise and reclaim man's right to immortality. The story claims that only one human had ever achieved immortality: an antediluvian king named Utnapishtim, whom the gods spared before they destroyed the world in a flood. In the epic, Utnapishtim tells Gilgamesh that immortality lies with a species of plant that exists only at the bottom of the ocean. Gilgamesh seeks out the flower of eternal life, but just as he is about to reach it, a serpent steals the plant and Gilgamesh must return home empty-handed. (See chapters 31, 35.)

falls from grace: *The Lost Angel* refers to the several falls from grace that the human race has experienced. They are moments when our species has been on the brink of extinction; according to Judeo-Christian teachings, there have been only three of these moments. (See chapters 27, 100.)

George Carver Jr. (1930–94): Carver was a CIA expert who was interested in Noah's Ark; his story is told at length in *The Lost Angel*. He was a twenty-six-year veteran of the CIA, joining in 1953 and handling important missions in West Germany and during the Vietnam War. During his many public lectures over the years, he confirmed that the CIA had discovered something "strange near the peak of Mount Ararat." That led other parties to ask for this information to be declassified under the Freedom of Information Act. This finally came to pass a year after Carver's death in 1995, and it confirmed that the CIA had in fact been interested in the "Ararat Anomaly" as far back as 1949. (See chapter 77.)

George Ivanovich Gurdjieff (1872?–1949): A mystic, writer and philosopher whom many consider one of the founding fathers of modern esotericism. Some of his theories on Yezidi superstitions are referenced in *The Lost Angel*, although Sierra does not get into Gurdjieff's enlightened ideas drawn from Buddhism, Hinduism, Christianity and, above all, Sufism. Some of the details in Gurdjieff's biography are curiously coincidental with some of the main themes in this novel. In his book *Meetings with Remarkable Men*, for example, he remarks that his own father was an *ashoj*, a Greek lyrical poet who often recited parts of the epic of Gilgamesh to his son from memory. Gurdjieff was so fascinated by the idea that the Armenian tales of Noah he had learned as a boy had such ancient roots that he began researching the hidden parts of history. That research led him to the Yezidi and to travel across all of Asia and Europe over the course of four decades.

Glory of God: Mentioned several times in the novel, it refers to a manifestation of God's devastating power. The expression is used in the Old Testament to describe a physical materialization of Yahweh. In it, God appears as a fiery cloud over Mount Sinai (Exodus 24) and as a glowing orb in the desert (Exodus 16). But this electromagnetic phenomenon is most commonly described as appearing over the Tabernacle (Exodus 29, Leviticus 9, Numbers 14), and each time it happens, the Temple must be evacuated. However, the most precise description of this phenomenon comes from the prophet Ezekiel, who comes face-to-face with it during his exile in Babylon. In *The Lost Angel*, Martin Faber,

Artemi Dujok and Nicholas Allen all must confront the Glory of God. (See chapters 58, 60.)

Great and Terrible Day: An Old Testament reference to the end of the world and the return of the prophet Elijah, which appears several times throughout the novel. "Behold, I will send you Elijah, the prophet, Before the day of the Lord comes, the great and terrible day." (Malachi 4:5)

Great Flood: Despite what many believe, this is not simply a Judeo-Christian myth. Just as Sierra writes in *The Lost Angel*, there are more than a hundred separate stories across the world that tell of humanity's destruction by a global flood. One of the most famous is the Hindu story of Manu and the fish that tells him of an impending flood. There's also the Aztec story of Tana and Nena, who escape the god Tlaloc's wrath after he tells them about his plan to drown all humans. And more famous still is the Greek myth of Prometheus, who warns his son, Deucalion, and Deucalion's wife, Pyrrha, about Zeus's plan to destroy them all. (See chapter 29.)

In the novel, Martin Faber is convinced—as are a growing number of climatologists—that the flood is a metaphor for the last great climatologic event, when the melting polar ice caps brought an end to the last ice age some eleven to twelve thousand years ago. That would have happened just before the first human civilizations, such as the Gobekli Tepe (in Turkey), are recorded to have appeared.

Hallaç: Name of the meteorite impact crater just a few miles from the Gurbulak pass, near the border between Turkey and Iran, where, according to *The Lost Angel*, Martin Faber and Julia Álvarez's adamants came from. It's this cosmic origin that makes the stones quite different from the stones found on Earth.

Javier Sierra next to the Hallaç crater, Turkey

heliogabalus: A luminous stone related to the adamants that is used to communicate with higher beings. The term traces to the city of Emesa (Homs in modern-day Syria) and comes from the name of the Syrian god by the same name (also called Elagabalus), who is depicted as a conical black stone that is, doubtless, a meteorite. (See chapter 58.)

Hopi: An important tribe of Native Americans that resides primarily in the American Southwest (see chapter 44). Their name means "peaceful people," although the tribe maintains the name has many other meanings as well. Sierra first visited their Arizona reservation in 1991 and returned in 1994. This land was ceded to them by President Chester Arthur in 1882, as is explained in detail in *The Lost Angel*. Actually a clan of more than thirty tribes, the Hopi Indians preserve their ancestral traditions to this day. Their land's spiritual center, Oraibi, is one of the longest continuously inhabited places in the United States. This is the birthplace of White Bear (also called Oswald Qo-tsa-Honow), the Hopi chief who makes a brief but significant cameo in *The Lost Angel* and is best known for sharing the tribe's oral history with writers Frank Waters and Josef Blumrich. White Bear explained that the Hopi break up humanity's eras into "worlds," which have come to an end after global catastrophes. The first world was destroyed by fire, the second by ice, the third by water. They believe we are living in the fourth world. And according to their beliefs, humanity will complete its evolutionary cycle once we reach the seventh world—which means our species must still confront three more global catastrophes. (See chapter 69.)

J

Ignatius Donnelly (1831–1901): A lawyer, congressman and former governor of Minnesota. His writings were extremely influential in his time, particularly his book *Atlantis: the Antediluvian World* (1882). It is still considered one of the most lauded works of its time. And many still refer to Donnelly's assertion that ancient Egyptian, Hindu and Central American cultures were founded by survivors of the global flood that destroyed Atlantis. Furthermore, he postulates that the royalty from Atlantis went on to be deified as the original gods of ancient mythology. He surmises that this explains commonalities across the globe, such as pyramids, common symbolism such as the spiral, and the obsession with astronomy.

Despite his controversial ideas, Donnelly is considered one of the most learned politicians ever to pass through Washington, DC—not just because of his writings about extinct civilizations, but also for his in-depth study of geology, botany and linguistics. One of his lesser-known works deals with trying to find hidden messages encrypted in the works of William Shakespeare. (See chapter 46.)

Jacob's ladder: A ladder or staircase of light that angels use to go back and forth between heaven and earth, as described by Jacob in the first book of the Bible (Genesis 28:11–19). It is a central premise in *The Lost Angel*. The concept first appeared in Sierra's work in his first book, *Las puertas templarias* (*The Templar Doors*), and resurfaces in this novel as the means for humans to communicate with celestial beings. In this book, the author focuses on the part of the Bible where Jacob envisions this ladder after he falls asleep against a mysterious black stone, which Sierra links to the adamants. (See chapters 35, 46, 48, 66, 93, 99.)

James Irwin (1930–91): This astronaut's search for Noah's Ark is detailed in *The Lost Angel* (chapter 91). Few know that he wrote a book about his travels to Ararat in his mission to prove the existence of the biblical ship. In *More Than an Ark on Ararat* (1985), Irwin, the eighth man to set foot on the moon, admits to his failed expedition but not to a crisis of faith. In the book, he concludes that the Ark would be discovered

Juan de Estivadas's tomb in Noia, Spain

Jacob's ladder

when God—not man—thought it was time, exposing Irwin's personal religious views on existence. After returning from the moon, he founded a Christian group called High Flight, through which he organized seven separate expeditions to Mount Ararat in search of the Ark. His perseverance and bravery as a test pilot served to save his life on more than one occasion but did not help him achieve his ultimate goal: to show that just as man walked on the surface of the moon, so did God on Earth.

The Jasons: An elite group of scientists, mathematicians and physicists from Princeton University who advised the US government on technology and defense during World War II. William Castle II is a member of this group in *The Lost Angel*. Its name comes from the months in which its members met, from July through November. (See chapter 91.)

John Dee (1527–1608): A complex and multifaceted man who lived during the reign of England's Queen Elizabeth, he was as lauded for his scientific knowledge as for his mastery over the occult arts. Despite lacking any actual supernatural ability, this Catholic "wizard" aligned himself in 1581 with a sketchy medium, one Edward Kelly, with the goal of communicating with angels and other beings on "the other side." He attempted to do this via a pair of stones, fully convinced that using magic and alchemy was as legitimate a way of speaking to God as any orthodox religion. He claimed to have received instruction from celestial beings on how to speak the language of angels, which he named Enochian, and how to build a talisman that facilitated this communication, one that shows up throughout *The Lost Angel*. Although his dealings in magic somewhat diminished his credibility, Dee was well known for his developments in geometry, cartography and astronomy, and he wrote sixty-nine works, most of which are stored in their original form in the Ashmolean Museum of Art and Archaeology in Oxford. (See chapter 13.)

Joseph Smith (1805–44): Sierra tells the story of the founder of the Mormon religion, who, he explains, possessed seer stones similar to the adamants that Julia Álvarez uses in *The Lost Angel*. Smith used the stones

Juan de Estivadas's tomb in Noia, Spain

given to him by angels, as John Dee did two hundred years earlier, to communicate with angels who taught him an unintelligible language—which he wrote down. Today, there are more than fourteen million followers of the Church of Jesus Christ of Latter-day Saints across the world, and all of them can recite the story of Smith's communion with an angel named Moroni. (See chapter 55.)

Juan de Estivadas: His tomb is perhaps the best known in the "church of tombstones," Santa María a Nova, in Noia, Spain. Sculpted in the fifteenth century, it shows the likeness of the former Galician businessman and merchant spectacularly carved in stone, his head resting against a stone pillow bearing his name. Hidden in his name is a code that is fundamental to *The Lost Angel*'s plot.

Kasskara: The mythical capital of the Hopi Indians' ancestors, it's cited as yet another version of the Greek philosopher Plato's story of the lost continent of Atlantis. According to the Hopi, our planet had several capitals that disappeared after successive global catastrophes. Kasskara was the third such capital and was at the center of a continent that supposedly disappeared beneath the Pacific Ocean. The story of Kasskara was first published in Spanish in March of 1980 in the magazine *Mundo Desconocido* (*The Lost World*), which was headed by a writer and journalist named Andreas Faber-Kaiser, who was the inspiration for Martin Faber's name in Sierra's novel. (See chapter 69.)

Kachinas: These Hopi deities today are depicted as gruesome tiny mud-and-stone figurines to, it is said, get the tribe's young children accustomed to their presence. The Kachinas, according to Hopi legends, were technologically advanced spirit beings who, among other things, could take flight aboard a kind of flying gourd that defied gravity thanks to "magnetic forces." Hopi traditions are steeped in the stories of the Kachinas, and they have inspired everything from dance to horrible ceremonial masks that seem taken from someone's worst nightmare. In *The Lost Angel,* they are described as helpful gods who taught the Hopi how to farm and raise livestock. They supposedly also were prophetic, foretelling that the Hopi would be visited by white men crossing the seas. They were capable of all kinds of supernatural feats, including reproducing without carnal knowledge, communicating telepathically, cutting and moving immense stones and even devising complex underground cities that still have yet to be discovered by modern archaeologists. (See chapter 69.)

Keyhole: A class of CIA spy satellite, one of which captured images of the "Ararat Anomaly," which was later identified as the possible remains of Noah's Ark. In *The Lost Angel,* they are often referred to as KH satellites. (See chapter 40.)

lapsis exillis: A Latin phrase that Father Benigno Fornés uses in the last chapter of *The Lost Angel* to describe the adamants. Wolfram von Eschenbach was the first person to use the term toward the end of the twelfth century in his work *Parzival.* The twenty-five-thousand-word epic poem tells the tale of the knight Parzival's search for the Holy Grail, which Eschenbach describes as a stone from the stars. Thus, *lapsis exillis* could be derived from the Latin *lapis ex caelis* ("celestial stone"), *lapsit ex caelis* ("it fell from the sky") or even *lapis laspus ex caelis* ("stone fallen from the sky"), though likely all those terms refer back to the celebrated *lapsis betilis*—a meteorite that was considered sacred in cultures throughout the ancient world, including Egypt. (See chapter 103.)

Melek Taus: Mentioned only once in the novel, this is a Yezidi deity. He is often represented as a peacock but he is supposed to be one of God's intermediaries. One of the original fallen angels, he redeems himself in the eyes of God and goes on to become mankind's patron saint. Taus is most likely a distortion of the name of the Greek god Zeus, so it stands to reason that Melek Taus would be an "angel of God." That would make the Yezidi among the world's only angel worshippers. (See chapter 65.)

monas hieroglyphica: This symbol created by John Dee encapsulates the formula needed to understand a new kind of science, one made up of kabbalah, alchemy and mathematics, which the expert Frances Yates says "would have allowed whoever mastered it to go up and down the levels of consciousness . . . up to the highest level where Dee believed he had found the secret to communicating with angels via mathematical computations." This singular symbol, often interpreted only as a magical entity, takes on a deeper meaning in *The Lost Angel,* where it comes to stand for an entire prophesy that can be understood through modern science.

Monas hieroglyphica also is the title of John Dee's most famous work. Published in Antwerp, Belgium, in 1564, it was written in just twelve days. It's largely regarded as a study in alchemy, but well-known semioticians (those who study signs and symbols) such as Umberto Eco believe it was Dee's attempt at recording a character-based alphabet. In fact, Dee twists, turns and parses the symbol to formulate twenty-four other theorems with distinct meanings. And so it fits Sierra's assertion that the symbol is a compendium of hidden cosmological information.

Mortlake Road: At the center of this street of brick houses, in the exclusive neighborhood of Richmond upon Thames, is the home of Shelia Graham, the keeper of the adamants that Martin Faber and Julia Álvarez receive on their wedding day. Sierra is accurate when he writes in *The Lost Angel* that there, at 9–16, is where John Dee's family home stood. The original building, since replaced, was first the home of Dee's mother until 1566, when it became the magician's domicile and library until his death at age eighty in 1608. He is buried in an unmarked grave at the nearby St. Mary the Virgin church on High Street. (See chapter 15.)

Nicholas Roerich (1874–1947): A Russian painter whose esoteric influences make his works some of the most displayed in his native country. His life was full of adventures and strange episodes, such as the day in 1925 when, in broad daylight near the Karakorum mountain range, he claimed to have seen an object in the sky that the "lamas" with whom he was traveling identified as a "sign of Shambhala," the underground kingdom that supposedly controls the world with an invisible hand. Roerich is mentioned in *The Lost Angel* in relation to the *chintamani*, a stone, like the adamants, that is said to be used to communicate with the heavens. But Roerich was a man with his feet firmly planted on the ground. He created our modern concept of culture and was so dedicated to the ideal of world peace that he was nominated for the Nobel Peace Prize. A flag he designed is recognized internationally as the flag of peace and a peak in the Altai mountain range is named for him. (See chapter 76.)

Noia (or Noya): The small town on the Costa da Morte that is the hometown of Julia Álvarez, *The Lost Angel*'s protagonist. Few know that the town's seal shows Noah's Ark run aground at the top of Mount Aro or that the town's name is derived from Noah's. One local legend has it that a daughter or granddaughter of Noah came to the shores of this town, to the *finis terrae,* and helped repopulate the world starting more than five thousand years ago. The town is peppered with remnants of prehistoric settlements more than five thousand years old. (See chapter 41.)

Noyon: Town in the French region of Picardy. *The Lost Angel* makes only a passing reference to it, although the author no doubt wanted to show yet another European connection to Noah's name. The reference also gives him entry to talk about another famous cathedral, Notre Dame, which forms a map of French temples whose layout exactly mirrors the constellation Virgo, just as Sierra describes in his other book *The Templar Doors*. (See chapter 77.)

Operation Elias: The fictionalized secret intelligence operation that US president Chester Arthur created at the end of the nineteenth century. Its objective is to control all manner of communication with any higher intelligence. It runs under the purview of the National Security Agency (NSA).

Noia's town seal

phonetic kabbalah: System by which the sounds of a word or phrase are used instead of the actual meaning to transmit a "secret" message. John Dee used this method in some of his writing. This method is the mother of homophone games, or plays on words. Martin Faber uses this method to transmit a hidden meaning to Julia Álvarez in his kidnapping video in the novel. (See chapter 43.)

PKK: Acronym for the Kurdistan Workers' Party. In *The Lost Angel*, it's described as an illegal political faction that has been at odds for decades with the Turks. It is considered a terrorist organization by the United States, the European Union and Turkey. (See chapter 9.)

Pórtico de la Gloria: This Master Mateo sculpture, which flanks the entrance to the cathedral in Santiago, took the place of a previous portico that commemorated the transfiguration of Jesus on Mount Tabor. It was a source of much consternation for those who understood the deep meaning behind the Way of St. James, since this transfiguration is precisely what those ancient pilgrims one day hoped to achieve. Father Benigno Fornés explains the tradition in detail in *The Lost Angel*. (See chapter 103.)

Quebec blackout: Often cited in the novel is the great blackout of March 13, 1989, that left most of Quebec, Canada, in total darkness. The event was real and began three days after a scientist half a world away detected a powerful eruption of energy on the sun's surface. The "solar wind" caused by the disturbance interrupted all satellite communications and even disrupted transmissions from radio stations such as those operated by Radio Free Europe, which originally blamed the Kremlin for trying to counter their broadcast into the Soviet Union. On March 12, aurora borealis could be seen as far south as Florida and Cuba. And on March 13 came the most serious repercussions, knocking out power to the city of Quebec and affecting power grids across the United States. In outer space, NASA's communications satellite TDRS-1 experienced as many as 250 anomalies and the Space Shuttle Discovery reported a malfunction in one of its hydrogen sensors. The series of unexplained events—including the accident with the oil tanker *Exxon Valdez* and the sea of blackness it left in its wake—caused by the solar wind convinced the scientific community that it was of utmost importance to monitor the sun's activity from then on. (See chapters 76, 94.)

Rachele Effect: Referenced in the novel, this event took place in June of 1936, just outside Rome. While the inventor Guglielmo Marconi was experimenting with long-range frequencies, all motorized engines in the vicinity—including the engine in the car of Rachele Mussolini, wife of the Italian prime minister—stopped working temporarily. This incident sparked a new era of experimentation with electromagnetic fields and their use as weapons. (See chapter 40.)

Santa María a Nova: This church is the site of one of the seminal scenes in *The Lost Angel*. It is built at the center of a medieval cemetery in the seaside town of Noia. Christened in 1327 and built over the ruins of a previous church, it houses hundreds of tombs, some of them up to

Santa María a Nova church, Noia, Spain

seven hundred years old. Most are inscribed with symbols of the guilds or trades of the people interred in them, though many symbols have still not been deciphered. However, some of these tombs—*lápidas* in Spanish—are empty, giving rise to endless theories for why this is. It remains, by far, one of the most mysterious churches in Galicia, even though it has been decommissioned and turned into a museum.

Solar eclipse of 1999: The novel refers to a complete solar eclipse that darkened much of Europe on August 11, 1999. Maybe because the event coincided with Sierra's birthday, but more importantly because Nostradamus foretold it, this celestial event plays a pivotal role in *The Lost Angel*. In the novel, the event brings the adamants to life, causing stones that have been hidden in locations all over the planet since the Middle Ages to reactivate once again. The novel later refers to this event during the Church Crisis of 1999 and refers the readers to one of Sierra's earlier works, *Las puertas templarias* (*The Templar Doors*). (See chapter 73.)

solar storm: Every so often, the surface of the sun erupts in giant bursts of plasma energy. If Earth were in the path of an eruption at that time, the electromagnetic radiation would reach us in as little as eight minutes and affect the workings and orbits of our communications satellites. *The Lost Angel* describes the damage that such a storm could cause. At the moment of impact, Earth would be showered in a rain of high-energy plasma that would alter electrical networks and deal a serious blow to the heart of our civilization. (Please see the entries for "coronal mass ejection" and "Quebec blackout" for more information.)

St. Echmiadzin: This cathedral is in the heart of Armenia's sacred city. It's the country's oldest Christian temple and one of the world's oldest, since Armenia was the first country to adopt Christianity as its official religion. While standing on the future site of the cathedral, Saint Gregory the Illuminator supposedly had a vision, wherein the heavens parted and a beam of light shone down to mark the spot. A procession of angels traveled down this beam of light with Jesus Christ leading them. He knocked on the ground three times with a golden hammer and two columns rose, one with a base of pure gold, another that was a pillar of fire that blazed into the sky. Legends aside, the fact is this sacred temple was built in the fourth century and houses venerable relics from throughout Christian history, including the very hand of St. Gregory; the Lance of Longinus, named for the Roman soldier who used it to pierce Jesus's side as he hung crucified; and a petrified piece of wood that is said to be part of Noah's Ark. That relic, carbon-dated at more than seven thousand years old, is noted in *The Lost Angel*.

STEREO: The acronym for Solar TErrestrial RElations Observatory, a pair of space probes NASA put into orbit in October of 2006 to study the electromagnetic energy between Earth and the sun. Their data has provided us previously unknown details about solar eruptions and they now form an essential part of our space meteorological program. In the future, they could alert us to solar storms that could damage our planet.

Uriel: A name that has several meanings, from "God is my light" to "God's fire." It belongs to one of the seven archangels mentioned by the prophet Enoch, an angel who presides over Tartarus, the underworld. Several biblical scholars believe it is the same angel who came to earth to battle with Jacob. And some Hebrew texts suggest he was the same angel who appeared to Noah to warn him of the impending flood. If that weren't enough, Uriel is also thought to be the angel who supposedly appeared in the form of a child in May 1581 to give John Dee his seer stone. (See chapter 87.)

Urim and Thummim: Hebrew names meaning "light" and "vessel." They are the names given to two sacred stones that were stored in Solomon's Temple in Jerusalem, as referenced in *The Lost Angel*. Apparently, ancient rabbis used the stones as a way to make their petitions to Yahweh (Exodus 28:3, Leviticus 8, Numbers 27:21). What the stones looked like is unknown. But they easily could have been small enough to be stored in the small case Sheila Graham shows Julia Álvarez on the eve of her marriage to Martin Faber. (See chapter 55.)

Uzza: According to the second book of Samuel in the Bible (chapter 6), it was the name of one of the slaves who carried the Ark of the Covenant and who died when he placed his hand on the ark while trying to keep it from hitting the ground. Despite the warnings from the Hebrew elders, he touched the casing that housed the Ten Commandments and was instantly struck down by "the wrath of God." (See chapter 77.)

VLA: Very Large Array telescope. Nestled in the Plains of San Agustin, New Mexico, this observatory is made up of twenty-seven antennas—each twenty-five meters across—and serves as the world's largest "ear" into the cosmos. Its purpose is to listen in on deep space, particularly for readings on pulsars, quasars and radio emissions from stars, and from the sun and planets in our own solar system. Although it became famous in the movie *Contact,* the VLA has never been used to search for radio communications from potentially intelligent life on other worlds. In *The Lost Angel,* it is used to track a particular electromagnetic signal that is at the heart of the plot.

William Seabrook (1884–1945): This author of *Adventures in Arabia* is mentioned in the novel in relation to the Yezidi people and their legend of the "towers of evil." According to Seabrook's work, there were seven of these towers built across the world, by which Satan could broadcast his evil globally. Seabrook, a world traveler and writer for the *New York Times, Vanity Fair* and *Reader's Digest,* earned the title of "traveler to the other side" because of the way mysticism flowed throughout his writing. In 1945, he swallowed a bottleful of pills and committed suicide after a spiraling descent into alcoholism. (See chapter 58.)

Yezidi: This relatively unknown religious and cultural minority—of which there are fewer than one hundred thousand members on earth—can be found peppered throughout Iraq, Iran, Turkey and Armenia, and it plays a pivotal role in *The Lost Angel.* And not just because one of the main protagonists, Artemi Dujok, is a member of this tribe of "fallen angels" descended from Melek Taus, but also because of their particular history. First off, the Yezidi believe they are direct descendants of Adam but not Eve. They believe in reincarnation and the innocence of the angel Lucifer and they revere snakes. All of this has cast them in the role of "devil worshippers," and opened them up to persecution by everyone from Muslims to the deposed Saddam Hussein. That history has drawn a wide variety of people to them, from writers such as H. P. Lovecraft—who immortalized them in his short story "The Horror at Red Hook"—to contemporary Satanists such as Anton LaVey.

They also have notable connections to the myth of the Great Flood. Ain Sifni, the largest city in Kurdish Iraq, is, according to the Yezidi, the place where the flood began. The city's name actually means "Noah's boat." On the outskirts of the city, people can visit the well that, according to legend, overflowed to begin the Great Flood. It is supposedly protected by Baba Sheikh (or the "Yezidi Pope"), who resides there to venerate the tomb of Adi, its founder.

The Santiago de Compostela Cathedral, where the novel begins

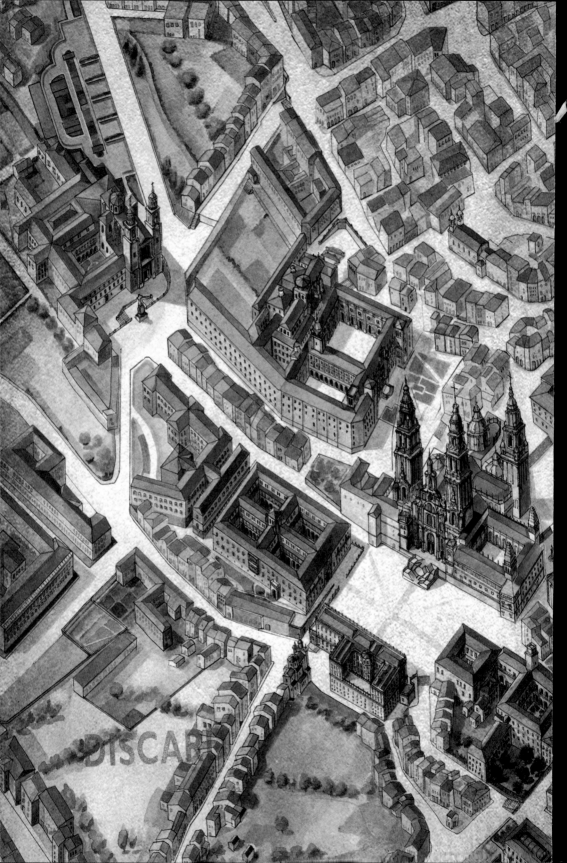